The Regency Season

DECADENT DUKES

CAROLE MORTIMER

Published in Great Britain 2018
By Mills & Boon, an imprint of HarperCollins*Publishers*
1 London Bridge Street, London, SE1 9GF

THE REGENCY SEASON: DECADENT DUKES © 2018 Harlequin Books S.A.

Rufus Drake: Duke of Wickedness © 2015 Carole Mortimer
Griffin Stone: Duke of Decadence © 2015 Carole Mortimer
Christian Seaton: Duke of Danger © 2015 Carole Mortimer

ISBN: 978-0-263-93157-0

52-0718

Our policy is to use papers that are natural, renewable and recyclable products and made from wood grown in sustainable forests.
The logging and manufacturing processes conform to the legal environmental regulations of the country of origin.

Printed and bound by
CPI Group (UK) Ltd, Croydon, CR0 4YY

RUFUS DRAKE: DUKE OF WICKEDNESS

The Regency Season

Carole MORTIMER
DANGEROUS DUKES
August 2017

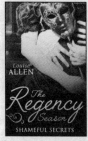
Louise ALLEN
SHAMEFUL SECRETS
September 2017

Sarah MALLORY
BLACKMAILED BRIDE
October 2017

Mary BRENDAN
RUINED REPUTATIONS
November 2017

Margaret McPHEE
GENTLEMAN ROGUES
December 2017

Ann LETHBRIDGE
PASSIONATE PROMISE
January 2018

Elizabeth BEACON
SCANDALOUS AWAKENING
February 2018

Sophia JAMES
CONVENIENT MARRIAGES
March 2018

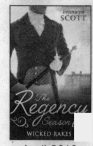
Bronwyn SCOTT
WICKED RAKES
April 2018

Anne HERRIES
HIDDEN DESIRES
May 2018

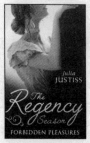
Julia JUSTISS
FORBIDDEN PLEASURES
June 2018

Carole MORTIMER
DECADENT DUKES
July 2018

To Peter, as always.

Carole Mortimer was born and lives in the UK. She is married to Peter and they have six sons. She has been writing for Mills & Boon since 1978, and is the author of 200 books. Carole is a *USA TODAY* bestselling author, and in 2012 she was recognised by Queen Elizabeth II for her 'outstanding contribution to literature.'

Visit Carole at carolemortimer.co.uk or on Facebook.

Chapter One

Late July, 1815
Northamptonshire, England

"Sir, are you aware that you are trespassing on the Duke of Northamptonshire's estate?"

Rufus Drake, who *was* the aforementioned Duke of Northamptonshire, had very recently jumped down from his horse on this warm July day. He'd undressed down to his drawers, with the intention of swimming naked in the pool situated in the woods of said estate, in the hopes it would refresh him after the dusty and tiring two days of riding up from London.

He instantly froze in the action of unfastening his drawers at the sound of the disembodied female voice, and instead gave a narrow-eyed glance about him to locate the owner of the huskily pleasant voice.

"I am up here, sir. And I would appreciate it if you would cover yourself before continuing this conversation!"

Rufus surveyed the surrounding trees, his dark brows rising above his vivid green eyes as he spotted a pair of female legs dangling down from a nearby horse-chestnut tree. Completely bare and very curvaceous female legs.

He abandoned the idea of removing his drawers, but did not replace his shirt as he strolled over to stand beneath the tree, slightly taken aback as he looked up into the dappled green branches and saw the young and beautiful owner of those legs. Her missing stockings and dainty cream boots were resting upon her knees as she perched on the branch slightly above his head.

Her slender fingers clutched the branch for balance, and were completely bare of rings, indicating she was an unmarried lady. Nor was there maid or companion with her anywhere that Rufus could see. Meaning she was very much alone here in the woods.

With him.

Huge blue eyes looked down at him from a flushed heart-shaped face, her nose slightly upturned, her lips surprisingly full and sensual. Riotous blonde curls were secured upon the crown of her head, with several damp tendrils falling about her creamy white shoulders above a white muslin gown decorated with tiny green leaves.

A gown that currently appeared to be caught on the branch above and behind her as she once again attempted, and failed, to pull the material down to cover her legs. The loosened bodice of the gown gaped open as she bent forward, to reveal the tops of full and creamy breasts.

A state of undress which would seem to indicate, added to her damp tendrils of hair curling at her throat and nape, that she had also recently been tempted by the lure of a cooling swim in the pond.

Rufus's appreciative gaze returned to that obviously discomforted face. "It would seem that you are in almost as much of a state of undress as I," he drawled dryly.

The blush deepened in her cheeks. "And I would appreciate it if you would stop *ogling*, sir!"

He gave an unapologetic grin as he continued to look up at her appreciatively. "Are you perhaps a wood nymph?" he teased.

Her eyes snapped with impatience. "There is no such thing as a wood nymph."

"No?"

"Absolutely not," she assured him with a practicality totally at odds with that throaty, seductive voice.

"You are not a wood nymph, and obviously you cannot be the Duke of Northamptonshire himself, so surely you must also trespassing?" he drawled pointedly.

Another firm shake of her riotous golden curls. "I have the duke's permission to…to stroll through the woods here."

Rufus raised an eyebrow beneath the fall of his ebony-dark hair. "Indeed?"

"Yes." She nodded emphatically.

As Rufus had never so much as set eyes on this enchanting female in all his two and thirty years, he knew that it was not *this*

Duke of Northamptonshire who had given his permission.

Of course it could have been either of his two cousins, or perhaps their father, his paternal uncle, before them.

As the only child of the second son born to the previous, previous, *previous* Duke of Northampton, Rufus had not expected to ever hold the title himself. Except that Rufus's own father had died shortly after he had been born, and unfortunately his uncle along with both his cousins had also perished in the past three years. The former to a seizure of the heart, his elder cousin to influenza, and the younger when he succumbed two days later to the injuries he had received at the battle of Waterloo.

Nor had either of his two cousins ever married and produced an heir. The elder because his inclinations ran in quite another direction, and he had refused to even contemplate the taking of a wife. The younger cousin, David, *should* have been married but had died before the wedding could take place.

Which had left Rufus, as the only Drake still alive, to inherit the Northamptonshire title and estates.

And damned irritating it was too, after all his years spent about Town as the infamous and rakish Mr Rufus Drake, the unashamedly vastly wealthy business entrepreneur. As the untitled third grandson of a duke, it had been required that Rufus provide his own fortune. Which, if he did say so himself, he had succeeded in doing exceedingly well, helped along by a small inheritance left to him by his maternal grandmother. He was now one of the wealthiest gentlemen in England.

His maternal cousin Zachary Black, the Duke of Hawksmere, had laughed uncontrollably when informed that Rufus was now the Duke of Northamptonshire. Mainly because Rufus had teased his cousin unmercifully over the years at

Zachary's certainty of inheriting their grandfather Black's title, while Rufus could continue merrily on, free of such responsibilities.

Admittedly, Hawksmere, once that humour had passed, had then invited Rufus to be an honorary member of the Dangerous Dukes, an exclusive group of gentlemen consisting of Zachary and his four closest friends. As an aside to that honorary membership, Rufus had further been invited to join them as an agent for the Crown. Which was Rufus's main reason for being in Northamptonshire at all.

Rufus had received a letter just days ago from Matthew Turner, the estate manager Rufus had personally hired the previous month to oversee the Banbury Hall estate, after receiving word that the previous estate manager, Jacob Harker, had absconded into the night. Turner had since discovered that Harker had also taken that month's rents from Rufus's tenants with him when he left, and suggested in his letter that perhaps Rufus might himself wish to look into the matter more fully himself.

Rufus had no interest in the pittance that had been stolen, but the previous estate manager's sudden disappearance was now of deep interest to him after what he had learnt from his cousin Zachary a week or so ago.

It transpired that just weeks before the battle of Waterloo there had been a plot afoot to assassinate the Prince Regent, and so throw the country into chaos. It had been discovered that several government secretaries along with servants in prominent households in England had been involved in that plot.

Rufus had decided it was now incumbent upon him to look more closely into why his previous estate manager had absconded so suddenly and, if possible, ascertain as to whether or not he had been part of the ring of spies working against the Crown.

That being so, Rufus had risen very early yesterday morning, instructed his valet to pack up enough of his clothes for months, just in case, and to then travel to Northamptonshire by coach. Then Rufus had set off alone on horseback for his ducal estate.

He had travelled a long way yesterday, and the inn he had stayed at the previous night had been passable at best. After another overly warm morning of travel he had been tempted, upon arrival at his estate, to take a dip in the pool he remembered so affectionately from his visits there as a child.

This delay was partly because of the need to refresh himself, but also, he admitted, to a reluctance on his part to actually make his presence known at Banbury Hall for a while longer.

Was it possible the enticing nymph in the tree was the daughter of his new estate manager? He vaguely recalled that Turner had told him that he was widowed but had a daughter. Although what the age of that daughter might be, Rufus had not enquired; a month ago he had merely been relieved to pass on the onerous task of running Banbury Hall to someone other than himself.

The young lady perched so prettily above him certainly looked as if she might be that worthy gentleman's daughter; whilst her gown was not of the finest quality, it was nevertheless modish in style, as was the set of her golden curls, and the cream leather boots were surely too fine to belong to a daughter of one of his tenants.

"May I enquire as to your name, miss?" he prompted huskily.

She looked slightly taken aback. "Are you not going to dress yourself first?"

Rufus held back a grin at her persistence in wishing to avoid looking at the nakedness of his chest. "Your name, miss?"

"I— It is— You may call me Juliet," she announced grandly.

Rufus knew instinctively that there was something not quite right with that statement. Admittedly, the name was fitting, considering her place above him in the tree. But he was certainly not her, nor any woman's, doting Romeo! "And is that actually your name?" he drawled sceptically.

"Well, not exactly," she conceded. "But it is my middle name, and comes from—"

"I am well aware of where it comes from," Rufus assured dryly. He was not a complete ignoramus; as the grandson of two dukes he had suffered through the requisite years at Eton and Oxford. The fact that this young lady also appeared to have received some education would seem to confirm Rufus's earlier assumption that she might very well be the daughter of his new estate manager. "I would simply prefer to address you by your given name."

She gave a heavy sigh. "It is nowhere near as pretty as Juliet."

Rufus held back a smile, finding himself exceedingly—and surprisingly—diverted by this young woman. The long years he had spent in London, and just a month of holding the title of duke, had rendered him more than a little jaded where the female sex was concerned. "Nevertheless…"

"It is Anna." She grimaced. "Plain, uninteresting Anna."

There was nothing in the least plain or uninteresting about this woman. The opposite, in fact. She was beautiful, diverting, and her state of dishabille was having the most delicious effect upon Rufus's libido.

"And might I also know your name, sir?"

Rufus had been grandly named after his two ducal grandfathers, his father and his mother's brother, as Harold Algernon Edward Rufus Drake, but from birth had been known to the family and friends alike by the last of his illustrious names.

"Rufus." He saw no sign of recognition of his name in her candid blue eyes. "Would you care to explain, Anna, why is it you are currently sitting up in that tree sans your stockings and boots if you were just strolling through the woods?"

Anna frowned her dismay, sensing, despite his politely enquiring expression, that he was somehow mocking her. And possibly with good reason, when she was indeed so scantily clad. He was also, Anna conceded, a gentleman more disturbing and handsome than she had ever encountered before.

Disturbing, because as an unmarried lady she had never before engaged in a conversation with a gentleman whilst he was dressed only his drawers. Indeed, she had never before *seen* a gentleman wearing only his drawers.

The skin of his bared torso was a warm olive-brown. His shoulders were broad, his chest and arms muscled. She observed with fascination the silky down of dark ebony that tapered down over his chest and stomach to disappear into the waistband of his drawers. She noted that his waist was lean and narrow above muscled thighs and legs.

From her position above him, Anna was also able to recognise that he was at least ten years older than her own twenty years, as well as exceedingly tall. True, most people were taller than her five feet, but this gentleman would surely tower over her by a foot or more.

He was a gentleman with fashionably over-long and tousled hair as black as midnight, and eyes the green of sparkling emeralds surrounded by thick, lush dark lashes, his nose long and aristocratic, with high cheekbones beneath taut flesh, and his mouth—

Oh dear me, *his mouth!*

This man had the most wickedly sensual and mocking mouth, the bottom lip slightly fuller than the top, set above a square and arrogant jaw.

As for the reason *why* she was currently sitting up in this tree, with her gown unfastened down her back and her stockings and boots upon her knees?

Propriety dictated she should not have been

walking alone in the woods at all, of course. Nor did she, as she had claimed earlier, have an acquaintance with the new Duke of Northamptonshire.

But the duke was safely in London, and Anna had not considered it would matter, once she reached this secluded pond amongst the woods of Banbury Hall, if she were to take a cooling dip.

Consequently, she had been happily indulging when she had heard the approach of a horse wending its way through the trees. She'd been left with no choice but to hastily wade out of the water and pull her gown on over the dampness of her chemise before hurriedly picking up the rest of her belongings and giving a hunted look about her surroundings.

She had hoped only to need to hide up in the tree until the horse and its rider had passed by, but had instead watched in horror as the man had halted and dismounted when he'd reached the pond.

He had then removed his hat and sat down on the grass to remove his black Hessians. He followed swiftly with his jacket, waistcoat, cravat and shirt, the latter revealing that magnificently muscled chest.

Anna's heart had begun to pound in her chest

when he had proceeded to unfasten and remove his pantaloons. Allowing him to see her own state of dress was completely scandalous, but watching this handsome gentleman *un*dress was surely even more so.

Except Anna had been unable to stop herself enjoying the experience.

Chapter Two

"Anna? I asked why you are currently sitting up in that tree…."

Guilty tears filled her eyes as she desperately sought for some explanation other than the truth. Her brother Mark would not be displeased but disappointed if he were to learn of her impetuous actions.

Perhaps if her mother had lived, Anna might have been able to talk to her of the terrible restlessness that sometimes overcame her. The aching need inside her for adventure and excitement, and the desire she felt to break free of the shackles her lowly station in life had placed upon her.

She had once talked to her papa about those feelings, and she had thought he understood, but not Mark. Her brother was so good and kind, and perfectly content with his life as parson of the parish. Which was, of course, to be commended.

Except…

Anna's own feelings of restlessness had become greater of late rather than less. So much so that she now often escaped the parsonage to be on her own, to pretend that she was not herself at all but was instead a lady of the world, and that she could travel to London if she cared to. To Cairo. The Americas. That she might go *anywhere* she chose.

But in none of those daydreams had Anna ever envisaged finding herself in such a scandalous situation, and with a gentleman as rakishly handsome as the one standing in front of her.

Everything about him spoke of wealth and privilege, from the beautiful black stallion he rode to the perfectly tailored clothes he had so carelessly dropped onto the grass as he undressed. He possessed that air of bored cynicism so many of the gentlemen seemed to wear about them like a mantle.

Could he not see, could none of them see, how lucky they were just to be men? To have the freedom to do what they wanted, and go where they wanted, whenever they wanted?

"I am still waiting, Anna."

She cast off the feelings of melancholy, raising her chin determinedly, even as she inwardly asked for forgiveness for the untruths she was about to tell. "As I have said, I was strolling through the woods——"

"Trespassing."

Anna ignored the jibe as she continued with her tale. "When I heard a poor little kitten meowing for help from up in a tree——"

"This very tree?"

"And being a good Samaritan," Anna continued doggedly, despite his mockery, "I, of course, had no choice but to climb the tree and offer my help."

"Would you not have climbed the tree more comfortably if you had continued to wear your boots?" her tormentor taunted as he leaned comfortably against the trunk and looked up at her, his arms folded across his chest, his eyes almost on a level with her bared limbs.

Anna tried again to pull her gown down—to no avail; it really was stuck fast on the branch slightly above and behind her. "I had to take off my boots so that I might remove my stockings. They are both expensive, you see, and I did not wish to damage them."

"Very commendable of you," he drawled.

"Unfortunately," she continued determinedly, "once I had climbed up here, the kitten decided it did not need my help after all and it jumped nimbly to the ground before running off."

"Very ungrateful of it," her tormentor nodded with a gravity that was completely nullified by the humour she could see glittering in his mocking eyes.

"Whereas I," Anna stated firmly, "appear to have caught my gown on a branch and am now stuck fast."

Rufus could see that, and he could recognise the blush of guilt colouring her creamy cheeks for exactly what it was. He had been a major in the king's army, and in charge of dozens of mostly reluctant soldiers, and as such he was certainly capable of identifying a lie when he was told one. "Tell me, Anna," he drawled as he straightened, "was there even one word of truth in that pretty story?"

That guilty flush deepened in her cheeks. "Are you calling me a liar, sir?"

"Oh yes," Rufus confirmed without hesitation. "As I said, it was a pretty tale, and very well narrated, but all a lie, nonetheless."

Blue eyes warred with his unwavering green ones for several long seconds before she lowered her lashes and gave a defeated sigh. "I really was strolling through the woods initially," she murmured softly.

"And latterly?"

She grimaced. "It has been so hot these past

few days, and the pool looked so inviting." She gave another sigh. "But then I heard your horse approaching through the trees, causing me to leave the water wearing only my chemise. I gathered up my things, and hoped by climbing the tree you would not see me as you rode past."

Rufus glanced across to where his horse, Caesar, was unconcernedly cropping grass, and inwardly cursed the black stallion for having made so much noise on their approach. Seeing this beautiful and outspoken young woman dressed only in her wet undergarments would no doubt have been extremely pleasurable.

Almost as pleasurable as when she had looked her fill of his bare chest.

"Except I did not ride past," he stated the obvious.

"No," she accepted heavily.

He nodded. "Your gown is stuck fast, you said?"

"Yes." She gave another ineffectual tug on the offending garment.

"Perhaps you might behave the gentleman and help me to become unstuck?" She added with what was no doubt intended to be a charming flutter of her long and silky eyelashes.

It was an affectation that had quite the opposite effect on Rufus as he was sure it was intended to have. He could no longer hold back his humour at the situation, as he first began to chuckle and then to laugh outright.

Anna did not see anything in the least amusing about her current dilemma, doubly offended as the gentleman rested his hands on his muscled thighs to bend over at the waist, completely overcome with laughter.

At her expense.

Which was not at all flattering when her intention had been to charm.

"I am glad you find this situation amusing, sir," she finally snapped frostily.

He continued to chuckle for several more moments before finally straightening. "I find *you* entertaining, Anna," he corrected gruffly. "Tell me, does the helpless fluttering of your eyelashes usually work on unsuspecting gentlemen?"

Anna gave a disgruntled frown as she admitted, "Always."

"Utter fools, all of them!" He gave a bemused shake of his head. "And what makes you think I might be a gentleman?"

Anna swallowed warily as she saw there was now a predatory edge to his gaze as he looked up at her in challenge, again making her aware of the depth of the danger she had placed herself in with her impulsiveness.

After all, she knew nothing about this man, other than he was obviously wealthy and that his name was Rufus. And that she was currently vulnerable to his every whim.

Anna moistened the dryness of her lips with the tip of her tongue.

"One must have faith in human nature, sir."

"Must one?" Rufus murmured as he watched the movements of that little pink tongue and imagined how its soft heat would feel running the length of him. Imagery which instantly sent his libido up another notch.

"Yes, of course one must," she answered him firmly. "As such, I would very much appreciate your assistance in disentangling me from this branch."

Rufus ran his tongue across his lips. "How much?"

She gave him a startled glance. "Pardon me?"

"How much would you appreciate my assistance in untangling you?" Rufus prompted huskily.

She blinked her long lashes, not with the intention of flirting this time, but out of nervousness. "I do not understand," she finally murmured uncertainly.

Rufus could see the truth of that in her gaze, and was reminded that this young woman was at least ten years his junior, and possibly also the innocent daughter of his new estate manager at Banbury Hall.

But no one could ever accuse Rufus of behaving sensibly.

At least, they had never accused Mr Rufus Drake of behaving sensibly.

Nor, Rufus decided impatiently, did he intend for the Duke of Northamptonshire to become so inured in that role he allowed himself to become staid and stuffy.

"It is quite simple, Miss Anna," he drawled mockingly. "What will you give me if I help to unhook your gown from the branch above you?"

Her slender throat moved as she gave another swallow. "I— As you can see only too well, I have nothing on my person I might give you."

"Except for yourself."

Her eyes widened in alarm. "I— How dare you!" she gasped in outrage. "I have not— I do not— I am not that type of woman."

Rufus could see by her indignation that she certainly *had* not. "I am only requesting a kiss, Anna, not marriage," he assured dryly, having discovered since inheriting the Drake title that a duke was a far more marriageable commodity than a mere mister, even one as independently wealthy as he was.

As such, the marriage-minded mamas of the ton had done nothing but thrust their daughters at him this past month whenever the Duke of Northamptonshire had appeared in public, to such a degree that Rufus had quickly learned not to appear in public. Even the sophisticated widows of the ton, with whom he had associated so congenially with before inheriting the title, now seemed to look upon him with avaricious eyes rather than come-hither ones.

Consequently Rufus had soon started to avoid those ladies too, resulting in there being a distinct lack of physical dalliance or relief these past few weeks.

Indeed, since inheriting the title Rufus had formed a new respect for his cousin Zachary and the other Dangerous Dukes, for having managed to avoid the parson's mousetrap for as long as they had.

Although that was no longer true, since his cousin and two of his close friends had all married in recent months.

Rufus had always relished his freedom too much to have even the vaguest intention of joining their number. He enjoyed too much being able to bed whomever he chose, whenever, to even think of marriage to one single woman.

But, as he had already stated, his thoughts

were not of marriage. "A kiss is not too much to ask for rescuing you, is it, Anna?" he now cajoled temptingly.

Despite her feelings of restlessness, those wistful hopes and dreams she had of a different, more exciting life, Anna had necessarily led something of a sheltered existence up till now. But not so sheltered that she had not suffered the occasional kiss on the cheek—or on one distasteful occasion, clumsily on the lips— from the young men in the area who had thought they might be allowed to court her.

The difference being, of course, that the man she knew only as Rufus was not a young beau interested in courting her, but a rakish gentleman who wished only to claim a kiss. He was also, Anna recalled with a quiver of delicious anticipation, a man who boldly claimed she should not assume he *was* a gentleman.

Here, standing before her, was the adventure, the illicit excitement she had so longed for.

And, really, how terrible could it be, to allow herself to be kissed by a man as handsome and assured as this one? A man Anna was sure would know exactly how to kiss a woman, so that she also enjoyed the experience?

"Are you visiting with people in the area?" she questioned warily. The last thing she wanted was to later discover that she had allowed herself to be kissed by a gentleman who was staying in Northamptonshire with friends or relatives she might also know.

His jaw tightened. "I am not."

"Then you are merely travelling through?" she prompted just to be certain.

He gave a wicked rake of a smile. "Merely travelling through the woods, yes," he nodded.

Anna gave a relieved sigh. "Very well, one kiss." She gave a haughty inclination of her head. "If you will help untangle my gown and assist me down from this tree."

"That would appear to be two kisses."

Her eyes widened. "I beg your pardon?"

"The price of the original kiss was for untangling your gown," her tormentor drawled. "The second is for helping you down from the tree."

Anna glared at him. "You, sir, are an opportunist."

"Yes," he confirmed unapologetically.

Anna was sure she had never met a man more infuriating, more audacious, more outrageous, more *intriguingly, meltingly roguish* as this one.

Chapter Three

"Should you not put on your pantaloons first?" Anna prompted in alarm as Rufus began to climb the tree with the dexterity of one of the primates she had once seen pictured in a book in her father's study.

He paused briefly, the warmth of his breath currently fanning across her exposed knees. "They are expensive and I would not wish to damage them," he mockingly returned her own earlier comment in regard to her lack of stockings and boots.

Anna's trepidation grew as she realised just how vulnerable she was to whatever this man might wish to take from her.

Or, more worryingly, what she might wish to *give*.

Heat suffused the whole of her body as he continued to climb the tree, and she realised as he did so just how big he was. Everywhere. His tanned shoulders really were impossibly wide, and the bareness of his chest, with that down of silky black hair, was far too warm and immediate as he reached up past her to grasp on to the branch above, so that he might release the back of her gown, before then twisting his body round to sit on the branch beside her.

A warmth and immediacy that caused Anna to tremble as he sat far too close to her, the bare skin of his shoulder warm against her own, and allowing her to smell citrus and spice on his body, his cologne, along with a musky, totally male smell that she found equally as enticing.

"One," he murmured pointedly.

Anna could make no pretence of not knowing what he was referring to, and her heart gave a leap in her chest as her gaze lowered to his chiselled lips just inches away from her own.

Sculptured lips. Wickedly sensual lips that surely did know *exactly* how to kiss a woman.

Her eyes widened as he slowly licked his bottom lip, before drawing it enticingly into his mouth with his teeth.

Rufus recognised Anna's flush of arousal for what it was, and he realised too that he was enjoying himself, more than he could remember doing in a very long time. Years, perhaps. If ever?

He had taken bachelor apartments in London after finishing with Oxford, and the past ten years had seen his fortunes change dramatically. He had no interest in cards or a life of idleness, but had instead concentrated on his investments, doubling his money within months, before investing further.

Until one day Rufus realised he had so much money he could easily buy himself a house in one of the most fashionable areas in London, along with the servants needed to run such a residence, whilst he quietly continued to amass even more wealth.

He had enjoyed the company of ladies during those years too, of course. Very much so. He had stayed well clear of married ladies, however, nor had he wished to become entrapped into a marriage with one of the simpering young debutantes of the Season.

The young debutantes and their families were desperate to make a match to one of the richest men in England. His family connection to the prestigious Dukes of Hawksmere and Northamptonshire were not to be dismissed, either.

Cynical perhaps, but Rufus had no illusions in regard to London Society and how those loveless

marriages were decided upon. And he wanted
no part of it—not the suitable marriage, nor the
demure miss, who would no doubt have been
advised by her mother to lie passive and unmoving in the marriage bed while her husband
impregnated her. After which she could banish
him from her bed until her lying in was over.
When the whole miserable cycle would begin
all over again.

An heir was now necessary, of course, but
Rufus had every intention of choosing his own
wife when the time came.

The young woman seated on the branch beside him was not of the *ton,* nor was she a married lady or a simpering debutante. Nor did the
circumstance of their meeting—she was currently as unclothed by choice as he was!—lend
itself to any outraged cries of ruination on her
part, if he should steal a kiss. Or two.

Which Rufus had every intention of doing.

Sitting as close as they now were, Rufus could
appreciate just how delectably kissable Anna's
slightly moistened lips were. They were naturally rosy in colour, and there was an endearing
dip in the centre of the fuller lower lip.

Her unfastened gown was still gaping down
slightly at the front, allowing him a tantalising
glimpse of her wet chemise as it clung damply

to the fullness of her breasts, tipped with pert nipples the same rosy-red colour as her lips.

To kiss or touch *those* would be going too far, but that did not mean Rufus could not be aroused by the sight of them.

He raised a hand to cup her cheeks, her skin feeling as soft and smooth as silk as he turned her face gently towards him.

Her eyes widened in alarm as Rufus held that gaze to slowly lower his head towards hers.

She gasped softly. "Perhaps we should not do this."

And perhaps, if Anna's breath had not been so soft and fragrantly warm against his lips, if she had attempted to avoid his kiss by turning away, then he might have been able to resist.

As it was, Anna did none of those things, but instead remained as still as a statue as Rufus placed his lips gently against hers

He pulled back only slightly. "Open," he encouraged gently.

"Open?" she asked, breathing softly.

Rufus ran the tip of his finger lightly across her lips, parting them slightly before once again claiming them with his own.

She tasted delicious. A combination of honey and mint, the latter a freshness that made his lips tingle, followed by that tempting sweetness.

The enticing dip in her bottom lip begged to be tasted by his tongue before he slid fully into the heat of her mouth.

Rufus continued to kiss her, to taste her, as he pressed back against the trunk of the tree, his arm about the slenderness of her waist as he pulled her in tight against him, the softness of her breasts pressed against the hardness of his bare chest.

He groaned low in his throat as he felt the shy, tentative stroke of Anna's tongue against his own. Then she became bolder still, sucking his tongue deeper into her mouth, slowly at first, and then more demandingly as her confidence grew.

Anna came to her senses with a gasp, wrenching her mouth from Rufus's the moment she felt a firm and hot hand cupping her breast, his knowing fingertips caressing the swollen and sensitised tip.

She used her free hand to push against his chest as he seemed reluctant to release her, her eyes wide, cheeks flushed, her breasts—the breasts he had touched so intimately!—rising and falling as she breathed quickly.

She had never experienced such a kiss, such *searing* intimacy, in all of her life before today.

She had meant the kiss to be merely a meeting of lips, in order to satisfy her side of the bargain, but the way that Rufus had kissed her—and she had kissed him—was nothing, absolutely nothing, like any other kisses Anna had suffered through in the past.

Instead she had felt *claimed* by him, by having his tongue in her mouth. Had felt as if she claimed *him* when she had felt drawn to return his passion.

His firm and chiselled lips had initially been surprisingly soft against her own, causing excitement to flutter wildly beneath her breasts. And her breasts had seemed to swell beneath the dampness of her chemise as the kiss continued, the rosy tips becoming an aching tingle, with an unaccustomed warmth spreading through the whole of her body before it had centred as a pleasant ache between her thighs.

It was an excitement that Anna had thoroughly enjoyed, until she had felt that hand cup her breast, and realised she had put a stop to these unexpected intimacies. Before it was too late.

The fact that she had needed to place her hand on the muscled nakedness of Rufus's chest in order to push him away, and that her hand still rested against it, caused her to recoil back so sharply that she lost her balance on the branch completely.

"Steady, Anna!" Rufus warned harshly as he reached out to clasp both of her arms to prevent her from falling, his back pushing harder, painfully so, against the rough bark of the tree trunk behind him in order to maintain his own balance. "Perhaps we should get down from here? Before one or both of us is injured," he added grimly, his lids narrowed to hide the expression in his eyes.

How had this woman aroused him so quickly and so heatedly? So thoroughly that he had touched her more intimately than he'd intended. To the degree that he had been on the edge of losing all control.

He was a man of two and thirty, and had bedded more women than he cared to remember since losing his virginity at the age of sixteen. The intervening years had rendered him both jaded and cynical where women were concerned, and he now approached all sexual liaisons with the same lack of emotions. All he wanted from his encounters was a release of his sexual tensions.

What happened just now had felt neither jaded nor cynical, but fresher and more arousing than anything Rufus had experienced before. Just as Anna herself possessed that same freshness of spirit.

Because she was fresh, you idiot, he rebuked

himself. Any fool could see that Anna, despite the sharpness of her tongue, was a virgin, an innocent.

He had not meant to go so far as he had. He'd intended only to kiss her, to have a little fun himself, whilst at the same time punishing Anna a little for her recklessness in being alone out here in the woods, making herself vulnerable to any man who happened by. That the man had been him was purely coincidental.

One touch of Anna's parted lips beneath his, the shy and then demanding caress of her tongue, and Rufus had felt himself stir with a pulsing, aching need for more. So very much more.

And that, Rufus old chap, is the road to perdition!

Because no father was going to allow a man— even a duke!—to take his daughter's virginity without demanding some sort of recompense.

"I shall go down first," Rufus rasped harshly before releasing her to turn away and begin his descent, his thoughts grim.

If Anna had not stopped him when she had—

Then both of them would have tumbled out of the tree and put an end to the disturbing interlude that way, Rufus assured himself, his good sense having returned to him the farther he removed himself from the lure of the warmth of Anna's mouth and body. There was not even the possibility, even if he were to have practised all of his considerable sexual inventiveness, that the two of them would have been able to deepen the intimacy whilst still up in the branches of a tree.

Of course, he still had to resist kissing her again once they were both down on the ground, but good sense told him he had best do exactly that if he did not wish to make this situation even worse than it already was.

How the two of them behaved towards each other when they met again, probably in the presence of Anna's father, was a subject for conjecture, but Rufus did not imagine that Anna would any more welcome her father knowing of her scandalous behaviour today than Rufus would.

No, it had been a pleasant interlude but it was not one Rufus believed it wise to repeat. His responses to her warned him that he should not demand that second kiss.

Rufus kept his movements brisk and impersonal, his gaze averted from that sensuous mouth and those creamy breasts, as he helped Anna to descend the tree. "Turn around," he instructed briskly once she stood in front of him, intending to refasten the buttons at the back of her still-gaping gown.

Anna felt slightly befuddled as she obediently

turned her back towards Rufus, disturbed by her reaction to being so thoroughly kissed, and by a man she had only just met.

His responses to her, the low groans in his throat, and the way his hands had roamed restlessly over her back before cupping her breast, had proved that he truly was not a gentleman.

Her confusion increased as she saw his expression was one of haughty remoteness as he turned away to pull on his own clothes. She sat down on the grass to put on her stockings and boots. It was almost as if he had not just kissed her so passionately, touched her more intimately than any other man ever had.

Nor had he made any demand for a second kiss in return for helping her down from the tree.

She eyed him uncertainly as she stood up slowly. "I...thank you for your help," she murmured hoarsely.

He was now fully dressed, his glance impersonal, as he swung easily up into the saddle of his restlessly prancing stallion. "I advise that you do not make a habit of venturing out in these woods alone." His mouth twisted into the semblance of a mocking smile. "Another man might not be so reluctant to take what you offer!"

Anna gasped at the deliberate insult. "I did not offer, *you* took!"

He looked down the length of his aristocratic nose at her. "You may tell yourself that if you wish."

Anna felt the guilty colour heat her cheeks as she knew she had been a more than willing participant to their lovemaking.

Something a gentleman would most certainly not have brought to her attention.

She glared up at him. "I do believe I dislike you intensely."

"Keep telling yourself that, my love, if it pleases you." Rufus gave a mocking laugh as he doffed his hat and bowed in a caricature of politeness. "I will wish you a good day, Anna Juliet." He placed his hat firmly back on his head before turning Caesar, not giving so much as a glance back as he urged the stallion through the canopy of trees and out onto the fields leading up to the majestic red-stoned residence that was the seat of the Duke of Northamptonshire.

Rufus continued to rebuke himself for his actions as he allowed Caesar his head. For allowing an innocent such as Anna to arouse him so completely he had forgotten who he was. Who *she* was.

A rebuke that became even more immediate when the first person he saw, as he rode into the cobbled stable yard of Banbury Hall, was Matthew Turner.

The older man was in conversation with one of the maids, but he excused himself immediately to hurry across the yard as he recognised Rufus. "It is very good to see you here, Your Grace," he greeted as he took Caesar's reins, a pleased smile lighting up his weathered face.

"I believe you wrote requesting my presence," Rufus reminded abruptly as he dismounted, not at all sure how he should deal with this man after the earlier liberties he had taken with Turner's daughter.

The older man immediately sobered. "Of course." He nodded. "But first let me introduce you to my daughter." He smiled proudly as he turned and beckoned for the maid to join them.

Well, this woman was clearly not the one he'd kissed so passionately in the woods just now.

And if Anna was not Matthew Turner's daughter, then who the hell was she?

Where was she?

Chapter Four

"I must say, I was very surprised to learn that it was the *parson's* sister who lied to me so brazenly on the last occasion we met."

Anna stiffened, her back turned towards the owner of the voice as she knelt in the parsonage garden weeding the bed of herbs.

It would be an understatement for her to claim she had been dreading this meeting after the village became abuzz with the news that the new Duke of Northamptonshire had arrived unexpectedly three days ago and was now in residence at Banbury Hall.

Anna had not believed the duke's unexpected arrival and her own meeting that same day with the stranger in the woods could possibly have been a coincidence; they simply did not have that many visitors riding through the parish in one day. Consequently, she had reluctantly been forced to accept that it was more than a possibility that the Duke of Northamptonshire was the same handsome gentleman who had stripped down to his drawers in front of her startled—and avid—gaze.

The same outrageous gentleman who had then teased and flirted with her.

The very same wicked man who had climbed a tree in order to assist her only so that he might claim a kiss as his reward! A kiss that had caused Anna to blush, warm and tremble with pleasure every time she had thought of it since.

She forced down those feelings as she rose slowly to her feet before turning to face the man who had surely come here to taunt and torment her for her past behaviour.

Anna was very much aware that he had once again found her in disarray; she always wore one of her oldest gowns for gardening, and her hair was slightly dishevelled from her exertions in the herb bed.

In comparison, the duke looked a picture of sartorial elegance, in a deep blue superfine with a silver paisley waistcoat over his snowy white linen.

He leaned confidently on the top of low wall surrounding the garden at the back of the parsonage as he nodded to her in mocking salute.

"I have asked forgiveness for the lie." Anna's gaze dropped from his. "Can you claim to have done the same, as you also lied to me when you said you were not visiting people in the area?" she reminded huskily.

"I did not lie, Anna," Rufus denied smoothly. "I admitted only to travelling through the woods. And I could hardly claim to be visiting myself," he reasoned.

Her eyes flashed deeply blue as she looked up at him. "A simple acknowledgement of being the Duke of Northamptonshire would have sufficed, as I am sure you are well aware."

Rufus could not help but smile at this show of her previous sharpness with him, laying his hat on top of the wall and placing a hand beside it before jumping nimbly over into the garden.

"What are you doing?" Anna took a step back, having raised her hands to her breasts in alarm.

He strolled unconcernedly down the pathway to join her. "I have no intention of conversing with a wall between us when anyone might walk past and overhear us talking."

That sentiment was all well and good, as Anna had no wish for anyone else to learn of the circumstance of their previous acquaintance either, but Rufus was now standing far too close to her.

So close, in fact, that he was able to reach out and take one of her hands in his. "There is no reason for you to fight me, Anna." He frowned as she instantly attempted to release her hand. "Better." He nodded as she reluctantly stilled but continued to regard him warily. "The truth of the matter is, I am still becoming accustomed to the fact that is who I now am. I was not born to be a duke, Anna," he added as her gaze became quizzical.

Anna gave a slow shake of her head. "I do not understand."

He smiled ruefully. "I am the third grandson of my grandfather, the only son born to his second son, and until five weeks ago I was just plain and uninteresting *Mr* Rufus Drake," he dryly reminded her of her opinion of her own name in the woods that day. "I should never have become a duke, Anna, and truly wish I had never inherited," he added grimly.

She gave a snort. "That is ridiculous!"

"Is it?" he mused softly.

"Of course," she dismissed impatiently. "What gentleman would not wish to become a duke?"

"This one," Rufus assured her, aware that his body was once again responding with its usual wilfulness at her close proximity.

Three days ago, Rufus had known his arousal

was such that he had to get away from this young woman, or else break every rule he had ever set himself in regard to innocents.

And to Rufus's chagrin and surprise, little else had occupied his thoughts *but* this young woman since.

No matter how hard he tried, he had been unable to rid himself of the memory of how soft and silky her skin had felt beneath his fingertips that day. How full and responsive her breasts. And her passion had been more than a match for his own as she'd returned the intimacy of his kisses. As for her taste… Rufus believed he had developed an addiction to that unique taste of honey and mint.

His mouth tightened as he recalled the last three frustrating days spent trying to ascertain the identity of his little wood nymph. Not as easy a task as it might have initially seemed.

He had not spent any time at Banbury Hall since he was a child; the Drake family was not a close or mutually sociable one, and as such he had absolutely no idea who Anna could be once he realised she was not Turner's daughter after all.

The situation was one of delicacy. To ask outright for the surname and whereabouts of a girl called Anna would have placed them both in a questionable position.

And so Rufus had spent his time with Matthew Turner discussing Jacob Harker, the previous estate manager. Rufus had decided that the man had in all likelihood been involved with the other traitors to the Crown, unfortunately still in so many of the homes of the English aristocracy. Rufus had already sent word to his cousin Zachary in London, giving a detailed description of the man. Helped by the fact, he hoped, that Harker apparently had a distinctive mole on the left side of his neck.

There was nothing else Rufus could do about that while he remained in Northamptonshire, and so he had turned his attention to asking Turner for the names of all the people residing in and around Banbury, on the excuse that he wished to become acquainted with all his tenants. To Rufus's frustration, during none of their conversations did Turner make mention of a young lady named Anna.

And then the young parson had called to see Rufus early yesterday evening, and introduced himself as Mark Bishop. Mark was the son of Andrew Bishop, the previous parson of the parish, and Rufus had learned through conversation with the younger man that he resided at the parsonage with his unmarried sister, Anna. A fact Matthew Turner, not being a churchgoer, had not seen fit to mention!

Rufus's first instinct had been to return immediately to the parsonage with Bishop and see the man's sister for himself. His second, more cautious response, had been to wonder whether it was possible that *his* Anna and the daughter and sister of two parsons could really be one and the same person. Rufus had questioned himself as to whether the spinster relation of two parsons would have behaved as she had in the woods that day.

But here Anna Juliet truly was, working in the parsonage garden, her blue gown slightly soiled from her endeavours, her hair softly ruffled by the lightly blowing breeze.

She looked utterly beautiful to him.

Utterly desirable.

Nor, he was pleased to have learned in the past few minutes, did her sharpness of tongue seem to have lessened in the least since learning his identity as the Duke of Northamptonshire.

"I did not wish to become a duke, Anna," he repeated ruefully. "I liked my life exactly as it was, free of the responsibility of others, of all restraint. Until five weeks ago I could go where I wanted, be who I wanted, *with* whom I wanted."

"And can you no longer do those things?"

He sighed. "Now I have numerous estates needing my attention, servants and tenants I am responsible for, along with all the other expectations of bearing the family title."

Anna had never thought of a duke as being someone who had restraints placed upon him.

Restraints that seemed so strangely similar to her own, when all her close family relations were connected to the church.

All her life she had been Anna Bishop, the respectable daughter and then sister of a parson, her actions and words always guarded so that she did not bring embarrassment or shame upon her father or her brother.

But inside, shamefully, Anna had always longed for the sort of excitement she had known in this man's arms three days ago.

"What are your own hopes and dreams, Anna?"

She looked at Rufus guardedly as he seemed to see, to recognise, her secret, wistful longings.

Her chin rose. "I have been the daughter of a parson all my life, sir, and now I am the sister of a parson, and since my mother died eight years ago, and I lost my father two years ago, I have been helpmate to my brother. I do not have any hopes, dreams or ambitions beyond that."

Rufus did not believe her. He had seen the

wistfulness of her expression just minutes ago; her cheeks flushed, the softness of her softly parted lips, as if she yearned for something just beyond her sight. Just beyond her reach.

"What if you should marry?" he probed softly.

She gave a humourless smile. "It is unlikely that I shall ever do so."

Rufus's relief at the realisation there was no particular young man in her life at present was instantly followed by surprise at why it should matter to him one way or the other.

His curiosity won out. "Why not?"

She shrugged slender shoulders. "I know all of the gentlemen in the area, and have no wish to marry any of them. Nor will I ever leave Banbury."

This time Rufus had no doubts as to the longing, the ache, he could hear in Anna's voice. "What if a gentleman were to take you away from here?"

She gave him a brief startled glance, whatever she saw in his face causing her to look quickly away again. "I told you," her jaw was tight, "I am helpmate to my brother."

"And what if your brother should marry and have children of his own?"

Anna gave a rueful smile, having no doubts that her brother would marry as he had recently taken quite an interest in Mary Turner, the pretty young daughter of the new estate manager at Banbury Hall. That Mark also hoped to entice Matthew Turner into his fold was no doubt an added incentive to that attraction. "Then no doubts I shall happily become the devoted sister-in-law to his wife and spinster aunt to his children."

"And with each month and year that passes will you also become increasingly bitter as your own life passes you by?"

"How dare you?" Anna demanded indignantly, even as she knew this man, this *duke,* spoke the truth.

That he somehow knew her.

Rufus Drake *knew* of the yearnings she had in her heart; for excitement, freedom, to travel and to see the world outside Banbury. Of how she longed to be wholly loved and cherished by the man she would wholly love and cherish in return.

Yearnings that she would never voice, never acknowledge, but would keep hidden inside her like a bitter, festering wound.

"I dare, Anna, because I see that same restless spirit in you that I know is inside me." He reached out to take a firm grasp of her chin as he tilted her face up towards his, so that Anna had no choice but to gaze up at him. "Admit it,

Anna, you wanted me that day in the woods," he encouraged gruffly. "You *wanted* me to kiss you, to make love to you."

"No!" She gave a desperate shake of her head in denial of his words. Sweet, truthful, *sinful* words that caused her heart to clench painfully in her chest.

"You want me to kiss you now…"

"No!" She gave another frantic shake of her head.

"Yes, Anna." Rufus raised her hand to stroke his lips across her knuckles, instantly aware of that same smell of mint he had tasted when he kissed her in the woods. "I love the way you smell," he groaned as he rubbed her hand against his cheek.

A cheek that was hot with embarrassment.

Or desire?

"It is only mint from my herb garden," she excused as she snatched her hand away from his and put it behind her back. "You must not do that. Anyone could walk by."

"We have introduced ourselves now, you could invite me into the parsonage," he suggested huskily.

"No, I— Our housekeeper will very soon be back from shopping in the village."

"And is that your only reason for refusing me?"

"You must go! I cannot— We cannot!"

Rufus looked down at her as he heard the distress in her voice, and noted the look of panic in her expressive eyes as she looked up at him pleadingly. He gave a sigh before stepping back. "I am not going anywhere, Anna. And we will meet again." It was a promise rather than a threat.

Anna's emotions were in complete turmoil as she watched Rufus cross the garden to jump lithely back over the wall. He collected and put on his hat, nodding to her briefly before going on his way.

As if nothing had happened.

As if seeing her again had not shaken up his whole world in the same way that her own world had just been shaken on its foundations by seeing him again.

Chapter Five

Two more days passed before Anna saw Rufus again, and at a time and place she was completely unprepared for.

Hurrying out of the rain, on her way into the church to arrange the flowers for tomorrow's Sunday services, she instead came to an abrupt halt as she saw a solitary man standing a short distance away in the churchyard.

Rufus.

He stood at the Drake crypt, head bent, seemingly unaware of the light rain falling and dampening his hat and clothes.

He looked so alone.

Which was a strange thought to have about a duke. A very wealthy and much-sought-after duke, as village gossip indicated that every well-connected family in the area had sent him invitations to dinner parties and hastily arranged balls.

Invitations Anna knew he had so far neither accepted nor refused.

She fought a battle within herself for several minutes as she continued to watch Rufus, part of her wanting to continue on into the church and begin her flower arranging and forget that she had ever seen him, the other part of her drawn to somehow try to alleviate some of his loneliness.

The softness of her heart meant the latter easily won out.

Leaving her flowers in the vestibule, Anna came back out of the church to walk down the pathway towards where Rufus stood.

Rufus knew almost instantly that he was no longer alone, sensing—no, *feeling*—Anna's presence behind him, at the same time as he smelled the faint hint of mint he now associated only with her.

He turned slowly to look at her from beneath the brim of his hat. "You should not be out here in the rain." The shawl she had draped about her shoulders was already showing damp, as was her pale green gown.

"Neither should you," she countered gently. "Were you very close?" She looked up at the crypt where the names of Rufus's uncle and two cousins had been added these past three years.

"Not close enough." He gave a sad shake of

his head as he too glanced up at his ornate family crypt. "I suppose we all think there's plenty of time, that next week, or next month, or next year, we will make an effort to spend time with family, with those we love. And then fate decides otherwise." He turned to look at her, "No, I was not close to my uncle and cousins, Anna. But I now wish that I had been."

"You have other family?"

"Oh yes," he smiled. "I have an interfering mother, and a maternal cousin who can be just as interfering."

"They both love you, else they would not take the time to bother."

Rufus looked at her incredulously for several moments and then he gave a rueful smile. "You are very wise for one so young."

She shrugged. "I am a parson's daughter."

She was the strangest parson's daughter Rufus had ever met. The *only* parson's daughter he had ever met.

Anna was only in her very early twenties, and yet there was such wisdom in her eyes, so much understanding for what he had been trying to convey with words that, to him, seemed too trite, too dismissive.

He *did* deeply regret that he had been too busy

with his own life to allow him to be close to his uncle and cousins, because now it was too late.

Was all of life like that? he wondered.

Was life, time, so fragile that it had to be grasped with both hands?

Was that how Anna had felt when they'd spoken two days ago? As if time, life, was passing her by? That it would continue to pass her by?

Was that how he now felt, standing in this churchyard, gazing up at his family crypt, where so many of his ancestors lay, including his own father? Did he feel that if he did not seize life, seize the things he really wanted, that he would lose them forever?

Rufus had become very introspective over the past couple of days as his thoughts dwelled on just that problem. Knowing that he hungered for something.

Or perhaps someone?

"I—" He stopped as the heavens suddenly seemed to open up above them, a deluge of rain falling down on them both. "Let's get you into the church out of the rain." He took a light hold of her arm as they hurried down the pathway.

Even with her shawl pulled up over her hair Anna was soaked through by the time the two of them reached the church vestibule.

"Do you love the rain as much as I?" She

laughed with happiness as she removed her shawl before looking up at Rufus. He removed his hat, sweeping the dampness of his dark hair back from his brow. "I always feel that it cleanses everything and makes it brand new." She continued to smile as she looked out of the arched entryway at the falling rain.

"Would it cleanse me, do you think, if I were to stand out in it?" Rufus mused unsmilingly.

She turned to look at him quizzically. "You already look very clean to me."

He smiled ruefully. "I am talking of my past, Anna. Do you think the rain would cleanse me of that?"

Anna's breath caught in her throat at the intensity of his gaze. "A person's past," she spoke carefully, "is exactly that, surely?"

"Is it?" He grimaced. "And what if that past has been less than reputable?"

"But honourable? Always honourable?"

His mouth twisted into a grimace of a smile. "Oh yes, always honourable."

"Then it must be accepted as the past." She shrugged. "For the past cannot be changed, we can only hope for the future."

Rufus felt something shift deep inside him, as if a key had just been turned to open a part of him that had been locked away.

"Anna," he murmured gruffly as he moved to take her in his arms. "Beautiful, wise Anna." He rested his cheek against the silkiness of her hair.

Anna had no idea what was happening. Did not fully understand what Rufus was saying. But she did understand that he was in need of warmth and understanding, possibly because of that visit to his family crypt, that she had not been mistaken in how alone he had seemed.

Her arms moved about his tapered waist as she rested her head against his chest, and she became instantly aware of the rapid beat of his heart.

They stood like that for some minutes. Long, delicious minutes, when Anna simply enjoyed holding and being held. A time out of time.

A time that surely could not last.

"Would you be ready to do the church flowers now, Miss Anna?"

Anna pulled sharply out of Rufus's arms, her face blazing with colour as she turned to look at Mrs Faulkner, the baker's wife. She had arrived to help arrange the flowers. As she did every Saturday...

Something Anna had completely forgotten in Rufus's company.

"His Grace was sheltering from the rain, and

I was keeping him company," Anna announced brightly as the elderly lady looked at the duke suspiciously. Unlike some in the village, Mrs Faulkner was not a gossip, thankfully.

Anna quickly made the introductions before announcing that it really was time for the two of them to go into the church and see to the flowers.

Rufus eyed her with amusement as he took his leave. "A pleasure to have met you, Mrs Faulkner. We will meet again soon, I hope, Anna," he added huskily.

Anna was too embarrassed to reciprocate, too mortified at being caught in the duke's arms by Mrs Faulkner, to even be able to look at Rufus again before he turned and left them.

"Did you arrange this deliberately?"

Rufus looked at Anna as she sat to the left of him at the mahogany table in the smaller dining-room at Banbury Hall, her head bent as she looked down at the folded hands on her knees, the softness of her voice sounding hurt rather than imbued with her usual fire.

No doubt that was because of the presence of Rufus's butler who, having served their meal, now stood in attendance near the door.

Rufus motioned for Watkins to leave them, waiting until the other man had closed the door behind himself before answering her. "I *am* responsible for calling upon your brother after our meeting at the church this morning, and also for issuing the invitation for you and your brother to dine here with me this evening," Rufus acknowledged. "But I certainly had nothing to do with your brother being called away to tend to one of his flock the moment our dessert had been served, leaving the two of us alone here together."

Although Rufus accepted that he *was* guilty of persuading the young parson to allow his sister to stay and finish her meal, after which Rufus had promised he would see she arrived home safely.

Anna looked so beautiful this evening, her gown a pale lemon, with matching slippers on her feet, her hair shining like burnished gold in the last of the evening's sun streaming through the dining-room windows, her eyes a deep and sparkling blue in her beautiful heart-shaped face.

"You are a duke, sir," she answered him waspishly as she finally raised her head to look at him, "and no doubt capable of arranging anything you please."

Ah yes, and there was that sharp little tongue that could amuse and arouse him in equal measure.

"Are you angry with me because of this morning?"

Anna eyed him impatiently, knowing it was not Rufus she was annoyed with, but herself. This morning she had allowed herself to forget who she was for a few pleasurable moments of being held in his arms. A pleasure she had paid for by suffering numerous questions from Mrs Faulkner as they'd arranged the flowers together, the elderly woman at last accepting that Anna had merely been comforting the duke, who had been overcome with emotion after visiting his family crypt.

"You did not have to come here this evening, Anna," Rufus spoke quietly. "You could have used any number of excuses not to accompany your brother."

Anna knew that.

But that part of her, which was wilful as well as impetuous, the part of her that so longed for adventure and excitement, had refused to allow her to do so.

Because she had wanted to see Rufus again. To *know* if her legs would once again become weak just at the sight of him. If her body would become aroused just by being near him...

A single glance at Rufus in his evening clothes and Anna had known without a doubt that she did indeed feel all of those things towards Rufus.

Achingly.

Futilely.

She was a parson's daughter, and Rufus Drake was a sophisticated London gentleman, not to mention a duke, and at least ten years older than she.

"Anna?" He frowned as he stood up to stand next to her chair, his eyes holding hers captive.

Her heart raced. "What are you doing?"

"I believe you are well aware of what I want, what I have wanted since the moment you arrived here this evening." His eyes gleamed with desire. "What we *both* want."

It was indeed a desire, a need, that Anna echoed. With all her heart.

She swallowed. "But we should not."

"I *must*, Anna."

He bent to swing her up into his arms and carried her over to a chaise in front of the window, laying her down upon it before joining her, the heat of his body pressed close against her own, a pleasure Anna had never thought to know with him again.

"You have no idea how much I have longed, hungered, to hold you in my arms, to be with you

like this again, Anna," he murmured throatily
as his head lowered and his lips captured hers.

If his hunger was even half as much as her
own was for him to hold her, and make love to
her, then Anna *did* know.

Chapter Six

It was as if the past six days had never been, as if they were simply continuing where they had left off that day by the pond, as Rufus's hot, marauding tongue swept confidently between Anna's parted lips, plundering, claiming, *demanding* that she respond in kind. A demand that Anna gave into willingly.

He gave a low groan of satisfaction as he felt the shy stroke of Anna's tongue alongside his own, her hands moving up from his chest and over his shoulders before her fingers became entangled in the dark silky hair curling at his nape. He felt himself once again lost to satisfying his addiction to her unique taste.

He moaned as his lips moved to her cheek, the length of her throat, the creamy tops of her breasts. "I have hungered for this again since the day I met you, Anna. For the *taste* of you. For *you*," he murmured urgently, knowing he spoke the truth, and that he had thought of little else, and no one else, since the two of them had first met six days ago.

"Rufus?"

"Yes, I am Rufus!" he urged fiercely. "Not Northamptonshire. Not a duke. With you I am only Rufus," he insisted urgently.

She looked up at him searchingly. "What is it you want from me?" she finally murmured softly.

"Everything!" he assured her heatedly, his gaze feverish. "I've longed to be with you again, to touch you again," he murmured achingly. "Will you allow me?" His hands were against the buttons at the back of her gown.

Anna swallowed before answering, knowing she should say no, that she would regret this madness tomorrow. That she would have time to regret it for the rest of her life.

But it was a regret she knew would be all the deeper if she now went against the dictates of her heart. She needed this memory with Rufus in order to make the rest of her life bearable without him.

"Yes," she breathed shyly.

Rufus unfastened her gown before gently tugging down the loosened material to reveal her breasts covered only by the thinness of her chemise. "You are so beautiful, Anna," he groaned as he revealed her rose-coloured nipples. "Do they ache, Anna?" He ran his fingertips across the tips. "Are they hot and aching for me to kiss them?" he encouraged raspily even as he lowered his head and took a rosy nipple into the heat of his mouth.

Anna was so awash with sensation, in the unmistakeable knowledge of Rufus's passion, and the desire he voiced for her so fiercely, she was unable to do anything more than arch her back as she groaned her surrender and gave herself up completely to the pleasure of being in his arms.

"You are so lovely," he murmured as the heat of his mouth moved to pay homage to her other breast. "So very lovely," he groaned before suckling the roused nipple deep into his mouth, lathing with his tongue, biting gently with sharp and stimulating teeth.

Rufus had never felt so aroused as he did making love to Anna. So deeply inflamed that he wanted to give her pleasure, to pleasure her, until she belonged to him completely. Anna. *His* Anna, whether she knew it yet or not.

He was moved by her beauty, entertained by her feistiness, enthralled with her delicious body. Her breasts were perfect, the taste of her nipples as addictive as her mouth, the skin of her thighs so silky soft as he caressed their length beneath her gown, between her thighs so wet and inviting as he touched her through the slit in her drawers.

"Rufus?" she gasped as he eased a finger inside the moist heat of her.

"Let me, love," he encouraged softly as he eased a second finger inside her, her inner muscles grasping his fingers, at the same time as he pressed his thumb rhythmically against her pulsing core.

Rufus suckled one of her nipples deeply into his mouth as he continued to stroke his fingers inside her, Anna arching against him as his thumb pressed harder against her.

His.

This woman was *his*.

"Rufus!" Anna cried out at the unimagined pleasure coursing wildly through every inch of her body, her hands clinging on to the muscled hardness of Rufus's shoulders as she arched up into his invading fingers. She needed— Oh goodness, she needed—

"Let go for me, Anna!" Rufus encouraged gruffly.

"I do not know how!" She shook her head from side to side as the pleasure seemed almost too much to bear.

"Let go, love," he groaned harshly. "Just let go!"

Anna gave another gasp as his words triggered something deep inside her and her pleasure washed over her in wave after wave of ecstasy such as Anna had never thought of or imagined in her wildest daydreams.

His, Rufus groaned in satisfaction, unrelenting as he rode Anna's climax to the very end of her pleasure. Until she lay limp and gasping in his arms, her eyes fever bright as she looked up at him in wonder.

"Tell me you want me too, Anna," Rufus urged hotly; his arousal a painful ache between his thighs. "Tell me I can have all of you."

"Rufus?" She looked up at him dazedly, uncomprehending.

"There is no one here to stop us," he explained heatedly. "Watkins will not return until he is called for, and your brother is occupied in the village."

Anna was breathing hard as she slowly came back to her senses and realised the intimacies she had allowed to happen. Exactly what her wanton hungers, her desire for excitement and adventure, had led her into doing.

And how much Rufus would despise her once he also came back to his senses.

Her face paled even as she pulled herself out

of his arms before moving quickly down to the bottom of the chaise and getting back onto her feet, her legs trembling as she turned away from him to pull her chemise and gown up over her swollen breasts.

What had she *done*? How could she have allowed this to happen?

To have allowed Rufus to touch her so intimately, and the building of that unbearable pleasure, so quickly followed by the release she could still feel between her thighs.

She had not realised when she gave herself up to his desire for her. Had not known where, or how far, her own passions would take her.

It was too much.

Rufus was too much.

He was also, no matter how much he might try to dismiss it, the Duke of Northamptonshire. And Anna would never be any more to him than another conquest. A woman to amuse him while he was in Banbury, so far away from the sophisticated amusements and equally sophisticated women he usually enjoyed in London.

She was merely an amusement to him.

A diversion, nothing more.

Anna had never met a man like Rufus before. A man so handsome. So self-assured. So intelligent. So wickedly amusing. So achingly, sinfully attractive.

She had realised the moment she'd seen him again that night, and the idea had grown as the two of them talked, as he made such delicious love to her just now, that somehow over the past six days her fascination with him had turned to budding love. A love that had burst into full bloom tonight. She was in love with Rufus Drake, the wickedly handsome Duke of Northamptonshire.

The fact that her heart was now breaking at that knowledge, as *she* now felt broken, would be of no interest to him. As she would be of no interest to him once he was back amongst his sophisticated London friends.

And she would not, *could* not, allow him to see, or even guess, her feelings for him, and the heartbreak of loving him. That would be the ultimate humiliation.

She raised her chin determinedly. "I had thought the *droit du seigneur* to have been abandoned several centuries ago?"

Rufus was taken aback. "You misunderstand my intentions totally."

"I do not think so," Anna murmured dismissively. "You invited my brother and me to dine here with you this evening, and then immediately proceeded to kiss me, to make love to me, the moment he was out of the room. You then pointed out that there is no one here to stop your attentions. And you— I— I am so ashamed!" She buried her face in her hands.

Rufus had done all of those things, but only because he had been so happy to be alone with Anna again. To be able to hold her. To make love to her.

He had obviously frightened her with the intensity of that lovemaking.

These possessive feelings were utterly new to him. Unprecedented. But that did not mean Rufus was not completely aware of what they were. What they meant to him. What Anna meant to him.

He had awoken every day these past six days full of anticipation, buoyant in the knowledge that he might see her again. Not only had he never before met a woman he desired as much as he did her, but he admired her intelligence, her sense of adventure, that wild imagination that had come up with the story of the kitten up in the tree. Anna made him laugh, at himself as much as anything else, and not in the bored or jaded way of his London friends.

She was also wise beyond her years in the way in which she had understood and soothed his feelings at the churchyard this morning. She'd helped him to see that life must be grasped, seized, before it was too late.

"Contrary to what you may think of me, Your Grace, I am not one of your London trollops!" Anna snapped as she turned her back on him, obviously waiting for him to refasten her gown.

Rufus frowned as he slowly refastened the tiny buttons. "I would never think that of you…"

"Nor," she continued firmly as she stepped away from him, "am I a country bumpkin, who would feel so flattered and grateful for the attentions of a duke, that she would simply throw herself down and worship at your feet."

This was why he wanted her, Rufus acknowledged ruefully. Because Anna, and damn it she would be *his* Anna, had shown him again this evening that she was not in the least in awe of him or his title. Instead she had treated him as if he were just the wicked gentleman she had met in the woods six days ago.

Rufus could not hold back a smile. "I believe I had in mind another part of my anatomy entirely which you might go down upon your knees and worship."

She drew in an indignant breath, even as her gaze moved to the front of his black pantaloons, where the evidence of his arousal was unmistakeable.

Her mouth firmed as she glared at him. "You, sir, are a cad. A lecher. A despoiler of innocents— I fail to see what is so amusing!" she snapped as he began to laugh.

"Ye gods, Anna," Rufus continued to chuckle. "I cannot wait to take you to London and introduce you to my friends, and most especially to my cousin Zachary!" He had no doubts that his cousin, of all the Dangerous Dukes, would understand exactly why and how this young woman had burrowed so deeply beneath Rufus's skin in so short a time.

Anna was a prize beyond any jewels, or any amount of money, was beyond freedom, beyond anything that Rufus had previously so highly valued in his life.

"What are you suggesting?" Anna looked at him in alarm. "That you would like to take me to London with you when you leave so that the two of you might *share* me in your bed?"

"Absolutely not," Rufus's humour faded as quickly as it had arisen, his expression grim as he stepped forward determinedly before once again placing his fingers beneath her chin and tilting her face up towards his, his lids narrowed in warning. "You will never be with any other man, Anna. No other man will ever be allowed to see your nakedness but me. Do you understand me?"

No, Anna did not understand him at all. She knew she had been playing with fire when she had thought him merely a gentleman passing through the area the day they met in the woods. She had behaved even more recklessly this evening, when her longings had allowed him to make love to her so pleasurably.

But this man, the arrogant words of this *duke*, were surely beyond her comprehension.

Except he seemed to be suggesting he would happily take her back to London with him when he went. As his mistress?

And perhaps she deserved such disrespect from him. Perhaps her shameful actions this evening had led him to assume, to believe, that she would accept such a role in his life.

"I understand you perfectly," she nodded abruptly.

Rufus looked down at her searchingly. "Do you?"

"Oh yes," Anna acknowledged dully. "I do not believe I will wait for your carriage to take me home. It is a warm and sunny evening, and I would prefer to walk."

"Anna—"

"Please do not say anything more to me this evening, Rufus."

Tears stung her eyes as she looked at him pleadingly. "I could not bear it."

Rufus frowned as he saw how deeply upset Anna was. No doubt because of their lovemaking earlier; he should not have allowed things to go as far as they had. Except he could not regret having touched and caressed her, having made love to her. Or deny the need he felt to caress and make love to her again as soon as was possible.

But not like this. Not with these misunderstandings standing between them.

He nodded abrupt acceptance of her decision to leave. "You will return to the parsonage in my carriage, as I assured your brother that you would." He rang for Watkins. "I will only agree not to accompany you," he continued as she seemed about to protest yet again, "on the condition *you* agree to meet me at two of the clock tomorrow afternoon at our pond—"

"No."

"Yes, Anna." Rufus knew that his own eyes must be as fiercely determined as her own.

He may not have wanted to become a duke, but there was no denying he was one, and in this particular instance, he intended to behave like one.

"Be there at two of the clock, Anna, unless you wish for your brother to know the extent of our friendship," Rufus's tone was soft, but nevertheless brooked no further argument.

Watkins knocked quietly on the door before entering the room. Rufus issued his instructions for the carriage, and waited for the other man to leave before turning back to Anna.

She frowned. "You would not really do that?"

No, of course Rufus would not do that, but he was determined that Anna would meet with him tomorrow. "Do not press me, Anna," he advised gently.

She looked at him searchingly for several long seconds before her lashes lowered and she gave a slight nod of acceptance. "Very well. I will meet you at two o'clock tomorrow afternoon."

"At our pond," he pressed.

"At the pond," she corrected purposefully.

Rufus stood at the window and watched a few minutes later as Anna hurried down the front steps of the house before stepping quickly up into his carriage.

As if the Hounds of Hell were at her heels.

Or the man who was determined to have her for his own.

Chapter Seven

The challenging expression on Anna's face when the two of them met at the pond the following day was not at all encouraging to Rufus in regard to his hopes of a successful outcome to the conversation to come.

He felt a clenching in his chest at how distant Anna seemed to him today, not in proximity, but in every other way that mattered. She looked beautiful of course, ethereally so, in a cream gown with her curls pure gold beneath the sun's rays. But her eyes were a dark and wary blue in the pallor of her face as she looked up at him, her mouth unsmiling.

She set her chin stubbornly. "Could we please get this conversation over with as quickly as possible?" her voice was brittle, as breakable as she appeared to be. "I have visits to make in the village this afternoon on my brother's behalf."

Rufus eyed her quizzically. "Why are you lying to me again, Anna?"

Colour suffused her cheeks. "I am not."

"Yes, I am afraid you are," Rufus rebuked gently as he crossed the short distance between them to stand directly in front of her. "My conversation this morning with your brother would have ensured he did not send you off on errands today."

"You have spoken to Mark?" she gasped, the colour once again draining from her cheeks. "But… I did not see you at the parsonage."

"We met at the church."

"Why?" Anna gave a pained groan. "What did you say to him? Did you complain of my behaviour yesterday evening? Tell him of my wantonness?" Tears stung her eyes at thoughts of that humiliation.

The same tears that had been falling down Anna's cheeks for all of the night and most of this morning. Tears of humiliation for her wanton behaviour yesterday evening. The tears of knowing she was in love with a man who would never, could never, return that love.

Anna had thought her life empty before this, her heart, her soul, hungering for *something*. But the thought of Rufus soon returning to London, of not seeing so much as a glimpse of him again for months, possibly years, filled her heart with a despair she could never have imagined.

To the point she had even considered accepting his offer that she return to London with him and become his mistress, for however long such arrangements lasted.

Only to sob even harder as she was forced to dismiss such a notion; such an arrangement may bring her some measure of happiness for a short time, but she could never bring such disgrace upon her brother by behaving in such a scandalous manner. And she could not avoid the pain that the end of such an alliance would bring.

No, the only course left open to her was to accept there was no future for herself with a man like Rufus, and to behave with all the dignity her deceased mother and father would have expected from her.

"I would not break my word to you in that way, Anna," Rufus reassured. "Nor do I have any complaints about your behaviour yesterday evening. On the contrary."

"Could we please *not* discuss the events of yesterday evening?" She turned sharply away from him, her lace-gloved hands tightly clasped together in front of her. "It is enough for us both to know it was a mistake. An aberration, brought about by…by…"

"Brought about by what, Anna?" Rufus prompted softly.

She gave an agitated shake of her head. "You are the more experienced one of us, so perhaps you will tell me what it was brought about by?"

His expression gentled. "Desire. Arousal. Love."

"I do not lo——" Anna stopped as she realised she was about to tell him yet another lie.

She *did* love Rufus. So very, very much. So much that it was breaking her heart to be with him again, just to be near him and know he could never be hers.

Rufus stepped forward to place his hands upon the slenderness of Anna's shoulders, deeply distressed at seeing her so upset. "Anna, the only reason I spoke with your brother this morning was because I needed to ask his permission before I dare ask you to marry me."

"No! No, no, *no!*" she cried emotionally as the tears cascaded unchecked down the paleness of her cheeks. "I cannot—— I will not allow you to. *Your* honour is not in question, Rufus," she assured him in a throaty voice. "*I* am the one who was at fault yesterday evening. I am the one who allowed you to make love to me. No man could have refused what I so freely offered. You should not now feel—— I will not hear of your offering to marry me because of my wantonness." She began to cry in earnest.

Rufus's heart had plummeted as Anna protested so vehemently against the idea of marrying him, only to feel ravaged as she offered up words of self-condemnation.

His heart now felt as if it were being wrenched from his chest as he witnessed the heartbreak of her tears.

He enfolded her tightly in his arms, his cheek resting against the silky softness of her golden curls. "I know we have not known each other for long, Anna, and that you will need time to feel for me as I do for you, but— Do you believe in love at first sight, Anna?" he prompted. "Do you believe it is possible to look at a person and know, instinctively *know*, that you are meant to be with that person for the rest of your life?"

Anna stilled in his arms before slowly pulling back to look up at him searchingly. "I do not— Are you saying that is what has happened to you? That you *love* me?"

"Oh yes," Rufus confirmed. "I admit I have spent all my adult life in total ignorance of the emotion, which is perhaps why I did not immediately recognise it for what it was, and instead believed it to be desire rather than love. But I am in no doubts now of my feelings, Anna. I cannot

live without you by my side." He had known it
three days ago when the two of them had spoken
in the churchyard. Had been totally convinced
of it when they'd made love together last night.
"I spoke to your brother this morning, before
discussing it with you, only because it was the
right thing to do, the gentlemanly thing to do."
He reached up to cradle each side of her face,
his eyes gazing unwaveringly into hers as his
thumbs stroked the tears from her cheeks. "I am
deeply in love with you, Anna Juliet Bishop, and
will always be so. And I would deem it an honour, a privilege, if you would one day consider
becoming my wife."

Anna gazed up at him in stunned disbelief,
never having thought to hear such words from
Rufus. From her wicked duke. From the sinful
gentleman she had last night realised she loved
with all her heart.

All of those reasons caused her doubts to linger. "Are you sure, Rufus?" She gave a shake of
her head. "I would not want you to feel obligated
into offering me marriage."

"I have never allowed feelings of obligation
to determine my actions, Anna," he assured her
dryly. "And certainly not when it comes to the
taking of a wife!" he added teasingly before sobering again. "I admit to having behaved some-

thing of a rake these past ten or twelve years, but that is because I did not know otherwise. As I tried to explain this to you on Saturday morning at the church. You have changed me, Anna," he assured earnestly. "My love for you has changed me, so much so that I no longer want any other woman but you. And I know that I never will. Will you at least give me leave to court you, Anna? To woo you, so that perhaps one day you might learn to feel that same love for me?"

Anna felt as if her heart had swollen with so much emotion it might burst out of her chest at any moment.

Rufus had told her he loved her!

More than that, he had said he did not feel obligated to offer for her but that he *wished* to marry her.

That he wanted to make her his forever beloved wife.

By loving her, by wishing to marry her, to be with her forever, Rufus offered her the freedom she had so restlessly hungered for all her life.

What better freedom was there than to love and be loved? To be with the man she loved, and who loved her? Forever.

"I already love you, Rufus." Anna knew her face glowed as she gazed up at him with all of that love shining in her eyes.

"You do?" His eyes darkened with emotion as he looked down at her searchingly. "Can you possibly? Is it really possible you are in love with me, my darling Anna?" He looked uncharacteristically uncertain.

An uncertainty that caused Anna's heart to ache. "I love you so very much. From that first moment, too, I believe. I just— I did not believe that you could ever feel the same way about someone like me."

"There is no one else like you, Anna!" Rufus assured gruffly as he held her fiercely in his arms. "You are unique. You are perfect. You are my beloved. Will you marry me, Anna, and make me the happiest man in the world? Will you be my duchess? The mother of our children?"

Anna's heart leapt at the realisation that if she said yes to his marriage proposal she would not only become Rufus's wife but also a duchess. "I am only the daughter of a parson." She reminded him then.

"And I am only a duke because of tragic family losses and being the unfortunate third grandson of a duke," Rufus assured wryly. "Can you not see how perfect we are for each other, Anna—the unexpected duke and the parson's daughter!" He looked almost boyish as he grinned down at her.

She winced. "It sounds like the title of a melodrama."

"To me it sounds like heaven," Rufus contradicted huskily. "Say yes, Anna. Say yes, and we shall have your brother marry us as soon as is possible, and then we shall leave England and go on an extended honeymoon. Would you like that, Anna?" he prompted as he saw the excitement glowing in her eyes. "Shall we leave England for a while and travel together, not to the Continent, because it is not safe as yet, but to all the other exotic places that so call to your heart?"

Rufus really did know her, Anna acknowledged wonderingly. He knew her *and* what was in her heart.

"I would be just as happy to remain here, or to go to London. As long as I am with you it does not matter where we are," she assured, knowing it was true, and that Rufus meant more to her than anything else. That *he* was her dream, loving him was her true freedom, and marriage to him would be the biggest adventure.

"We will travel," Rufus insisted. "I am looking forward to sharing all the wonders of the world with you. To seeing them through your beautiful eyes. I love you so much, Anna Juliet. So very, very much," he added fiercely.

"I love you too, Rufus," she answered him just as earnestly.

"Then marry me and make me the happiest of men."

"As you will make me the happiest of women."

Anna had no doubts it was a vow, and a love, they would both treasure for the rest of their hopefully long lives together.

They made their official vows before family, friends and God just weeks later, Anna somewhat overwhelmed by meeting so many titled members of the ton, most especially the five Dangerous Dukes, and several of their wives, who were all Rufus's closest friends.

But she need not have worried, the three duchesses could not have been more welcoming, and the dukes were all exceedingly charming to her. Apart from Griffin Stone, Duke of Rotherham, who was pleasant enough, but seemed to be of a naturally taciturn disposition.

"Do you think he is leaving early because he disapproves of me?" Anna whispered to her new husband after Rotherham had taken his leave to depart for his estate in Lancashire.

"I would not care if he did," Rufus assured her with his usual arrogance. "But I am sure he does approve of you, my darling." He kissed her soundly in front of all their wedding guests. "Rotherham is… It is only that weddings are not his favourite occasions." He grimaced.

Rufus had told Anna all there was to know about him. His past, his present, their future. And she loved him still, in spite of it.

But there was no reason for him to talk on their wedding day of his and the other Dangerous Dukes' work for the Crown. No need to explain that Griffin was returning to his estate because they had received word that Jacob Harker, Rufus's errant estate manager, had possibly been seen in Lancashire.

"Oh?" Anna looked up at him enquiringly.

"Never mind your curiosity about Griffin." Rufus tapped her lightly on her nose. "You shall have your hands far too full of your husband, and our happiness together for many years to come, to be able to indulge your inquisitive nature in regard to Rotherham. Besides which, he would not thank you for it," he added with certainty.

"Really, husband?" Anna looked up at him mischievously. "And how shall we occupy ourselves for these many years to come?"

Rufus grinned down at her. "I am sure we shall think of something."

The two of them laughed softly together, the

promise of a long and happy life together ahead of them. The adventure they had both longed for and now found in each other.

* * * * *

GRIFFIN STONE: DUKE OF DECADENCE

To all of you for loving the
Dangerous Dukes as much as I do!

Chapter One

July 1815, Lancashire, England.

'What the—?' Griffin Stone, the tenth Duke of Rotherham, pulled sharply on the reins of his perfectly matched greys as a ghostly white figure ran out of the darkness directly in front of his swiftly travelling phaeton.

Despite his concerted efforts to avoid a collision, the ethereal figure barely missed being stomped on by the high-stepping and deadly hooves, but was not so fortunate when it came to the back offside wheel of the carriage.

Griffin winced as he heard rather than saw that collision, all of his attention centred on bringing the greys to a stop before he was able to jump down from the carriage and run quickly round to the back of the vehicle.

There was only the almost full moon overhead for

illumination, but nevertheless Griffin was able to locate where the white figure lay a short distance away.

An unmoving and ghostly shape was lying face down in the dirt.

Two strides of his long legs brought him to the utterly still figure, where he crouched down on his haunches. Griffin could see that the person was female; long dark hair fell across her face and cascaded loosely down the length of her spine, and she was wearing what, to him, looked suspiciously like a voluminous white nightgown, her feet bare.

He glanced about them in confusion; this private way through Shrawley Woods was barely more than a rutted track, and as far as he was aware there were no houses in the immediate vicinity. In fact, Griffin was *very* aware as the surrounding woods and the land for several miles about them formed part of his principal ducal estate.

It made no sense that this woman was roaming about his woods wearing only her nightgown.

He placed his fingers about her wrist, with the intention of checking for a pulse, only to jerk back as she unexpectedly gave a pained groan the moment his fingers touched her bared flesh. It let him know she was at least still alive, even if the sticky substance he could feel on his fingertips showed she had sustained an injury of some kind.

Griffin took a handkerchief from his pocket and wiped the blood from his hand before reaching out to gently stroke the long dark hair from over her face, revealing it as a deathly pale oval in the moonlight.

'Can you hear me?' His voice was gruff, no doubt from the scare he had received when she'd run out in front of his carriage.

Shrawley Woods was dense, and this rarely used track was barely navigable in full daylight; Griffin had only decided to press on in the darkness towards Stonehurst Park, just a mile away, because he had played in these woods constantly as a child and knew his way blindfolded.

There had been no reason, at eleven o'clock at night, for Griffin to take into account that there would be someone else in these woods. A poacher would certainly have known his way about in a way this barely clothed female obviously did not.

'Can you tell me where you are injured so that I can be sure not to hurt you again?' Griffin prompted, his frown darkening when he received no answer, and was forced to accept that she had once again slipped into unconsciousness.

Griffin made his next decision with the sharp precision for which he had been known in the army. It was late at night, full dark, no one had yet come crashing through the woods in pursuit of this woman, and, whoever she might be, she was obviously in need of urgent medical attention.

Consequently there was only one decision he could make, and that was to place her in the phaeton and continue on with the rest of his journey to Stonehurst Park. Once there they would no longer be in darkness, and he could ascertain her injuries more accurately, after which a doctor could be sent for. Explanations for her state of undress, and her mad flight through the woods, could come later.

Griffin straightened to take off his driving coat and lay it gently across her before scooping her carefully up into his arms.

She weighed no more than a child, her long hair cascading over his arm, her face all pale and dark hollows in the moonlight. He rested her head more comfortably against his shoulder.

She was young and very slender. Too slender. The weight of her long hair seemed almost too much for the slender fragility of her neck to support.

She made no sound as he lifted her up onto the seat of his carriage, nor when he wrapped his coat more securely about her. He took up the reins once again and moved the greys on more slowly than before in an effort not to jolt his injured passenger unnecessarily.

His decision to come to his estate in Lancashire had been forced upon him by circumstances. The open war against Napoleon was now over, thank goodness, but Griffin, and several of his close friends, who also bore the title of Duke and were known collectively as the Dangerous Dukes, all knew, better than most, that there was still a silent, private war to be fought against the defeated emperor and his fanatical followers.

Just a week ago the Dangerous Dukes had helped foil an assassination plot to eliminate their own Prince Regent, along with the other leaders of the alliance. The plan being to ensure Napoleon's victorious return to Paris, while chaos ruled in those other countries.

A Frenchman, André Rousseau, since apprehended and killed by one of the Dangerous Dukes, had previously spent a year in England, secretly persuading men and women who worked in the households of England's politicians and peers to Napoleon's cause. Of which there were many; so many families in England had French relatives.

Many of the perpetrators of that plot had since been either killed or incarcerated, but there remained several who were unaccounted for. It was rumoured that those remaining followed the orders of an as yet unknown leader.

Griffin was on his way to the ducal estates he had not visited for some years, because the Dukes had received word that one of the traitors, Jacob Harker, who might know the identity of this mysterious leader, had been sighted in the vicinity.

It just so happened that three of the Dangerous Dukes had married in recent weeks, and a fourth wed just a week ago, on the very day Griffin had set out for his estate in Lancashire. With all of his friends being so pleasurably occupied, it had been left to him to pursue the rumour of the sighting of Harker.

Running a young woman down in his carriage, in the dark of night, had not been part of Griffin's immediate plans.

She hurt.

Every part of her was in agony and aching as she attempted to move her legs.

A wave of pain that swelled from her toes to the top of her head.

Had she fallen?

Been involved in an accident of some kind?

'Would you care for a drink of water?'

She stilled at the sound of a cultured male voice, hardly daring to breathe as she tried, and failed, to recall if she recognised the owner of it before she attempted to open her eyes.

Panic set in as she realised that he was a stranger to her.

'There is no reason to be alarmed,' Griffin assured her firmly as the young woman in the bed finally opened panicked eyes—eyes that he could now see were the dark blue of midnight, and surrounded by thick lashes that were very black against the pallor of a face that appeared far too thin—and turned to look at him as he sat beside the bed in a chair that was uncomfortably small for his large frame.

She, in comparison, made barely an outline beneath the covers of the bed in his best guest bed-chamber at Stonehurst Park, her abundance of long dark hair appearing even blacker against the white satin-and-lace pillows upon which her head lay, her face so incredibly pale.

'I assure you I do not mean you any harm,' he added firmly. He was well aware of the effect his five inches over six feet in height, and his broad and mus-cled body, had upon ladies as delicate as this one. 'I am sure you will feel better if you drink a little water.'

Griffin turned to the bedside table and poured some into a glass. He placed a hand gently beneath her nape to ease up her head and held the glass to her lips until she had drunk down several sips, aware as he did that those dark blue eyes remained fixed on his every move.

Tears now filled them as her head dropped back onto the pillows. 'I—' She gave a shake of her head, only to wince as even that slight movement obviously caused her pain. She ran her moistened tongue over her lips before speaking again. 'You are very kind.'

Griffin frowned darkly as he turned to place the glass back on the bedside table, hardening his heart against the sight of those tears until he knew more about the circumstances behind this young woman's flight through his woods. His years as an agent for the Crown had left him suspicious of almost everybody.

And women, as he knew only too well, were apt to use tears as their choice of weapon.

'Who are you?'

It was a reasonable question, Griffin supposed, in the circumstances. And yet he could not help but think he should be the one asking that.

When they'd arrived at Stonehurst late last night he had left the care of his carriage and horses to his head groom, before hurriedly taking her into his arms and carrying her up the steps into the house. Once inside he had hurried her up to the bedchambers, much to the open-mouthed surprise of his butler, Pelham.

Rather than send for a doctor straight away Griffin had taken a few moments to assess the condition of the young woman himself. After all, until he knew the reason for her flight through the woods it might be prudent to ask her some questions. Was she in some sort of danger?

Griffin had been grateful for his caution once he had placed his burden carefully down atop the bedcovers and gently folded back the many capes of his topcoat.

As he had thought, the woman was young, possibly eighteen, or at the most twenty, and her heart-shaped face was delicately lovely. She had perfectly arched eyebrows beneath a smooth brow, though the slight hollowness to her cheeks possibly spoke of a deprivation of food. Her nose was small and straight, her mouth a pale pink, the top lip slightly fuller than the bottom, her chin softly curved.

She had been wearing a filthy white cotton nightgown over her slender curves, revealing feet that were both dirty and lacerated beneath its bloodied ankle length. A result, he was sure, that she'd begun her flight shoeless.

There had also already been a sizeable lump and bruising already appearing upon her right temple, no doubt from her collision with his carriage.

But it was her other injuries, injuries that Griffin knew could not possibly have been caused by that collision, which had caused him to draw in a shocked and hissing breath.

The blood he had felt on his fingers earlier came from the raw chafing about both her wrists and ankles. She'd obviously been restrained by tight ropes for some time before her flight through his woods.

There were any number of explanations as to why she'd been restrained, of course, and not all of them were necessarily sinister.

Though he did not favour the practice himself, he was nevertheless aware that some men liked to secure a woman to the bed—as some women enjoyed being secured!—during love play.

There was also the possibility that this young woman was insane, and had been restrained for her own safety as well as that of others.

The final possibility, and perhaps the most likely, was that she had been restrained against her will.

Until such a time as Griffin established which explanation it was he'd decided that no one in his household, or outside it, was to be allowed to talk to her but himself.

His decision made, Griffin had immediately instructed the hovering Pelham to bring him hot water and towels, and to appropriate a clean nightgown from one of the maids. After all, there had been nothing to stop Griffin making his uninvited guest at least a little more comfortable than she was at present.

Still, he had been deeply shocked, once he had used his knife to cut the dirty and bloodied nightgown away from her body, to discover many bruises, both old and new, concealed beneath.

There had been no visible marks on her face, apart from the bruise on her temple, but there had been multiple purple and black bruises covering her body, with other, older bruises having faded to yellow. The ridge of her spine had shown through distinctly against that bruised skin as evidence that this woman had not only been repeatedly kicked and or beaten, but that she had also been starved, possibly for some days if not weeks, of more than the food and water necessary to keep her alive.

If that was the case, Griffin was determined to know exactly who was responsible for having exerted such cruelty on this fragile and beautiful young woman, and why.

After assuring she was as comfortable as was possible, Griffin had then gone quickly to his own room to bathe the travel dust from his own body, before changing into clean clothes and returning to spend the night in the chair at her bedside. He'd meant to be at her side when she woke.

If she woke.

She had given several groans of protest as Griffin had bathed the dirt from her wrists, ankles and feet, before applying a soothing salve and bandages, her feet very dirty and badly cut from running outdoors without shoes, and also in need of the application of the healing salve. Otherwise she had remained worryingly quiet and still for the rest of the night.

Griffin, on the other hand, had had plenty of time in which to consider his own actions.

Obviously he could not have left this young woman in the woods, least of all because he was responsible for having rendered her unconscious in the first place. But the uncertainty of who she was and the reasons for her imprisonment and escape meant the ramifications for keeping her here could be far-reaching.

Not that he gave a damn about that; Griffin answered only to the Crown and to God, and he doubted the former had any interest in her, and for the moment—and obviously for some days or weeks previously!—the second seemed to have deserted her.

Consequently Griffin now had the responsibility of her until she woke and was able to tell him the circumstances of her injuries.

Just a few minutes ago Griffin had seen her eyes

moving beneath her translucent lids, and her dark lashes flutter against the pallor of her cheeks, as evidence that she was finally regaining consciousness. And her voice, when she had spoken to him at last, had at least answered one of his many questions; her accent was refined rather than of the local brogue, and her manner was also that of a polite young lady.

'I am Griffin Stone, the Duke of Rotherham.' He gave a curt inclination of his head as he answered her question. 'And we are both at Stonehurst Park, my ducal estate in Lancashire.' He frowned as she made no effort to reciprocate. 'And you are?'

And she was...?

Panic once again assailed her as she sought, and failed, to recall her own name. To recall *anything* at all from before she had opened her eyes a few minutes ago and seen the imposing gentleman seated at her bedside in a bedchamber that was as unfamiliar to her as the man himself.

The Duke of Rotherham.

Even seated he was a frighteningly large man, with fashionably overlong black hair, and impossibly wide shoulders and chest. He was dressed in a perfectly tailored black superfine over a silver waistcoat and white linen, and his thighs and legs were powerfully muscled in grey pantaloons above brown-topped Hessians.

But it was his face, showing that refinement of feature and an expression of aloof disdain, surely brought about only by generations of fine breeding, which held her mesmerised. He had a high intelligent brow with perfectly arched eyebrows over piercingly cold silver-grey eyes. His nose was long and aquiline between high cheekbones, and he'd sculptured unsmiling lips above an arrogantly determined jaw.

He was an intimidating and grimly intense gentleman, with a haughty aloofness that spoke of an innate, even arrogant, confidence. Whereas she...

Her lips felt suddenly numb, and the bedroom began to sway and dip in front of her eyes.

'You must stay awake!' The Duke rose sharply to his feet so that he could take a firm grip of her shoulders, his hold easing slightly only as she gave a low groan of pain. 'I apologise if I caused you discomfort.' He frowned darkly. 'But I really cannot allow you to fall asleep again until I am sure you are in your right mind. So far I have resisted calling the doctor but I fear that may have been unwise.'

'No!' she protested sharply. 'Do not call anyone! Please do not,' she protested brokenly, her fingers now clinging to the sleeves of his jacket as she looked up at him pleadingly.

Griffin frowned his displeasure, not in the least reassured by her responses so far. She seemed incapable of answering the simplest of questions and had now become almost hysterical at his having mentioned sending for the doctor. Had last night's bump to the head caused some sort of trauma to the mind? Or had her mind been affected before?

Griffin knew the English asylums for housing those pitiful creatures were basic at best, and bestial at worst, and tended to attract as warders those members of society least suited to the care of those who were most vulnerable. Admittedly, some of the insane could be violent themselves, but Griffin sincerely doubted that was true in the case of this young woman. She was surely too tiny and slender to be of much danger to others? Unless her jailers had feared self-harm, of course.

Distasteful as that thought might be, Griffin could not deny that it was one explanation for both the bruises on her body, and those marks of restraint.

Except, to his certain knowledge, there was no asylum for the mentally insane situated within fifty miles of Stonehurst Park.

'At least tell me your name,' he said again, more gently this time, for fear of alarming her further.

'I cannot.' The tears now flooded and overflowed, running unchecked down her cheeks and dampening her hair.

Griffin frowned his frustration, with both her tears and her answer.

He was well aware that women cried for many reasons. With pain. In fear. Emotional distress. And to divert and mislead.

And in this instance, it could be being used as a way of not answering his questions at all!

But perhaps he was being unfair and she was just too frightened to answer him truthfully? Fearful of being returned to the place where she had been so cruelly treated?

It would be wrong of him to judge until he knew all the circumstances.

'Are you at least able to tell me why you were running through the Shrawley Woods in the dead of night wearing only your nightclothes?' he urged softly. He was not averse to using his height and size to intimidate a man, but knew only too well how easily those two things together could frighten a vulnerable woman.

'No!' Her eyes had widened in alarm, as if she had no previous knowledge of having run through the woods.

Griffin placed a gentle finger against one of her bandaged wrists. 'Or how you received these injuries?'

She looked blankly down at those bandages. 'I— No,' she repeated emotionally.

Griffin's frustration heightened as he rose restlessly to his feet before crossing the room to where the early morning sun shone brightly through the windows of the bedchamber, the curtains having remained undrawn the night before.

The room faced towards the back of the house, and outside he could see the stirrings of the morning: maids returning to the house with pails of milk, grooms busy in the stables, feeding and exercising the horses, several estate workers already tending to the crops in the far fields.

All normal morning occupations for the efficient running of the estate.

While inside the house all was far from normal.

There was an unknown and abused young woman lying in the bed in Griffin's guest bedchamber, and he knew that his own mood was surly after the long days of travel, and the upset of the collision followed by lack of sleep as he'd sat at her bedside.

Griffin was a man of action.

If something needed to be done, fixed, or solved, then he did, fixed or solved it, and beware anyone who stood in his way.

But he could not do, fix or solve *this* dilemma without this woman's cooperation, and, despite all his efforts to the contrary, she was too fearful at present to dare to confide so much as her name to him.

He knew from personal experience that women often found him overwhelming.

He was certainly not a man that women ever turned to for comfort or understanding. He was too physically large, too overpowering in his demeanour, for any woman to seek him out as their confidant.

No, for their comfort, for those softer emotions such as understanding and empathy, a woman of delicacy looked for a poet, not a warrior.

His wife, although dead these past six years, had been such a woman. Even after weeks of courtship and their betrothal, and despite all Griffin's efforts to reassure her, his stature and size had continued to alarm Felicity. It had been a fear Griffin had been sure he could allay once they were married. He had been wrong.

'I am not—I do not—I am not being deliberately disobliging or difficult, sir,' she said pleadingly. 'The simple truth is that I cannot tell you my name because—because I do not know it!'

A scowl appeared between Griffin's eyes as he turned sharply round to look across at his unexpected guest, not sure that he had understood her correctly. 'You do not know your own name, or you do not have one?'

Well, of course she must have a name!

Surely everyone had a name?

'I have a name, I am sure, sir.' She spoke huskily. 'It is only—for the moment I am unable to recall it.'

And the shock of realising she did not know her own name, who she was, or how she had come to be here, or the reason for those bandages upon her wrists—indeed, anything that had happened to her before she woke up in this bed a few short minutes ago, to see this aloof and imposing stranger seated beside her—filled her with a cold and terrifying fear.

Chapter Two

The Duke remained still and unmoving as he stood in front of the window, imposing despite having fallen silent after her announcement, those chilling grey eyes now studying her through narrowed lids.

As if he was unsure as to whether or not he should believe her.

And why should he, when it was clear he had no idea as to her identity either, let alone what she had been doing in his woods?

What possible reason could she have had for doing something so shocking? What sort of woman behaved so scandalously?

The possible answer to that seemed all too obvious.

To both her and the Duke?

'You do not believe me.' She made a flat statement of fact rather than asked a question.

'It is certainly not the answer I might have expected,' he finally answered slowly.

'What did you expect?' She struggled to sit up higher against the pillows, once again aware that she had aches and pains over all of her body, rather than just her bandaged wrists. Indeed, she felt as if she had been trampled by several horses and run over by a carriage.

What had Griffin expected? That was a difficult question for him to answer. He had completely ruled out the possibility that she'd sustained her injuries from mutual bed sport; they were too numerous for her ever to have enjoyed or found sexual stimulation from such treatment. Nor did he particularly wish to learn that his suspicions of insanity were true. And the possibility that this young lady might have been restrained against her will, possibly by her own family, was just as abhorrent to him.

But he had never considered for a moment that she would claim to have no memory of her own name, let alone be unable to tell him where or from whom she had received her injuries.

'You do not recall any of the events of last night?'

'What I was doing in the woods? How I came to be here?' She frowned. 'No.'

'The latter I can at least answer.' Griffin strode forcefully across the room until he once again stood at her bedside looking down at her. 'Unfortunately, when you ran so suddenly in front of my carriage, I was unable to avoid a collision. You sustained a bump upon your head and were rendered unconscious,' he acknowledged reluctantly. 'As there are no houses in the immediate area, and no one else was about, I had no choice but to bring you directly here to my own home.'

Then she really *had* been trampled by horses and run over by a carriage.

'As my actions last night gave every appearance of my having known who I was *before* I sustained a bump on the head from the collision with your carriage, is it not logical to assume that it was that collision that is now responsible for my loss of memory?' She eyed him hopefully.

It *was* logical, Griffin acknowledged grudgingly, at the same time as he appreciated her powers of deduction in the face of what must be a very frightening experience for her. He could imagine nothing worse than awakening in a strange bedchamber with no clue to his identity.

Nor did he believe that sort of logic was something a mentally unbalanced woman would be capable of.

If indeed this young woman was being truthful about her memory loss, which Griffin was still not totally convinced about.

The previous night she had been fleeing as if for her very life, would it not be just as logical for her to now *pretend* to have lost her memory, as a way of avoiding the explanations he now asked for? She might fear he'd return her to her abusers.

'Perhaps,' he allowed coolly. 'But that does not explain what you were doing in the woods in your nightclothes.'

'Perhaps I was sleepwalking?'

'You were running, not walking,' Griffin countered dryly. 'And you were bare of foot.'

The smoothness of her brow once again creased into a frown. 'Would that explanation not fit in with my having been walking in my sleep?'

It would, certainly.

If she had not been running as if the devil were at her heels.

If it were not for those horrendous bruises on her body.

And if she did not bear those marks of restraint upon her wrists and ankles.

Bruises and marks of restraint that were going to make it difficult for Griffin to make enquiries about this young woman locally, without alerting the perpetrators of that abuse as to her whereabouts. Something Griffin was definitely reluctant to do until he knew more of the circumstances of her imprisonment and the reason for the abuse. Although there could surely be no excuse for the latter, whatever those circumstances?

He straightened to his fullness of height. 'Perhaps for now we should decide upon a name we may call you by until such time as your memory returns to you?'

'And if it does not return to me?' There was an expression of pained bewilderment in her eyes as she looked up at him.

If her loss of memory was genuine, then the collision with his carriage was not necessarily the cause of it. Griffin had seen many soldiers after battle, mortally wounded and in pain, who had retreated to a safe place inside themselves in order to avoid any more suffering. Admittedly this young woman had not been injured in battle, nor was she mortally injured, but it was nevertheless entirely possible that the things that had been done to her were so horrendous, her mind simply refused to condone or remember them.

Griffin did not pretend to understand the workings of the human mind or emotions, but he could accept that blocking out the memory of who she even was would be one way for this young woman to deal with such painful memories.

For the moment he was willing to give her the benefit of the doubt.

For the moment.

'Bella.'

She blinked her confusion. 'Sorry?'

'Your new name,' Griffin said. 'It means beautiful in Italian.'

'I know what it means.' She *did* know what it meant!

Could that possibly mean that she was of Italian

descent? The hair flowing down her shoulders and over her breasts was certainly dark enough. But she did not speak English with any kind of accent that she could detect, and surely her skin was too pale for her to have originated from that sunny country?

And did the fact that the Duke had chosen that name for her mean that he thought her beautiful?

There was a blankness inside her head in answer to those first two questions, her queries seeming to slam up against a wall she could neither pass over nor through. As for the third question—

'I speak French, German and Italian, but that does not make me any of those things.' The Duke was obviously following her train of thought. 'Besides, your first instinct was to speak English.'

'You could be right, of course,' she demurred, all the while wondering whether he did in fact find her beautiful.

What would it be like to be the recipient of the admiration of such a magnificently handsome gentleman as Griffin Stone? Or his affections. His love…

Was it possible she had ever seen such a handsome gentleman as him before today? A gentleman who was so magnificently tall, with shoulders so wide, a chest so muscled, and those lean hips and long and elegant legs? A man whose bearing must command attention wherever he might be?

He was without a doubt a gentleman whom others would know to beware of. A powerful gentleman in stature and standing. A man under whose protection she need never again know fear.

Fear of what?

For a very brief moment she had felt as if she were on the verge of something. Some knowledge. Some *insight* into why she had been running through the woods last night.

And now it was gone.

Slipped from her grasp.

She frowned her consternation as she slowly answered the Duke's observation. 'Or maybe because you spoke to me in English I replied in kind?'

This woman might not be able to answer any of Griffin's questions but he had nevertheless learnt several things about her as the two of them had talked together.

Her voice had remained soft and refined during their conversation.

She was also clearly educated and intelligent.

And, for the moment, despite whatever experiences had reduced her to her present state, she appeared completely undaunted by either his size or his title.

Of course that could be because for now she had much more personal and pressing things to worry about, such as who she was and where she had come from!

Nevertheless, the frankness of her manner and speech towards him was a refreshing change, after so many years of the deference shown to him by other gentlemen of the ton, and the prattling awe of the ladies.

Or the total abhorrence shown to him by his own wife.

He had been but five and twenty when he and Felicity had married. He'd already inherited the title of Duke from his father. Felicity had been seven years younger than himself, and the daughter of an earl. Blonde and petite, she had been as beautiful as an angel, and she had also possessed the other necessary attributes for becoming his duchess: youth, good breeding and refinement.

Felicity might have looked and behaved like an angel but their marriage had surely been made in hell itself.

And Griffin had been thinking of that marriage far too often these past twelve hours, possibly because the delicacy of Bella's appearance, despite their difference in colouring, was so similar to Felicity's. 'We have talked long enough for now, Bella,' he dismissed harshly. 'I will go downstairs now and organise some breakfast for you. You need to eat to regain your strength.'

'Oh, please don't leave! I am not sure I can be alone as yet.' She reached up quickly with both hands and clasped hold of his much larger one, her eyes shimmering a deep blue as she looked up at him in appeal.

Griffin frowned darkly at the fear he could also see in those expressive eyes. A fear not of him—else she would not be clinging to him or appealing to him so emotionally—but certainly of everything and everyone else.

There was a certain irony to be found in the fact that this young woman was showing her implicit trust in him to protect her, when his own wife had so feared the very sight of him that she had eagerly accepted the attentions and warmth of another man.

Damn it, he would not think any more of his marriage, *or* Felicity!

'I am sorry.' Bella hastily released her grasp on the Duke's hand as she saw the scowling displeasure on his face. 'I did not mean to be overly familiar.' She drew her bottom lip between her teeth as she fought back the weakness of tears.

The bed dipped as he sat down beside her, his eyes filled with compassion as he now took one of her hands gently in his. 'It is only natural, in the circumstances, that you should feel frightened and apprehensive.' He spoke gruffly. 'But I assure you that you are perfectly safe here. No one would dare to harm you when you are in my home and under my protection,' he added with that inborn arrogance of his rank.

Bella believed him. Absolutely. Without a single doubt.

Indeed, he was a gentleman whom few would ever

dare to doubt, in any way. It was not only that he was so tall and powerfully built, but there was also a hard determination in those chilling grey eyes that spoke of his sincerity of purpose. If he said she would come to no harm while in his home and under his protection, then Bella had no doubt that she would not.

Her shoulders relaxed as she sank back against the pillows, her hand still resting trustingly in his. 'Thank you.'

Griffin stared down at her uncertainly. Either she was the best actress he had ever seen and she was now attempting to hoodwink him with innocence, or she truly did believe his assurances that he would see she came to no harm while under his protection.

His response to that trust was a totally inappropriate stirring of desire.

Was that so surprising, when he had seen her naked and she was such a beautiful and appealing young woman? Her eyes that dark and entrancing blue, her lips full and enticing, and the soft curve of her tiny breasts—breasts that would surely sit snugly in the palms of his hands?— just visible above the neckline of her—

What was he thinking?

Griffin hastily released her hand as he rose abruptly to his feet to step back and away from the bed. 'I will see that breakfast and a bath are brought up to you directly.' He did not look at her again before turning sharply on his heel and exiting the bedchamber, closing the door firmly behind him before leaning back against it to draw deep breaths into his starved lungs.

He had just promised his protection to the woman he had named Bella, only to now realise that *he*, and the unexpected stirring of his long-denied physical desires, might have become her more immediate danger.

'You are feeling more refreshed, Bella?'

Griffin knew the question was a futile one even as he asked it several hours later, as she stood in the doorway to his study. The walls were lined with the books he enjoyed sitting and reading beside the fireside in the quiet of the evening, a decanter of brandy and glass placed on the table beside him.

At least he *had* intended to enjoy those things the evenings he was here; the advent of his unexpected female guest meant that he might possibly have to spend those evenings entertaining her instead.

He now felt extremely weary following his days of travel and sitting at her bedside all of the previous night.

Bella appeared very pale and dignified as she remained standing in the doorway, her hair still wet from her bath, scraped back from her face and secured at her crown. She also looked somewhat nondescript in the overlarge pale blue gown borrowed from his housekeeper. It was the best Griffin had been able to do at such short notice, although he had instructed Mrs Harcourt to see about acquiring more suitable clothing for her as soon as was possible.

And if he was not mistaken, Bella had flinched the moment he'd spoken to her.

Unfortunately he knew that flinch too well; Felicity had also recoiled just so whenever he'd spoken to her, so much so that he'd eventually spoken to her as little as was possible between two people who were married to each other and often residing in the same house.

'My feet are still too sore for me to wear the boots provided,' Bella told him quietly, eyes downcast.

Griffin scowled slightly as he looked down at her stockinged feet. She gave all the appearance of a little girl playing dress up in those overly large clothes.

Or the waif and stray that she actually was.

He stood up impatiently from behind his desk. 'They will heal quickly enough,' he dismissed. 'I asked if you are feeling refreshed after your bath,' he questioned curtly, and then instantly cursed himself for that abruptness when Bella took a wary step back, her eyes wide blue pools of apprehension.

The fact that Griffin was accustomed to such a reaction did not make it any more pleasant for him to see it now surface in Bella. But perhaps it was to be expected, now that she was over her initial feelings of disorientation and shock in her surroundings, and had had the chance to fully observe her imposing host?

He leant back against the front of his desk in an effort to at least lessen his height. 'Have you perhaps recalled something of what brought you to Shrawley Woods?'

Bella had been horrified when, after eating a very little of the breakfast brought up for her, she had undressed for her ablutions and seen for the first time the extent of her injuries to her body. She could only feel grateful that she'd seen fit to refuse the attendance of a maid before removing her nightgown as she stared at the naked reflection of her own body in the full-length mirror placed in the corner of the bedchamber.

She was literally covered in bruises. Some of them were obviously new, but others had faded to a sickly yellow and a dirty brown colour, and were possibly a week or so old. As for those strange abrasions, revealed when she removed the bandages from her wrist and her ankles...

How could she have come by such unsightly injuries?

She had staggered back to sit down heavily on the bed as her knees had threatened to buckle beneath her, her horrified gaze still fixed on her naked reflection in the mirror.

She had stared at her bedraggled reflection in utter bewilderment; her long dark hair had been tangled and dull about her shoulders, and there was a livid bruise on her left temple, which the Duke said she had sustained when she and his carriage had collided the night before.

But those other bruises on her body were so unsightly. Ugly!

She had realised then how stupid she had been to think that he had chosen the name Bella for her because he had thought her beautiful!

Instead it must have been his idea of a jest, a cruel joke at her expense.

'No,' she finally answered stiffly.

Griffin had issued instructions to all of the household staff, through Pelham, that knowledge of the female guest currently residing on the estate was not to be shared outside the house, and that any attempt to do so would result in an instant dismissal. No doubt the servants would do enough gossiping and speculating amongst themselves in that regard, without the necessity to spread the news far and wide!

Griffin, of course, if he was to solve the mystery, had no choice but to also make discreet enquiries in the immediate area for knowledge of a possible missing young lady. And he would have to do this alongside his research into the whereabouts of Harker. But he would carry out both missions with the subtlety he had learnt while gathering information secretly for the Crown. A subtlety that would no doubt surprise many who did not know that the Duke of Rotherham and his closest friends had long been engaged in such activities.

It would have been helpful if the maid who had taken up Bella's breakfast, or any of the footmen who had later taken up her bath, had recognised Bella as belonging to the village or any of the larger households hereabouts. Unfortunately, Pelham had informed him a few minutes ago that that had not been the case.

Confirming that Griffin now had no choice but to try and identify her himself.

In the meantime he had no idea what to do with her!

'Do you play cards?'

She eyed him quizzically as she stepped further into the room. 'I do not believe so, no.'

Griffin watched, mesmerised, as she ran her fingers lingeringly, almost caressingly, along the shelves of books, his imagination taking flight as he wondered how those slender fingers would feel as they caressed the bareness of his shoulders, and down the tautness of his muscled stomach. How soft they would feel as they encircled the heavy weight of his arousal...

'You obviously have a love of books,' he bit out tensely, only to scowl darkly as she immediately snatched her hand back as if burnt before cradling it against her breasts. 'It was an observation, Bella, not a rebuke.' He sighed his irritation, with both his own impatience and her reaction.

'Do not call me by that name!' Fire briefly lit up her eyes. 'Indeed, I believe it to have been exceedingly cruel of you to choose such a name for me!'

Griffin felt at a complete loss in the face of her upset. Three—no, it was now four—of his closest friends were either now married or about to be, and he liked their wives and betrothed well enough. But other than those four ladies the only time Griffin spent in a woman's company nowadays was usually in the bed of one of the mistresses of the demimonde, and then only for as long as it took to satisfy his physical needs, and with women who did not find his completely proportioned body in the least alarming. Or did not choose to show they did.

His only other knowledge of women was that of his wife, Felicity, and *she* had informed him on more than one occasion that he had no sensitivity, no warmth or understanding in regard to women. Not like the man she had taken as her lover. Her darling Frank, as she had called the other man so affectionately.

Damn Felicity!

If not for Harker, then Griffin would not have chosen to come back here to Stonehurst Park at all. To the place where he and Felicity had spent the first months of their married life together. He had certainly avoided the place for most of the last six years, and being back here now appeared to be bringing back all the bitter and unhappy memories of his marriage.

But if he had not come back to Stonehurst Park last night then what would have become of Bella?

Would she have perhaps stumbled and fallen in the woods in the dark, and perished without anyone being the wiser?

Would the people who had already treated her so cruelly have recaptured her and returned her to her prison?

For those reasons alone Griffin could not regret now being at Stonehurst Park.

Now if only he could fathom what he had said or done to cause Bella's current upset.

His brow cleared as a thought occurred to him. 'I have already asked my housekeeper to send to the nearest town for more suitable gowns and footwear for you to wear.'

'Suitable gowns and footwear will not make a difference to how I look!' There was still a fire in her eyes as she looked at him. 'How could you be so cruel as to—as to taunt me so, when I am already laid low?'

Griffin gave an exasperated shake of his head. 'I have absolutely no idea what you are talking about.'

'I am talking about this!' She held up the bareness of her bruised arms. 'And this!' She pulled aside the already gaping neckline to reveal her discoloured shoulders. 'And this!'

'Enough! No more, Bella,' Griffin protested as she would have lifted the hem of her gown, hopefully only to show him her abraded calves, but he could not be sure; an overabundance of modesty did not appear to be one of her attributes!

'Bella.' He strode slowly towards her, as if he were approaching a skittish horse rather than a beautiful young woman. 'Bella,' he repeated huskily as he placed a hand gently beneath her chin and raised her face so that he could look directly into her eyes. 'Those bruises are only skin deep. They will all fade with time. And they could never hide the beauty beneath.'

Bella blinked. 'Do you truly mean that or are you just being kind?'

'I believe we have already established that I am cruel rather than kind.'

'I thought—I did not know what to think.' She now looked regretful regarding her previous outburst.

Griffin arched that aristocratic brow. 'I am not a man who is known for his kindness. But neither am I a deceptive one,' he added emphatically.

She gave a shake of her head. 'When I undressed for my bath and saw my reflection in the mirror I could only think that, by giving me such a beautiful name, you must be mocking me for how unsightly I look. I truly believed that you were taunting me.'

'I would never do such a thing to you, Bella,' he assured her softly as he drew her into his arms. 'Never!'

Bella breathed a contented sigh as she lay her head against the firmness of his chest, her arms moving tentatively about the leanness of his waist. He felt so big and strong against her, so solid and sure, like a mountain that would never, could never, be moved.

'Who could have done this to me?' She shuddered as she imagined the beatings she must have received.

Griffin's arms tightened about Bella as he felt her tremble. 'I do not know.' Yet!

For he would learn who was responsible for hurting this young woman. Oh, yes, Griffin would find those responsible for her ill treatment. And when he did—

'Do you think that—?' She buried her head deeper into his chest. 'Could it be that I am a married woman and that perhaps my husband might have done this to me?'

That was a possibility Griffin had not even considered in his earlier deliberations!

Perhaps because she had initially appeared so young to him.

Perhaps because she wore no wedding ring on her left hand.

And perhaps he had not thought of it because he had not wished for her to be a married woman?

But he knew better than most the embarrassment of a cuckolded husband, and Griffin's physical response to Bella was not something he wished, or ever wanted to feel for a woman who was the wife of another man. Not even one who could have treated her so harshly.

Indeed, marriage could be the very worst outcome to Griffin's enquiries regarding Bella; unless otherwise stated in a marriage settlement, English law still allowed that a woman's person, and her property, came under her husband's control upon their marriage. And, if it transpired that Bella was a married woman, then Griffin would be prevented by law from doing anything to protect her from her husband's cruelty, despite his earlier promise to her.

His arms tightened about her. 'Let us hope that does not prove to be the case.'

Bella had sought only comfort when she snuggled into the Duke's arms, seeking an anchor in a world that seemed to her both stormy and precarious.

Since then she had become aware of things other than comfort.

The way Griffin's back felt so firmly muscled and yet so warm beneath her fingers.

The way he smelled: a lemon and sandalwood cologne along with a male earthy fragrance she was sure belonged only to him.

Of what she believed must be his arousal pressing so insistently against the softness of her abdomen as he held her close.

Was it possible that this gentleman, this breath-takingly handsome Duke, this towering man of so-lidity and strength, was feeling that arousal for *her*?

Griffin became aware of just how perfectly the softness of Bella's curves fitted against his own, much harder body. So perfectly, in fact, that she could not help but be aware of his desire for her.

He pulled back abruptly to place his hands on the tops of her arms as he put her firmly away from him, assuring himself of her balance before he released her completely and stepped back and away from her.

'I have important estate business in need of my urgent attention this morning, so perhaps you might find some way of amusing yourself until luncheon?' He moved to once again sit behind his desk.

He put a necessary distance between the two of them, while the desk now hid the physical evidence of his arousal.

Hell's teeth, he was an experienced man of two and thirty, and far from being a callow youth to be so easily aroused by a woman he had just met. He was also a man who would never again allow him-self to fall prey to the vulnerabilities of any woman.

That particular lesson had also been taught to him only too well. His softness of heart had been one of the reasons he had allowed Felicity to charm him into taking her as his wife. Unbeknown to him, Felicity's father, an earl, had been in serious financial difficulties, and a duke could hardly allow his father-in-law to be carried off to debtors' prison!

Bella felt utterly bewildered by Griffin's sudden rejection of her.

Had she done something wrong to cause him to react in this way?

Been too clinging? Too needy of his comfort?

If she was guilty of those things then surely it had been for good reason?

She felt totally lost in a world that she did not recognise and that did not appear to recognise her. Could she be blamed for feeling that Griffin Stone, the aloof and arrogant Duke of Rotherham, was her only stability in her present state of turmoil?

Blame or otherwise, Bella now discovered that she had resources of pride that this austere Duke's dismissal, the ugliness of her gown, or her otherwise bedraggled and bruised appearance, had not succeeded in diminishing.

Her chin rose. 'I believe I do like books, Your Grace.' Stiltedly she answered his earlier question. 'Perhaps I might borrow one from this library and find somewhere quiet so that I might sit and read it?'

Griffin was feeling a little ashamed of the abruptness of his behaviour now. The more so because he had seen Bella's brief expression of bewilderment at his harsh treatment of her.

Before it was replaced with one of proud determination.

Even wearing that overlarge and unflattering pale blue gown, her feet bare but for her stockings, and with her hair styled so unbecomingly, Bella now bore an expression of haughty disdain worthy of his severe and opinionated grandmother.

The tension eased from his shoulders at that expression, and he settled back against his leather chair. 'If you wish it you might ask Pelham for a blanket, and then go outside and sit beneath one of the trees in the garden. Although I advise that you walk on the safety of the grass until your new footwear arrives,' he added dryly.

Her look of hauteur wavered slightly as she now eyed him uncertainly. 'I might go outside?'

'You are not a prisoner here, Bella,' Griffin answered irritably. 'Any restrictions placed on your movements, while you are here, will only be for your own safety and never as a way of confining you,' he added with a frown.

The slenderness of her throat moved as she swallowed before answering. 'And what if we were never to discover who I really am?'

Then he would keep her.

And buy her dozens of pretty gowns of a fit and colour that flattered her, and the slippers to match. Then he would feed her until she burst out of those gowns and needed new ones, her cheeks rosy with—

Griffin's mouth firmed as he brought an abrupt halt to the unsuitability of his thoughts. He could not *keep* Bella, even if she were foolish enough to want to stay with him. She was not a dog or a horse, and a duke did not *keep* a young woman, unless she was his mistress, and Bella was far too young and beautiful to be interested in such a relationship with a gentleman so much older than herself.

Nor did Griffin have any interest in taking a mistress. A few hours of enjoyment here and there with the ladies of the demi-monde was one thing, the setting up of a mistress something else entirely.

Even if his physical response to Bella was undeniable.

Chapter Three

'**P**eople do not just disappear, Bella,' he now bit out grimly. 'Someone, somewhere, knows exactly who you are.'

Bella supposed that had to be true; after all, she could not have just suddenly appeared in the world as if by magic.

Oh, but it had been so wonderful, just for those few brief seconds, to imagine being allowed to stay here. To remain at Stonehurst Park for ever, with this proud and arrogant Duke, who she was sure had a kind heart, despite the impression he might wish to give to the contrary. After all, he had not hesitated to care for her, despite the circumstances under which he had found her.

She felt sure that a less kind man would have handed her over to the local magistrate by now, in fear she might be a criminal of some sort, rather than allowing her to remain in his household. For if it transpired she was a thief, then he could not be sure she might not steal all the family silver before escaping into the night. And she might do so much more if she were more than a thief…

No, despite his haughty aloofness, his moments of harshness, and that air of proud and ducal disdain, Bella could not believe Griffin to be anything other than a kind man.

Besides which, she had not imagined the physical evidence of his desire for her a few minutes ago.

She looked at him shyly from beneath her lashes. 'Then I can only hope, whoever they might be, that they do not find me *too* quickly.'

Exactly what did she mean by *that*? Griffin wondered darkly.

He had come to Stonehurst Park for the sole purpose of finding Harker; the last thing he needed was the distraction of a mysterious woman he found far too physically disturbing for his own comfort!

A conclusion he was perhaps a little late in arriving at, when that young woman currently stood before him, barefoot, and a guest in his home…

The mysteries of her circumstances aside, Bella was something of an unusual young woman. The slight redness to her eyes was testament to the fact that she had been recently crying, which he was sure any woman would have done given her current situation. But most women would also have been having a fit of the vapours at the precariousness, the danger, of their present dilemma. Bella appeared calm, almost accepting.

As evidence that she did not, as he suspected, suffer from amnesia at all?

He looked at her coldly from between narrowed lids. 'The sooner the better as far as I am concerned.'

Bella frowned at the coldness of his tone. Just when she had concluded that Stone must be a kind man he did or said something to force her to decide the opposite. As if in self-defence?

She turned away to look at the shelves of books so that he should not see the hurt in her eyes, glad when the heaviness of her heart lightened somewhat just at the sight of those books. As proof that she did indeed like to read?

She took a novel down from the shelf. 'I believe I shall read *Sense and Sensibility*. I have read it before, but it has long been a favourite of—' Bella broke off, her expression one of open-mouthed disbelief as she realised what she had just done. 'Oh, my! Did you hear what I said?' she prompted eagerly.

The Duke's mouth twisted without humour. 'I believe that happens sometimes with people who have lost their memory. They recall certain likes and dislikes, such as a foodstuff, or a book they have read, but not specifics about themselves.'

'Oh.' Bella's face dropped in disappointment. 'I had thought for a moment that I might be recovering my memory, and so relieving you of my presence quite soon, after all.'

Griffin knew that he deserved her sharpness, after speaking to her so abruptly and dampening her enthusiasm so thoroughly just now. He had been exceedingly rude to her.

But what was he to do when he was so aware of every curve of her body, even in that ghastly gown? When she had felt so soft and yielding in his arms just minutes ago? When the clean womanly smell of her, after the strong perfume and painted ladies of the demi-monde, was stimulation enough? When just the sight of her stockinged feet peeping out from beneath her gown sent his desire for her soaring?

Why, just minutes ago he had been thinking of *keeping* her!

Damn it, he could not, he *would* not, allow himself to become in any way attached to this young woman, other than as a surrogate avuncular figure who offered her aid in her distress. Chances were Bella would be gone from here very soon, possibly even later today or tomorrow, if his enquiries today should prove fruitful.

He deliberately turned his attention to the papers on his desk. 'Do not go too far from the house,' he instructed distractedly. 'We have no idea as yet who is friend or foe.' He glanced up seconds later when Bella had made no effort to leave or acknowledge what he'd said.

'What?' He frowned darkly.

She eyed him quizzically. 'I was wondering if that follows you around constantly.'

Griffin's irritation deepened at her enigmatic comment. 'If what follows me around?' He had owned a hound as a child but never as a man...

'That black thundercloud hanging over your head.'

Griffin stared at her for several long seconds as if he had indeed been thunderstruck. He had also, he realised dazedly, been rendered completely speechless.

Did he have a thundercloud hanging over his head?

Quite possibly.

There had been little in his past, or of late, for him to smile about. Nor, he would have thought, too much to cause amusement to this young woman either, but Bella now gave him a mischievous smile.

'If that should be the case, I sincerely hope it does not rain on you too often.'

Impudent minx!

Despite his best efforts he could not prevent the smile of amusement from curving his lips, followed by a sharp bark of outraged laughter as Bella continued to look at him with that feigned innocence in her candid blue eyes.

Bella's breath caught in her throat as Griffin began to chuckle, finding herself fascinated by the transformation that laughter made to the usual austereness of his face. Laughter lines had appeared beside now warm grey eyes, two grooves indenting the rigidness of his cheeks, his sculptured lips curling back to reveal very white and even teeth.

He was, quite simply, the most devastatingly handsome gentleman she had ever seen!

Perhaps.

For how could she say that with any certainty, when she did not so much as know her own name?

She gave a shiver as the full weight of that realisation once again crashed down on her. What if she *should* turn out to be a thief, or something worse, and last night she had been fleeing from imprisonment for her crimes?

She did not *feel* like a criminal. Had not felt any desire earlier, as she'd made her way through this grand house to the Duke's study, to steal any of the valuables, the silver, or the paintings so in abundance in every room and hallway she passed by or through. Nor did she feel any inclination to cause anyone physical harm—except perhaps to crash the occasional vase over the Duke's head, when he became so annoyingly cold and dismissive.

Except there weren't any vases in this room, Bella realised as she looked curiously about the study. Nor had she seen any flowers in the cavernous hallway to brighten up the entrance to the house.

That was what she would do!

When she asked Pelham for a blanket to sit on

outside, she would also enquire about something with which to cut some of the flowers, growing so abundantly in the garden she could see outside the windows, and she'd ask for a basket to put them in.

Just because she had no idea who she was, or what she was doing here, was no reason for her not to attempt in some small way to repay the Duke's kindness in allowing her to remain in his home. And this beautiful house would look so much more welcoming with several vases of flowers placed—

'What are you plotting now?' Griffin's laughter had faded as suddenly as it had appeared, and he now eyed Bella warily as he saw the light of determination that had appeared so suddenly in her eyes.

She frowned as her attention snapped back to him. 'Why do you treat me with so much suspicion?' She gave a shake of her head. 'I know that the circumstances of my being here are unusual, to say the least, but that is hardly my fault, or a reason for you to now accuse me of plotting anything.'

Griffin heaved a weary sigh, very aware that he was projecting his wariness and suspicions onto Bella, emotions so familiar to him because of Felicity's duplicity. Which was hardly fair or reasonable of him.

He nodded abruptly. 'I apologise. Perhaps I am just tired after my disturbed night's sleep,' he excused ruefully. 'Please do go and enjoy reading your book out in the garden, and try to forget that I am such a bad-tempered bore.'

Griffin was far from a bad-tempered bore to her, Bella acknowledged wistfully. No, the Duke of Rotherham was more of an enigma to her than a bad-tempered bore. As he surely would be to most people.

So tall and immensely powerful of build, he occasionally demonstrated a gentleness to her that totally belied that physical impression of force and power. Only for him to then address or treat her with a curtness meant, she was sure, to once again place her at arm's length.

As if he was annoyed with himself, for having revealed even that amount of gentleness.

As if he were in fear of it.

Or of her?

Bella gave a snort at the ridiculousness of that suggestion as she glanced at him, and saw he was already engrossed in the papers on his desk. He did not even seem to notice her going as she took her book and left the study to walk despondently out into the garden.

No, the differences in their stature and social standing—whatever her own might be, though it surely could in no way match a duke's illustrious position in society?—must surely ensure that Bella posed absolutely no threat to Griffin. In any way.

In all probability, the Duke was merely annoyed

with being forced to continue keeping the nuisance of her, and the mystery of her, here in his home.

She had not *asked* to be here, or to foist the puzzle of who she was upon him.

Nevertheless, that was exactly what had happened.

But where else could she go, and *how* could she go, when she had no friends or money with which to do so?

Like a moth to a flame Griffin found himself getting restlessly back onto his feet and wandering over to the window within minutes of Bella leaving the library, the papers on his desk holding no interest for him whatsoever.

At least, none that could compete with his curiosity in regard to the mystery that was Bella.

She had already spread a blanket on the grass and was now sitting beneath the old oak tree he could see from the window, the book open in her hand, the darkness of her still-damp hair loose again about her shoulders, now drying in the dappled sunlight filtering through the lush branches above her.

What *was* Griffin going to do with her, if his enquiries as to her identity should prove unsatisfactory?

She could not remain here indefinitely; if it turned out that she came from a family in society, as he suspected she might, then her reputation would be blackened for ever if anyone should realise she had stayed in his home without the benefit of a chaperone or close relative.

Inviting *his* only close relative to come to Stonehurst Park and act as that chaperone was totally unacceptable to Griffin; he and his maternal grandmother were far too much alike in temperament to ever be able to live under the same roof together, even for a brief period of time.

Perhaps he should send word to Lord Aubrey Maystone in London? He worked at the Foreign Office, and was the man to whom Griffin reported directly in his ongoing work for the Crown.

The puzzle of Bella was not a subject for the Foreign Office, of course. Nor was it cause for concern regarding the Crown. But Maystone had many contacts and the means of garnering information that were not available to Griffin. Most especially so here in the wilds of Lancashire.

Except…

Maystone had been put in the position of shooting one of the conspirators himself the previous month, and after that he'd become even fiercer in regard to the capture of the remaining conspirators. If Griffin were to tell the older man about Bella, he could not guarantee that Maystone would not instruct that Bella must be brought to London immediately for questioning, for fear she too was involved in that assassination plot in some way.

He might never see Bella again—

His gaze sharpened as he saw that while he had been lost so deep in thought, Bella had risen to her feet and left the shade of the oak tree to walk across the garden. She now stood in conversation with the gardener who had been working on one of the many flower beds.

This was not the elderly Hughes, who had been head gardener here even in Griffin's father's time, but a much younger man Griffin did not recognise. A handsome, golden-haired young man, in his early twenties, who was obviously enjoying looking at Bella as that dark hair hung loosely about her shoulders, as much if not more than the conversation.

Just as Bella appeared perfectly relaxed and smiling as the two of them chatted together.

Griffin did not give himself time to think as he turned to stride forcefully out of his study to walk down the hallway, leaving the house by the side door usually only reserved for the servants, before crossing the perfectly manicured lawn towards the still-conversing couple.

A handsome young man and beautiful woman so engrossed in each other they did not yet seem aware of his presence.

Bella broke off her conversation and her eyes widened in alarm the moment she spied the tall and fiercely imposing Duke storming across the grass towards her, his face as dark as that thundercloud he carried around above his head.

Her heart immediately started to pound in her chest, and the palms of her hands felt damp. What on earth could have happened to cause such a reaction in him?

'Your Grace?' She looked up at him uncertainly as he reached her side.

'Who are you?'

The glowering Duke ignored her, his countenance becoming even more frightening as he instead looked at the young gardener with cold and frosty eyes.

'Sutton, Your Grace. Arthur Sutton.' The young man touched a respectful hand to his forelock, his face becoming flushed under the older man's cold stare.

'You may go, Sutton.' Griffin nodded an abrupt dismissal. 'And I would appreciate it if you would take yourself off to work elsewhere on the estate for the rest of the day,' he added harshly, causing the bewildered young man to turn away and quickly collect up his tools ready for departing.

Bella felt equally bewildered by the harshness of Griffin's tone and behaviour. It was almost as if he suspected her and the gardener of some wrongdoing, of some mischief, when all they had been doing was—

'Oh!' She gasped after glancing towards the house to see that the library window overlooked this garden, and realised *exactly* what Griffin had suspected her and the handsome gardener of doing.

Bella made sure that the young gardener had walked far enough away out of earshot, before she glared up into the harshly drawn face looking down at her so condescendingly. 'How could you?'

The Duke quirked that infuriatingly superior eyebrow. 'How could I what?'

'You know exactly what I am talking about.' Bella sighed her impatience. 'How can you have been so disgusting as to have thought—to suggest, that I—that we—?' She was too angry to say any more as she instead turned sharply on her stockinged heels to run back towards the house.

Hateful man.

Hateful, suspicious, disgusting man!

Griffin stood unmoving for several seconds after Bella had departed so abruptly, totally taken aback by her reaction. To the anger she had made no effort to hide from him as she'd spoken to him so accusingly.

Why was she angry with him, when *she* was the one who had been—?

The one who had been what?

Exactly what had Griffin actually seen from the library window?

The beautiful Bella in her overlarge gown, with her gloriously black hair loose and curling down the length of her spine, in conversation with one of his under-gardeners.

A young and handsome under-gardener, accepted,

but Bella had not been standing scandalously close to Sutton, nor had she been behaving in a flirtatious manner towards him. Admittedly she had been smiling as she chatted so easily with the younger man, but even that was not reason enough for Griffin to have made the assumption he had.

Could it be that he had been *jealous* of her easy conversation and laughter with the younger man?

Was it possible that he thought, because of the unusual circumstances of Bella being here with him at all, that her smiles and laughter belonged only to him?

That *she* now somehow belonged to him?

'Bella?'

She stiffened and ceased her crying, but made no effort to lift her head from the pillow into which it was currently buried as she lay face down on the bed.

She made no verbal acknowledgement of Griffin's presence in her bedchamber at all. Correction, *his* bedchamber. As all of this magnificent house, and the extensive estate surrounding it, also belonged to him.

And she, having absolutely no knowledge of her past or even her name, was currently totally beholden to him.

But that did not mean Griffin Stone had the right to treat her with such suspicion. That he could virtually accuse her of flirting with Arthur Sutton. Or worse...

The under-gardener had been *nice*. A young man who had not been in the least familiar in his manner towards her, but rather accepted her as a guest of the Duke, and had treated her accordingly.

Not that she could expect Griffin to believe that when his mind was so obviously in the gutter.

What had she done to deserve such suspicion from him?

Admittedly, the circumstances of their meeting had been unusual to say the least, but surely there had to be an explanation for that?

Even if she had no idea as yet what that explanation was...

Besides which, she was so obviously battered and bruised, it was ludicrous to imagine that any man might find her attractive in her present state.

Although, there was no denying that Griffin himself had physically reacted to her close proximity earlier.

Perhaps it was just that he was a little odd, if he was attracted to a woman who was covered in bruises!

Which was a little worrying, now that Bella considered the possibility fully.

The Duke did not look like a gentleman who enjoyed inflicting pain, but that was no reason to suppose—

'I apologise, Bella.'

The bed dipped beside her as the Duke, obviously

tired of waiting for her response to his initial overture, now sat down on the side of the bed.

'Bella?'

Her body went rigid as he placed a hand lightly against her spine. 'We both know that is not my name.' Her voice was muffled as she spoke into the pillow.

'I thought we had agreed that it would do for now?' he cajoled huskily.

Until they discovered what her name really was, Bella easily picked up on his unspoken comment.

If they ever discovered what her name really was, she added inwardly.

Which was part of the reason she had been so upset when she'd returned to the house just now.

Oh, there was no doubting this aloof and arrogant Duke had behaved appallingly out in the garden just now; he had spoken with unwarranted terseness to Arthur Sutton, and had certainly been disrespectful to her. His implied accusations regarding the two of them had been insulting, to say the least.

Bella's previous treatment, as well as her present precarious situation, meant that her tears were all too ready to fall at the slightest provocation...

Griffin Stone's behaviour in the garden had not been slight, but extreme.

Bella slipped out from beneath his hand before rolling over to face him, hardening her heart as she saw the way he looked down at her in apology. She had been enjoying her time out in the garden, and he had now spoilt that for her.

For those brief moments she had spoken with Arthur Sutton she had felt *normal*, and not at all like the bedraggled and beaten woman the Duke had found in the woods the previous night.

Her chin rose challengingly. 'Your behaviour in the garden—the cold way you spoke to Arthur Sutton, as well as to me—was unforgivably condescending.'

Griffin only just managed to hold back his smile as Bella administered the rebuke so primly. To smile now would be a mistake on his part, when Bella was so obviously not in the mood to appreciate the humour.

'And wholly undeserved,' she added crossly as some of that primness deserted her to be replaced by indignation. 'You may well be overlord here, Your Grace, but that does not permit you to make assumptions about other people. Assumptions, I might add, that in this case were wholly unfounded.'

Oh, yes, this young woman was certainly educated and from a titled or wealthy family, Griffin acknowledged ruefully; that set-down had been worthy of any of the grand ladies of the ton!

Did Bella even realise that? he wondered.

Possibly not, when she had no knowledge of anything before her arrival here last night.

Appeared to have no knowledge, he again reminded himself.

There was still that last lingering doubt in Griffin's mind regarding her claim of amnesia. Added to, no doubt, by his having just observed her in conversation with one of his under-gardeners.

What if she had been passing information on to Arthur Sutton? If her arrival here in his home had been premeditated?

Shortly before the assassination plot against the Prince Regent had been foiled several of Maystone's agents had been compromised. Griffin had been one of them.

There was always the possibility that Bella had been deliberately planted in his home, of course. That she was here to gather information from him as to how deeply their circle had been penetrated.

And he was becoming as paranoid as Maystone!

Nor was it an explanation that made sense, when Griffin considered those marks of restraint upon Bella's wrists and ankles.

Alternatively perhaps she had been talking to Arthur Sutton in an effort to find some way in which she might leave Stonehurst Park without his knowledge.

And what if she had?

If Bella were to disappear as suddenly as she had arrived, then surely it would be a positive thing, as far as Griffin was concerned, rather than a negative one?

He would not have to give her a second thought

this afternoon, for example, when he rode out to pay calls on his closest neighbours, in his search for information on Harker.

Nor would there be need to write to Aubrey Maystone in London to ask for his assistance, and possibly at the same time alert the other Dangerous Dukes to his present dilemma by doing so; in their work as agents for the Crown they all of them had or still reported to Maystone. Ordinarily Maystone would not discuss any individual agent's business with a third party, but the older man was well aware of the close friendship between the Dangerous Dukes, and might feel obliged to mention his concerns to them.

The last thing Griffin wanted was for one or all of his closest friends to decide to come to Stonehurst Park to offer him their assistance.

Lord knew he had felt displeased, even proprietorial, merely watching Arthur Sutton in conversation with Bella, so how would he feel if any of his much more attractive friends were to come here and proceed to exert their considerable charms on her?

Admittedly only Christian Seaton, the Duke of Sutherland, still remained single out of those five friends, but Christian possessed a lethal charm as well as handsome looks. Women had been known to swoon when confronted by them.

'What were you and Sutton talking about, Bella?' Griffin demanded harshly, determined to remain in control of his wandering thoughts.

Bella frowned as she pushed herself up against the pillows; she felt at far too much of a disadvantage with Griffin looming over her in that way. 'Should you not offer me an apology before making demands for explanations?'

The Duke's jaw tightened. 'I apologised a few minutes ago. An apology you chose not to acknowledge.'

'Because it was far too ambiguous,' she told him impatiently. 'As it did not state what it was you were apologising for.'

The Duke closed his eyes briefly, as if just looking at her caused him exasperation. As no doubt it did. He had not asked to have her company foisted upon him, and whatever his own plans had been for this morning he had surely had to abandon them. Also because of her.

His eyes were an icy grey when he raised his lids to look at her. 'It was not my intention to upset you.'

Bella raised dark brows. 'Then what was your intention?'

Griffin wondered if counting to ten—a hundred!— might help in keeping him calm in the face of Bella's determination to demand an explanation from him. 'I was concerned that Sutton might have been bothering you.'

A frown appeared between her eyes. 'How could that be, when I was obviously the one who had walked over to where he was working, rather than him approaching me?'

Griffin's mouth thinned as he acknowledged that fact. 'And I ask again, what were the two of you talking about?'

'The weather, perhaps?' she snapped, her irritation obvious.

'I warn you not to try my patience any further today, Bella,' Griffin rasped coldly.

Bella *was* deliberately provoking Griffin, and she knew she was. But with good reason, she believed.

She might not recall anything about herself, but this proud and arrogant Duke did not know anything about her either, and she resented—deeply— that, having seen her in conversation with Arthur Sutton, he had made certain assumptions regarding her nature.

She sat up fully to wrap her arms about her bent knees. 'If you must know, I was asking Arthur for a trug and something to cut the flowers to put in it.'

'Why?' Heavy lids now masked the expression in Griffin's eyes, but his increased tension was palpable, nonetheless.

'This is such a beautiful house and the addition of several vases of flowers would only enhance—'

'No.'

Bella blinked her uncertainty at the harshness of his tone. 'No?'

'No.' He stood up abruptly, towering over her, his hands linked behind his back as he once again looked down the length of his aristocratic nose at her. 'I do not permit vases of flowers in any of my homes.'

'Why on earth not?' She gave a puzzled shake of her head. 'Everyone likes flowers.'

'I do not,' he bit out succinctly, a nerve pulsing in his tightly clenched jaw.

He was currently at his most imposing, his most chilling, Bella acknowledged. She had no idea why the mention of a vase of flowers should have caused such a reaction in him. 'You are allergic, perhaps?'

His laugh was bitterly dismissive. 'Not in the least. I am merely assured that the beauty of flowers is completely wasted on a man such as me.'

'Assured by whom?' Bella frowned her deepening confusion.

His eyes glittered coldly. 'By my wife!'

His *wife*?

Griffin, the Duke of Rotherham, the man who had saved her from perishing alone and lost in the woods, the man she felt so drawn to, the same man who had physically reacted to her close proximity this morning, had a *wife*?

Chapter Four

Why was Bella so surprised to learn that the Duke of Rotherham had a wife?

He was a very handsome gentleman, and wealthy too, judging by the meticulous condition of this beautiful estate. *Of course* such a man would have a wife. A beautiful and accomplished duchess, to complement his own chiselled good looks and ducal haughtiness. And, no doubt, to provide him with the necessary heirs.

Was it possible he already had several of those children in his nursery?

Bella swallowed before speaking again. 'I did not know... I had no idea... I had assumed—' She had *assumed* that Griffin was unmarried. That the way she felt so inexplicably drawn towards him was acceptable, even as she acknowledged it was altogether impossible that that interest would ever be felt in return for the vagabond she currently was. 'Why have I not yet been introduced to your wife?'

A nerve pulsed in his tightly clenched cheek. 'Obviously because she is not here.'

Bella felt totally bewildered by the coldness of his tone.

'Then where is she?'

His eyes were now glacial. 'She has been buried in the family crypt in the village churchyard these past six years.'

Oh, dear Lord!

Why had she continued to question and pry? Why could she not have just left the subject alone, when she could see that it was causing Griffin such terrible discomfort? The stiffness of his body, the tightness of his jaw, and the over-bright glitter of his eyes were all proof of that.

But no, because she was irritated with him over his earlier behaviour, those ridiculous assumptions he had made concerning her conversation with Arthur Sutton, she had continued to push and to pry into something that was surely none of her business. Into a subject that obviously caused this proud and haughty man immense pain.

'Do you have children, too?'

His mouth tightened. 'No.'

'How did she die?' Bella knew she really should not ask any more questions, but the look on Griffin's face indicated that if she did not ask them now she might never be given another opportunity. And she wanted to *know*.

Besides which, Griffin could only be aged in his early thirties now, and he said his wife had been dead for six years, so surely that wife could not have been any older than her early to mid-twenties when she died?

'She drowned,' he bit out harshly.

'How?' Bella gasped.

'I will not discuss this subject with you any further, Bella!'

Bella knew she really had pushed the subject as far as Griffin would allow, as he turned away to look out of the bedroom window.

She hesitated only briefly, her gaze fixed on the rigid set of his shoulders and unyielding back as she swung her legs to the floor, before rising quickly to her feet to cross over to where the Duke stood. 'Now it is my turn to apologise.' Her voice was huskily soft as she stood behind him. 'I should not have continued to ask questions about something that so obviously distresses you.'

He made no response, indeed he gave no indication he had even heard her.

Bella waited for several long seconds before lifting her arms up tentatively and sliding them gently about his waist, hearing him draw in a hissing breath as she did so. She could feel the way that his body became even more rigid beneath her hands as she rested them on his abdomen.

Realising her mistake, she started to draw away.

'No!' Griffin's hands moved up to hold those slender arms about his waist. 'Stay exactly where you are,' he ordered as his body relaxed against Bella's warmth and the soft press of her breasts against his back.

It had been so long since any woman had voluntarily offered him the comfort of her arms other than for that brief prelude occasionally offered before the sexual act began.

Griffin's eyes closed as he now savoured the sensation of just being held. Of having no expectations asked of him, other than to stand here and accept those slender arms about his waist. At the same time as Bella's softness continued to warm him through his clothing.

Griffin had not realised until now just how much he had missed having a woman's undemanding and tenderness of feeling. He had not allowed himself to feel hunger for those things that he knew could never be his.

He had to marvel at Bella, giving that tenderness and warmth so freely, when circumstances surely dictated she was the one in need of that comfort.

For the moment Griffin did not want to think about those circumstances, to give thought to the fact he knew nothing about this young woman. Why should he, when he had known even less about the women in whose bodies he had taken his pleasure these past six years? No, for now he intended to simply *enjoy* the moment.

Bella had not moved since Griffin had instructed her not to. But she still couldn't stop thinking about the wife he'd lost so tragically.

Had Griffin been very much in love with her?

Had their marriage been a happy one?

Had Griffin been nursing a broken heart since losing his wife?

Could that broken heart be the reason he had never remarried?

'Your thoughts are so loud, Bella, I can almost hear them,' Griffin chided dryly.

'Can you?' she breathed shallowly, sincerely hoping that was not the case. Griffin seemed such a private man, so closed off within himself, that she was sure he would not appreciate learning of the many questions about him still raging inside her head.

'Oh, yes,' he murmured as he slowly turned in her arms.

Bella's breath caught in her throat as she found herself so suddenly facing him. It had been so much easier to hold Griffin when she was not looking up into his mesmerising and handsome face.

When she could still breathe.

When her thoughts had not suddenly turned to mush.

When he could not see how her body was betraying her responses to him. Her face felt flushed, eyes fever-bright, and the tips of her breasts had become swollen and sensitive beneath the material of her overlarge gown. She also felt an unfamiliar sensation low down between her thighs.

Griffin's large hands moved up to cup her cheeks as he tilted her face up to his, looking down searchingly. 'Are you a witch?' he murmured gruffly.

Bella could not look away from the compelling heat in those silver eyes. 'I do not think so.'

He gave a slow shake of his head. 'I think you must be.'

'Why must I?'

His eyes darkened, his expression grim. 'Because you have made me want you!'

Her heart leapt in her chest at the fierceness with which he delivered the admission.

There was such an unmistakeable underlying anger in Griffin's voice, telling her that he resented those feelings.

Because he still loved his dead wife, and the desire he now felt for Bella was a betrayal to those feelings?

Or was his anger with himself rather than her, for feeling that desire for someone he did not know or completely trust?

He gave a humourless laugh. 'You can have no idea how much I envy you, Bella!'

She blinked at the strangeness of the comment.

'Why on earth would you envy me?' At the moment she had nothing. No past.

No future. No *name*. Even the dress she was wearing belonged to another woman.

Griffin's hands tightened against her cheeks. 'Because your lack of knowledge about your past means you have no memory of pain or loss, either. Or the mistakes you might have made,' he rasped harshly. 'Because the blank of that past allows you to start afresh. To decide what that past might have been, and to make the future your own.'

That was one way of looking at this situation, Bella supposed.

Except she would much rather know her past. Whatever that past might be.

To not know who or what she was gave her the constant feeling of walking along the edge of a precipice, when one misguided step or action would hurtle her over the edge of that precipice to her certain death.

She moistened her lips with the tip of her tongue. A movement Griffin followed hungrily, causing Bella's heart to falter in her chest as she found herself suddenly unable to speak.

'You *are* a witch,' Griffin groaned throatily, no longer able to resist the lure of wanting to feel those lush and rosy-coloured lips beneath his own. He lowered his head towards hers.

Her gently parted lips felt as soft as rose petals beneath his, as he held back his hunger to plunder and claim but instead kissed her with restrained gentleness, her taste as sweet as the nectar between those petals. A nectar Griffin wanted to lap up greedily with his tongue.

Dear Lord!

Griffin groaned low in his throat, hungrily deepening the kiss as he felt the tentative sweep of Bella's tongue against his own like hot enveloping silk, her arms now clinging tightly about his waist as she pressed the soft length of her body eagerly against his much harder one. So eager, so trusting.

Damn it, he had made a promise to Bella to protect her while she remained in his household. And she had left him in no doubt that she now trusted him to ensure her safety. Even from himself.

It took every effort of willpower on his part, but he finally managed to gather the strength to wrench his mouth from hers, breathing heavily as he put her firmly away from him before releasing her.

He hardened his heart against the look of pained rejection in Bella's reproachful gaze. If he weakened, even for a moment, he would give in to the temptation to take her back into his arms. And he knew that this time he would be unable to stop kissing her, touching her, caressing her, and it would end with him craving more than she was ready to give.

'It is past time I returned to my study,' he barked before turning sharply to cross the room to the door.

Bella reached out a hand to grasp the back of the chair nearest to her, barely able to stand on her own two feet. The onslaught of emotions she had known in Griffin's arms had left her feeling light-headed.

'I will be going out for some time after luncheon, paying calls to some of my neighbours,' the Duke—for that was surely who Griffin now was; that aloof and disdainful Duke whom she had met this morning!—informed her distantly.

'Do you wish me to accompany you?' Bella had no idea how she felt about leaving the safety of this estate. Fear, perhaps, at going out into a world she did not know?

As much as she felt a nervousness at the thought of Griffin being nowhere nearby for her to call to if she should need him?

'I believe, for the moment, you should remain here, out of sight,' he dismissed coldly, his back still turned towards her as he paused with his hand on the door handle of the bedchamber. 'You may pick some flowers from the garden, and bring them into the house, if you wish.'

There was no doubt in Bella's mind that he made the concession as an apology. Whether that apology was for his mistaken accusations over Arthur Sutton, or for kissing her just now, she had no idea.

Either way, Bella did not need to be humoured as if she were a child!

She had been a willing participant in their kisses

just now, and she had revelled in the experience, in the rush of emotions she had felt at being held so tightly in Griffin's arms: pleasure, arousal, heat.

His rejection just minutes later had been as if a shower of cold water had been thrown over her.

She gathered herself up to her full height as she stepped away from the chair. 'I do not wish, thank you.'

Griffin gave a wince as he heard the hurt beneath Bella's haughtiness of tone.

Because he had called a halt to their kisses?

Because she had enjoyed them as much as he had?

But what other choice did he have but to stop? She was a young woman staying as a guest in his household. A vulnerable young woman he had offered his protection to for as long as she had need of it. She said she trusted him.

Yet surely he had just violated that trust?

He would not be accused of violating her too!

Griffin gave a terse inclination of his head. 'Do as you please,' he dismissed coolly even as he wrenched open the door to the bedchamber and made good his escape.

Bella blinked back the tears of self-pity that now blurred her vision. She would not allow herself to cry again.

She refused to cry simply because Griffin so obviously regretted kissing her.

But what a kiss!

Delivered with a depth of feeling, a passion, that had shaken her to the core.

Had it also shaken Griffin?

He had been so cold when he'd pulled away from her so suddenly. Very much the Duke of Rotherham.

He was tired of her, tired of the burden she'd become.

Perhaps it would be best for both of them if she were to leave here.

To leave Griffin.

Griffin's mood was one of deep impatience by the time he rode through the Shrawley Woods on his way back to Stonehurst Park late that afternoon.

If his neighbours had been surprised to receive a visit from the Duke of Rotherham then they had quickly masked the emotion, their manner effusive as they'd offered him tea and fancies.

Even when Felicity had been alive Griffin had always hated, had actively avoided, such visits.

The fact that he was now a widower, and an eligible duke at that, obviously had not escaped the notice of his neighbours. The Turners and the Howards had taken advantage of the opportunity to introduce him to any and all of their daughters who were of a marriageable age, the MacCawleys to a niece who was residing with them for the summer.

Only the Lathams had no daughter or niece to thrust at him, and unfortunately they were away from home at present. The butler had informed him that Sir Walter, an avid member of the hunt, was currently in the next county looking to buy a promising grey, and his wife was away until the end of the week visiting friends.

Not that the latter was any great loss to Griffin; several inches taller than her rotund and jovial husband, Lady Francesca Latham was exactly the type of woman Griffin least admired. A blond-haired beauty, admittedly, but Lady Francesca also had a cold and sarcastic sense of humour, and spoke with a directness that Griffin found disconcerting, to say the least.

All of those visits had been a waste of his time and energy anyway, as he had not managed to ascertain any information from his conversations in regard to Bella, or Jacob Harker.

So the slowness of Griffin's pace on his journey back to Stonehurst Park was not due to any lingering enjoyment of his afternoon, but more out of a reluctance to see and be with Bella again.

He no longer trusted himself to be alone in her company.

The way he had responded to her earlier was unprecedented. He'd experienced a depth of arousal that had resulted in his continued discomfort for more than an hour after the two of them had parted. He had breathed a sigh of relief when she had asked to have her luncheon on a tray in her bedchamber, leaving him to dine alone in the small family dining room.

But Griffin knew he could not continue to avoid her. They would have to put those kisses behind them, by ignoring the incident, if by no other means. Although Griffin doubted he would be able to forget his response.

'Oh, thank goodness you are returned, Your Grace!'

A harried-looking Pelham came hurrying down the front steps of the house as Griffin dismounted and handed his reins to the waiting groom.

'There's been such a to-do! I did not know what to do for the best.'

'What is it, Pelham?' Griffin frowned his concern; Pelham had been butler here at Stonehurst Park since Griffin was a boy, and as far as he was aware this was the first time he had seen the elderly man in the least discomposed.

'It is Miss Bella.'

'Bella?' Griffin quickly looked up towards the house. 'Has she fallen? Been injured in some way? Did someone come here while I was out?' he demanded belatedly. He knew someone would almost certainly be looking for Bella, following her escape, but Griffin had not thought they would dare to come here, to Stonehurst Park. 'Out with it, man!' he barked his impatience at his butler.

Pelham obviously did his best to calm himself, although there was still a light of panic in his eyes.

'We were just finished afternoon tea in the servants' dining room when we heard such a screaming and carry on.'

'Bella?' Griffin knew he was the one who was now less than composed. 'Did someone attack her? If someone has dared to harm her—'

'No, no, it is nothing like that, Your Grace. It seems that she must have fallen asleep some time after lunch, and had a nightmare. Mrs Harcourt is up in her bedchamber with her now, but Miss Bella is inconsolable, and we did not know what to do for the best.'

Griffin was no longer there for the older man to explain the situation to; he was already ascending the front steps two at a time in his rush to get to Bella's side, throwing his hat aside as he hurried across the hallway to ascend the wide staircase just as hurriedly, all the time berating himself for having left Bella.

He should not have left her alone after all that she had so obviously suffered.

Nor should he have parted from her so angrily earlier, when *he* was the one who had been at fault for kissing her.

He was an unfeeling brute, who did not deserve—

'Griffin!'

He had barely stepped inside the bedchamber, his heart having contracted the moment he took in the sight of Bella's tear-stained face, when she jumped up suddenly from the bed to rush across the room and launch herself into his arms.

His own arms closed tightly about her as he held her slenderness securely against him, feeling as he did the terrible trembling of her body.

'I am here now, Bella. I am here,' he assured her softly as she continued to sob and cling to him.

Her face was buried against his chest. 'It was… I was… It was so dark I could not see, only hear, and—'

'You may leave us now, Mrs Harcourt.' Griffin curtly dismissed the housekeeper; there was no need to add to the mystery of Bella's presence at Stonehurst Park. 'Perhaps you might have Pelham bring us up some tea in half an hour or so?' he added, to take the sting out of his dismissal as he saw the housekeeper's crestfallen expression.

'Yes, Your Grace.' She bobbed a curtsy before hurrying from the room, obviously as discomfited as Pelham by this upset.

'You are safe now, Bella,' Griffin assured her as he bent to swing her up in his arms and carry her across the bedchamber, where he sank down into the armchair, settling Bella on his knees as her body still shook uncontrollably.

She buried her face against the side of his throat. 'That is not my name.'

Griffin stroked a soothing hand down the length of her spine even as he lightly brushed the tangle of dark hair from her face. 'We have agreed it shall be for now.'

'No,' she sobbed emotionally. 'I meant that it really is not my name.' She raised her head and looked at him, eyes red, lashes damp, her cheeks flushed. 'I believe my—my real name is—I heard someone in my dream call me Beatrix.'

She had spent a miserable morning in her bedchamber, pacing up and down as she'd tried to decide what she should do for the best. What was best for Griffin, not herself.

He was so obviously a man who preferred his own company.

A singular gentleman, who did not care to involve himself in the lives of others.

A wealthy and eligible duke, who had not remarried after his duchess died six years ago.

And *she* was responsible for disturbing the constancy of his life.

What Bella *should* do now was leave here. Remove herself from his home. Before news of a woman's presence at Stonehurst Park became known, as it surely would be if she remained here for any length of time. The last thing she wanted was to blacken Griffin's name.

Except she still had nowhere else to go, nor the means to get anywhere.

The tears of frustration she had cried had not

helped to lessen the helplessness of Bella's situation in the slightest.

Any more than her best efforts to try not to think of the way Griffin had kissed her earlier. Or that he had called her a witch for having tempted him.

It had been in that state of despair and emotional turmoil that Bella had finally fallen into an exhausted asleep.

The dreams had seemed harmless at first. Just images, really. Of a smiling, laughing young lady, with fashionably styled dark hair, dressed in a beautiful gown of gold silk as she'd twirled about the room with another lady, older, but so like the first that they had to be mother and daughter. A seated gentleman had looked on and smiled at the two of them indulgently.

Then had come the overwhelming sadness as that image had faded and she'd seen the young lady again, dressed in black this time, her face ravaged by grief.

And she'd known, without a doubt, that the young woman in the dream was herself, and that she stood at the graveside of the same man and woman who had looked so happy in the previous image. She'd known instinctively that the man and woman were her father and her mother.

That image had faded to be replaced by hands reaching for her in the darkness. A hand placed over her mouth. The warning not to scream, before something, a cloth of some kind, had been placed over her mouth and her eyes, and she'd been dragged kicking from her bed before something had hit her on the side of the head and she'd known no more.

She had tried then to wake herself from the terror she'd felt, but she had not succeeded, that terror only increasing as instead the next image had been of waking to the painful jolting of a travelling carriage as she'd lain huddled and bound on the hard floor, unable to see, speak or move.

Even so, she'd known she was not alone in the carriage, had been able to smell an unwashed body and hear another person breathing, sometimes snoring, as they'd slept, but never speaking, except when the carriage had stopped and she had been dragged outside and told to relieve herself. She had refused at first, having had no idea where she was or who was watching her, but had roughly been warned she would be left in her own mess if she did not do as she was told.

The dream gave her no idea of time, of how long she had been in the carriage when it had finally stopped and she'd been dragged outside. There had been the sound of a door opening and closing, a degree of warmth, before she had been pushed to the floor and she'd felt ropes being twined about her wrists and ankles as she had been secured in place. The cloth about her mouth had been ripped away and she'd gagged as some stale bread had been pushed between her cracked and dry lips, followed by blessedly cool water.

She'd had images then of being forced to eat more stale bread, followed by that delicious cold water.

Even the smell of unwashed bodies had become normal as the time had passed and she'd known herself to be a part of that smell. As all she'd known had been that fear and hunger and cold. Until her jailer had been joined by another. And that was when the pain had begun.

The man's rough voice would ask her questions, and another person, someone who remained absolutely silent, had administered the kicks and slaps when she'd failed to give them the answers they'd seemed to want from her.

All that had existed for Bella was sitting alone in the darkness, being forced to eat the stale bread and water, followed by those questions being repeated over and over again. Followed by the painful kicks and slaps. The abuse had been accompanied by the harsh warnings of the first jailer when Bella had cried out that she did not understand the questions let alone have the answers they wanted.

Her nightmare, if it was a nightmare, and not actually a memory, had seemed to go on endlessly. Pain, cold and hunger.

Until Bella had finally awoken to the sound of her own screams as she'd sat up in the bed. Those feelings still with her even though she was now fully awake; the shaking of her body beyond her control.

Pelham had burst through the bedchamber door first, quickly followed by the housekeeper, the two of them doing all that they could to soothe and calm her.

Except Bella could not be calmed or soothed. Not once she'd accepted that she had not been dreaming. That they were memories that had returned to her.

Along with the knowledge that her beloved parents were both dead.

So what did her captors want?

What did she overhear?

Who had she told?

Tell me, tell me, tell me!

She sat up suddenly, eyes wide as she turned to look at a grim-faced Griffin. 'Jacob,' she breathed harshly. 'The man who held me prisoner was called Jacob!'

Chapter Five

Bella's, or rather Beatrix's, gasped statement was not what Griffin had been expecting to hear.

She had been so caught up in her nightmares still, so lost in those awful memories, that Griffin was sure she did not realise she had been talking out loud the whole time as she'd recounted the details of the visions that had caused her to wake screaming.

And as she'd remembered Griffin had felt himself becoming angrier and angrier at all she had suffered. It was a cold and vengeful anger, which he knew would only be assuaged when he found, and punished, the two people responsible for having treated Beatrix so cruelly.

Yet hadn't he also been guilty of mistreating her? By refusing to trust her and treating her with suspicion?

Admittedly, his many years as an agent for the Crown had created a deep cynicism and distrust within him. To the point where he was now wary of anyone who was not family or a close friend. This left him with a very small circle of people: his grandmother, the Dangerous Dukes and their wives, and Aubrey Maystone. And recent events had only added to his distrust and wariness.

However, was it possible that she was innocently involved in his own reason for being in Lancashire? 'Jacob?' he repeated softly. 'Could this man you refer to possibly be called Jacob Harker?'

She gave a pained frown. 'I never heard his last name, only his first, and I believe even that was by accident.'

'Can you describe him?' Griffin prompted gently. 'Did he have any distinguishing marks? A scar, perhaps? Or a mole?' Recalling that Harker had a mole on the left side of his neck.

She shuddered. 'I never saw him.'

Griffin frowned his puzzlement. 'I do not understand.'

'Usually there was a blindfold secured back and over my ears. On the day I heard his name they had been questioning me again, and had not covered my ears sufficiently, so that I could hear a muffled conversation, more like an argument, between the two of them outside of where I was kept prisoner.' She swallowed. 'The second jailer was angry, and remonstrating with the first, I think because they had once again failed to get the answers from me they wanted.

One shouted that I would be dead before they had their answers. That is when I overheard one of them refer to the other as Jacob.'

Complete deprivation of sight, sound and touch, along with a minimum of food and water, with the added threat of dying a painful death; it was a standard method of torture.

That those things had been done to this helpless young woman made Griffin feel positively murderous.

If her parents were both dead, then where was her guardian, her closest male relative? Someone, somewhere had surely been entrusted with the care of her after her parents' deaths? Whoever they were they deserved to be shot for their negligence.

Of course young ladies did sometimes run away in the middle of the night during or after the London season, but usually they returned several days or weeks later, either in disgrace or with a husband!

There was always the possibility that her guardians believed she had eloped.

'Bella—Beatrix?' Griffin hesitated over the name.

'Bea,' she corrected flatly. 'I believe my parents referred to me as Bea.'

Griffin did not miss the past tense in that statement, or the look of pained bewilderment in Bea's eyes. A pained bewilderment that he perfectly understood if, in fact, her parents were both dead, as she had dreamt they were. 'Do you remember them?'

'Only in the dream,' she answered dully. 'And only that one instance, when I was dancing giddily with my mother.'

That was, Griffin now strongly suspected, because shock and fear were responsible for causing her amnesia. The memories were obviously returning to her, even if only subconsciously, but her imprisonment, the harshness of her treatment, meant it would probably take time for all of her memories from before her abduction to return to her completely.

He might have wished she could forget her imprisonment and torture too!

Griffin's attempts today, to see if Bea belonged to a family in the area, had come to naught.

On his way out this afternoon he had instructed Reynolds, his estate manager, to check on any of the empty cottages and woodcutters' sheds within the estate, in the hopes that he might find some sign of where Bea might have been held prisoner. Her flight through the woods the previous night surely meant that Bea could not have run far dressed as she was and without footwear.

Bea.

How strange that he had chosen a name for her not so far from her own.

Tears dampened her lashes as she pulled abruptly out of his arms before standing up. 'I do not know how or when my parents died, but it must have been recently I think, because in my dream I attended their funeral, and I did not look so different then, except for the bruises, from how I am now.' The tears fell unchecked down the pallor of her hollowed cheeks.

'I am sorry for that, Bea,' Griffin consoled as he stood up to go to her, taking a light grasp of her arms as he looked down at her. 'I am so very sorry for your loss.'

'I do not remember them.' She shook her head sadly as she drew her bottom lip between her teeth in an effort to stop any more tears from falling. 'I only know of them at all because I saw myself standing at their gravesides, and knew that I loved and grieved for them both.'

How Bea had survived, even as well as she had, after all that had recently been done to her, Griffin could not even begin to comprehend.

She might have survived physically, he corrected himself grimly, but emotionally it was a different matter. It appeared now that Bea's mind had simply shut itself down and refused to remember.

Except in her dreams.

But the things that Bea had now recalled about herself in those dreams were something Griffin might use in order to further try and identify who she was. She was obviously well spoken and educated, which indicated that in all likelihood her parents had been also. A further adage to that was they had, in all probability, been members of society; there could not be too many couples in society who had both died at the same time, and recently, and with a daughter named Beatrix.

Being so far away from London himself, Griffin now knew he had no choice but to write to Aubrey Maystone and ask him to look into the matter for him.

'Bea, I hate having to ask you to dwell on this any further just now, but…'

'If I have the answer I will gladly give it,' Bea assured him sadly, the grief, the dark oppression of her dreams, obviously still weighing her down.

He nodded. 'The questions the man Jacob asked. What were they?'

'They were the same two questions, over and over again. How much did I overhear? Who had I told?' She frowned as she gave a shake of her head. 'I did not know the answers then, and I do not know them now.'

Griffin realised that someone obviously *believed* that she knew something they would rather she did not.

And it was in all possibility something to do with the reason why Jacob Harker had left Northamptonshire so suddenly several weeks ago, and travelled up to Lancashire.

Something of relevance to the foiled assassination plot of the Prince Regent just weeks ago?

Harker's possible involvement in Bea's abduction would seem to imply that was in all probability the case.

Griffin filed the information away in his head. 'How did you finally manage to escape?'

She frowned. 'The man, Jacob, had taken to unfastening my hands and feet when I was allowed to use—' She gave a shake of her head, her cheeks becoming flushed. 'I believe I struck him on the side of the head with the bucket before ripping off my blindfold and simply running and running. Does this man, Jacob, mean something to you?' She looked up at him sharply.

Griffin frowned grimly. 'It is not important.'

'It is important to *me*!' Some of her earlier fire returned as her eyes flashed darkly.

Griffin gentled his voice. 'I believe the best thing for now would be for you to rest.'

'No!' Bea pulled out of the Duke's grasp before stepping back. 'I cannot. I do not wish to rest.' Even the thought of going to sleep again, of having more nightmares, was enough to fill her with panic. 'I should like to know what relevance this man Jacob Harker has to you. Why, upon hearing the name Jacob, did you immediately assume he might be this Harker you speak of?'

'He is a known troublemaker in the area, that is all,' Griffin soothed.

Bea was not fooled for a moment by that explanation. 'That still does not explain why—'

'Bell—Bea,' he corrected apologetically. 'It is not the best time for us to talk about him, when you are already so upset.' He looked grim. 'I am more interested in the questions that were asked of you, and what significance they— Damn it!' he muttered in frustration as there was a brief knock on the bedchamber door. 'We will talk of this again once we are alone again.'

'I really do not think I can discuss my actual imprisonment any more just now, Griffin.' Her voice broke emotionally. 'It is too—distressing.' She was slightly ashamed of this show of weakness on her part, but was unable, for the moment, to think any more of her imprisonment and what her dreams had already revealed.

Her worst fear now—a fear she dared not talk of out loud—was that she might also have been violated.

She did not remember it, did not feel in the least sore between her legs. But perhaps she would not have noticed that soreness amongst the other bruises, cuts and abrasions on her body?

Just the thought of that smelly and disgusting man laying so much as a finger on her—

The dreams, revelations, that she had already had, about her most recent life, before Griffin had found her in the woods last night, along with the things she had not yet remembered, made Bea's position here now seem even more precarious than it had been previously.

If that were possible.

She was an orphan. And one whom no one seemed

to have claimed or loved, for if they had then surely her sudden disappearance would have caused a hue and cry, and in all likelihood Griffin would now know exactly who she was.

Instead of which he was obviously as much in the dark as to her identity as she was.

Although the name Jacob had certainly meant something to him. Something he did not wish to discuss with her.

'Come in, Pelham,' the Duke now instructed impatiently as a second knock sounded on the door. The door opened and the butler entered with the tray of tea things, quickly followed by the housekeeper carrying a large box.

'Some of Miss Bella's gowns, Your Grace,' she explained hastily as the Duke scowled at her presence.

'My goddaughter would prefer that we call her Bea in future,' Griffin announced haughtily.

Earlier today Bea had been almost excited at the prospect of new gowns, ones that actually fitted her. But the events since had reduced their arrival to mediocrity.

And Griffin's claim now, that she was his goddaughter, further robbed her of speech.

Although she appreciated that their present situation must be as awkward for him as it was for her. If not more so.

He was a duke, and a widower, and this was his

primary ducal estate, and Bea's dreams now indicated they would not discover who she was, or to what family she belonged, as quickly as he might have hoped. Bea could hardly continue to stay here without some further offer of explanation being made to his household staff as to the reason for her sudden presence in their employer's home.

But surely her late arrival last night with the Duke, wearing only her soiled nightgown, gave instant lie to the claim she was his goddaughter?

If Pelham or Mrs Harcourt found his choice of explanation in the least surprising, then they gave no indication of it. The butler placed the tray of tea things on the table in front of the window, and the housekeeper placed the box containing Bea's new gowns on the bed, both acknowledging their employer respectfully before departing the bedchamber.

'I am sorry I could not pre-warn you of my announcement, Bea.' He grimaced ruefully once they were alone together. 'As I am sure you can appreciate, following this afternoon's upset, some further explanation for your presence here now has to be given.'

As Bea also knew, without his having to say it, that Griffin was a man who disliked intensely having to explain himself to anyone.

As the powerful and wealthy Duke of Rotherham he no doubt rarely felt the need to do so!

Except Bea needed some further explanations herself.

Since waking she had several times thought of her dishevelled state when Griffin had found her the previous night. 'Who undressed and bathed me last night, and then dressed me in a clean nightgown?' she prompted slowly; she had certainly not been wearing the soiled or bloodstained garment from her dreams when she woke this morning.

'I did,' he dismissed briskly. 'I thought it best that none of my household staff be made privy to your bruises or abrasions,' he added abruptly as Bea's eyes widened.

Instead this breathtakingly handsome man had undressed her before bathing her completely naked body.

That he had seen her in that dirty and disgusting state was humiliating enough. To think of him stripping her, washing her, and then dressing her in a clean nightgown was far too intimate to contemplate.

'And my old nightgown?'

'I gave it to Pelham and instructed him to burn it this morning,' Griffin said coolly. 'Do not look so aghast, Bea; Pelham has been at Stonehurst Park for most of my life. He is and always has been the height of discretion, and you may rest assured he will not discuss the matter with anyone else.'

Bea was far more concerned with Griffin having seen her total humiliation, her unwashed and bruised body, than she was with the kindly butler's sensibilities.

She kept her eyes downcast as she turned away to look at the laden tea tray, noting the two cups and saucers. 'Will you be joining me for tea?'

'I think not, thank you,' Griffin refused stiffly, accepting that Bea was unwilling to discuss this any further just now, and knowing it was past time he removed himself from her bedchamber.

Despite her earlier upset, and his claim now of being her godfather, it was still not acceptable that he spend so much time alone with her in her bed-chamber.

Even if a part of him wished to do so.

Being reminded of the intimacy of bathing her the night before, of kissing her, and holding her in his arms, listening as she talked of the nightmares, Griffin felt the tenuous strands of an emotional bond being forged between the two of them.

And it would not do.

He was not truly Bea's godfather, but a healthy and virile man of two and thirty who was totally un-related to her, and who had several times responded to her in a physical way that was definitely not in the least godfatherly!

They did not as yet know Bea's true circum-stances or age, but Griffin now felt sure she came from a good family, and that he was at the very least ten years her senior.

He had suffered through an unhappy marriage, and his experiences with women these past six years had not lessened that disillusionment in the slightest. He was distrustful of them at best, cynical at worst.

He had once believed that Felicity felt an affection for him, and that the two of them would be together for the rest of their lives. He had been fond of Felicity, if not deeply in love with her, and totally faithful and loyal to their marriage. Both had been thrown back in his face when Felicity had chosen another man's affections and body over his own.

He would have to marry again one day, of course, if only to provide his heir, but Griffin was determined his second wife would be a woman for whom he held only respect, as the future mother of his children. Nor would he expect his duchess to feel any unwanted affection for him.

He had not been in the past, and he was not now, nor could he ever be, any young woman's romantic image of a knight in shining armour.

Still, at the moment he was sure Bea must feel a certain gratitude towards him, an emotion based solely on his having rescued her the previous evening.

As such, his own physical response to her, as well as his growing feelings for her, were both totally inappropriate.

'We will meet again at dinner, if you feel up to joining me downstairs?' he asked coolly.

Did Bea feel up to bathing and dressing in one of her new gowns before joining him for dinner?

It would certainly be a *normal* activity, in a world that now seemed even more alien to her than it had before. Besides which, her afternoon spent alone had resulted in those mind-numbing nightmares, and she wished to avoid the possibility of experiencing any more of those for as long as was possible.

'Dinner downstairs would be lovely, thank you,' she accepted equally coolly, fully intending to ask Pelham if she might have a bath before then. She felt unclean after the vividness of her dreams, as if some of that filth and squalor in which she had been kept prisoner still clung to her.

Griffin gave her a formal bow. 'Until eight o'clock, then.'

Bea kept her lashes lowered demurely as she gave a curtsy, and remained so until she heard the door quietly closing as Griffin left her bedchamber.

At which time she released a heavily sighing breath.

Her dreams had truly been nightmares.

Her fragmented memories, of her parents, her abduction and imprisonment, the frantic madness of her flight from her jailer, were even more so.

And there was still that lingering doubt that she might have been physically violated by her captors.

If so, was it possible she might have buried that particular horrific memory so deep inside her it might never show itself again?

Until such time as she married and her husband discovered she was not a virgin bride.

If she ever married.

And if she ever remembered who she truly was.

'You are looking very lovely this evening, Bea,' Griffin complimented politely once the two of them were seated opposite each other at the small round table in the family dining room.

Bea did indeed look very beautiful; the house-keeper had managed to find a gown the colour almost the same deep blue as her eyes. Her hair was fashionably styled upon her crown, with several enticing curls at her temples and nape. She was a little pale still, but that only added to her delicacy of appearance, which bordered on ethereal.

Griffin felt heartily relieved that it was not yet dark enough for Pelham to light the candles in the centre of the table; a romantic candlelit dinner for two would be the height of folly in the circumstances.

'Thank you,' she accepted lightly. 'You are looking very handsome this evening too.'

They sounded like polite acquaintances passing the time as their dinner was served, when in reality they were far from that. After leaving Bea earlier he had gone immediately to the library to send an urgent letter to Maystone, prompting the other man to use his considerable influence and acquaintances

to ascertain any and all information he could about
a missing young lady named Beatrix.

It would take several days but Griffin had felt better in the knowledge he had at least done something
positive in that regard.

His estate manager had also asked to see him
earlier, as he believed one of the disused woodcutters' sheds in Shrawley Woods might have recently
been inhabited. Griffin had immediately ridden out
to look for himself.

It was situated about a mile from where Griffin
had found Bea, and whoever had stayed in the barely
furnished shed had attempted to cover their tracks.
But it was impossible to hide the stench of unwashed
bodies, or the presence of a bloodstained bucket in
the corner of one of the downstairs rooms—the same
bucket Bea had struck Jacob Harker about the head
with?

Griffin believed it was and his rage had grown
tenfold as he'd stood and looked about him. The shed
consisted of just two rooms, the floors were of dirt,
just a single broken chair and table in one of the
rooms, and no other furniture. The roof overhead
sagged, and no doubt leaked in several places too.
Several dark rags had been draped over the single
square cut out of one of the wooden walls. No doubt
to prevent anyone from looking in. Or out.

There was nothing else there to show recent habi-
tation, no ragged blankets, fresh food or water, but it

was impossible to miss the recent odour of unwashed bodies, or the stench of rotting food.

And the distinctive smell of fear.

Bea's fear...

Griffin had given Reynolds a grim-faced nod before leaving the shed to ride back alone to Stonehurst Park, an impotent rage burning deep within him. And as he'd ridden the heavens had opened up, as if the angels themselves cried for all that Bea had suffered.

He had not told her as yet that he believed he had discovered the place of her imprisonment, and he was not sure that he intended to. She appeared so composed this evening, and was so elegantly attired, and Griffin had no wish to disturb that composure by once again taking her thoughts back to her imprisonment.

It was impossible to deny it had happened, of course; Griffin could still see some of the bruises on her shoulders and arms, although she had attempted to fasten a cream lace shawl over them in an effort to hide the worst of the abuse she had suffered. Matching lace gloves covered her bandaged wrists, and the length of her gown covered her bandaged ankles.

Covering signs of her abuse that once again incited Griffin's displeasure.

'I will ring for you when we have finished eating our soup,' he tersely dismissed Pelham, finding even the butler's quiet presence in the room to be an intrusion.

Griffin realised his mistake as soon as the older man left the room as the intimacy of earlier suddenly fell over the two of them like a cloak.

Bea knew a sudden discomfort at being alone with her dashing Duke. Well, he was not *her* Duke. Griffin was most certainly his own man. Self-contained, aloof, and demanding of respect. But he *was* her very handsome rescuer, and several times Bea had sensed an awareness between the two of them that was not avuncular. And earlier today he had kissed her.

'The soup is delicious,' she remarked to fill the sudden silence.

'My cook here is very good.' He smiled slightly, as if aware of her discomfort.

Because he felt it also? Bea would be very surprised if too much discomforted this confident gentleman.

'Thank you for my new gowns.' There had been three gowns in the box Mrs Harcourt had brought to her bedchamber earlier, two day dresses and one for the evening, the blue gown Bea was now wearing, along with undergarments, a shawl and slippers. 'I hope—I hope that once I am restored to—to being myself again, that I shall be in a position to repay you.'

'A few second-hand gowns altered by the local

seamstress will not bankrupt my estate, Bea!' the Duke rasped impatiently.

'Nevertheless.' Bea was not to be gainsaid on the subject; she had taken enough from this gentleman already, in the form of his kindness and hospitality, and she did not intend to be indefinitely in his debt financially too.

Griffin frowned his irritation with this conversation. 'You must concentrate your energies on becoming completely well again, and not worry yourself over such trivialities.'

Her chin rose. 'I assure you, they are not trivial to me.'

Griffin eyed her curiously. 'I have a feeling that, whatever your true identity might be, you are an independent and determined young lady!'

The fullness of her lips curved into a rueful smile. 'I would hope so.'

Griffin was sure that she was. He believed that many young women who had been as ill treated as Bea had would now be prostrate with the vapours. And possibly remain so for many days. Bea might feel that way inside, but outwardly she was calm and collected.

'You have the courage and fortitude of a queen,' he complimented huskily as he all too easily pictured the hovel in which she had been kept prisoner.

A blush slowly warmed her cheeks, lashes lowered over her eyes. 'I do not feel like a queen.'

Griffin looked at her searchingly. 'Something else is troubling you.' It was a statement, not a question. 'What is it, Bea?' he asked sharply. 'Have you remembered something else?'

Tears glistened in her eyes as she looked at him. 'It is what I do not remember that now troubles me.'

'Such as?'

She gave an abrupt shake of her head, no longer meeting his gaze.

'I would rather not put it into words.'

Griffin frowned darkly. Bea had been physically beaten, emotionally tortured, what else could there possibly be to—? 'No, Bea!' he gasped harshly. 'Surely you do not think—? Do not believe—?'

'Why should I not think that?' Bea dropped her spoon noisily into her bowl as she gave up all pretence of eating. 'I was alone with these men, and at their complete mercy for goodness knows how long. Surely in those circumstances it would be foolhardy to assume that—that one did not—' She could not finish the sentence, could not put into words this last possible horror of her captivity.

Once it had been thought of, Bea had been unable to put the possibility of physical violation from her mind. She had tried to appear calm as she'd joined Griffin in the dining room. Had been determined not to speak of her worries with him.

But the what-ifs had continued to haunt her.

To plague her.

Until it seemed it was all she could think of.

Griffin also looked suitably horrified at the possibility of violation as he now placed one of his hands firmly over both of her trembling ones clasped tightly together on her thighs. 'Bea, I am sure that did not happen.'

'You are no surer than I am!' she instantly rebutted, eyes glittering. 'I want these men found, Griffin. I want Jacob found and the truth beaten from him if he will not give it any other way!' Two bright spots of fevered colour heated her cheeks.

'Bea!'

'If you will excuse me, Griffin?' She pulled her hands away from his and threw her napkin on the tabletop before standing up noisily from the table. 'I do not believe I am hungry, after all.' She turned on her heel and almost ran from the room.

Griffin sat alone at the dining table, once again at a loss to know what to do where Bea was concerned.

Should he go after her and offer her more words of comfort?

Or should he leave her alone and allow her time to come to terms with her thoughts?

Was Griffin himself not in need of several minutes in which to fully take in the shocking implication of Bea's suspicion regarding her treatment at the hands of the man called Jacob?

Chapter Six

Bea found it impossible to fall sleep. She was *afraid* to fall asleep. For fear that more of those dreams might come back to haunt her. For fear that she might learn more from those dreams than she was comfortable knowing…

So instead of sleeping, she threw back the dishevelled bedclothes and paced her bedchamber long after she had heard Griffin pass her door, no doubt on the way to his own bedchamber further down the hallway.

What must he now think of her?

Nothing she did not think of herself, Bea felt sure!

Of course, she was not to blame if she had been violated, but that would not make it any less true. Any less of a disgrace. Whether she had been forced or otherwise, it would not change the fact that Bea was no longer—

Bea raised her hands and pressed her palms

tightly against each of her temples, sure she would go mad if she did not stop this circle of thought from going constantly round and round inside her head.

It felt as if there were no longer any air in her bed-chamber for her to breathe!

Not enough room in here for her.

She needed to flee.

To escape!

'I believe you are safer, here with me, than you would be anywhere else, Bea.'

She had no sooner thrown open her bedchamber door and stepped out into the hallway, her night-gown billowing about her bare legs, her hair loose about her shoulders and down her back, when she came to a halt at the sound of Griffin's calm and reasoning voice.

Her eyes widened as she turned and saw him lean-ing casually back against the pale pink silk-covered wall just a short distance down the hallway.

He had removed his jacket, but still wore the rest of his evening clothes. He somehow looked younger now that he was less formally clothed, and with the darkness of his hair tousled on his brow, his grey eyes heavy with exhaustion.

Bea eyed him uncertainly. 'I thought you had gone to your bedchamber some time ago.'

'I did.' Griffin straightened away from the wall to walk down the hallway towards her, his movements as silent and graceful as a large cat's. 'But I heard you pacing and muttering to yourself as I walked past your bedchamber, and guessed that you would find it difficult to sleep tonight. That you would perhaps have thoughts of running away?' He came to a halt just inches in front of her, hooded lids preventing Bea from seeing the expression. 'The things you remember suffering are bad enough on their own, Bea. Do not torture yourself further with thoughts of something that might not have happened.'

Tears stung her eyes as she gave a shake of her head. 'That is all well and good for you to say, Griffin, but you cannot possibly understand.'

'Bea, I was once held prisoner myself.'

'You were?' She blinked up at him uncertainly as he spoke quietly.

'I was captured by the French after the battle of Talavera,' he admitted grimly; it was not a time he normally chose to talk about. To anyone. And yet he knew that he had to. That it was his only way of assuring Bea that he knew a little of how she was feeling tonight. 'I do not pretend to understand the devils tormenting you, but I know what it is like to lose your freedom, to have suffered physical torture. To know of the scars it leaves on the soul.'

'How long were you held prisoner?'

He shrugged. 'A week or so, until I too escaped. What I am really saying, Bea, is that we all carry scars about with us we have acquired from life, whether they be physical or emotional.'

Bea felt shame wash over her at learning Griffin had been held a prisoner of the French in the war against Napoleon. She had also forgotten, caught up in her own self-pity as she had been, that Griffin must grieve still for his dead wife, making her doubly ashamed at her own self-indulgence.

'Life can be so cruel!' She rested her forehead against Griffin's wide and muscled chest, at once able to feel his reassuring warmth through the material of his waistcoat and shirt, and the steady, comforting beat of his heart. 'Truth be told, I am afraid to fall asleep,' she admitted huskily.

'Understandably.' Griffin's arms moved about her as he held her close against him.

She could not seem to stop the trembling. 'I— Would you—? Could you possibly sit with me for a while? Knowing you are there, and that I am safe, perhaps I will sleep and not dream?'

Griffin tensed at the request, knowing that his self-control was not at a premium where Bea was concerned. Just holding her in his arms like this, being completely aware of her nakedness beneath her nightgown, of her beautiful silky dark hair flowing loose down the length of her spine, was sorely testing that control.

At the same time he knew that it would be cruel of him to deny Bea this small comfort. He had already borne witness to her distress this afternoon, following her nightmares. The concern she had voiced earlier, about what else might have happened to her, disturbed him almost as much as it did her.

The thought of any man—*any man*—laying hands on Bea, let alone the animals who had kept her a prisoner in such filthy conditions, who had abused her both emotionally and physically, was enough to fill Griffin with a murderous rage.

His hands now closed into fists as he fought against that anger, knowing that it served no purpose right now; Bea needed his reassurance, not his rage.

The time for Griffin to let loose the full extent of his fury would come if—*when*—he caught up with Jacob Harker.

Because he would find him. And when he did the other man would suffer as he had made Bea suffer.

'Of course,' he now agreed briskly. 'What else are godfathers for?' he added lightly, and knowing he was deliberately using that tenuous claim in the hopes of amusing her, but also as a means of attempting to place their relationship on a platonic footing.

As a means of convincing himself that his feelings towards Bea were indeed platonic.

A husky laugh caught in Bea's throat as she straightened. 'I believe I shall like having you for my godfather.'

Griffin had never felt less like someone's godfather—Bea's godfather, in particular—than he did as he followed her inside her bedchamber and closed the door behind them.

A single candle burned on the bedside table to alleviate the darkness of the room, the bedclothes badly rumpled from where Bea had obviously gone to bed earlier, but had only tossed and turned, before rising again when she had been unable to sleep. When she had been too afraid to sleep, Griffin corrected himself grimly.

He moved to briskly straighten the bedclothes before turning them back invitingly. 'Ready?'

Bea felt more than a little self-conscious now that they were alone together in the silent intimacy of her bedchamber, the very air about them seeming to have stilled.

Almost with expectation?

She kept her gaze averted as she climbed back into bed, laying her head back on the pillows as Griffin rearranged the covers over her and tucked them beneath her chin. Bea almost expected him to place a fatherly kiss upon her brow!

When her own feelings towards him were far from paternal.

Griffin, instead of kissing her brow, now moved to carry the chair over from the window and place it beside the bed, before folding his long length down into it as he sat down beside her.

What would they have thought of each other if they had met under normal circumstances, at a society ball, or perhaps a musical soirée?

Bea almost laughed as she asked herself that question; even if Griffin were to ever attend such frivolities, which she seriously doubted, then she did not believe he would have noticed her existence.

Just as she had absolutely no doubt that she most certainly *would* have noticed Griffin, whatever the circumstances of their meeting!

He had such presence, was so tall and handsome, it would be impossible for any woman not to notice, or to be attracted to the charismatic Duke of Rotherham.

And yet he had never remarried.

Because he had loved his wife so much the idea of marriage to another woman repulsed him?

That had to be the explanation, Bea accepted wistfully.

Oh, but it would have been so wonderful to meet Griffin under different circumstances. For him to have asked to dance with her at a ball. To have him accompany her into supper. To have him call or send flowers the following day.

Bea brought her thoughts up sharply as she realised that all of those things seemed perfectly natural to her. That perhaps they had happened in her previous life?

Oh, not with Griffin, more was the pity, but she was sure she had danced at balls, and been accompanied into suppers by handsome gentlemen, and that they had called or sent flowers the following day.

Slowly, too slowly for Bea's peace of mind, her memories seemed to be returning to her.

Griffin sat quiet and unmoving as he watched Bea slowly relax, her lids fluttering and then falling softly downwards, dark lashes caressing the paleness of her cheeks, her lips slightly parted, as she fell asleep.

He breathed out a soft and relieved sigh as he relaxed back into the same uncomfortable chair in which he had dozed fitfully the previous night. Sitting at Bea's bedside seemed to be becoming something of a habit! He continued to watch her for several minutes longer, before his own lack of sleep the night before finally caught up with him and he lay his head back against the chair and fell asleep himself.

Bea woke to the feel of the warmth of the sun caressing her cheeks, and a deeper warmth down the left side of her body, and with a not uncomfortable weight across her abdomen and her legs. Almost as if—

She quickly opened her eyes, slowly turning her head to the left as she looked beside her, her breath catching in her throat as she saw that Griffin lay next to her, one of his arms curved about her waist, a leg thrown over the top of both of hers.

As if he were protecting her, even in his sleep.

He lay above the covers rather than under them, Bea discovered on closer inspection, the darkness of his hair more tousled than ever as his head lay on the pillows beside her own, his harshly chiselled features appearing much softer in sleep.

Bea's fingers itched to trace those finely arched brows. The sharply etched cheeks and the length of his aristocratic nose. As for those chiselled lips...

They looked so much softer when Griffin's mouth was not set in the habitually grim and determined shape it bore when he was awake. Lips so soft and inviting, in fact, that Bea's temptation to taste them became too much for her, her lids fluttering closed as she began to move her face closer towards his.

'What are you doing?'

Bea froze with her own lips just inches away from Griffin's, guilty colouring warming her cheeks as she looked up at him; she had been so intent on kissing the softness of his lips, she had failed to notice that Griffin had raised his own lids and was now looking at her with stormy grey eyes.

Angry eyes?

She moistened her own parted lips before answering him. 'I was...merely taken aback at finding you here in bed beside me.' She turned the explanation into a challenge, having no intention of owning up to the yearning she had known to kiss him, to taste the soft temptation of his lips.

Lips that were once again set in that grim, uncompromising line as he sat up in the bed before swinging his legs to the floor and standing up.

'I apologise,' he rasped gruffly as he looked down at her between narrowed lids, his back stiff and unyielding, shoulders tensed. He had removed his boots, and unbuttoned his waistcoat, but otherwise was still as fully dressed as he had been the night before. 'I meant only to hold you for several minutes after your upset, and that blasted chair is so uncomfortable.' He scowled at the offending piece of furniture. 'I must have drifted off to sleep myself once you were settled.'

Only one part of that explanation held any significance for Bea. 'After my upset?' Her face paled at the thought she might have had another nightmare. One that might possibly have revealed even more of the events of her captivity.

'You did not wake, just became restless and disturbed, and muttered a little in your sleep.' Griffin frowned as he recalled how he had been woken from his own fitful dozing in the chair in the early hours of the morning to see Bea thrashing restlessly in the bed, her words incomprehensible to him as she muttered and protested and cried out in her sleep.

Except for...

He looked down at her searchingly. 'Who is Michael?'

Bea returned his gaze blankly, her face unnaturally pale.

'Michael?' she repeated uncertainly.

'Michael,' Griffin confirmed abruptly. 'You called out for him in your sleep.'

'I did?' Her expression remained uncomprehending.

He nodded. 'You kept repeating his name, and then you said, "Michael must be so alone, so very alone!" and then you began to cry.'

Griffin could still remember the clenching of his gut as Bea had called out for the other man in her sleep, and how she had shed tears because she could not be with him.

He had no memory of having fallen asleep on the bed beside her after he had sought to comfort her, but he did recall the weight of her obvious love for the other man as weighing heavily on his chest.

Because he had enjoyed kissing her?

Because he wanted to kiss her again?

Because he was growing fond of Bea himself?

Griffin briskly dismissed such thoughts as nonsense. He merely felt responsible for Bea, and was concerned as to what had happened to her and why. Saddened for her, too, because she seemed to be so alone in the world.

Except she obviously was not as alone as he had thought she was. Because she was obviously concerned for—loved?—a man named Michael.

Did this Michael love her in return?

Of course he did; how could any man not fall in love with Bea if she chose to give her love to him?

Then where was this Michael now?

Why was he not the one here to comfort Bea when she was so lost and in pain? And why was he not ripping the country apart in his efforts to find her? To rescue her?

As Griffin was sure he would have done, in the same circumstances!

An obvious answer to those questions was that perhaps the other man was dead.

That the reason this Michael was not searching for Bea was because the people who had taken her might possibly have killed her lover during that abduction? It might even be that it was the shock of that death that was responsible for her amnesia, rather than the blow she had received to the head, or the horror of her abduction.

Bea gave a shake of her head, tears glistening in her eyes. 'I do not recall knowing anyone named Michael. Who could he be?' she added agitatedly.

'Please do not upset yourself, Bea.' Griffin heard the clock out in the hallway striking the hour of six. 'I believe I must now return to my own bedchamber.' He grimaced. 'The maid will arrive with my morning tea very shortly, and my valet not long after, to prepare my bath and lay out my clothes.'

'I— Of course.' Bea blinked. 'I have inconvenienced you far too much already, without the added scandal of your being found in my bedchamber at this hour, and in a state of undress.'

It would certainly be a first in this house for Griffin to be found in any lady's bedchamber in the morning, he acknowledged grimly. Even in the early days of their marriage Felicity had rarely allowed him entry to her bedchamber, and when she did she had always insisted that he leave again immediately after one of their less than satisfactory couplings, with the claim that she could not possibly fall asleep with his bulk in the bed beside her.

As Bea had done so easily and comfortably the night before.

And making comparisons of the way in which the two women regarded him was not only unproductive but also painful. It was like comparing night and day, rain or shine, when Bea was so obviously daylight and sunshine, after the dark and stormy years of being Felicity's barely tolerated husband.

His mouth tightened at those memories. 'I really do have to go now.' For the sake of his sanity, if nothing else! 'We will talk of this further over breakfast, if you wish.' He gave a terse bow before collecting up his boots and departing the room.

Bea was left momentarily stunned at the abruptness with which Griffin had left her. She felt guilty as she realised how her presence here was a constant inconvenience to him. Firstly, by his being forced into the position of becoming her saviour at all. And latterly, her presence here, an unaccompanied and young lady, surely bringing his reputation into question within his own household.

And who could this man Michael be? Someone she obviously felt an affection for, if she was calling out for him in her sleep. Perhaps he was a brother or other relative? Or a fiancé?

The thought of a fiancé caused Bea to go cold inside.

She had only known Griffin for a day, but it had been a significant and highly emotional time. And her attraction to him, her physical response to his having kissed her, her complete trust in him, could not be denied.

So perhaps her restlessness last night, her calling out for this man named Michael, had been because of a guilty conscience on her part, because she now found herself so inexplicably drawn to the man who had become her rescuer?

Whatever the reason, she resolved to be as little of a burden to Griffin as was possible in the coming days.

And nights.

'Sir Walter Latham has called to see you, Your Grace.'

Griffin looked up from the papers on his desk to first look at Pelham and then to glance frowningly across his study at Bea, as she sat curled up in a chair beside the fire reading a book. He noted pleasurably how the afternoon sun made her hair appear a particularly beautiful shade of blue-black against the pale lemon of her gown.

These past three days had been surprisingly companionable ones, with just the two of them sitting here together in the library during the day, he working on estate business, Bea quietly engrossed in her book, before they dined together in the evenings. Their conversations together had flowed surprisingly easily, Bea proving to be an intelligent woman, knowledgeable and able to discuss many subjects, despite her continued lack of memories of her own former life.

Much as Griffin had once imagined he would spend tranquil days and quiet evenings at home with his wife. Except Felicity had never wanted to sit companionably with him anywhere. In fact, towards the end of their marriage, it had become almost too much to expect her to even occupy the same house as him.

He frowned as he once again firmly put thoughts of Felicity from his mind to turn and look at his butler standing in the doorway. 'Show Sir Walter into the blue salon, if you please, Pelham,' he instructed impatiently.

'Very good, Your Grace.' The butler bowed out of the room, closing the door quietly behind him.

'Sir Walter Latham?' Bea repeated curiously as she closed her book.

'A neighbour who was away from home when I

called upon him three days ago,' Griffin dismissed as he stood up from behind his desk to pull on his jacket. 'He is obviously home again now and simply returning my visit to him. I think it might be for the best if you were to remain here while I speak with him.'

'Of course.' Bea readily agreed to the suggestion; she had absolutely no interest in meeting any of Griffin's neighbours.

People who would no doubt be curious as to who she was, and what she was doing here.

People who might know Griffin well enough to know that he did not have a goddaughter named Beatrix.

Although she was a little disappointed at having their tranquillity interrupted. A surprising tranquillity, considering the unusual manner in which they had first met, and the uncertainty that still surrounded Bea's past.

Her bruises were rapidly fading, and she no longer wore the bandages on her wrists and ankles, but unfortunately her memory beyond her abduction and imprisonment continued to remain elusively out of her reach.

By tacit agreement it seemed, the two of them had not referred again to Bea's disturbed dreams of three nights ago, or of her having called out for another man. Bea felt distinctly uncomfortable at the thought she might have a fiancé pining away for her somewhere, and Griffin was no doubt respecting her own silence on the subject.

Consequently they had fallen into an easy routine during the past three days. Bea, in keeping with her decision not to be any more of a burden to Griffin than necessary, had chosen to suffer her sleepless nights in silence. Although she often fell asleep here in the library beside the fire during the daylight hours, reassured, no doubt, by Griffin's presence across the room.

'I am perfectly content to remain in here until after your visitor has gone,' she now assured him lightly.

'This should not take long.' He deftly straightened the cuffs of his white shirt beneath his jacket, looking every inch the Duke in his perfectly tailored dark grey superfine, black waistcoat, pale grey pantaloons and highly polished black Hessians. 'Amiable he might be, but one can only listen to so much of Sir Walter's conversation on the hunt and the magnificent horse flesh in his stable!' he added dryly.

Bea chuckled softly. 'He sounds a dear.'

Griffin considered the idea. 'He is most certainly one of the more congenial of my closest neighbours.'

'And is there also a Lady Latham?'

'She is something less than a dear,' Griffin assured him with feeling, more than a little relieved that Lady Francesca appeared not to have returned as yet to accompany her husband on this visit to Stonehurst Park.

Why was it, he wondered, that amiable men such as Sir Walter more often than not burdened themselves with a controlling wife? An attraction of opposites, perhaps? Although Griffin could not claim to have ever seen much of that attraction in regard to Francesca Latham and Sir Walter!

'Would you like me to ask Pelham to bring you some tea in my absence?' he added briskly.

'That would be lovely, thank you.' Bea gave him a grateful smile.

Griffin drew in a deep breath as he felt himself bathed in the warm glow of that smile, before just as quickly giving himself an inner shake as he reminded himself that this current arrangement could only ever be a temporary one. That, in fact, he might not have the right to enjoy Bea's companionship at all, or to wallow in the warmth of her smiles.

That those things might all belong to a man called Michael.

Hopefully Aubrey Maystone would have received his letter by now, and might at this very moment be making the enquiries Griffin had requested, and thus soon putting an end to the mystery that was Bea.

Griffin's feelings on the subject had become mixed over these past three days. The longer Bea remained here at Stonehurst Park, the more he came to enjoy her company. At the same time it was foolish to do so, when at any moment her memories might come back to her, and she would then be returned to her former life, her time spent at Stonehurst Park, and with Griffin himself, both things she would rather put to the farthest reaches of her mind.

Griffin had ensured there had been no opportunity for a repeat of the kiss they had shared that first day, but that did not mean he did not feel desire every time he so much as looked at her.

A desire that Bea, so innocently trusting, obviously did not see or recognise.

Or return.

'I won't be long,' Griffin said harshly before turning sharply on his heel and leaving the room, instructing Pelham regarding Bea's tea, and striding determinedly into the blue salon to join Sir Walter.

At the same time as he determined he must put all thoughts of kissing Bea again from his mind.

Or try to, at least.

Chapter Seven

'Good to see you again, Rotherham!' The older and much shorter man rose at Griffin's entrance, his round face flushed, his riding jacket dark brown, the gaudily checked waistcoat beneath stretched to its limits over the portliness of his stomach, his brown Hessians dusty from his ride over to Stonehurst Park. 'You don't come to Stonehurst nearly enough!'

'Sir Walter.' Griffin nodded his cool acknowledgement of the other man. 'May I offer you some refreshment?' He chose to ignore Latham's comment regarding the frequency of his visits here; since Felicity died Griffin only came to Stonehurst perhaps once or twice a year, the memories of that disastrous marriage far too oppressive and immediate here, the place where Felicity had died.

'Thank you, but no.'

'Your visit into Yorkshire was successful, I hope?' He lowered his bulk down into one of the armchairs.

'Oh, my, yes.' The older man grinned as he resumed his seat opposite. 'I managed to buy myself a beautiful grey hunter.' He nodded his satisfaction.

Griffin nodded. 'Your butler informed me that Lady Francesca is away from home at the moment?'

'She was in London for part of the Season, acting as chaperone to my young niece. The two of them are presently making their way to Lancashire via several house parties.' The older man grimaced. 'I cannot abide London, or house parties, but for some reason Francesca enjoys all that social nonsense.'

Griffin smiled in sympathy; he too hated all that social nonsense, but had been forced to attend a certain amount of those functions when he was Felicity's husband. 'I am sure you will be pleased to have her and your niece returned to you.'

'Without a doubt,' Sir Walter agreed jovially. 'A house needs a woman's presence in it to feel anything like a home— Ah, but I apologise, Rotherham.' He frowned his consternation. 'That was in particularly bad taste, even for me.'

'Not at all,' Griffin dismissed dryly, having become accustomed to Sir Walter's bluntness over the years.

Besides which, Felicity's presence in any of his ducal homes had always made them feel less like a home to Griffin, and towards the end of their marriage that had been reason enough for him to wish to vacate those houses rather than suffer being in her frosty company a moment longer than was necessary.

A feeling in direct contrast to these past few days of ease he had shared living with Bea.

Damn it, he did not *live* with Bea, she was merely a guest in his home until such time as he could reunite her with her family.

And her lover.

'Although there is a rumour about the village that you have brought a young lady here with you this time?' Sir Walter eyed him curiously.

Griffin had known that he could not keep Bea's presence here a secret for long, despite his previous threats to his household staff regarding gossip.

The rarity of Griffin's visits to Stonehurst was a cause for gossip in itself, and the village of Stonehurst was simply too parochial for it to escape the notice of the locals that a young lady had accompanied the Duke of Rotherham to Stonehurst Park. There was no doubt much speculation as to her identity.

'I believe you are referring to my goddaughter.' He nodded haughtily. 'Her parents have both recently died, and I have now taken guardianship of her.' Griffin felt no hesitation in enlarging upon the lie he had already perpetrated regarding the reason for Bea's presence here.

'She is but a child, then?'

'Not quite,' Griffin dismissed, having no idea of

Bea's precise age, although he did not believe she could be any older than twenty.

The older man's eyes lit up with interest. 'Then no doubt Lady Francesca, once returned, will wish to invite you both over to dinner one evening while you are here, so that my niece and your goddaughter might become acquainted?'

'That will not be possible, I am afraid,' he refused smoothly. 'My goddaughter is still in mourning.'

'But surely a private dinner party is permissible?'

'I am afraid not. Bea's emotions are still too delicate at present for us to give or receive social invitations. Another time, perhaps,' he dismissed briskly as he stood up and rang for Pelham in conclusion of the conversation.

'Of course.' Sir Walter rose to his feet as he took the hint it was time for him to leave. 'It really is good to see you back at Stonehurst Park again, Rotherham,' he added sincerely.

'Thank you.' Griffin nodded.

'You must at least ride over and see my new hunter when you have the time.'

'Perhaps,' Griffin replied noncommittally.

'No doubt the young ladies in the area are also delighted at your return,' the older man added dryly.

Griffin did not dispute or agree with the statement as Pelham arrived to escort Sir Walter out, knowing it was his title the young ladies coveted. And he had learnt his lesson the hard way, in that regard!

* * *

'You did not return to the library earlier, once your guest had departed?' Bea prompted curiously as she and Griffin once again enjoyed a quiet dinner together in the small family dining room, Pelham having just left the room to go to the kitchen to collect their main course.

Griffin had been feeling too restless, too impatient with his current circumstances, to return to his work in the library.

And Bea.

Because he had realised, as he'd refused Sir Walter's dinner invitation on behalf of Bea as well as himself, that his protectiveness where Bea was concerned, his possessiveness towards her, the desire he felt for her, were growing deeper as each day passed.

And it was fast becoming an intolerable situation.

One that surely could not continue for much longer, without the danger of doing something he would sorely regret!

It certainly did not help that several more gowns had been delivered to Bea just yesterday, and that she wore one of those new gowns this evening.

Now that most of her visible bruises had faded, the pale peach colour of her new gown gave her face the appearance of warm and delectable cream, and her throat was a delicate arch, the bareness of her arms long and elegant. The darkness of her hair was swept up in a sophisticated cluster at her crown, with several loose wisps at her temples and nape.

She looked, in fact, every inch the beautiful and composed young lady of society that these past three days had convinced Griffin she truly must be.

A *unprotected* young lady of society, whom Griffin was finding it more and more difficult to resist taking in his arms and making love to!

'I do have other ducal responsibilities besides you, Bea,' he answered her with harsh dismissal. 'I cannot spend all of my time babysitting and mollycoddling you!'

'Of course.' It was impossible for Bea not to hear and inwardly flinch at the impatience in Griffin's tone. Or to feel hurt at being referred to as a responsibility. Even if that was what she so obviously meant to him.

It had been very silly of her to allow herself to grow so comfortable in Griffin's company these past few days. So comfortable, in fact, she had hoped that their time together might continue indefinitely.

Griffin was a duke, and, more importantly, he was a very handsome and eligible one. Her presence here, her unknown origins, must also be curtailing his own movements. Was it so surprising he did not wish to be burdened indefinitely with the responsibility of a young woman he did not even know, and, moreover, one who might very well turn out to be anything, from a thief to a murderess!

Bea carefully placed her napkin on the table beside her plate before standing up. 'I hope you will excuse me. I believe I have eaten enough for tonight.'

Griffin looked at her through narrowed lids as he stood up slowly, easily noting the pallor of her cheeks. 'You are unwell?'

'Not in the least.' Her chin rose. 'I am merely feeling a little fatigued.'

Griffin sighed at the distance he heard in her tone. 'I did not mean to be harsh with you just now.'

'You were not in the least harsh,' she assured him with that continued coolness. 'My presence here *is* a responsibility for you. And moreover it is one you did not wish or ask for.'

'Bea…'

'Please do not say any more just now, Griffin.' Tears glistened in her eyes as she looked up at him. 'Please allow me some dignity.' Bea turned and fled the room rather than finishing the sentence.

Griffin was once again left standing alone in a room after Bea had fled it in tears. And feeling just as impotent as to know what to do as he had the last time. As he had done in the past on those occasions when Felicity had chosen to remove herself from his company after he had said or done something she did not like. Admittedly she had rarely been in tears, but always with an air of coldness that had told him quite clearly she could no longer tolerate his company.

What was a man expected to do in such circumstances as these?

Bea was not his wife, nor was she related to him in any way, but for the moment she was his ward, and those tears glistening in her eyes indicated that, even if she was not crying, she was at the least very upset.

Should he follow Bea, and once again offer his apologies for his harshness? Or should he leave her to the solitude she was so obviously in need of?

He had respected Bea's need for solitude last time. Just as in the past Griffin had always respected Felicity's obvious aversion to his company, and his apologies for having offended her in some inexplicable way, by choosing not to intrude upon her solitude. But Bea was nothing like Felicity, and furthermore Griffin was well aware that it was he who was now responsible for her upset.

Bea was, without a doubt, a woman of great strength and fortitude, as she had demonstrated by her survival of her captivity and beatings, followed by her eventual escape. But even she must have her breaking points, and it appeared that Griffin's ill temper was one of them.

No doubt because he had become the only true stability in her world at present.

Griffin did not fool himself into thinking Bea felt any more for him than that. She was totally dependent upon him for everything, including the clothes she wore. At present, he was the only thing standing between her and the people who had abducted her. The same people who were no doubt searching for her even now. Unaware of her amnesia, they would hope to recapture her before she was able to tell anyone what had happened to her.

No matter that Griffin had been motivated by a sense of self-preservation just now, a defence against his increasing desire for Bea, he should not have been so short with her.

And whether she wished to see him again this evening or not, he *did* owe her an apology.

Bea was very aware that she had overreacted to Griffin's comment just now. That she was being unreasonable in expecting him to be in the least bit happy with their living arrangements. As no doubt Sir Walter Latham's visit earlier today had only emphasised.

Griffin had hardly left the four walls of Stonehurst Park these past three days, and usually only to go to the stables, or to talk with his estate manager. And rather than being able to relax and enjoy Sir Walter's visit earlier today, he had likely been forced to be restrained in his manner and to keep the visit short for fear a misspoken word might reveal Bea's presence here.

Whatever her own feelings of hurt just now she had behaved unreasonably by leaving the dinner table so abruptly, and she owed him an apology for possibly having caused him embarrassment when Pelham returned to the dining room and found her gone.

She drew in a deep steadying breath as she fortified herself for going downstairs and facing Griffin again.

Only to come to an abrupt halt the moment she opened the door to her bedchamber and found Griffin standing outside in the hallway, his hand raised as if in preparation for knocking.

She gave a nervous smile. 'I was just coming downstairs to speak with you.'

'As I am here to speak to you.'

Bea stepped back in order to open the door wider. 'Please, come inside.'

Griffin stepped reluctantly into the bedchamber, aware that it was probably not wise. He noted how at home Bea had become in just a few days; there were combs and perfumes on the dressing table, the gown she had worn that day was draped over the chair, with a pair of matching satin slippers left on the floor beside it.

He turned back to Bea as she stood nervously in the centre of the bedchamber. 'I feel I owe you an apology and explanation for my behaviour earlier,' he began.

'I wish to apologise for having been so unreasonable earlier—'

Bea broke off as she realised that they had both

begun to speak at the same time. And on the same subject. 'You have nothing to apologise for.' She gave a shake of her head. 'I am still somewhat emotional at the moment, and you have done so much for me already. My new gowns and slippers, the combs and perfumes.'

'I do not require your gratitude, Bea!' Griffin winced as he realised he had spoken harshly yet again. 'My impatience now, and earlier, is not with you, but due solely to frustration with this situation. I feel as if I should be doing more for you, not less, but until I receive word, or otherwise, from the friend I have contacted in London, my hands are tied.' He paced the bedchamber restlessly.

Bea knew of the letter he had sent to a well-connected acquaintance in London a few days ago. 'When do you expect to hear back from him?' The sooner he did, the sooner Bea might have the information she needed to remove herself from Stonehurst Park; she would no longer be a burden on Griffin's generosity.

She would be sad to leave here, and even sadder to leave Griffin, but had already accepted it was inevitable.

Griffin sighed. 'Perhaps in another three, possibly four days. I realise that is a lengthy time,' he acknowledged as Bea grimaced. 'But I do not see how I can expect to hear news any earlier than that when we are two hundred miles away from London.

And there is always the possibility that there will be no news at all, or that Maystone may be away from home when my letter arrives,' he added grimly.

Bea accepted there might be delays that might occur in the delivery of Griffin's letter. Even if his friend did receive the missive, there was no guarantee that he would be able to garner any information about her. If that should be the case, she had no idea what she was going to do next. She could not remain with Griffin; that would be expecting too much, even from a man as generous as he. In which case, she had a week at most in which to formulate plans for her own future.

'You are not to worry about this, Bea.' Griffin frowned as he saw her look of concentration. 'There is no rush for you to leave here. You eat no more than a mouse, and are almost as quiet as one!'

A mouse?

Was that truly how Griffin regarded her? As a *mouse*?

Bea might have no memories of flirtation or society, but even so she was sure that being described as *a mouse* was not in the least complimentary. Or that she behaved in any way like one.

Griffin realised from Bea's dismayed expression that he had somehow spoken out of turn again, when he had meant only to reassure. The dealings between men and women really were as volatile to him as a powder keg; he had not felt this much out of his depth even with Felicity.

Perhaps that was because he actually cared what Bea thought of him? Whereas he had known that nothing he did or said was ever going to find approval from Felicity.

He frowned his impatience with the idea. 'That was not meant as an insult, Bea. Truth is, I have enjoyed the contented silence of your company these past few days,' he acknowledged grudgingly, never having believed he would ever say that to any woman.

Her face brightened. 'You have?'

Griffin once again acknowledged the danger of being alone with Bea in her bedchamber. Yet another habit he would have to break, if he was to continue behaving the gentleman.

Except his thoughts at this moment were far from gentlemanly!

He *had* enjoyed her company at the same time as he had been aware of everything about her. Bea's skin was so soft and creamy, her figure so womanly, her manner towards him so warm, and he had been too long without the warmth of any woman.

The logical part of his brain knew not to extend this dangerous situation any longer and that he should leave the bedchamber forthwith; while the part of his brain ruled completely by his desire told him to take what was in front of him, and to hell with the consequences!

Would Bea accept or reject him if he were to take her in his arms and kiss her again?

Would she accept him out of gratitude, for all that he had done and was still doing for her?

Griffin did not want any woman to accept his kisses out of gratitude.

Bea frowned at Griffin's continued silence. She believed that before her abduction she must have been a tactile person, a woman who liked to touch and be touched in return.

Because at this moment she wished for nothing more than to reach out and touch Griffin, to feel his arms close about her, to be crushed against the hardness of his chest and thighs, to lose herself in his strength and power, to feel *wanted*.

Was she imagining the hunger she saw burning in the depths of eyes? Was it possible he felt the same need for touch, for warmth, that she now did?

His wife had died six years ago but Bea did not deceive herself into believing a man as handsome as Griffin would not have occupied many women's beds in the years since.

Dared she hope, dream, that he now wished to occupy *her* bed, and it was only his sense of honour that was holding him back from doing so?

She moistened her slightly parted lips with the tip of her tongue. 'Griffin...'

'I have some estate work I need to complete this evening.' Griffin's expression was unreadable before he turned on his heel and walked to the closed door, his back towards her as he spoke again. 'I will instruct Pelham to bring you up a light supper tray. You did not eat nearly enough at dinner.'

'But, Griffin—'

'I wish you a good night, Bea,' he added firmly before opening the door and then closing it softly behind him as he left.

Bea felt the chill of disappointment at the abruptness of Griffin's departure. It was intolerable when she wanted, needed, *ached* to be close to him.

If Jacob Harker or his accomplice had violated her during her imprisonment then Bea had no memory of it—thank heavens. She shuddered. What she did know, with all certainty, was that her body had become attuned to Griffin's every move these past few days. Her breasts swelled beneath her gown as she sat in the study with him, and a fire burned between her thighs whenever she watched him walk across the room, his movements unknowingly sensuous and graceful. She ached low in her belly whenever she imagined his large hands upon her own body, caressing, cupping, *stroking*.

She was sure she would have had these feeling towards Griffin no matter what the circumstances under which they had met.

Was she a wanton, to have such yearnings?

Could the warm feelings she now felt towards Griffin be so very wrong?

Her life was already in such turmoil, did she really want to add to that confusion by complicating things even further?

The answer to that question was *yes*!

It had become sheer torture for her to be so much in Griffin's company these past few days, and at the same time so aware of the barrier of formality he had erected between the two of them. To be aware of his deliberately avuncular attitude towards her.

A deliberation that had not been present in those glittering eyes just minutes ago when Griffin had looked at her so hungrily.

Were her own feelings, her emotions, sure enough at present for her to know exactly what she would be doing if she were to meet the fire she believed she had seen in his gaze?

A mouse, he had called her, when in truth the only reason for Bea's quiet these past few days had been in the hopes of making her presence here more tolerable for him, to make herself less visible, so that she appeared less of a burden to him.

Whatever her station in life might have been before her amnesia, Bea knew with absolute certainty that she could not possibly have been *a mouse*. Griffin had also called her a woman of fortitude, and Bea did not doubt she was a woman of determination and resolve. Anything less and she would not have survived her abduction and the beatings, nor would she have managed to secure her own escape.

However, it was clear now that she would be gone from here soon, one way or another.

Away from Griffin.

She might never see him again!

She was not a mouse, and she would not have Griffin think of her as such, but was instead determined he would see the strong and capable woman she knew herself to be.

A woman who knew exactly who and what she wanted.

Chapter Eight

So much for his claim that he needed to work, Griffin acknowledged several hours later as he sat sprawled in the chair behind the desk in the library, a single lit candle on his desktop and the glow of the fire in the hearth to alleviate the darkness of the room behind him.

He had removed his jacket and cravat from earlier, several buttons of his shirt he'd also unfastened for added comfort, his thoughts ranging far and wide, before inevitably coming back to the exact same subject.

Bea.

His fingers clenched on the arms of his chair as he once again pictured her as she had looked in her bedchamber earlier: her hair slightly dishevelled, her cheeks flushed from the tears she had cried, her eyes dark with hurt, the swell of her breasts softly rising and falling as she breathed, her arms long and slender, hands and fingers delicately elegant. Hands he ached to have touch and stroke him.

She was desire incarnate!

A desire that was slowly but surely eating into Griffin's very soul, and driving him out of his mind.

'Griffin?'

Griffin turned so quickly in his chair at the unexpected sound of Bea's huskily soft voice, when he had been thinking of her so intensely, that he was in danger of falling out of it!

He almost did as he took in her appearance. She was framed in the doorway; her hair loose and silky about her shoulders, and she was wearing only her nightrail, with a thin silk robe over it and a matching belt fastened about the slenderness of her waist.

Griffin stood up, as was his custom when a lady entered the room, his brow lowering into a glower as he felt his body react instantly to Bea's appearance, and even more intensely than the uncomfortable and throbbing ache at dinner.

'What on earth are you still doing awake at this time of night?' His voice was husky as he tried to temper his tone, recalling how he had upset her when he had spoken to her harshly earlier.

She stepped into the room and closed the door quietly behind her before moving further into the shadowed library, the corners of the room completely dark. Only Griffin, his hair tousled, as if he had run his fingers through it several times in the past few hours, stood out in stark relief against that darkness. The unfastened shirt at his throat revealed a hint of dark hair covering his muscled chest.

Her chin rose determinedly before she lost her nerve and turned on her heel and fled. 'Has Pelham retired for the night?'

Griffin continued to glower. 'I believe so, yes.'

She nodded. 'I waited upstairs in my bedchamber after my bath until I believed he might have done,' she informed him softly.

His eyes narrowed warily. 'Why?'

Now that she was here, face to face with this physically mesmerising man, Bea was starting to wonder that herself!

It had all seemed so simple up in her bedchamber earlier. She would take a leisurely bath, wait for the household to go to bed before then going downstairs to seek out Griffin, with the intention of tempting him into kissing her again. With the intention of showing him she most certainly was not *a mouse*. Here and now, faced with the sheer masculinity of the man, she felt decidedly less confident.

What did she possibly have to offer a man of such sophistication and self-confidence as him? A man, a duke, who only had to snap his elegant fingers to have any woman he chose?

In her present loss of memory, homeless, friendless state, absolutely nothing.

Her nerve completely failed her. 'I have been

afraid to fall asleep these past few nights because of the nightmares that occur when I do.' She drew in a deep and ragged breath.

Of course, Griffin acknowledged with a wince, he'd noticed these past few days, during their hours spent together in the library, that she occasionally dozed in her chair beside the fire. As if, he now realised, she had not slept at night.

'Would you like me to sit with you again until you have fallen asleep?' he suggested gruffly.

At the same time as he wondered if he was capable of being alone again with Bea in her bedchamber without making love with her. Or, more likely, once again suffering the tortures of hell as he tried to resist the urge to do so!

Her hair moved silkily against the soft swell of her breasts as she shook her head. 'I want—' She drew in a deep breath and began again. 'I should very much like it if you were to hold me in your arms again.'

He was doomed. His fate writ high in the heavens, as the man who had absolutely no defences when it came to the innocence of the very woman he was supposed to be protecting.

He cleared his throat before speaking. 'That would not be a good idea, Bea.'

She eyed him curiously. 'Why not?'

Griffin clenched his hands together behind his back. 'Please just accept that it would not.'

Bea studied him from beneath lowered dark

lashes, easily noting the slightly fevered glitter in his eyes, and the flush high on those sharply etched cheekbones. There was a nerve pulsing in his tightly clenched jaw, and the width of his chest rapidly rose and fell as he breathed. 'I should like it very much if you did,' she insisted softly.

He eyed her impatiently. 'What are you doing?' he barked even as his hands came quickly from behind his back as she hurtled across the room and into his arms.

Her arms were about his waist as she burrowed into the comforting hardness of his chest. 'I feel so safe when you hold me in your arms, Griffin.'

Safe? Griffin echoed the word incredulously.

Bea felt *safe* when he held her?

It was the very *last* thing she was when his body reacted so viscerally to the feel of the warm softness of her body nestled so closely against it. He was a man of flesh and blood, not a blasted saint!

As the swell of his arousal testified.

Bea sighed her contentment. 'This is so very nice.'

His gaze sharpened with suspicion as she looked up at him. Was that a glint of mischief he could see in her eyes? A curve of womanly satisfaction to the fullness of her lips?

It was, damn it!

He pulled back slightly so that he could see her face more clearly; yes, he could definitely see challenge now in the darkness of her gaze, and her creamy cheeks were flushed. 'Bea, are you playing a game with me?'

'A game?'

Griffin wasn't fooled for a moment by her too-innocent expression. 'A dangerous game.' He nodded grimly.

'Dangerous?' she echoed softly, her fingertips playing lightly across his chest.

'Very dangerous,' he assured her firmly as his hands moved to grasp the tops of her arms to hold her firmly away from him. 'I advise that you leave here now, Bea, or suffer the consequences,' he warned.

Heat and caution waged war within Bea. The heat of the desire she felt for Griffin, to be closer to him. And the caution of realising that the man who now stood before her was not that same easy companion of the past few days. Or the gentleman who had pledged to protect her until her true protector could be found.

This Griffin was not a gentleman at all, but was instead pure, predatory male. A man who was rakishly handsome and wholly sensual, his gaze now feasting hungrily on the firm swell of her breasts visible above her nightrail and robe.

Perhaps she did have something to offer him, after all?

Bea moistened her lips with the tip of her tongue before she spoke slowly. 'I believe I will choose the consequences.'

'Then you are a reckless fool!' Griffin grated even as he pulled her into his arms and his mouth laid siege to hers.

Bea groaned her satisfaction as she gave herself up to the savagery of his kiss, eagerly standing on tiptoe as she moulded her body against his much harder one.

Her hands moved up his chest, feeling the soft hair visible there, lingering for several seconds, caressing that silkiness, as he moaned softly. She then slid her hands over the muscled width of his shoulders, her fingers becoming entangled in the darkness of the hair at his nape as the heat between them intensified and grew.

Bea whimpered low in her throat as Griffin now widened her stance to grind the hardness of his arousal into the inviting softness between her thighs, drawing her breath in sharply through her nose as he touched a part of her that caused the heated pleasure to course wildly through her veins.

She was lost in a maelstrom of emotions as his mouth continued to devour hers, even as his large hands restlessly caressed the length of her spine before settling on her bottom as he pulled Bea in even closer. The rhythmic stroking of his arousal now sent heated pleasure through the whole of her body; her nipples were full and aching, and between her thighs was swollen and warm.

Reckless fool or not, Bea didn't want Griffin to

stop. She wanted this pleasure to go on and on. To lose herself utterly, in both Griffin's arms and his unmistakeable passion.

Griffin wanted all Bea had to give. His hands cupped beneath the weight of her breasts and the soft pad of his thumbs caressed the swollen and sensitive tips. Bea's passion, Bea's pleasure, every inch of Bea's body.

Her kisses revealed the first, her groans, as he caressed her breasts showed the second, and the third—

Griffin pulled back abruptly to draw ragged breath into his starved lungs as he looked down at her with heated eyes. 'You should go back to your bedchamber, Bea. Now!'

Her hair was tousled, her eyes heavy with passion, cheeks flushed and feverish, her lips swollen from their kisses. 'I would rather stay here, with you.'

'It will very shortly be too late for me to stop, Bea.'

She looked up at him searchingly. 'Do you want to stop?'

What he wanted was this woman's body spread naked before him, so that he could kiss and taste every inch of her, from her head to her toes!

He clenched his jaw. 'No, I do not want to stop.'

'Then neither do I,' she assured him gently, her gaze continuing to hold his as her fingers moved purposefully to unfasten the two remaining buttons of his shirt.

His breath caught in his throat as she pulled his shirt free of his pantaloons before sliding it slowly up his chest. 'You really are playing with fire, Bea,' he gave her one last, growled warning.

She smiled up at him impishly. 'Then at least I shall be kept warm!' She pulled his shirt up, removing it completely. Her eyes were hot and devouring as she gazed at the muscled bareness of his chest before tentatively touching. 'You truly are magnificent, Griffin!' she breathed wonderingly as she smoothed her hands across his chest and over his nipples.

Her words, and her touch, caused Griffin's desire for her to rage out of control.

He had no memory of when a woman had last desired him for himself, and not because of his title or because she was being paid to want him. A sad state of affairs, indeed, but he had felt too raw after Felicity—

No!

He would not think of Felicity now.

Why should he think of her when there had been such an impenetrable coldness to his wife? A coolness he already knew Bea did not share.

Bea was warm—so very warm. She was responsive. Even now the hard berries of her nipples throbbed heatedly against the soft pads of his thumbs. And the scent of her arousal teased and tempted his senses, a mixture of honey and earthy, desirable woman.

Perhaps he should spare a thought for the man Michael, the man she had called for in her sleep.

Griffin saw no reason why he should consider him when Bea seemed bound and determined not to!

'Are you sure this is what you really want?' Griffin knew *he* was the one who had to be sure; he had to know that Bea wanted him as much as he desired to make love to her.

'Very sure,' she answered without hesitation.

He gave her one last searching glance, seeing only sincerity in her expression, before taking her hand and drawing her over to the warmth of the fireplace. He came to a halt and turned to face her, his gaze deliberately holding hers as he unfastened the robe at her waist before slipping it from her shoulders and allowing it to drop onto the rug on which they both stood.

She wore only her nightrail now, a diaphanous garment easily penetrated by the flickering firelight, and revealing every dip and curve of Bea's body as Griffin gazed down at her hungrily. Her breasts were full and tipped by ruby red and swollen berries, her waist slender above the womanly flare of her hips. Dark curls nestled temptingly between her thighs, and her legs were smooth and shapely above slender bare feet.

Bea sensed that Griffin hesitated still, not because he did not want her—the evidence of that was all too apparent in the tenting of his pantaloons—but because he was, after all, a gentleman, even in his desire for her.

How lucky his wife had been to have such a considerate husband. To have such a wonderful man in love with her. To be so privileged as to possess the care and devotion of such a man.

The desire Griffin now felt for her might only be a shadow of the emotions he had once felt for his dead wife, but surely it was enough?

Bea would make it be enough!

She continued to look into his eyes rather than down at her own body as her hands moved down to take hold of her nightgown. She slowly drew the material up to reveal her calves, then her thighs. The blush deepened in her cheeks as she raised the garment to her waist and saw Griffin's eyes darken, his heated gaze fixed on the V of silky ebony curls between her thighs.

'Higher,' he encouraged tightly.

Bea's hands trembled as she slowly pulled her nightrail up over her waist and breasts, her legs starting to shake as she heard his harshly indrawn breath as she removed the garment completely, dropping it down beside her robe as she stood naked before him.

'How beautiful you are,' he murmured as he sank to his knees in front of her, his large hands cupping both her breasts as he drank in his fill before slowly leaning forward to suckle one of her aching and engorged nipples into the moist heat of his mouth.

Bea reached out to grasp his bared shoulders as sharp pleasure engulfed her. She was afraid her legs would no longer support her if she didn't. His chest was bathed in firelight, warm and dry beneath her fingers, and she could feel the play of muscles beneath his skin as Griffin caressed her.

Bea had never dreamt that such pleasure existed as that created by the complete intimacy of having Griffin on his knees before her, his bared flesh beneath her caressing fingertips, her aching nipple in his mouth.

The pleasure intensified as he now drew hungrily on her swollen berry, the fingers and thumb of his other hand stroking and squeezing its twin, and sending waves of heated pleasure coursing through Bea's body straight down to between her thighs.

Soft moans began to penetrate the silence of the room, and Bea realised they were her own as one of her hands moved to clasp the back of Griffin's head, her fingers becoming entangled in the dark thickness of his hair as she held him to her, never ever wanting this pleasure to stop.

Wanting *more*.

But having no idea what more there was.

Griffin looked up at Bea as he felt her restlessness; her eyes were closed, long lashes resting on flushed cheeks, her lips parted slightly as she breathed raggedly, her throat arched in pleasure as she thrust her breasts forward.

He lightly caressed her waist as he slowly released her nipple from his mouth.

'Griffin!' She looked down at him, need shining brightly in the feverish glow of eyes.

He took a few seconds to enjoy the sight of her engorged nipple, so moist and red and swollen from his suckling, before his gaze moved lower, his hands now resting on her hips as he held her in place before him and gently nudged her legs apart with his knees.

She was so aroused. For him. Because of him. Because of her desire for him.

'Griffin?' Bea's voice quivered her uncertainty as she watched his long fingers gently part the ebony curls between her thighs before he once again lowered his head towards her.

He glanced up at her, so close now the warmth of his breath brushed softly against a part of her that felt swollen and aching. 'Do you trust me, Bea?' he prompted huskily.

'Of course I trust you.' If she did not trust Griffin, then she could never, would never, trust anyone again.

'Then trust me now.' He blew delicately against that swollen ache between her thighs, causing her to shudder and tremble with the pleasure of that caress. 'Do you like that?'

'Yes,' she groaned weakly, fingers now digging painfully into his muscled shoulders. Although Griffin seemed unaware of any pain.

'And this?' He slowly lathed the rough length of his tongue against her swollen flesh.

'Yes!' Bea's cheeks suffused with embarrassed colour at the intimacy even as she rose up on tiptoe as the force of that pleasurable caress ripped through the whole of her body.

He moved back slightly before taking her hand and tugging lightly until she sat down on the rug beside him. 'I will not hurt you, Bea,' he assured her gruffly. 'I will never do anything to hurt you or endanger you.' He cupped her face in his hands before his lips gently claimed hers.

Bea was so befuddled by the end of that long and satisfying kiss that she offered no further hesitation as Griffin pushed her gently down onto the rug before parting her legs and settling the width of his shoulders between them.

She groaned low in her throat at the first touch of his tongue against that swollen ache between her thighs. Her hands fell limply to her sides, eyes closing as she became lost in the pleasure of that moist and rhythmic caress. A pressure began to build inside her that she did not understand. Did not need to understand. She needed only to *feel*, as Griffin's hands cupped the cheeks of her bottom to tilt her up to him, like a sacrifice on an altar.

'Griffin!' She gasped as the pressure built and built. Until it grew so high, so intense, she felt as if her whole body might explode from the joy of it.

Until she did explode, deep inside her, the intense pleasure radiating outwards as well as inwards until she lay weak and gasping.

'Wh—what was that?' she gasped weakly.

Griffin moved to lie beside her as he slowly licked her juices from his lips. 'The French call it *le petit mort*—the little death,' he translated huskily.

Bea certainly felt as if she had died and gone to heaven and she was sure that she had never experienced pleasure like it.

'The English refer to it as a climax, or an orgasm.' Griffin smoothed the hair back from the dampness of her brow.

'I— Does that—does that always happen to a woman when—when a man and woman are t-together?' she prompted shyly.

'Only if the man cares enough to ensure her pleasure, which sadly too many rarely do.' His jaw tightened. 'And if the woman allows herself to become excited or stimulated.'

Bea gazed up at him searchingly, detecting a bitterness beneath his tone and the sudden bleakness of his expression. She was too satiated, too lethargic to care at that moment as she lay unabashedly naked beside him. Modesty seemed a little silly when Griffin had not only looked at her most intimate of places, but had also licked and tasted her there.

All bitterness fled as he smiled down at her, his

gaze warm. 'You are a singular woman, Bea. Very passionate and giving.'

She smiled. 'I believe *you* are the one who is remarkable, for having ignited that passion. I— Does a man experience that same climax?'

Griffin drew in a sharp breath, unsure of how to answer her. It was obvious Bea was an innocent, that her own responses just now had surprised her, her orgasm was a shock to her. How much more shocked would she be if she were to see him achieve his climax?

'Griffin?'

He closed his eyes briefly before looking at her. 'I do not know how to answer you, Bea,' he admitted honestly.

'With the truth?'

Griffin's lids lowered. 'My own arousal is more physically visible than your own.'

'The swelling in your pantaloons?'

'The swelling in my pantaloons,' he confirmed uncomfortably.

She sat up slightly. 'Would you—? Can I see it?'

He swallowed as he saw how pretty her breasts looked as she sat forward, so firm and uptilting, her nipples still swollen and rouged from his earlier ministrations.

He gave a shake of his head. 'That would not be a good idea.' Felicity had visibly paled the first time she had seen him naked. Despite all his efforts to arouse her, to ease his passage, she had screamed the first time he had penetrated her, until he had retreated again when her sobs had become too much for him to bear. The second time had been no better, nor the third, thus setting a pattern for their physical intimacy that had never changed.

Not that he intended to penetrate Bea. She was an unmarried lady, an innocent still, whether she believed it or not, and once inside her Griffin knew he would be unable to stop himself from spilling his seed.

No, far better that he should send Bea back to her bed before he returned to his own chamber, where he could douse himself in cold water! 'I believe you might sleep now if you were to return to your bedchamber.'

Bea was sure that she would, her body having an unaccustomed lethargy, a feeling of fullness and satiation, and no doubt resulting from her orgasm.

But she did not feel like falling asleep. She did not want their time together to be over just yet, and there was still that intriguing bulge in Griffin's pantaloons to explore.

'May I please see?' She looked at him encouragingly.

His jaw tightened as he obviously waged his own inner battle. Quite what that battle was, Bea had no idea, but she knew that there was one from the stormy grey of his eyes and the clenching of his jaw.

'You really are a witch!' He groaned his defeat and began to unfasten his pantaloons. 'The moment you are frightened you will tell me to stop.'

'Frightened?' Bea looked at him incredulously as she watched that unfastening in fascination. 'Why would I be frightened?'

'You are a genteel lady and I am…overlarge, in that area,' he acknowledged reluctantly as he unfastened the tie of his drawers.

'But that is surely because you are altogether an overlarge man?'

'Yes,' he bit out grimly. 'But some ladies find me unpleasantly so. Especially here.' He folded back his drawers as he spoke the last word, allowing his arousal to spring free of all restraint as he lay back on the rug and stared up at the shadowed ceiling.

Almost as if he could not physically bear to watch her reaction, Bea realised.

She sat up completely, her fascinated gaze fixed on his member; surrounded by dark curls at its base, it was indeed an impressive size, but Bea saw no reason at all for fear. She looked up at Griffin's face, frowning as she saw how pale and strained he looked. 'Does it hurt to be so swollen?'

'No.' His voice sounded strange, strangulated.

'Then may I touch it?'

'Bea…' He broke off his angry outburst as she flinched back, his eyes glittering darkly. 'If you touch me I am afraid I shall—I shall be unable to maintain control myself!' he bit out forcefully.

'You will climax?'

'Without a doubt I shall, yes!'

Bea gave a confused shake of her head. 'Why should you not, when I have already done so?' Her cheeks felt warm.

Griffin drew in a deep and controlling breath. 'You asked to see and I have shown you. Are you not fearful? Overwhelmed by my size?'

'If I am overwhelmed then it is at your magnificence,' she assured him softly. 'And, no, I am not in the least frightened. Why should I be when this is a part of you?' She touched him gently with her fingertips, incredulous at how soft his skin felt when he was obviously so fiercely hard.

He was steel encased in warm velvet, her touches becoming bolder still as Griffin made no further objection to her explorations, although the grinding of his teeth spoke of his inner fight to remain in control as her hand cupped him.

He drew his breath in sharply as Bea's other hand then moved to close about him, and, recalling how Griffin had made love to her, she began to lower her head with the intention of feeling him with her mouth, her tongue.

'No, Bea!' Griffin groaned weakly in protest even as his body burned for more of her touch.

'Will it hurt you if I do?'

'No. But— *Saints protect me!*' He groaned as her tongue tentatively licked his length.

Griffin groaned his pleasure as she licked and tasted, causing Bea's fingers to tighten as she began to stroke until he began to thrust up into her encircling fingers. She reacted instinctively as she widened her lips and took him into the heat of her mouth.

'You are killing me, Bea!' Griffin gasped weakly, hands reaching out to grasp her shoulders.

Bea did not believe that for a moment, knew from the throb and heat of him in her hands, and the fact that he was holding her closer rather than pushing her away, that Griffin would shortly experience that same intense pleasure as she had just minutes ago.

The *petit mort*.

The little death of pleasure.

And she wanted to give this to him. Wanted to *share* this with him.

She had no idea why any other ladies should ever have been frightened of him. Why he should have been so reluctant to let her see and touch him, when his body was so truly magnificent. Nor did she care. At this moment, here and now, there was only herself and Griffin.

Heat engulfed her own body for a second time at the sounds of Griffin's groans of pleasure.

'Stop now, Bea! For goodness' sake, you have to stop…' Griffin's protest turned to a loud and aching groan as his own pleasure overtook his control, his fingers digging painfully into her shoulders as he continued to gasp his pleasure.

The arousal of Bea's own body rose with each hot and pulsing jet of Griffin's release, heat engulfing her as she climaxed for a second time, adding her own groans of completion to Griffin's.

Chapter Nine

Griffin was at a loss as to know what to do next, his fingers lightly stroking the dark silkiness of Bea's hair as she lay with her head against the dampness of his thighs, his body now totally spent.

As he now felt totally relaxed and at ease in Bea's company.

Had he ever felt such a connection to any woman?

Had any other woman ever given to him so wholeheartedly as Bea just had?

Had any other woman climaxed just from giving him pleasure, as he knew Bea had?

Never, came the instant answer to all those questions.

But what to do now?

The complications of what they had just done together weighed heavily on Griffin's shoulders. He did not need to offer marriage, of course. Precarious as Bea's life seemed at the moment, she did not need to add to that uncertainty by taking such a socially inept man as her husband!

But should he at least insist she return to her own bedchamber before going to his?

Would she be happy with that, or would she want him to stay with her tonight?

Just thinking of lying beside her for the whole night, his body wrapped protectively about hers, was enough to cause his body to throb in anticipation of further lovemaking.

Lovemaking that should not—could not—happen again.

Tonight they had given each other pleasure with their mouths and hands, but if it was allowed to happen again how long before they—*he*—wanted more? Before he wished to possess Bea totally? How long before making love put them both at risk, so that marriage was no longer an option but a certainty?

Bea was warm and giving, yes, but Griffin did not need her to say the words to know that she would not want to tie herself to a man such as him for ever because of an unborn child.

Especially so when somewhere a man called Michael was awaiting her return.

'You are very quiet,' Bea said as she raised her head to look at him.

Griffin breathed in deeply before speaking. 'I was just thinking that—' He paused with a frown as there came the sound of a loud knocking. 'What the devil?'

He sat up abruptly, a scowl marring his brow as he turned towards the door.

Bea also frowned at the interruption; she was desperate to know what Griffin had been thinking as he'd lain so quiet and unmoving beneath her.

Was he as happy as she was, overwhelmed by the warmth of emotions flowing between them?

Or was he regretting what had just happened between the two of them, and seeking some way in which to gently but firmly express those regrets?

'You must dress immediately,' he instructed harshly as there came the sound of another loud pounding, causing him to rise quickly to his feet before hastily fastening his pantaloons. 'Now, Bea.' He scowled darkly as she still sat naked upon the hearthrug. 'It would seem we have a visitor, and you cannot be seen like this!' He gathered up her nightrail and robe and pushed them into her trembling hands. 'Make haste, Bea,' he encouraged impatiently as he pulled his shirt on over his head before turning away.

Bea felt bereft as she watched Griffin march across the room to the door and leave the library without sparing her so much as a second glance.

As if he had already forgotten the intimacies the two of them had just shared.

And perhaps he had. Perhaps men did not feel the same way about such things? Did they not appreciate the vulnerability that occurred inside a woman when she placed her trust, her naked self, so completely into the hands of another human being?

Certainly Griffin would not have been celibate in the years since his wife's death and yet he remained unencumbered by a second marriage, which would seem to imply that his affections had never been engaged in any of those liaisons.

Had Bea been foolish to believe that she was somehow different from the other women he had made love to, and that Griffin held some measure of affection for her?

Or was it just, in her determination to show Griffin she was not the mouse he believed her to be as well as her need to be with him, that she had deliberately chosen to *believe* that he cared for her?

Her memories of her own past might be seriously lacking at present, but still she knew instinctively that men were different from women, in that their physical desires were not necessarily accompanied by the same feelings of affection or love.

Love?

Did she *love* Griffin?

She certainly cared for him a good deal, and would be very sad to part from him when the time came, but was that love?

'Perhaps now that I have persuaded Pelham to go back to bed you will explain what the hell you are doing here!' she heard Griffin hiss fiercely from outside in the hallway.

'I would rather we were alone together in a private room before doing that,' a male voice replied unconcernedly. 'With the door closed so that we cannot be overheard— Hello, who have we here?'

Bea viewed the newcomer nervously as he stepped inside the library, one blond eyebrow raised in mocking query as he slowly took in her appearance from the top of her head to her toes.

Lavender eyes.

The man had lavender-coloured eyes, Bea realised inconsequentially.

Bright, wickedly sparkling eyes, set in a face of such aristocratic handsomeness that he was likely to take a woman's breath away at a glance.

His eyes were fringed by thick dark lashes, his nose was perfectly straight between high pronounced cheekbones, chiselled lips curved into a speculative smile above a surprisingly determined jaw.

As tall as Griffin, and almost as broad across the shoulders, the blond-haired gentleman was dressed in the height of fashion, despite the lateness of the hour. His superfine was a perfectly tailored black, his linen snowy white, a diamond pin nestled in the folds of his neckcloth. He had a tapered waist and hips, long legs, the layer of dust on his black boots the only evidence that he had almost certainly arrived here on horseback.

He turned his quizzical gaze on his host. 'Griff?'

'Bea, this is my friend Christian Seaton, the Duke of Sutherland,' Griffin introduced tersely.

The thing he had dreaded when he'd sent that letter to Maystone, that one of the Dangerous Dukes would hasten to Lancashire, had indeed come to pass. The question was, how much had Maystone imparted regarding the situation here?

He and Christian had a long-standing affection for each other, having attended Eton together, along with the other Dangerous Dukes, but even so Griffin knew that Christian was everything that he was not. Elegant. Charming. Fashionably dressed, no matter what the occasion.

Women had been known to swoon at Christian. Sensible women, matronly women, as well as the twittering debutantes who appeared in society every Season.

And Bea, Griffin noted somewhat sourly, had been unable to take her eyes off the man since he'd appeared in the doorway!

Was that *jealousy* Griffin felt towards his friend's easy charm and good looks?

Ridiculous.

And yet those feelings of bad humour persisted as he finished the introduction. 'Christian, this is my goddaughter, Beatrix.'

Bea offered Christian a shy smile. 'I prefer to be called Bea, Your Grace,' she invited huskily.

'I am pleased to meet you, Bea.' Christian nodded before turning to look at Griffin with narrowed, mocking eyes. 'Your goddaughter, Griff? Was that the best you could come up with?'

Griffin scowled darkly. 'The situation is not what you have assumed it to be.'

'Maystone has made me fully aware of what the situation is, Griff,' Christian assured him as he strolled further into the room to take Bea's hand in his before raising it to his lips. 'I trust you are now recovered somewhat from your unpleasant ordeal?'

Griffin's mouth tightened as he realised that Christian did indeed know exactly how Bea had come to be a guest at Stonehurst Park. Just as he could see, by the sudden wariness in Bea's expression, she was also aware of Sutherland's insight into the reason for her presence here.

'Maystone sent you?' Griffin queried abruptly.

Christian finally released Bea's hand as he turned to Griffin.

'Maystone is also on his way here. By carriage. I was able to travel faster on horseback.'

Griffin had not expected his letter of query to Maystone to have elicited quite such a reaction as this. It did not bode well regarding the outcome of that query.

'I am to assist in protecting your...goddaughter until Maystone arrives and explains all,' Christian added grimly.

Bea was uncomfortable at learning that the Duke

of Sutherland seemed aware of the details of her current situation. Most especially so because she had never heard of the gentleman until his arrival a few minutes ago. 'Griffin?' she asked uncertainly.

Griffin moved to stand at her side. 'Christian is a trusted friend, Bea,' he assured her gruffly.

That might well be true. But was it not humiliating enough that Griffin knew of her circumstances, without the charmingly handsome Duke of Sutherland being aware of them too?

She turned to look at the man now. 'Do you know my true identity, sir?'

'I do,' he confirmed abruptly.

'And?' she prompted as he added nothing to that statement.

He winced. 'I have been instructed not to discuss the matter until Lord Maystone arrives.'

Bea stared at him incredulously. 'That is utterly ridiculous. Surely I have a right to know who I am? Why those things were done to me?' Two bright spots of angry colour burned in her cheeks as she glared at Christian Seaton.

'You have every right, yes.' He sighed. 'Unfortunately, I am not presently at liberty to discuss it.'

'Griffin?' Bea turned her angry gaze on him.

Griffin was as much at a loss as Bea. Except to know that Christian's silence on the subject, his added protection, implied Bea's situation was even graver than he had anticipated it might be. 'I believe that, for the moment, Bea, we will have to accept Sutherland's reticence on the subject.' His gaze remained on Christian as he answered Bea, knowing by the other man's expression that he was not remaining silent out of playfulness but necessity.

'By "we" I am to presume you mean me.' She glared. 'For no doubt the two of *you* will discuss the matter at your earliest convenience!'

Griffin winced. 'Perhaps it is time you returned to bed, Bea?'

'I shall do no such thing!' she said angrily. 'I am not a child to be ordered to my room. This man— this *Duke*—knows exactly who I am, and yet says he is not at liberty to reveal it. And you *agree* with him!' She glared at Griffin incredulously.

As Bea had no knowledge of the work he and Christian had been involved in for the Crown for so many years, she could not possibly understand the need there often was for secrecy, even from each other. 'Christian must have his reasons.'

'None that are acceptable to me, I assure you!' She was breathing hard in her agitation, and with each breath Griffin was able to make out the hard, aroused pebbles of her nipples against her robe.

Which meant that Christian must be able to see that delectable display too.

Griffin's jaw tightened. 'I really think it best if you return to your bedchamber now, Bea.'

'And I have said that I have no wish to return to my bedchamber!'

'The two of us will talk again in the morning,' Griffin concluded firmly.

Bea glared first at Griffin and then at Sutherland, and back to Griffin. 'You are both mad if you believe I will calmly accept this silence until this Lord Maystone arrives!' She gathered up the bottom of her robe with an angry swish. 'I will give you both until morning to discuss the matter, and then I shall *demand* to know the answers!' She turned on her heel and marched angrily from the room.

'What a fascinating young woman,' Christian breathed as he gazed after her admiringly.

'You will keep your lethal charms to yourself where Bea is concerned.' Griffin was in no mood at present—or any other time, he suspected—to listen to or behold another man's admiration for Bea.

Christian gave him a long and considering stare. 'As you wish,' he finally drawled softly. 'In the meantime, perhaps you might care to explain to me just exactly what it was you were doing in the library with your "goddaughter" at this time of the night?'

Griffin felt his face go pale.

Hateful.

Hateful *and* impossible, Bea decided as she angrily paced the length and breadth of her bedchamber.

Both of them!

How *could* Griffin, especially after the intimacies they had so recently shared, possibly side with the hateful Duke of Sutherland?

Why was her identity such a secret?

Who was she, and what had she done, that Christian Seaton refused to discuss it in front of her?

Bea sank down on the side of her bed, weariness overtaking her as the events of the evening finally took their toll on her.

Just a short time ago she had been so happy, had felt so utterly desired, so satiated in that desire, yet now it was as if that closeness between herself and Griffin had never taken place. As if there was a distance between them so wide it might never be bridged.

Her cheeks heated as she thought of the intimacies they had shared. The pleasure Griffin had given her with both his hands and mouth. The unmistakeable pleasure she had given him in return. The taste of him on her lips.

Oh, dear Lord, would Seaton *know* that the two of them had been making love shortly before his arrival?

Griffin's appearance had certainly been dishevelled enough; he had not bothered to resume wearing his neckcloth or waistcoat and jacket before striding out into the hallway, and his hair was in disarray from her caressing fingers. Just as his lips had looked as puffy and swollen as her own now felt.

Would Christian Seaton, wickedly handsome, and so obviously a sophisticated gentleman of the world, have been able to tell, just from looking at the two of them, that she and Griffin had been making love together when he arrived?

Oh, dear Lord, could this night become any more humiliating?

Bea gave a muffled sob as she buried her face in the pillow, once again afraid. Of the knowledge of her past. Of what her future might hold.

Of having to leave Griffin.

'I would not care to discuss it, no,' Griffin answered the other man tightly as he moved to lift the decanter on his desk, pouring brandy into two of the crystal glasses before handing one to his friend. 'Who is she, Christian? And why all the secrecy?'

Christian took a grateful swallow of the amber liquid before answering him. 'We believe her name to be Lady Beatrix Stanton. She is nineteen years of age, and the unmarried daughter of the Earl and Countess of Barnstable. You will recall that both the Earl and his countess perished in a carriage accident last year? As for the rest...' He grimaced. 'The demand for secrecy is all Maystone's doing, I am afraid.'

Bea's name was Beatrix Stanton. She was the unmarried *Lady* Beatrix Stanton, Griffin corrected grimly, relieved at the former and satisfied that his previous conviction that Bea was a lady was a true one.

He had known her father, damn it; the two of them had belonged to the same club in London. Unfortunately Griffin had been out of the country when Barnstable and his countess had died so he had been unable to attend the funeral.

But he had known Bea's father!

Griffin threw some of the brandy to the back of his own throat, face grim as his thoughts raced.

Bea's dream of having attended her parents' funeral had been a true one.

So, then, must be the dream of her abduction, imprisonment, and the beatings.

Not that Griffin had ever had any doubts regarding the latter even if he did not know the reason for it.

And what of the man, Michael? He then must also be real.

Exactly who was he, and what did he mean to Bea?

He looked sharply across at Sutherland as the other man now slouched down in one of the chairs before the fire, no doubt tired from the strains of his hurried journey. 'If her parents are both dead, then who is now her guardian?'

The other man looked up at him beneath hooded lids. 'Apart from having you as her godfather, you mean?'

'Christian—'

'I am sorry, Griff, but I believe you are now crossing into the area where Maystone has demanded secrecy.' Sutherland grimaced.

Griffin's eyes widened. 'You are refusing to tell me who Bea's guardian is?'

The other man's mouth tightened. 'I am ordered not to tell you, Griff. There is a difference. This does not just involve the young lady you have claimed as your goddaughter,' he bit out harshly as Griffin looked set to explode into anger. 'The lives of other innocents are also at stake.'

Griffin stilled, eyes narrowed. 'What others?' he demanded. 'I always could pummel you into the ground, Christian,' he reminded grimly as the other man sipped his brandy rather than answer his question.

Sutherland sighed heavily as he relaxed back in the chair. 'Then you will just have to pummel away, I am afraid, Griffin, because I am not—'

'You are not at liberty to tell me,' Griffin finished grimly. 'Maystone believes Bea's life is still in danger?' he added sharply.

'It is the reason I have travelled here so quickly,' Christian confirmed.

Part of Griffin bristled at Maystone having doubted that he alone could protect Bea. Another part of him was grateful to have Christian's assistance.

If Bea truly was still in danger, then he welcomed any assistance in ensuring her safety.

He sighed heavily. 'How long before Maystone arrives, do you estimate?'

'Another day at best, possibly two, or even three at worst.'

Griffin inwardly chafed at the delay. 'And in the meantime?'

'In the meantime we do not let your young ward out of our sight. And, Griffin?'

'Yes?' He answered warily; he might welcome Christian's help in keeping Bea safe, but he was not altogether happy with the thought of the other man keeping such a close watch over Bea.

'Have a care where she is concerned, will you?' Christian suggested gently.

His shoulders tensed. 'I would not harm a hair upon her head!'

'I was thinking more of your own welfare than of hers.'

Griffin's eyes narrowed. 'I am only concerned for Bea, for the harsh treatment she has suffered, and the reason behind it. Nothing more.'

'I know you, Griffin.' Christian sighed. 'On the outside you are harsh and gruff, keeping the world and others at a distance, but on the inside—'

'On the inside I am just as harsh and gruff,' Griff assured him with some of that harshness. 'And whatever you may think you witnessed here this evening, let me assure you that you are mistaken if you believe that either my own or Bea's emotions were seriously engaged. It was…a mistake, an impulse, of the moment. She was upset, I attempted to comfort her, and the situation spiralled out of control. It will not happen again.'

'No?'

'No!' Even as he had made the explanation, and now the denial, Griffin knew that he was not being altogether truthful. With himself or Christian.

He *had* been attempting to comfort Bea earlier, but she had made it clear that she needed something else from him, something more.

Something he had been only too willing to give her.

And would willingly give time and time again if asked.

Bea, listening outside the study door, having cried her tears and decided to return down the stairs with the intention of demanding that Seaton give her the answers to her many questions, instead now felt as if her heart were breaking hearing Griffin describe their lovemaking as a mistake that he would not allow to happen again…

Chapter Ten

'You must try to eat something more than toast, Bea,' Griffin encouraged as they sat at the breakfast table the following morning, where she only nibbled at a dry piece of toast and took the occasional sip of her tea.

Griffin had been unsure of what Bea's mood would be today, after their…closeness the previous evening, and followed by Christian's unexpected arrival, and Bea's own heated departure from the room.

After her threats he had certainly not expected her uncharacteristic silence this morning, other than when she replied with stilted politeness to whatever remark he or Christian addressed to her directly.

'Thank you, but I am not hungry,' she answered him in just that manner now.

'Did you have more nightmares last night?' Griffin asked with concern, having noted the pallor of Bea's face the minute she'd entered the breakfast room, where he and Christian were already seated and enjoying breakfast. Her pallor did not in any way, though, detract from her fresh beauty, dressed as she was today in a pretty yellow gown that complemented her creamy complexion and gave an ebony richness to her hair.

Bea looked coolly across the table at him. 'How am I to tell, when my life has become nothing but a continuous nightmare from which I would rather awaken?'

Griffin scowled as he saw the corners of Christian's lips twitch with amusement as the other man obviously heard the sharp edge to Bea's reply.

A reply that implied she considered their lovemaking last night to be a part of that nightmare existence.

It had been Griffin's intention to apologise to her this morning at the earliest opportunity for the serious lapse in his behaviour and judgement but he now found himself bristling with irritation instead.

At the same time as he knew it was illogical of him to feel regret for his own actions, but feel offended when Bea expressed she felt the same way.

If only Christian were not here, perhaps he might have tried to explain to Bea *why* he regretted it.

'If you will both excuse me?' As if aware of Griffin's thoughts, Sutherland placed his napkin on the table before rising to his feet, an expression of studied politeness on his face as he bowed to them both.

'It is such a pleasant morning, I believe I will take a stroll about the grounds.'

'I believe I asked last night to be given answers this morning?' Bea reminded tightly.

'Not now, Bea.' Griffin glanced pointedly at Pelham as he stood beside the breakfast salvers.

'Then when?' she demanded, eyes glittering. 'Very well,' she bit out angrily when neither man answered her. 'As you are obviously no more inclined to answer my questions this morning than you were last night, I believe I will join His Grace for a walk in the grounds.' Bea also rose to her feet, her napkin falling to the floor in her haste. 'If I would not be intruding?' she added to Sutherland before bending to retrieve the napkin.

Griffin and Christian exchanged a glance over the top of Bea's bent head as Griffin rose politely to his feet. Christian's look was questioning, while his own was of scowling displeasure at the thought of Bea alone in the garden with the other man.

An emotion Griffin knew he did not have the right to feel. He was not truly Bea's guardian, so could not object. He would not, could not, claim to be Bea's lover, so again he had no right to object to her enjoying the company of another man.

'I will accompany you, Bea, if you wish to go outside,' he offered instead.

'No, thank you.' Bea did not as much as glance at him. 'Your Grace?' She looked at Sutherland.

'I have no objection if Griffin does not?' Christian still eyed him questioningly.

Bea bristled resentfully at the mere suggestion that it was any of Griffin's business what she chose to do after the conversation she had overheard between the two men last night. Griffin had dismissed not only her, but also their lovemaking, as a mistake that meant nothing to him.

'I believe I shall stroll in the garden, in any case,' she stated determinedly. 'If we should happen to meet, Your Grace—' she glanced coolly at Seaton '—then perhaps we might stroll along together.'

'Bea—'

'If you will excuse me, I believe I will go to my room and collect my bonnet.' Again Bea ignored Griffin as she turned on her heel and marched determinedly from the room, her head held high.

'As I remarked last night,' Sutherland mused softly as he watched her leave, Pelham following, at Griffin's discreet nod for the butler to do so, 'Bea is a fascinating young woman.'

'And as I replied, you are to stay away from her.' Griffin glared.

'Can I help it if she prefers my company to yours today?' the other man drawled dryly.

'This is not a laughing matter, Christian.'

'I could not agree more.' Sutherland sobered grimly. 'Will you accompany Bea on her walk, or shall I? In any case, she should not be left to stroll outside in the grounds alone and unprotected,' he added firmly.

Griffin eyed him sharply. 'The threat is still near, then?'

'Very near.'

He breathed his frustration with the situation. 'If you would only confide—'

'I cannot, Griff!' The refusal obviously caused Christian some discomfort. 'There are other lives at risk, and for the moment all I can do is offer to assist you in keeping Bea safe.'

Griffin could see by the strain about Sutherland's eyes and mouth that his regret was genuine over his enforced silence. 'Can you at least reassure me that Bea will be safe as long as one of us is with her?'

'I— Not completely,' the other man confessed. 'The stakes are high, Griff, and Bea may have information that is the key.'

'As I explained to Maystone in my note, she has no memory of who she is, or the events before her abduction.'

'But those memories could return at any moment,' Sutherland reasoned. 'And we believe there are people who would like to ensure they do not.'

Griffin shook his head. 'I have had the estate workers keep constant watch for strangers since the night I found her wandering in the woods and brought her here. They have assured me they have

seen no one who doesn't belong here in the immediate area.'

The other man raised blond brows. 'Then perhaps
the people in question are not strangers?'

Not strangers? Did that mean that the person, or
people, who had abducted and harmed Bea might
belong to the village of Stonehurst? That one of his
own neighbours, possibly one of the ones whom he
had visited just days ago, might be in cahoots with
Jacob Harker, whom Griffin was still convinced had
been Bea's jailer?

It did make more sense if that were the case, than
that Jacob Harker had randomly chosen one of Griffin's own woodcutters' sheds on the estate in which
to hide and then mistreat Bea.

But which of his neighbours could have been involved in such infamy? One of those social-climbing
couples he had visited, and whose only interest had
appeared to be to show off their marriageable daughters to him? Or the jovial Sir Walter? One of Griffin's own tenants? Someone who actually worked
here in the house?

If it was the latter, then surely there would have
been another attempt to silence Bea before now.

'I believe you must be the one to accompany Bea
this morning, Christian,' he murmured softly as he
heard her coming back down the stairs after collecting her bonnet. 'While you are gone I will ride over
to visit a neighbour who has invited me to come and

admire his new hunter. It is a terrible bore, but there is always the possibility I might learn something new while I am there.'

'Which neighbour would that be?' Sutherland enquired casually.

Too casually?

Griffin studied his friend's face as he answered him. 'Sir Walter Latham.'

'I do not believe I have ever met the gentleman.'

Had Griffin imagined it, or had something flickered in his friend's eyes at mention of Sir Walter?

He found it hard to believe that Latham would involve himself in intrigue and kidnapping; Sir Walter cared only for his wife, his horses and his hounds—and not necessarily in that order!

He shrugged. 'Latham does not care for London society and prefers to remain in the country. Although I believe his wife was in London for the Season.' He could not keep the distaste from his voice as he spoke of the woman who had been such a close friend to Felicity.

'You do not care for Lady Latham?'

Griffin's jaw tightened. 'She was a friend of my wife.'

'Ah.' Christian nodded knowingly. 'No doubt the dislike is mutual, then?'

'Without a doubt,' he confirmed with feeling.

The other man chuckled wryly. 'Marriage is a complicated business, is it not?'

'Women in general are complicated, I have recently been reminded.' Griffin grimaced.

The other man smiled. 'Have no fear, Griff, between the two of us we will ensure that no harm comes to your Bea.'

'She is not my Bea,' Griffin bit out harshly.

'No?'

'No,' he repeated emphatically.

No, nor would she ever be. Once Bea's memory was restored to her, and this business was over with, she would be able to return to whatever family she had left.

And the mysterious Michael.

'You really should not hold Griffin responsible for this present situation, you know,' the Duke of Sutherland remarked quietly, Bea's gloved hand resting lightly on his arm as the two of them strolled about the garden together.

No, Bea did not know.

She was grateful to Griffin for all he had done for her this past week, but that kindness could not excuse his deliberate silence over her identity. He did know now, she felt sure of it.

Nor could she forgive him for so easily dismissing the intimacies between them last night when he had spoken with Seaton.

Most of all she could not forgive him for that!

Their lovemaking had been beautiful. A true giving and receiving of pleasure such as Bea had never dreamt possible. A closeness she had believed must surely form a bond of some kind between the two participants.

Only for Griffin to have dismissed their time together so casually just minutes later.

Obviously it had not meant the same to him as it did to her.

Because he desired to make love to her but did not love her.

As Bea was so afraid she might have fallen in love with him.

And she was afraid, deeply so, that an unreciprocated love could only lead to heartbreak.

Her own heartbreak.

'I am sure Griffin is more than capable of putting forward his own defence if necessary, Your Grace,' she came back waspishly.

'But he will not.'

Bea glanced up at the handsome gentleman at her side. 'Why do you say that?'

He sighed. 'Because Griffin does not believe himself to be deserving of anyone's affection.'

Bea removed her hand from his arm as she turned fully to face him. 'I beg your pardon?'

Sutherland grimaced. 'Griffin and I have known each other for a long time, you understand. We were at school together.'

'I did not know that.'

He nodded. 'I do not believe I am being indiscreet by revealing that Griffin was placed in the school by his father when he was only eight years old. He was not a cruel man, merely elderly, and had been widowed since Griffin's birth. He did not, I believe, know quite what to do with his young son and heir, other than to place him in the competent hands of first a wet-nurse, then a nanny, and, finally, school.'

'But how lonely that must have been for Griffin!' Bea frowned at the thought of that lonely little boy, motherless, and sent away from the company of his father at such a tender age.

'Just so.' Seaton grimaced. 'We others did not join him until four years later. There were five of us altogether, all heir to the title of Duke. We were, and still are, a close-knit bunch. We became our own family, I believe, and have always looked out for each other,' he added enigmatically.

Bea's interest quickened. 'Then you also knew his wife?'

'I did, yes.' Seaton's expression became blandly unrevealing.

She nodded. 'Griffin loved her very much.' And no wonder, if he had led such a lonely childhood as Seaton had described. Griffin must have been so gratified to have someone of his own at last. Someone to love and want him.

Blond brows rose. 'Did he tell you that?'

'Well, no.' Bea frowned. 'But surely it is obvious?'

'How so?'

She shrugged. 'I understand it has been six years since his wife's death, and he has not remarried in that time.'

'Perhaps that is because one marriage was enough?' the Duke drawled.

Bea gazed at him speculatively. 'But surely it was a happy marriage?'

'I believe that is something you must ask Griffin, not me.'

'He refuses to talk to me of his marriage or his wife.'

'And I will not speak of it, either.' Sutherland grimaced. 'My only reason for discussing Griffin with you at all is in an effort to persuade you not to think too harshly of him for his silence about you. We have been, all five of the Dangerous Dukes, bound in our actions these past five years by a higher authority,' he added softly.

Other than God—and Bea did not believe Griffin or Christian Seaton to be overly religious men— what higher authority could there possibly be than a duke of the realm? Oh.

Bea looked sharply up at Seaton as she searched his handsome face for some indication that her surmise was correct. His expression, as he steadily returned her gaze, remained infuriatingly bland.

And yet the idea persisted that Griffin and his four

closest friends had all—perhaps still?—worked in some way for the Crown.

It would explain so much about Griffin. The deft and efficient way in which he had dealt with her own unexpected and unorthodox appearance into his life. The fact that he had connections in London, like Lord Maystone, whom he might call upon discreetly to help him in discovering her identity.

It was perhaps also the reason Griffin had never married again; working secretly for the Crown could no doubt be a hazardous occupation, even in times of peace, as it now finally was. Already a widower, he was not a man who would allow his own actions to risk making his wife a widow.

Could that be the reason he was choosing to discourage her own affections?

No, it was more likely that Griffin simply did not feel that way about her.

But the rest of it?

Oh, yes, knowing Griffin she could well believe the rest of it.

Griffin was above all a man of honour, of deep loyalties, and once that loyalty had been given she had no doubt that he would never betray it. For anything or anyone.

'I see.' She nodded slowly.

'I hope that you do.' Sutherland gave a slight inclination of his head. 'Griffin is a good man, and I should not like to see you treat him with unnecessary harshness.'

Bea gave a rueful shake of her head. 'I believe you mistake our friendship, Your Grace. Circumstances have put Griffin in the role of an older brother to me, or—or an uncle.'

Blond brows rose up to the Duke's hairline. 'I trust you do not truly expect me to believe that?'

Bea could feel the blush in her cheeks at thoughts of last night. 'Whatever Griffin has said to you in regard to me—'

'I am sure you know him better than to believe he would ever be so indiscreet as to discuss his friendship with a lady with a third party. Even one of his closest friends,' Seaton stated firmly. 'But I do have eyes, Bea, and the power of deduction, and I do not believe that Griffin was behaving as an older brother or an uncle to you when I arrived late last night.'

The heat deepened in her cheeks. 'That was all my own doing, not Griffin's.'

'Perhaps we should not discuss this any further, Bea?' Seaton suggested ruefully. 'Such conversations have the power of stirring the blood, I am far from London, and sadly the only beautiful woman in the vicinity is far more taken with my friend than she is with me.'

'You are a flirt, sir.' Bea could not help but laugh.

'Indubitably.' He gave an unrepentant grin as he once again placed her gloved hand upon his arm so that they might continue their walk about the gardens together.

But that did not mean that Bea did not continue to think of their conversation. For her heart to ache for the lonely little boy Griffin must once have been. For the sad and lonely widower he must also have been these past six years since he'd lost his wife.

For Bea to feel ashamed of her harshness towards him this morning, when she had spoken and treated him so coldly.

As no doubt the wily Duke of Sutherland had intended her to feel...

'Yes, Bea?' Griffin eyed her warily as she appeared in the doorway of the library, where he currently sat alone, drinking whisky and contemplating the unpleasantness of his visit to Latham Manor this morning.

She hesitated. 'I am not interrupting anything?'

'Only my thoughts,' he acknowledged dryly.

Lady Francesca had arrived back at Latham Manor the previous evening, and, as Griffin had quickly learnt, her acerbic tongue had not been in the least tempered by having spent the Season in London, followed by several weekend parties on her leisurely journey back into Lancashire.

'Thoughts I can well do without,' he added dismissively as he stood up and indicated that Bea should enter and take her usual seat by the fire, before he sat down opposite her.

He had missed her company this morning, truth be told, allowing him to realise that he had become accustomed to her presence in the library as he worked on estate papers. Seeing her strolling about the gardens before he left, her hand resting companionably on Christian's arm, had not improved his mood in the slightest. Finding Lady Francesca Latham back at home had only exacerbated his ill humour.

Nor had he learnt anything useful from the visit. Sir Walter was his usual jovial self, even more so now that his wife was returned to Lancashire, but the lady's jarring presence had not allowed for any private conversation between the two gentlemen.

The only good thing about the visit was that Griffin had not had to suffer through meeting Lady Francesca's whey-faced niece; she, no doubt having spent quite enough time in the company of her sharp-tongued aunt, had wisely chosen to remain a little longer at the home of one of her friends.

All in all, Griffin's day so far had not been a successful one. Bea had opted to eat lunch in her bedchamber, and Griffin had absented himself from afternoon tea on the excuse that he was busy working on estate business.

'I owe you an apology.'

Griffin tensed as he raised his gaze sharply to look searchingly at Bea. 'An apology for what?'

She sighed. 'I believe I was—unfair to you, both last night and this morning. The Duke of Sutherland was kind enough to explain a little about the restraints put upon the two of you, in regard to revealing my true identity.'

Griffin felt a certain satisfaction in hearing her still refer to Christian formally; he did not think he could have born to suffer through listening to Bea referring to the other man in a familiar way.

He was not so pleased with the rest of the content of her apology, however. 'And how did Christian do that?'

Bea sensed the reserve in Griffin's tone. 'His Grace was not in the least indiscreet, Griffin,' she hastened to reassure. 'He merely helped me to understand that there is more involved in all of this than my own personal wants and needs.'

'Indeed?'

Griffin sounded even more cool and remote when all she had wished to do was settle the unease that now existed between the two of them.

She had not forgotten overhearing his dismissal of their lovemaking last night, nor would she, but Christian Seaton *had* helped her to understand that there was a much broader picture to this situation, one that required she put her personal feelings of hurt to one side.

To be dealt with later.

She looked up at him quizzically. 'You would rather he had not said anything?'

Griffin would rather *he* had been the one to do the explaining.

Feelings of jealousy rearing their ugly head again?

Feelings he did not have the right to feel.

Feelings he would be unwise to feel.

He looked at Bea closely, noting the pallor to her cheeks. 'You have suffered no ill effects from our intimacy last night, I hope?'

'No, of course not.' Those cheeks immediately warmed with colour, her gaze avoiding meeting his. 'What ill effects should I have suffered?' she added waspishly.

Griffin, totally unfamiliar with a woman's pleasure, had no idea. It had merely been something for him to say once he had noticed her pallor. Something he obviously should not have said, when it seemed to have inspired a return of tension between the two of them.

He grimaced. 'I should not like to think that I had caused you any physical discomfort.'

'I have no idea what you are talking about, Griffin,' she dismissed impatiently, obviously in great discomfort at this moment, her arms tense as they rested on the brocade-covered arms of the chair, the knuckles of her fingers showing white as she tightly gripped the wooden ends.

He stood up restlessly. 'I am trying, in my obviously clumsy way, to put things right between us. To—to—I wish to have the old Bea returned to me!' he rasped.

Bea had to harden her heart to the frustration she could hear in his voice, knowing she could never again feel so at ease in his company after the events of last night. Not because she regretted them in the slightest, because she did not. It was overhearing Griffin voice *his* regrets over those events that now constrained her.

He loomed large and slightly intimidating over the chair in which she sat. 'Bea, if I could turn back the clock, and make it so that last night had never happened, then I would,' he assured her with feeling. 'I would do it, and gladly!'

Bea felt the sting of tears in her eyes. She had not thought that Griffin could hurt her more than he already had, but obviously she had been wrong.

A numbing calm settled over her. 'If anyone is responsible for the events of last night, then it is me. You did warn me against proceeding, but I refused to listen. You are not to blame, Griffin,' she repeated firmly as she stood up. 'I have made my apology, now if you will excuse me?'

'No!' Griffin reached out to grasp hold of her arms as she would have brushed past him. 'No, Bea, I will not, I cannot let you leave like this. Beatrix Stanton!' he bit out grimly as she kept her face turned away from looking at him directly. 'Your name is Lady Beatrix Stanton,' he repeated, no longer caring about Christian's warning of caution. Only Bea mattered to him at this moment, and putting an end to the estrangement between the two of them. 'You are the daughter of Lord James and Lady Mary Stanton, the Earl and Countess of Barnstable.'

Her face paled as she stared up at him for several long seconds with dark unfathomable eyes before finally crying out, 'Mamma! Pappa!' Before very quietly, and very gracefully, sinking into a faint in Griffin's waiting arms.

Chapter Eleven

'Did you not consider how dangerous it could be to tell an amnesiac the truth so bluntly?'

'Obviously I know now.' Griffin turned to scowl his impatience at Christian as the other man restlessly paced the length of the library and back.

Griffin sat beside Bea on the chaise, where he had placed her tenderly just minutes before, and now held one of her limp hands in his.

The other man frowned. 'I thought we had agreed last night that we would not tell Bea anything until after Maystone's arrival?'

'*You* agreed that with Maystone, not I,' Griffin growled. 'And in making that agreement the two of you seem to have forgotten that Bea is a person not an object, and that she at least had the right to know who she is.'

Christian ceased his pacing before slowly nodding. 'I apologise.' He grimaced. 'You are right, of course.'

Griffin raised surprised brows. 'I am?'

'Do not look so shocked, Griff, you are sometimes right, you know.' Christian smiled ruefully. 'I freely admit I was wrong to agree otherwise, no matter what Maystone's directive.'

'You have had a drastic change of mind since yesterday?' Griffin eyed him suspiciously.

Christian turned away. 'I discovered, while walking in the garden with Bea earlier today, that she is a lady about whom it is easy to feel…concern.'

Griffin scowled darkly at his friend's obvious admiration for Bea.

An admiration Griffin shared but now found himself resenting. Deeply. 'Is that the reason you chose to confide in her as to the nature of our association with Maystone?'

Sutherland looked uncomfortable. 'As I said, she is one in whom it is easy to…feel empathy.'

Griffin stiffened. 'Indeed?'

'Oh, not in that way, Griff,' Christian snapped his impatience. 'She is just so vulnerable, and so very alone. Damn it, Griff, you were the one making love to Bea when I arrived late last night, not I!' He scowled his exasperation with Griffin's scowl. 'And do you really know me so little that you believe me to be capable of ever attempting to usurp one of my closest friends in the play for a lady's affections?'

'I am not making a play for Bea's affections.'

'Perhaps that is because you do not need to do so!' the other man bit out tersely.

'You misunderstand the situation, Christian.' Griffin gave a shake of his head. 'Bea is grateful to me for my part in her rescue; that is all.'

Christian now eyed him pityingly. 'You are a fool if you believe that to be all it is.'

His eyes glittered in warning. 'I am not having this conversation, Christian.'

'Why on earth not? Griffin,' he continued in a reasoning tone, 'it is wrong of you to allow the events of the past to dictate how you behave now.'

'It is none of your affair, Christian.'

The other man continued to eye him in exasperation for several moments more before nodding abruptly and changing the subject. 'Do you think it possible that revealing Bea's name to her may have triggered a return of her memories?'

'Why?' Griffin looked at his friend through narrowed lids. 'What is it that she knows, Christian, that is of such importance Maystone sent you here almost immediately he received my letter? Why does he need to come here himself?'

Christian straightened. 'I have allowed that Maystone and I were wrong in deciding to keep Bea's identity from her until he arrives, but I will not concede any further than that. Please try to understand, Griff,' he added persuasively. 'I assure you Maystone is not being difficult, but he has his own reasons for remaining cautious. Reasons I cannot as yet confide.'

'I believe *I* might perhaps shed at least a little

light on the matter,' Bea spoke softly as she opened her eyes and attempted to sit up on the chaise. A move hampered somewhat by the fact that one of her hands was being held firmly clasped in both of Griffin's. She avoided meeting his concerned gaze as she carefully but determinedly released her hand before sitting up and looking up at Christian Seaton.

'Lord Maystone mistakenly believes, as did my kidnappers, that I have information detrimental to their plans. Is that not so, Your Grace?'

Most, but not all, of Bea's memories had painfully returned to her the moment Griffin had revealed her full name. Along with the raw pain of losing the parents she had loved so dearly, both of whom had been killed during a winter storm when a tree had fallen onto and crushed their carriage with them both inside.

One memory she was profoundly grateful to have returned to her, however: neither Jacob Harker nor his accomplice had violated her. He had been an unpleasant man, and cruel in his care of her, but he had not physically harmed her in any way. Even the beatings had all been carried out by his accomplice, who had upbraided her jailer that day and so allowed Bea to overhear that his name was Jacob.

'Mistakenly?' Christian repeated slowly.

'Yes. Might I have a glass of water or—or perhaps some brandy, do you think?' Bea requested faintly as she lay her head back on the chaise, her mind once again swirling as some of the memories still danced elusively out of her reach.

'Of course.' Griffin stood up immediately to cross the room to where the decanter and glasses sat upon his desk top, pouring the dark amber liquid into a glass before returning.

Bea had managed to sit up completely in his absence, slippered feet placed firmly on the floor, her hands shaking slightly as she accepted the glass before taking a reviving sip of the drink.

So many of her memories had now returned to her. Her parents' death the previous winter was the most distressing.

They had been such a happy family. Her parents were still so much in love with each other, and it was a love that had included rather than excluded their only child. So much so that they had been loath to accept any of the offers of marriage Bea had received that previous Season, determined that their daughter should find and feel the same deep love for and from her husband. They wished for her to find a happy marriage, such as they had enjoyed together for twenty years.

After their sudden deaths her guardianship had been given over to her closest male relative— Oh, dear Lord!

'Bea?' Griffin prompted sharply.

She looked up at him with pained eyes. 'Please be patient with me, Griffin. It is such a muddle still inside my head.' Could it really be possible that the answer to her abduction and present dilemma was so close at hand?

Well, of course Bea's head was a muddle, Griffin accepted, feeling that he was in large part responsible for her present distress. Her face was deathly pale, her hands shaking slightly as she held tightly to the brandy glass. Christian had been quite right to up-braid him for his stupidity in having revealed Bea's name to her so unthinkingly that she had fainted from the shock.

At the time he had thought only of preventing her from leaving when things were so strained between the two of them. Instead his outburst had caused Bea immeasurable pain, and the distance between them now seemed even wider than it had been before he had spoken.

Much as it grieved him, Griffin realised that most of that distance was coming from Bea herself. Because her memories were too distressing? Or because she was still angry with him? Whatever the reason, Griffin had no choice but to respect her feelings, and so continued to keep his distance as Christian now took his place on the chaise beside Bea.

She gave the other man a tentative smile. 'I fear Lord Maystone's visit here may be a futile one in re-gard to myself,' she voiced regretfully. 'Even with my memories returning to me, I still do not have any idea what it is that my abductors thought I might know.'

'No idea at all?' Seaton looked disappointed.

'No,' she confirmed heavily before turning to Griffin. 'However, Griffin, I am now aware of who my—'

'Lord Maystone, Your Grace.' Pelham had appeared unnoticed in the library doorway, quickly followed by the visitor.

Bea turned in surprise to look at the visitor as he strode hurriedly into the room without waiting for Griffin's permission to do so.

Lord Maystone was a man possibly aged in his mid to late fifties, and he appeared a little travel-worn, as might be expected. But he was a handsome man despite his obviously worried air, with his silver hair and upright figure.

Bea did not recall ever having seen or met him before this evening.

Griffin scowled darkly as he looked across the room at Maystone. 'It's about time you arrived and gave an explanation for this whole intolerable situation!' He turned all of his considerable anger and frustration onto the older man.

'Griff—'

'I will thank you not to interfere, Christian.' Griffin eyed his friend coldly.

'I believe Aubrey might be in need of some refreshment before we do or say anything further?' Christian pointedly reminded Griffin of his manners.

Griffin shot his friend an irritated glance before turning to the silently waiting butler. 'Another decanter of brandy, if you please, Pelham, and possibly some tea,' he added with a glance at Bea, waiting only long enough for the butler to depart before speaking again. 'Neither I, nor Bea, I am sure, appreciate this ridiculous need you feel for secrecy, Maystone.'

'Griffin!' Bea was now the one to reprove him sharply as she stood up quickly to cross the room to Aubrey Maystone's side. 'Can you not see that Lord Maystone does not look at all well?'

She placed her hand gently on the older man's arm as she looked up at him in concern.

Griffin *had* noticed that Maystone looked slightly pale about the mouth and eyes, but he had assumed it was from the exhaustion of travelling so far and so quickly at his advanced years.

On closer inspection Griffin could also see that the older man had lost weight since he'd last seen him. To a considerable degree: his face was thinner, his jowls no longer firm, and his well-tailored clothing seemed to hang loosely upon his upright frame.

'Come and sit down, My Lord,' Bea encouraged gently, her arm gentle beneath Maystone's elbow as she guided him over to sit on the chaise.

'I am sure I shall feel perfectly well again soon, my dear.' Maystone patted Bea's hand reassuringly as she sat down beside him. 'Possibly after I have drunk a reviving glass or two of brandy.'

'Griffin?' Bea prompted pointedly, her attention and concern all on Aubrey Maystone.

Griffin caught the mocking glint in Christian's eyes as he moved to pour Maystone a brandy. As if the other man found Bea's somewhat imperious behaviour towards him amusing. Or, more likely, Griffin's reaction to it…

As far as he was concerned, this situation had already caused more than enough of an upset between himself and Bea, and he did not intend to tolerate much more of it. His scant patience had come to an end.

He moved stiffly away to stand before the window once he had handed over the glass of brandy to Maystone. 'I assure you, I am nowhere near as tolerant of this situation as Bea!'

'Griffin!'

'Griff!'

He scowled as he was simultaneously reprimanded by both Bea and Christian.

'Rotherham is perfectly within his rights to feel irritated by my request for secrecy.' Lord Maystone sighed deeply once he had swallowed a large amount of the brandy in his glass and some of the colour had returned to his cheeks. 'It is—' He broke off as Pelham returned with a tray carrying the second decanter of brandy, the pot of tea also in evidence. 'This is something of a lengthy tale, so I suggest we all make ourselves comfortable by sitting down and having tea or a brandy while I tell it,' he suggested heavily once the butler had departed at a nod from Griffin.

Bea continued to sit on the chaise beside the older man as Griffin first poured a cup of tea for her and placed it on the table near her, before replenishing Lord Maystone's glass, and then pouring brandy into two more glasses for himself and Christian, those two gentlemen then taking up occupancy of the chairs on either side of the fireplace.

There were several significant things she had now remembered that she needed to discuss with Griffin, but perhaps those things would become clearer to her, to all of them, once Lord Maystone had told his lengthy tale.

She believed there was something else beneath Lord Maystone's obvious pallor and fatigue. Possibly an air of despair? Or perhaps even grief?

'Firstly, my Lady Bea,' Maystone began wearily, 'let me apologise to you for your having innocently become involved in this situation.'

She squeezed his arm reassuringly. 'I do not believe that it is your apology to make, My Lord, but that of the people responsible for my abduction and imprisonment.'

He grimaced. 'Nevertheless, I might have done something to prevent it. I am not sure what,' he added distractedly, 'but... Are you aware that I work within the Foreign Office?'

'I am, yes.' Bea gave Griffin a sideways glance from beneath her lashes.

Maystone nodded. 'Then I must also reveal that both Rotherham and Sutherland have for some time kindly assisted me in my less public work for the Crown.'

'I am aware of that also, Lord Maystone.' Bea turned away from Griffin's scowl to give the older man a reassuring smile. 'I am sure that you can appreciate it was necessary, for my own protection, that I be made aware of it?'

'I am sure Griffin acted only for the best.'

'I was the one to inform Lady Bea of the reason for my hurried presence here, not Griffin,' Seaton interjected decisively.

Lord Maystone's brows rose. 'Indeed?'

'Could we just get on with this?' Griffin glared his impatience over the delay; he just wanted to get this whole sorry business over and done with.

So that he might talk alone with Bea.

So that he might apologise for upsetting her earlier.

So that he might *be* alone with her.

He had always enjoyed Christian's company in the past, and the same was true of Aubrey Maystone, but here and now they both represented a deepening of that barrier between himself and Bea that he found so intolerable.

'Of course.' The older man sighed as he turned

back to Bea. 'Several months ago there was a plot to assassinate the Prince Regent. A plot that was effectively foiled, my dear,' he added as Bea gasped and raised a hand to her throat. 'With the aid of Rotherham, Sutherland, and several other worthy gentlemen.' He nodded. 'After which, most of the perpetrators were found and arrested.'

'But not all?'

Griffin had long appreciated Bea's intelligence, and he could see it had not failed her now either, and that she was beginning, if not completely, to understand the restraints that had been placed upon his own conversations with her this past week.

'Not all, unfortunately,' Maystone acknowledged heavily. 'We have all of us been attempting, these past few months, to find those of the plotters who have infiltrated society itself. Do not be alarmed, my dear.' He placed a reassuring hand on Bea's arm as she drew her breath in sharply. 'I am sure you are perfectly safe here with both Rotherham and Sutherland to protect you.'

Griffin sincerely hoped that was the case, although he still suspected—and feared—that Jacob Harker was in hiding somewhere within the district.

It made no sense to him, with Bea now free and able to talk of her captivity, to assume that the other man would have completely disappeared from the area. Finding Bea, and possibly silencing her once and for all, would now be Harker's mission. After all, he could have no idea that Bea had suffered a temporary loss of her memories following the trauma of her abduction and frightening escape.

Nor did Griffin believe, with the information Christian had imparted to him, that Harker was acting upon his own initiative.

One, or perhaps more than one, other person was most assuredly in control of these events.

'My concern was not for myself,' Bea now assured Lord Maystone huskily; in truth, her present alarm was all on Griffin's behalf upon learning that he had been involved in the risky business of preventing a plot to assassinate the Prince Regent.

That Griffin might have been killed before she'd even had opportunity to meet him.

'What a sweet and caring child you are.' Lord Maystone smiled at her warmly before that smile turned regretful. 'Which only makes my guilt all the deeper regarding my own involvement in your sufferings— Not her abduction, Rotherham.' He frowned as Griffin tensed in his chair. 'Do give me a little credit, please. I was not even aware of Lady Bea's abduction until after you wrote and told me of it.'

'But you most certainly knew something was afoot,' Griffin put in testily. 'As is someone else; Bea's real guardian must also have been aware of it when she completely disappeared.'

'Griff—'

'Allow him to have his say, Sutherland.' Maystone sighed. 'Truth be told, I have handled this situation very badly, and as a consequence I deserve any approbation Griffin may care to lay at my feet.'

'I disagree.'

'Enough!' Griffin rose restlessly to his feet. 'Will you please just state the events, Maystone, and cease leaving Bea and I in this infernal state of uncertainty?'

Bea did not rebuke him this time; she knew from the pallor of his face and the nerve pulsing in his tightly clenched jaw that Griffin really was at the end of his patience.

And who could truly blame him? He had no doubt initially travelled to his country estate with the intention of enjoying some peace and quiet. Instead he had happened upon a woman in the woods who must have appeared to him to be deranged, quickly followed by the arrival of the Duke of Sutherland and now Lord Maystone. The poor man must have thought himself caught in the middle of bedlam this past week.

With no end to his suffering in sight.

He also had no idea as yet that Bea had now remembered the name of her guardian.

Lord Maystone emptied the rest of the brandy from his glass, his voice flat and unemotional when he spoke again. 'Three weeks ago an eight-year-old child was abducted, taken from his home, his parents and his family, for the sole intention of using the threat of taking his life as leverage in gaining access to certain information that might, indeed undoubtedly would, help in their cause against the Crown.'

'Good God!' Griffin breathed softly.

Maystone looked up at him with bloodshot eyes. 'That child is my grandson.'

Griffin closed his eyes in shame for his earlier rebukes and the anger he had shown towards Maystone since his arrival.

The man's grandchild had been abducted, his life threatened.

As Bea's had.

No wonder Maystone had added two and two together—his grandson's abduction followed by Griffin informing him Bea had suffered the same fate—and come to the conclusion of four!

Especially so when Griffin had stated in his letter to Maystone that there was a possibility that Jacob Harker, known to have been involved in the plot to assassinate the Prince Regent, and a man who just a few weeks ago had been seen in the area of Stonehurst, might have been involved in Bea's abduction and imprisonment. Bea's memory of the man's name being Jacob had, as far as Griffin was concerned, confirmed that suspicion, which he had also stated in his letter to Maystone. That had obviously caused both Sutherland and Maystone to travel so quickly to Stonehurst.

And no wonder, if Maystone's own grandson had also been abducted and kept prisoner.

Had the boy been kept a prisoner, or was there the possibility that he was already—?

The idea the boy might already be dead was so unthinkable that Griffin could not even finish the thought.

Although Maystone's bloodshot eyes and severe weight loss would seem to imply the older gentleman had also thought of that possibility these past agonising weeks. Far too often.

Griffin straightened briskly. 'The kidnappers have made their demands for the boy's release and safe return?'

'Most certainly,' Maystone confirmed leadenly. 'Demands with which I cannot possibly comply.'

'Oh, but—'

'I know what you are going to say, my dear.' Lord Maystone squeezed Bea's hand in understanding. 'But you must understand that my first loyalty has always been, must always be, to the Crown I have served all these years.'

No, Bea did not understand. A boy's life was at stake, this gentleman's own grandson—surely it was worth anything to have him returned safely to his family?

She gave a firm shake of her head. 'I admire your loyalty, of course, but there must be some way in which you can maintain that loyalty and still rescue your grandson?'

'We must respect Lord Maystone's views, Bea.' Griffin had easily seen and recognised that stubborn set to her mouth as the precursor to her frankly stating her own views on the subject.

'Why must we?' She stood up abruptly, those flashing blue eyes now including him in her anger. 'We are talking of a little boy, Griffin,' she added emotionally. 'A little boy who has been taken from his parents, from all that he loves. He must be so frightened. So very, very frightened.' Her hands were so tightly clasped together her knuckles showed white, as she so obviously lived through memories of her own abduction and imprisonment. When she had suffered through that same fear of death, of dying.

'You must remain calm, Bea.' Griffin quickly crossed the room to clasp her clenched hands within his own.

'I do not see why.' Tears swam in those pained blue eyes as she looked up at him. 'Consider how you would feel, Griffin, if the child who had been taken were your own? How you would feel if your own son had been snatched from—?' She broke off as there came the sound of choking, both of them turning to look at Aubrey Maystone.

Just in time to see him fall back against the chaise, a hand clutching at his chest, his face as white as snow.

Chapter Twelve

'I did not mean— I had not thought to distress Lord Maystone so much that he— I am so very sorry!' Bea buried her face in her hands as the falling of her tears made it impossible for her to continue.

'It is not your fault, Bea,' Griffin consoled huskily as he reached out to cradle her in his arms.

The two men had managed, between them, to carry Lord Maystone up the stairs to one of the bed-chambers, and Bea, Christian, and Griffin were now all seated about the library as they waited for the doctor to come back down the stairs after attending to his patient. Christian reclined in an armchair, Bea and Griffin once again sat together on the chaise.

'It is my fault,' Bea sobbed. 'I should not have said— I should have thought.'

'Nothing you said tonight was anything May-stone has not already said to himself many times during this past three weeks, Bea,' Seaton assured her comfortingly. 'The man has been beside himself with worry, and I have no doubts that this prolonged strain, and these added days of travelling, are the only reason for his collapse tonight.'

'Why did he not confide in me?' Griffin gave a pained frown. 'We could all have assisted in searching— No,' he guessed heavily. 'I am sure one of the kidnappers' demands was for Maystone's silence on the affair.'

Indeed, Griffin had thought of Bea's accusation prior to Maystone's collapse: How *would* he have felt if it had been his child who had been taken? Would he have turned England upside down in an effort to find his son? Or would he have done what Maystone had done, and suffered in silence himself rather than put the child's life in jeopardy?

If he had known Bea prior to *her* abduction, would he have been able to stay silent when she was taken, in the hopes it might save her life?

The answer to that was he had already been doing exactly that for this past week.

As had the man Michael for whom she had cried out in her sleep? The man whom she must surely now remember?

Perhaps that was what she had been about to tell Griffin earlier, when Maystone had arrived and interrupted her.

Christian stood up restlessly. 'Maystone decided that, as you were leaving to follow up the rumour of

Harker's sighting in Lancashire, and the other Dangerous Dukes were all busy with their new marriages, it must be me that he took into his confidence in this matter.' He looked grim. 'It has been difficult enough for me, knowing there is a child's life at stake, so goodness only knows how Maystone has coped with this prolonged strain.'

'And the boy's parents?' Bea lifted her head from Griffin's chest, her cheeks tear-stained. 'They must be beside themselves with worry.'

'His mother is prostrate and his father sits at her bedside a great deal.' Sutherland nodded grimly.

'But what do the kidnappers' people want?' Griffin frowned. 'Something from Maystone, obviously, but what?'

Sutherland gave a grimace. 'Initially they had hoped he would use his influence to persuade the Prince Regent and the government into allowing Bonaparte to reside in England.'

Griffin narrowed his eyes. 'We are all aware that cannot be allowed to happen.'

'Of course not,' Christian acknowledged briskly. 'As we are also aware, there is still the hope amongst Bonaparte's followers that if he did reside in England they might one day be able to put him back on the French throne.'

'But that is ludicrous! Is it not?' Bea looked at the two men uncertainly as they exchanged a pointed glance.

'It certainly will be once Bonaparte is safely delivered and incarcerated on—' Sutherland broke off abruptly, giving an impatient shake of his head. 'At the moment there are legal moves afoot by Bonaparte's followers, to ensure that he remains in England. That is something the Crown and government simply cannot allow to happen.'

'Understandably,' Bea acknowledged softly.

Christian grimaced. 'That legal process has been deliberately delayed, for obvious reasons, so that— Suffice it to say that, for the moment, for the matter of a few more days only, it is still possible for Bonapartists in England to foil the arrangements made for his incarceration. After which they are no doubt hoping to see him safely returned to France, at which time a civil war will once again break out, allowing Bonaparte to prevail through the ensuing chaos.'

'But surely the French people have already spoken, by accepting the return of their King?' Bea did not pretend to know a great deal about politics, few ladies of her age did, but even she did not believe that the usurper Napoleon could reign without the will of the majority of the people.

Sutherland gave a rueful shake of his head. 'A number of French generals have spoken, as has the British government and its allies, but they alone are responsible for the Corsican's complete defeat, and returning Louis to his throne. Napoleon's charisma has always been such that no one with any sense believes it will be possible to proclaim the man thoroughly subdued until after he is dead.'

Bea eyed him curiously. 'You sound as if you might have met him.'

'I have recently had that dubious honour.' Christian nodded ruefully. 'I expected to dislike him intensely, for the mayhem he has created here for so many years, as well as on the Continent, and for the lives lost because of it, many of them my own friends. Instead, I am sorry to say, I found him every bit as intelligent and charismatic as he is reputed to be.' His jaw tightened. 'Enough so that I perfectly understand Maystone's concerns should he give in to the demands of his grandson's kidnappers, and so allowing the Corsican's followers opportunity to free him.'

'And these demands are?' Griffin asked softly.

Christian's shoulders slumped. 'Can you not guess?'

He nodded. 'They wish to know the secret details and destination of Bonaparte's exile, so that they might intercede either before or during his journey.'

'Details Maystone is obviously completely aware of.' Christian gave an acknowledging inclination of his head. 'And time, unfortunately, is running out.'

Bea was unsure as to whether he meant time was running out for the plans of Bonaparte's followers or for Lord Maystone's grandson. Either way, determined steps must be taken to find the little boy and return him to his parents and grandfather, before it was indeed too late.

Just the thought of an eight-year-old boy suffering the same cruel imprisonment that she had was beyond bearing.

'Griffin?' she appealed.

Griffin had never felt as impotent as he did with Bea looking up at him so trustingly. As if she believed he was capable of solving this situation when Maystone and Christian had been unable to in the past three weeks.

But he dearly *wanted* to deserve that look of complete trust, to be the hero that Bea believed him to be.

He turned to Christian. 'Have you and Maystone made any progress at all?'

Christian grimaced. 'We have arrested several more people involved in the original assassination plot, but all claim to know nothing of the kidnapping of Maystone's grandson. Consequently they did not have any information on where the boy is being held. Your information of Lady Bea's abduction, so similar to that of Maystone's grandson, is the first real indication we have had that mistakes are being made. Desperation is setting in, and when that happens...'

'The whole begins to unravel,' Griffin finished with satisfaction.

'But I have told you both that I do not know why I was taken! That I do not know anything.' Bea hesitated. 'That is not completely true. I now know *where*

I was when I was abducted!' Her eyes lit up excitedly. 'I know who was at the house party that weekend. Surely once I have told you their names it can only be a matter of time— You have both said there is no time!' She groaned her frustration.

Griffin frowned in thought. 'You were abducted from a house party?'

'Yes. Sir Rupert Colville and his wife had invited my aunt and I— I am such a fool!' Bea pounded the palm of her hand against her forehead. 'Griffin, I tried to speak with you earlier. I know now who my guardian is—' She broke off to look up at Seaton. '*That* is the reason you have kept your own counsel since you arrived! Why you have been so protective of me.'

'Yes,' he confirmed grimly.

'Would someone care to enlighten me?' Griffin raised an impatient brow.

Bea turned back and unthinkingly clasped both his hands in hers.

'It is Sir Walter Latham, who is my late mother's cousin and now my guardian!'

Griffin gave a start, pulling sharply away from Bea before standing up. 'Sir Walter?' he repeated disbelievingly. Bea was the niece Sir Walter had spoken of so affectionately? The niece who had been in London with her aunt but whom Latham now claimed to be staying with friends? 'But he has no interest in politics or society.' Griffin frowned. 'He is a pleasant and jovial enough fellow, but otherwise— You already knew of this connection, Christian, and said nothing?' he accused, recalling how he had sensed his friend's air of reservation when they had spoken of Sir Walter earlier.

The other man gave a frustrated shake of his head. 'The fact that Lady Bea is his ward does not make Sir Walter guilty of any more than negligence at the moment, in having failed to report her as missing. And there are often other reasons than kidnapping for a young lady's sudden disappearance,' he added dryly.

Griffin turned back to Bea. 'You said your aunt accompanied you to this house party?'

'Yes,' she confirmed hesitantly.

That Lady Francesca Latham, always so cold and mocking, might be involved in intrigue and kidnapping, Griffin certainly *could* believe.

Especially so, when only this morning she had told him herself that her niece had decided to stay with friends rather than immediately accompany her aunt to her new home to Lancashire.

Unless…

Unless he was allowing his own dislike of Lady Francesca, and her past influential friendship with his wife, to colour his judgement?

The possible explanation for Lady Francesca's lie, as to her niece-by-marriage's whereabouts, might be that she was under the same warning of silence as

Lord Maystone if she wished to have her niece safely returned to them.

Did Sir Walter know of Bea's abduction too, but was keeping up his jovial front in an effort to prevent that truth from becoming public, also in an effort to protect the life of his niece?

There were far too many questions yet unanswered for Griffin's liking!

And he was prevented from asking any more of them as the doctor came back into the room with his report on Aubrey Maystone's state of health.

Apparently the older man had suffered a slight seizure of the heart, but would recover fully, in time. For the moment, it was best that Lord Maystone rest as much as possible.

'I believe I will go and sit with Aubrey for a while,' Christian quietly excused himself once the doctor had gone.

Leaving Griffin and Bea alone together.

Bea was instantly aware of a change in the atmosphere, a charged tension totally unlike the one that had existed when they had all spoken together of the unfortunate situation regarding the Corsican usurper, and how the deposed Emperor seemed to be the connection between the two kidnappings.

Did Griffin feel that tension too?

A glance from beneath her lashes revealed his expression to be one of wariness. As if he feared what she might say to him.

It was ridiculous of him to feel wary of her. Admittedly, she was still hurt at overhearing his rejection of their lovemaking. But she could never be truly angry with Griffin. She cared about him too much for that to ever be true. He could not be blamed for not having that same depth of feeling for her.

'What are—?'

'Are you—?'

They both began speaking at once, both stopping at the same time.

Bea looked across at Griffin shyly as he politely waited for her to speak first. 'What are we to do next, do you think?'

'Regarding the recovery of Maystone's grandson?'

'What else?' she prompted softly.

What else indeed, Griffin acknowledged, knowing it was ridiculous of him to think that Bea would have any interest in discussing the subject of their closeness last night when she now knew exactly who she was.

Who Michael was.

It irked that as yet she had still made no mention of the other man in her life.

Out of embarrassment and awkwardness, perhaps, because of their own closeness last night?

Bea need have no qualms in that regard where Griffin was concerned; what had happened between the two of them had been madness. A wonderful sensual madness, but it had been madness nonetheless.

A beautiful young woman such as Lady Beatrix Stanton could have no serious interest in a man such as him. A man so many years older than her, also a widower, and still suffering the emotional scars of his disastrous marriage.

He nodded abruptly. 'I believe we will have to wait until we are able to consult with Maystone on that situation.'

'Of course we must,' Bea allowed. 'What were you going to ask me just now?'

Griffin frowned for a second, and then his brow cleared. 'Ah. Yes. I wondered if you have a fondness for your aunt Francesca?' he enquired with deliberate lightness; after all, his own dislike of the woman was personal, and might not be shared by others, least of all her niece-by-marriage.

Bea gave a husky chuckle. 'She is a little over-whelming, I concede. But I do not know her terribly well—my mother and Sir Walter were not close,' she explained at Griffin's puzzled expression. 'As such I did not have opportunity to meet either Sir Walter or Lady Francesca often until after my parents—until after they had both died,' she added quietly.

'I really am so sorry for your loss, Bea.' Griffin took a step towards her and then stopped himself; there was absolutely no point in causing further awkwardness between the two of them by taking her in his arms—most especially when he could not guarantee the outcome.

He seemed to be fighting a constant battle within himself where she was concerned. The need to be close to her, to make love to her again, was set beside the knowledge that he did not have that right. That Bea belonged to another man.

Even if she had chosen not to speak to him of that man, as yet.

How could she, when he had taken such liberties? When just to think of the two of them together last night must now cause her immeasurable embarrassment and guilt?

No, better by far that he respect her silence, and the distance now between them, rather than cause them both further embarrassment.

'Griffin, do you think that I should go to—?'

'No!' he protested violently.

Her eyes opened wide at his vehemence. 'You do not know what I was about to say.'

'Oh, but I do,' he assured her dryly. 'You have shown yourself to be both a courageous and resourceful woman this past week.'

'I do not believe that to be true.' She shook her head sadly.

'Oh, but it is,' Griffin countered. 'You are very determined. What's more you have refused to allow fear to dictate your movements. Consequently it is not in the least difficult for me to reason that you are thinking of offering yourself up as human bait, by going to your uncle and aunt's home in the hope that one or both of them might give themselves away as being involved in this plot of treason and kidnapping.'

As that had been exactly Bea's intention, she could not help but feel slightly put out that Griffin had so easily guessed what she had been about to suggest. 'But surely it is the obvious answer to this dilemma? A way of knowing, without doubt, if one or both of my relatives are involved, when I am able to see their reaction to my safe and unexpected return?'

'And what if that should turn out to be the case? What of the danger to yourself?'

'What of the danger to that little eight-year-old boy?' she said, tears glistening in her eyes. 'Griffin, you do not believe that he might already be—'

'No,' Griffin assured her abruptly. 'Certainly not.'

Bea eyed him quizzically for several long seconds. 'You are not a very good liar, Griffin,' she finally murmured sadly. 'At least, not when you are speaking to me.'

He drew in a ragged breath as he thought of the abused state in which he had found Bea. For a young child to suffer such ill treatment would surely cause irrevocable emotional damage, as much as physical. Although they had no reason to suppose that Maystone's grandson would be beaten, the boy was being held to ransom, and not because he personally was in possession of knowledge wanted by his kidnappers, as Bea apparently had.

'You really have no idea of what it is you might have overheard to cause your abduction?'

'None at all.' She gave a pained grimace. 'As far as I recall, it was just a weekend party, with the usual bored group of people attending.'

Griffin wished he dare ask if Michael had been one of those people, but again knew it would not be fair to place Bea in such a place of awkwardness. 'We will find Maystone's grandson, Bea, have no fear,' Griffin stated with determination. 'And if anyone is going to visit the Lathams then it will be me,' he added grimly.

'But would it not look suspicious if you were to visit them again so soon?'

He smiled tightly. 'Not if my purpose was to make Sir Walter an offer for his new hunter. He will refuse, of course, and have the satisfaction of owning a piece of horseflesh he believes coveted by his neighbour.'

'You must be terribly good at the secret work you do for the Crown,' Bea murmured ruefully. 'That is what you and the Duke of Sutherland do for Lord Maystone, is it not?'

'We should not speak aloud of such things, Bea.'

'But why do you do it, Griffin?' She looked up at him in confusion. 'Why have you chosen to deliberately put yourself in danger?'

It had begun as a way for him to evade thoughts

of his failed marriage and his dead wife, but had all too soon become a way of life. One that he did not think of so very much any more, but merely accepted the assignments he was given. Such as he had in his search for Jacob Harker.

And instead he had found Bea.

She had, he realised, become a part of his household this past week. Someone that he looked forward to seeing across the breakfast table every morning. To spending the mornings in companionable silence with. To talking and arguing with over dinner, as they conversed on a number of subjects, some of which they did not agree on, and a larger number of which they did.

He could not imagine being here without Bea.

And yet he knew that she must leave him.

Not to go to the Lathams' as yet. Not until they had first ascertained if the Lathams were directly involved in Bea's kidnapping, and that of Maystone's grandson. Or if they were merely remaining silent regarding Bea's disappearance out of concern for their niece's safety.

But once that situation was concluded? Yes, then a home must be found for Bea, either by returning her to her uncle and aunt, or with some other relative if one or both of them should be revealed as being involved in these kidnappings.

'There is no one to care what I do, and so I do what has to be done,' Griffin answered her bluntly.

Bea *cared*!

She cared very much what happened to Griffin. Now and in the future.

Even if he did not want or need her concern.

'That is unfortunate—Your Grace!' She turned concernedly to the Duke of Sutherland as he appeared in the doorway. 'How is Lord Maystone feeling now?'

He stepped into the room. 'He wishes to speak with both of you now, if that is convenient?'

'Why?' Griffin eyed the other man suspiciously.

Sutherland looked grim. 'Best you speak to Maystone, Griff.'

Griffin had a fair idea of what Aubrey Maystone wished to discuss with him—at this point in time the older man was feeling desperate enough to go to any lengths to achieve the return of his grandson.

Even suggesting, as Bea had already done, that her immediate return to the Lathams' home might bring forth the breakthrough in this impasse that was so sorely needed.

Chapter Thirteen

'Absolutely not! I will not hear of it!' Griffin barked furiously in reply to Maystone's suggestion. The older man was looking very pale and tired as he lay back against the pillows in one of the guest bedchambers at Stonehurst Park.

'But, Griffin—'

'I tell you I will not hear of it, Bea!' He turned that glare on her. 'Whatever it is that Bea is supposed to know, she has no knowledge of it now—' he turned back to the other two men '—and to even think of sending her back amongst that possible nest of vipers, completely unprotected, is totally unacceptable.'

'But she will not be unprotected,' Christian put in softly. 'It has been proposed that I will accompany Lady Bea, along with her maid.'

'She has no maid.'

'Then we shall find her one,' Christian said reasonably.

Bea could not bear to be the cause of contention between Griffin and the gentlemen, who were obviously two of his closest friends. 'It is no more than I offered to do myself just minutes ago, Griffin,' she reminded softly.

'And if you recall I turned down that offer. Unequivocally!' he came back fiercely.

'But surely you can see it is the only course of action that makes any sense?' she reasoned. 'I will go to Latham Manor, having travelled from my friend's house under the kind protection of the Duke of Sutherland. At which time, my aunt and uncle will then either react with gladness at my safe return after my abduction, and so proving their innocence. Or they will both sincerely thank the Duke of Sutherland for having safely returned me from my visit with friends, and we will know that in all probability my aunt has lied. It all makes perfect sense to me.'

'It makes *no* sense to me!' Griffin bit out as he ran an exasperated hand through his hair.

'But—'

'It is far too dangerous, Bea,' he ground out harshly as he continued to glare down at her. 'Added to which, I absolutely forbid it!'

She sat back in surprise, not only at the fierceness of Griffin's emotions, but also because he felt he had the right to forbid her to do anything.

Admittedly he had been claiming to be her godfather and guardian this past week, as a means of explaining her presence here at Stonehurst Park, but it was a sham at best, and a complete untruth at worst. Griffin could not seriously believe that tenuous arrangement gave him the right to forbid any of her actions?

'Have a care, Griff,' Christian warned ruefully as he obviously saw the light of rebellion in her eyes. 'It has been my experience, in my many dealings with my younger sister, Julianna, that it is a mistake for any man to forbid a strong-minded woman to do anything—unless he expects her to do the opposite. For myself, in regard to Julianna, I am more than gratified to have passed that particular responsibility over to Worthing!' He grinned ruefully.

Griffin drew in a harsh, controlling breath, well aware of the contrariness of a woman's actions; he had been a married man for a year, after all.

'This is all my fault,' Maystone rallied apologetically. 'For having suggested such a plan in the first place.' His expression gentled as he looked up at Bea. 'Perhaps Griffin is in the right of it, my dear, and we should not proceed with this.'

'Griffin is most certainly *not* in the right of it!' Bea stood up, her expression one of indignation, eyes glittering rebelliously as she glared at Griffin. 'Lord Maystone's suggestion is a sound one. And I shall do just as I please,' she added challengingly as Griffin would have spoken. 'I have no doubt I shall be perfectly safe under the protection of the Duke of Sutherland.'

That was one of Griffin's main objections to the plan!

Besides the obvious one of Bea deliberately placing herself in the path of danger.

Whether either of the Lathams were involved in her abduction or not, Bea's reappearance at their home would still leave her vulnerable to the people who had been responsible. To Jacob Harker, at the very least.

Besides which, if anyone was to act as Bea's protector then it should be him. In this particular situation that was an impossibility, when the Lathams lived but a mile away from Stonehurst Park, and he was supposed to be unacquainted with the Lathams' niece. And if Griffin could not be at her side, once she was returned to the uncertainty as to the innocence of the inhabitants of Latham Manor, then he could not, in all conscience, approve of Bea going there either.

Or bear the thought of her spending so much time alone with Christian.

Griffin knew his own nature well enough to realise he could be taciturn and brusque, and that his looks were not, and never would be, as appealing as Christian's. Just as he knew Bea could not help but be charmed by the man, as so many other women in society had been and still were, if the two of them were to be so much together at Latham Manor.

If Christian, charming and gentlemanly, were perforce to become Bea's rescuer in Griffin's stead.

What made the situation worse was that Griffin knew how ridiculous it was for him to feel this way.

Even petty and childish.

Griffin knew he would be lying if he claimed to not already feel jealous at having to share Bea, first with Christian, and now with Maystone too.

This current conversation was a prime example of just how frustrating he found having this situation taken out of his control! 'I believe I should like to go to the library and discuss this alone with Bea, if you two gentlemen have no objection?' He eyed the other two men stonily.

'And if *I* should object?' In point of fact, Bea did not have any objections to going anywhere with Griffin, but she did resent his high-handed attitude in not so much as consulting with her on the subject.

He turned that stony gaze on her. 'Do you?'

She drew her breath in slowly, sensing, despite his chilling and controlled appearance, that Griffin was teetering on the edge of another explosion of temper. 'I merely wish you to have the courtesy of consulting me,' she finally replied softly.

'Very well.' His jaw had tightened. 'If you would care to accompany me to the library, Bea, so that we might discuss this matter further and in private?'

It was impossible, facing the three gentlemen as she was, for Bea to miss the knowing look that passed between Seaton and Lord Maystone, even if she did not quite understand it.

'By all means I will accompany you to the library, Griffin. Gentlemen.' She nodded politely to Sutherland and Maystone. 'But be aware, Griffin,' she added as he moved to politely open the door for her so that she might precede him out of the bedchamber, 'I have no intention of allowing myself to be bullied. By you or anyone else,' she warned as she swept past him and out into the hallway.

Was it even sane of him, Griffin wondered as he had to hold back a smile as he accompanied Bea down the curved stairs to the library, to feel both admiration and frustration for her at one and the same time?

Admiration for the way in which she had conducted herself just now.

And frustration with the light of determination he had seen so clearly in her eyes as she gave him that set-down.

'I am aware our conversation was interrupted earlier, Bea,' he remarked as he closed the library door firmly behind them. 'But nevertheless, I cannot have left you in any doubt as to my disapproval of this scheme.'

Bea faced him as she stood in the middle of the

room. 'Even if it were to save the life of a small child?'

Griffin's hands were clenched together behind his back. 'I do not believe it sensible to save one life by putting the life of another at risk, no.'

She eyed him reprovingly. 'I am sure, during your own work for the Crown all these years, that you must have done so many times in the past?'

'I...' Griffin hesitated in order to draw in a deeply controlling breath.

He knew Bea too well now, realised that the remark he had intended to make—that he was a man, and so the situation was different—would only result in Bea becoming even more intransigent.

'I may well have done,' he conceded. 'But the risk to you in this situation is too great. Bea, you might conceivably have died of the cruel injuries deliberately inflicted upon you the last time you were held prisoner,' he added gruffly.

And instantly regretted it, as he saw the colour immediately leave her cheeks.

He stepped forward quickly to grasp her shoulders as she would have swayed. 'I did not mean to upset you by reminding you of such things,' he bit out. 'Can you not understand, Bea—' he attempted to temper his tone '—that I am concerned for your safety?'

Tears swam in her eyes. 'It would indeed be a pity to undo all the good work you have done this past week by tending my cuts and bruises and feeding and clothing me.'

Griffin drew back as if Bea had struck him. Indeed, it felt as if she had just done so. 'That was an unforgivable thing for you to say, Bea.'

It was, Bea knew that it was. It was just that she'd felt so disconnected from Griffin since Christian Seaton's and Lord Maystone's arrival. As if the closeness the two of them had shared this past week had been completely rent asunder by the arrival of his other visitors.

She *missed* Griffin.

As she missed their previous closeness. Their conversations. Their bantering and occasional laughter. Their lovemaking.

But that was still no reason for her to have been so mean to Griffin just now.

She bowed her head in shame. 'I apologise, Griffin.' She looked up at him, tears blurring her vision. 'This is just such an awful situation for everyone, and I cannot bear the thought of that little boy being all alone, and suffering as I did. I want to *do* something to help him, Griffin.'

Griffin was well aware that she felt as impotent as he did over this situation. But, still, he could not bear the thought of her once again being placed in danger, and this time by a decision consciously made.

He knew he looked defeat in the face because of

the depth of her determination. 'I do not suppose I can stop you if you have made your mind up to help.'

'Oh, thank you, Griffin!' She beamed up at him as she reached out to clasp both of his hands in her own. 'I will feel so much better about doing this if I have your blessing.'

Griffin was not sure she did have his blessing, but he did welcome the breaking of the tension that had existed between the two of them for most of today. As he welcomed her voluntarily touching him again.

He looked down at her gravely as his fingers tightened about hers. 'You will be careful, Bea? And you will accept Seaton's instructions in regard to your safety?' He almost choked over the directive, still far from happy that Christian would be the one to accompany Bea to Latham Manor, but knowing that he now had no choice, in the face of Bea's stubbornness, but to accept it with good grace.

Most especially so when he now held Bea's hands in his own and knew himself bathed in the warmth of her smile.

'I will do as you ask.' Bea moved instinctively up on her tiptoes to kiss him lightly on the cheek, her own cheeks immediately becoming flushed and warm as she looked up at him shyly. 'I cannot thank you enough for being so very kind to me this past week, Griffin.'

A nerve pulsed in his tightly clenched jaw. 'You are a woman whom it is easy to be kind to.'

The two of them remained looking at each other for several long moments, before Bea broke the connection as she sternly reminded herself of the conversation she had overheard last night between Griffin and his friend. She must not make the mistake again of thinking that his kindness towards her, his concern for her welfare, was anything deeper than that of a man who cared deeply for others—hence his work for the Crown these past years—even if he did not care to show it in the often stern exterior he presented to the world at large.

She released his hands before stepping away. 'I shall need to go up to my bedchamber and pack what few belongings I now have. I shall have to give the excuse to my aunt and uncle that, having accepted the Duke of Sutherland's protection for the journey, the rest of my luggage will be arriving later by carriage,' she added with a frown.

Griffin still believed this whole concept, of Bea going to Latham Manor, was fraught with the possibility of mistakes being made, of someone getting hurt. Possibly Bea herself. Mistakes she, or Griffin, or even Christian, would not have any control over.

Which was not to say Griffin did not intend to find some way in which he might watch over her himself.

'Do not scowl so, Griffin!' Bea advised teasingly the following morning as she sat in the coach opposite Christian Seaton, prior to their departure for Latham Manor. She wore a pretty yellow bonnet over her curls to match her gown, with her hands and arms covered to the elbows by cream lace gloves.

She looked, in fact, to Griffin's eyes at least, a picture of glowing health and happiness. All of the visible bruising had now faded from her creamy skin, and her eyes shone brightly with the excitement of what she was about to do.

As she stepped willingly—even eagerly—into a possible lion's den.

Albeit with Christian at her side.

Griffin's jaw tightened as he looked at his friend, seated across the carriage from Bea. 'It is understood that at the first sign of danger you are to bring Bea away from there?'

The other man gave a mocking inclination of his head. 'Do not fear, Griffin,' he drawled as he stretched his legs out across the carriage. 'You may rest assured I shall take good care of our little Bea.'

Griffin's eyes narrowed at his friend's obvious mockery. 'You will send word immediately with Miss Baines if I am needed.' He nodded in the direction of the young woman sitting beside Bea. She was a niece to his housekeeper, Mrs Harcourt, who had agreed to accompany Bea to Latham Manor as her maid. 'I shall be visiting Sir Walter this morning, in any case.' He was also well aware that he might possibly arrive too late, if there was an immediate reaction to Bea's arrival. But this proposed visit to take another look at Sir Walter's hunter was the best that Griffin could come up with in the circumstances.

At least this way he might have opportunity to be formally introduced to Bea as Sir Walter's niece.

The irony of his eagerness now to be introduced to Sir Walter's niece, when he had not cared to meet the daughters and nieces of any of his other neighbours, was not lost on Griffin.

Nor was the possibility of Lady Francesca Latham being involved in the plot to secure Bonaparte's freedom.

Again Griffin questioned as to whether or not he was being influenced in this suspicion by his personal dislike of the woman. Lady Francesca had been far too much of a negative influence on his late wife, he suspected, in regard to their marriage, and him. And she'd enjoyed being so, if the mocking smiles Lady Francesca had so often given Griffin were an indication.

'Is that altogether wise, Griffin?' Christian frowned at Griffin's proposed visit to Latham Manor.

Wise, or otherwise, it was Griffin's intention to visit shortly after Christian and Bea had arrived. 'I shall be calling upon Sir Walter this morning.' He nodded.

'As you wish.'

'It is exactly as I wish.' Griffin gave another terse nod before stepping back and closing the carriage door.

His last sight of Bea as she left Stonehurst Park—and him—was as she turned her head away from the window in order to answer something said to her by Christian.

'Stay calm, Griffin,' Aubrey Maystone advised softly half an hour later as he and Griffin travelled down the driveway of Latham Manor in the ducal coach.

Griffin stilled immediately as he became aware of the fact that he was sitting on the edge of his seat, as well as tapping his hat impatiently against his thigh. An impatience exacerbated by the fact that he had been forced to travel by coach at all, out of concern for Maystone's health, when he would have much preferred the faster travel of horseback.

Truth was, he would have preferred to call upon the Lathams by himself, and he had told Maystone as much when the older gentleman had announced his intention of rising from his bed and accompanying him.

Maystone was not to be gainsaid, however, and in the end Griffin had no choice but to capitulate when he could see how pale and agitated the older man was in his need for news of his young grandson.

As agitated, in fact, as Griffin was in regard to news of Bea's reception on her arrival at Latham Manor.

He shot Maystone an impatient glance. 'I warn you now, I cannot answer for my actions if anyone has harmed so much as one hair upon Bea's head!' His teeth were clenched, a nerve pulsing in the tightness of his jaw.

The older man's expression softened. 'Perfectly understandable, when you are in love with her.'

'I— What?' Griffin looked at the other man incredulously. 'Of course I am not in love with Bea,' he denied harshly. 'I am concerned for her safety, that is all.'

'Of course you are.'

'I have had to suffer enough of Christian's sarcasm these past two days, and can quite well do without your adding to it!' Griffin scowled darkly.

The older man gave an acknowledging nod. 'It was not intended as sarcasm. Very well, I will say no more on the matter,' he acquiesced as Griffin continued to glare coldly across the carriage at him, before politely turning away to look out of the window at the trees lining the driveway.

Leaving Griffin alone with his thoughts.

Was he in love with Bea?

Of course he was not! The mere idea of it was preposterous, ridiculous.

Preposterous and ridiculous or not, was it possible that the feelings of jealousy, of possessiveness, which Griffin so often felt where Bea was concerned, might indeed be attributed to a growing affection for her?

No!

He did not love Bea or any other woman. Nor would he ever do so.

And Bea?

Griffin had no choice, once this present situation had resolved itself, other than to allow Bea to return to Michael. The man she obviously loved.

After which she would likely not give Griffin so much as a single thought. Unless it was out of gratitude for having saved her from her abductors. And for having returned her safely to the man she would no doubt give the rest of her life, and her love, to.

'We are arrived, Griffin,' Maystone announced softly as the carriage came to a jostling halt at the end of the driveway.

Griffin barely managed to contain his impatience long enough to allow his groom to open the carriage door, and then wait while Maystone preceded him down onto the cobbled driveway, before quickly jumping down from the carriage himself.

He drew in a deep and steadying breath as he placed his hat back upon his head to look up at the grim grey-stone visage of Latham Manor.

Knowing that Bea was somewhere inside this inhospitable-looking house…

Chapter Fourteen

'The Duke of Rotherham and Lord Aubrey May-stone,' the Lathams' butler announced from the door-way of the salon in which Bea, Christian and Sir Walter Latham sat together drinking the tea she had recently poured for them.

She and Seaton had arrived at Latham Manor just thirty minutes previously, to be greeted enthusiastically by Sir Walter. And in such a manner as to indicate that the gentleman had no knowledge of Bea's abduction, but had in fact believed her to be visiting with friends.

Thus confirming Lady Francesca's guilt?

Unfortunately they had no answer yet as to whether that was indeed the case; Lady Francesca was out this morning, paying courtesy calls upon her neighbours.

The question now was whether or not Lady Francesca had actively lied to her husband regarding the reason for Bea's disappearance two weeks ago. Or whether that lady herself believed that Bea had eloped, and she had merely told the lie of Bea visiting with friends in order to prevent her husband from worrying about his ward.

Sir Walter's pleasure in having Bea back with him could not be doubted, nor his gratitude to the Duke of Sutherland for having escorted her here.

Now that Bea's memory was returning to her she had recognised the rotund gentleman on sight, of course. And remembered him with affection, if not great acquaintance; her real acquaintance with Sir Walter had only occurred upon her parents' deaths last winter, when he and Lady Francesca had attended the funeral and then, as her guardians, taken her to live with them in their London home. Sir Walter had not remained long in Town with the two ladies once the Christmas holiday was over, preferring to return to his country estate and his pursuits there.

Bea stood up now as Griffin entered the salon first, followed more slowly by a white-faced Lord Maystone; surely that gentleman should not have come here at all, when he had been ordered by the doctor to rest. Although Bea had no doubt Lord Maystone would feel less anxious if he was allowed to actively do something in regard to bringing about the return of his missing grandson.

'Your Grace!' Sir Walter greeted warmly, obviously slightly overwhelmed by the visit of yet more exulted company this morning.

'Latham.' Griffin nodded abruptly. 'My recently arrived guest, Lord Aubrey Maystone,' he introduced just as tersely, having eyes for no one else but Bea as she stood so still and composed across the room.

He could read nothing from her expression. Nor, as he glanced at Christian, did his friend give him any more than a shrug. One that seemed to imply frustration, rather than an indication that Christian had come any closer to learning the truth of this situation.

And the reason for that frustration soon became obvious as Sir Walter apologised because his wife, Lady Francesca, was presently not at home.

Lady Francesca's many absences from home might be perfectly innocent, but Griffin sensed, more than ever, that the woman had information that would give them the answers to the reason for Bea's abduction.

And might also lead to the whereabouts of Maystone's young grandson.

'More cups, if you please, Shaw,' Sir Walter instructed the butler once he had made Aubrey Maystone's acquaintance. 'I am sure you gentlemen must both already be acquainted with my guest, the Duke of Sutherland,' he continued jovially. 'And please allow me to introduce my ward, Lady Beatrix Stanton.'

Griffin nodded abruptly to Christian before he

quickly crossed the room to where Bea now stood. As if he had been drawn there by a magnet.

As indeed he had been; just this short time of Bea being out of his sight, out of his protection, had been a sore trial to his already frayed temper.

'A pleasure to meet you at last, Lady Beatrix.' He took the gloved hand she held out to him, holding her gaze with his as he brushed his lips across her knuckles while maintaining that hold upon her hand. 'Sir Walter omitted to mention your beauty when he spoke of you.'

To say that Bea felt reassured upon seeing Griffin again, even though it had only been half an hour or so since the two of them had parted, would be putting it too mildly. His mere presence had the effect of making her feel safe.

Even if that feeling of safety was a false one.

Inside Latham Manor was, to all intents and purposes, almost as comfortably appointed as Stonehurst Park. Not quite so grandiose perhaps, but the furnishings were lavish, the paintings and statuary were also beautiful.

Even so there was a chill to the atmosphere in this house that had not been present in Griffin's home, despite his not having visited there for some time.

That chill seemed to emanate from the fabric of the house itself, as if placed there by its owners.

'I agree, dear Beatrix is everything that is charming and lovely, Your Grace,' Sir Walter acknowledged Griffin's compliment warmly.

Sir Walter appeared to be everything that was jovial and friendly, leading Bea to conclude that the chill of the house must have come from Lady Francesca.

During their months spent in London together Bea could not say that she had found the other woman to be of a type she might make into a bosom friend, but she had not found her to be unfriendly either. They were merely of a different age group, Lady Francesca nearing forty years of age, and Bea not yet twenty. Nor did Lady Francesca appear to possess the maternal instinct that might have drawn the two women closer together. That the Lathams' marriage was childless perhaps accounted for the latter.

Bea had no idea if she was merely being fanciful about her aunt-by-marriage, or allowing some of Griffin's obvious aversion to Lady Francesca to influence her own feelings towards the wife of her guardian.

No doubt they would all learn more upon that lady's return.

Bea felt a blush warm her cheeks as she became aware that the other three gentlemen in the room were now eyeing her and Griffin curiously. No doubt that was because Griffin still had a hold of her hand.

'May I pour you two gentlemen some tea?' She deftly slid her fingers from between Griffin's, before once again making herself comfortable on the sofa, waiting until Shaw had entered the room and placed the extra cups on the tea tray in front of her before pouring more of the brew.

She was barely aware of Lord Maystone's acceptance as Griffin chose that moment to make himself comfortable on the sofa beside her.

The hard length of his thigh pressed warmly against her own.

'Tea would be perfect, thank you, Lady Beatrix,' he accepted huskily.

Bea turned slightly to give him a sideways frown from beneath her lashes. The two of them were supposed to have only now been introduced to each other, and from what she had gathered of Griffin's relationship with his neighbours, and his indifference towards remarrying, she did not believe he usually singled out any of his neighbours' nieces—for his particular attentions. Much more of this and Sir Walter would be demanding that the Banns be read on the morrow!

Aware of the reason for Bea's censure, Griffin moved his thigh slightly away from her own. But he could not bring himself to move away from her completely, finding some comfort in at least being close to her.

'I hear you have recently added a fine grey hunter to your stable, Sir Walter?' Aubrey Maystone smoothly stepped into Griffin's breech in manners after receiving his cup of tea. 'You must allow us to see this fine horseflesh before we depart!'

Griffin took advantage of Sir Walter's fulsome praise of the other man's hunter in which to talk quietly with Bea. 'You are well?'

'Quite well, Your Grace,' she replied quietly as she handed him his tea. 'We only parted a short time ago,' she added even more softly.

Griffin put the cup and saucer down on the table beside him untouched as he kept the intensity of his gaze fixed upon Bea. 'And I have hated every moment of it!'

Bea gave him a searching glance, cautioning herself not to read too much into Griffin's statement; he could just be once again referring to the danger she had placed herself in rather than any deeper meaning.

Such as that he loved her as she surely loved him?

Bea had known it for a fact the moment the carriage had pulled away from Stonehurst Park earlier this morning. Had felt an ache in her heart such as she had never known before. An emptiness that could only be filled by Griffin's presence.

She loved him.

Not because she was grateful to him for having rescued her. Not because he had continued to protect her once he'd realised she had no idea who she was. Nor because they had made such beautiful love together.

She loved Griffin.

All of him. The bad as well as the good.

His manners, for instance, could be exceedingly rude. His nature could occasionally be morose, even terse. As for his suspicions concerning her friendliness towards the gardener, Arthur Sutton, and Christian Seaton—they had been altogether unacceptable.

But there was a kindness to Griffin, a caring, that he hid beneath that gruff exterior. Perhaps because of his lonely childhood. Or the sad end to his marriage. Whatever the reason, Bea saw beneath that gruffness to the man beneath, and she loved him.

Unreservedly.

When all of this was over she did so hope that the two of them could remain friends, at least. She did not think she could bear it if they were to never see each other again.

But she must not let her own feelings for Griffin colour her interpretations of his comments. When he said he had hated every moment she had been away from him, he had surely meant in the role he had undertaken as her guardian.

'Perhaps once Lady Francesca has returned we might all be better informed as to how we might proceed,' Bea spoke again softly.

Griffin clenched his jaw at the mere mention of the other woman. 'It is to be hoped so.' He really did not think that he could leave Bea behind when he departed Latham Manor. Just the thought of it was enough to make him clench his fists in frustration.

And he knew that feeling no longer had anything to do with thoughts of Bea remaining here in the company of Christian, and everything to do with—

'My dears, what a lovely surprise it is to see you all gathered together in my drawing room!' Francesca Latham swept into the room, blond head tilted at a haughty angle, blue eyes aglow with that mocking humour she so often favoured. 'I could barely credit it when Shaw informed me of our exulted company, Latham.' She moved to her husband's side. 'And I see dear Beatrix has also returned to us, in the company of the Duke of Sutherland.' That hard blue gaze now settled on Bea.

Griffin had stood up upon that lady's entrance. 'I am sure that must be as much of a pleasant surprise to you as it was to Sir Walter?'

'But of course.' That hard blue gaze now met his challengingly.

Griffin placed his clenched fists behind his back as he resisted the urge he felt to reach out and shake the truth from this woman.

Now that he was here he knew he could not leave here today until he knew whether this woman was Bea's friend or foe. And to hell with the politeness of manners! He was tired of this tedious social dance. He wished now only for the truth. 'You had perhaps not expected her to be here at all?'

Lady Francesca shrugged her elegant shoulders. 'I am sure Latham is not so strict as to begrudge Beatrix time spent with her new friends.'

Griffin's nostrils flared. 'But you, of all people, must know she was not staying with friends.' No matter what the situation, whether Francesca Latham believed Bea to have eloped or been kidnapped, she almost certainly knew that Bea had not been visiting friends these past weeks.

'Griffin—'

'Rotherham—'

'Is that not so, madam?' Griffin ignored both Christian and Aubrey as they rose to their feet in protest at his blunt methods, his gaze now locked in a silent battle with Francesca Latham.

'I am not sure I care for the way in which you are addressing my wife, Rotherham,' Sir Walter blustered uncomfortably.

Still Griffin's gaze remained locked with that hard and mocking one of Francesca Latham's. 'Your wife, sir, is either a liar or a traitor—and I for one wish to know which it is!'

'Griffin?' Bea looked up at him anxiously as he appeared to have forgotten everything the four of them had spoken of this morning, before she had departed for Latham Manor with Christian Seaton. Indeed, Griffin now appeared so coldly angry, as he and her aunt locked gazes, that it seemed the two of them had forgotten they were even in the company of others.

Implying a past rift much deeper than merely that he did not care for his neighbour's wife.

It appeared so to Bea. And she could think of only one reason why such tension might have arisen between two such handsome people. A past love affair that had not ended well.

The idea of Griffin having been intimately involved with Lady Francesca so sickened Bea that she could raise no further protest regarding the bluntness of his conversation.

'What on earth are you on about, Rotherham?' Sir Walter was red-faced with anger. 'You are either foxed or mad. Either way, you will apologise to my wife forthwith.'

'I will neither apologise nor retract my statement,' Griffin bit out harshly. 'You will answer the accusation, Lady Francesca. And you will do so now.'

'Remember my grandson, Griffin,' Lord Maystone cautioned softly.

'I have not forgotten,' Griffin assured him gruffly. 'As I have not forgotten the manner in which I found Bea, following her abduction and days of being held prisoner.' His voice hardened as he continued to look coldly at Lady Latham.

'Abducted? Held prisoner?' Sir Walter looked totally bewildered. 'But Beatrix has been staying with friends—is that not so, Francesca?'

Throughout the whole of this exchange Francesca Latham had remained strangely silent, a contemptuous smile curving her lips as she continued to meet Griffin's gaze unflinchingly.

'Is that so, Lady Francesca?' Griffin now snapped scathingly.

She remained silent for several more long seconds before she gave a weary sigh as she stepped away from her husband and into the centre of the room. 'Is there any point in my continuing with the farce?' she finally taunted in a bored voice.

Griffin's jaw tightened. 'None whatsoever.'

'Very well.' She gave a disgusted shake of her head as she turned to look at Bea. 'So you have been warming Rotherham's bed for this past week.'

'Do not make this situation any more difficult for yourself than it already is,' Griffin warned through clenched teeth.

Hard blue eyes swept over him mockingly. 'I do not in the least begrudge you the warmth, Rotherham,' she drawled. 'Why should I, when I had your wife warming my own bed for so many months before she died?'

Bea felt the colour leave her cheeks even as she saw Griffin stumble back a step.

His own face became deathly pale as he now stared at Francesca Latham in horror. '*You* are "darling Frank"?'

She bared her teeth in a humourless smile. 'So Felicity liked to refer to me as, yes.'

'The two of you were lovers?'

'For many months.' Francesca Latham nodded with satisfaction.

'Francesca!'

'Oh, do be quiet, Walter,' his wife snapped dismissively as she gave him a contemptuous glance. 'We have not shared a bed for years, and now you know the reason why. I have always preferred my own sex,' she continued conversationally. 'Of course, Felicity did become a tad over-possessive and demanding, forcing me to end our association, but whoever would have thought the little ninny would have drowned herself for love of me? Quite tedious, I do assure you.' She gave an irritated shake of her head.

Bea had not been able to take her eyes off Griffin since her aunt had announced her past intimate relationship with his late wife.

Or to wonder if, as Seaton had implied yesterday, she had been mistaken in believing that the happiness Griffin had known in his marriage was the reason he had never remarried. He might have loved his wife, certainly, but he also seemed to have known that his wife's love had not belonged to him.

'But we digress,' Lady Francesca continued pleasantly. 'I take it the two other gentlemen here also wish to see justice done? As I thought.' She nodded at the silence that greeted her question. 'What happens next? Am I to be dragged away in shackles and tortured until I tell you everything I know?'

Griffin roused himself from the shock of hearing the truth of Felicity's betrayal, of their marriage bed and of him. Of learning that his wife's lover, Frank, had not been a man at all, but a woman. Francesca Latham, in truth.

At the same time as he could not help but feel a certain lightening of his heart at learning it had not been *him* in particular whom Felicity had found so physically repellent. That her sexual preference would have made her feel disgust at the idea of a physical relationship with any man.

That her suicide, by drowning herself in the lake at Stonehurst Park, had not been as a way of escaping him and their marriage, but because the woman she loved had rejected her.

Strange to experience such a sense of euphoria in the midst of such chaos. And yet that was exactly how Griffin now felt. As if a heavy weight of guilt and self-loathing had been lifted from his shoulders.

As if that truth had now freed him to try to win Bea's heart for himself.

Were it not for the existence of Michael, of course.

'Was that not what you did to Bea?' Griffin now accused hardly. 'Are you not the one responsible for beating Bea, with the help of your associate Jacob Harker?'

'What is he talking about, Francesca?' Sir Walter

seemed to have deflated into being a shell of himself in the past few minutes, his rosy cheeks now a sickly shade of grey.

'Do not tax your brain about it, Latham,' his wife dismissed mockingly. 'You would be far better to attend to your horses and your hounds.'

Latham attempted to rouse himself. 'You will answer me, madam. Who is this man Harker? What have you done that Rotherham now accuses you of being a traitor? It is something to do with that worthless half brother of yours, is it not?' He puffed angrily. 'I always knew he would be nothing but trouble.'

'Be silent, Latham!' His wife turned on him angrily, cheeks flushed. 'You are not fit to so much as speak my brother's name.'

'Half brother,' Sir Walter rallied defiantly. 'Sir Rupert Colville is only your half brother. A weak, lily-livered anarchist bent on bringing down the Crown.'

'I said be quiet!' Lady Francesca flew at him, hands raised, fingers bent into talons, her face an ugly mask.

Christian was closest to the couple, managing to grasp Francesca Latham about her waist and pull her back before she could reach her husband with those talons. Once she was in his grasp, he secured her more tightly by pulling her arms down and also holding them captive within his grasp as he stood behind her.

Bea had found herself unable to move or speak as the horror of this scene was played out before her.

The revelations about Griffin's wife and Francesca Latham.

The knowledge that it had in all possibility been Francesca Latham herself who had administered Bea's beatings during her week of captivity. Hence the reason she had never spoken in Bea's presence?

As the events of that weekend she had spent with her aunt at the home of Sir Rupert Colville now came back to her. 'You were completely mistaken in your suspicions towards me at your half brother's home, madam.' She got up to stand in front of Francesca Latham. 'At the time I did not understand any of the conversation I overheard between you and Sir Rupert. How could I, when I did not know then that an eight-year-old boy had been cruelly taken from his parents and was being used as blackmail against his influential grandfather?' She gave a shake of her head before turning to Aubrey Maystone. 'My Lord, I think you will find your grandson is being held prisoner at Sir Rupert Colville's home in Worcestershire.'

'Why, you little—'

'Have a care, madam!' Christian warned through gritted teeth as his prisoner would have made a lunge for Bea. 'You have seriously wronged two gentlemen who are close friends of mine, and you have caused great distress and pain to a lady wholly undeserving of such treatment. As such I will have no compunction in taking steps to silence you if you should give me reason to do so.'

'Do as you wish with me.' Francesca tossed her head unconcernedly. 'You may cut off the head of the snake but two more will grow in my place!'

'I do not believe for one moment that you are the head of this particular snake,' Griffin scorned. 'Nor your milksop brother, either. Neither of you is intelligent enough,' he added with hard derision. 'And I believe we will leave it to the Crown to decide whether or not to cut off both your heads.'

All the colour now drained from Francesca's cheeks. 'How can you remain loyal to such a man as the Prince Regent? A man who overindulges himself in every way possible, spending money he does not have on things he does not need, and to the detriment of his own people.'

'Oh, please, spare us your warped idea of patriotism!' Maystone dismissed. 'Also be assured, madam, that if my grandson is not returned to me unharmed, then I shall personally recommend the hardest sentence imaginable to the Prince Regent, for your crimes against both him personally and to England,' he added grimly.

Hatred now gleamed in those cold blue eyes. 'My brother should have disposed of the boy when I advised him to.'

'You will be quiet, madam!' Bea was shaking

with anger at this woman's added cruelty, when Lord Maystone had already suffered so much during these past weeks of uncertainty as to whether his grandson still lived. 'Your grandson is unharmed, Lord Maystone,' she reassured him gently.

He blinked his uncertainty. 'You are sure?'

She nodded. 'I realise now that I was abducted and beaten because it was he that Lady Francesca and her brother spoke of that day I overheard the two of them talking together. Sir Rupert Colville was adamant that he would care for the boy as if he were his own. At the time I thought he spoke of an orphaned ward or nephew. Having recently been orphaned myself, my heart ached for the little boy. For the loneliness he must feel. I had no idea of the truth of the conversation I had overheard.' She gave a bewildered shake of her head.

'Michael truly is unharmed?' There was such hope in Lord Maystone's voice.

Bea gave a puzzled frown as she heard Griffin draw his breath in sharply before she answered the older man gently. 'I truly believe that Sir Rupert Colville will have ensured Michael has remained unharmed, yes. Sir Rupert is not a man who enjoys physical violence.'

'Unlike you, madam, who enjoys nothing more than beating those who are more helpless than yourself.' Griffin's eyes glittered with anger as he looked contemptuously down his nose at Francesca. 'Where is Harker now?'

Francesca now seemed less defiant than she had a few moments ago. 'I presume he is in his hovel of a cottage, where I was forced to stay hidden during the week of Beatrix's imprisonment.'

Griffin's eyes widened. 'Harker lives in a cottage on my own estate?'

'His name is not Harker but Harcourt, and he is nephew to your own housekeeper,' Lady Francesca taunted.

Which explained, Griffin realised, why none in the area had reported seeing anyone suspicious or unknown to them. But did that also mean that Mrs Harcourt—?

'The old dragon has no idea of Jacob's political views, if that is what you are now thinking,' the blonde-haired traitor dismissed mockingly. 'Not that any of this matters now.' She took in everyone present in the room with one sweeping glance. 'You may rescue Maystone's grandson, arrest Jacob, Rupert and myself, do with us what you will. But, as I have stated, there are plenty of others who will happily take our place in securing Napoleon's freedom.'

'There are even more of us who will ensure they do not succeed,' Christian assured her grimly.

And no doubt Griffin would have to be one of them, he accepted heavily.

But once Maystone's grandson, Michael, was

freed and returned to his family, once the Corsican was safely away from England and secured in exile, *then* he might discharge his duties to the Crown once and for all, and return to his estate in Lancashire.

Return to Bea.

Chapter Fifteen

Ten days later

'His Grace, the Duke of Rotherham, is here to see you, My Lady,' Shaw announced from the doorway of the drawing room in Latham Manor.

Bea's heart leapt in her chest at the news that Griffin was back in Lancashire, and she tensed as she looked up from the book she had been reading, as she sat in the window seat enjoying the last of the day's sunlight. 'You are sure the Duke is here to see me and not Sir Walter?'

Bea had not seen Griffin since Lady Francesca and her associate, Jacob Harcourt, had been placed in custody, and he had set off immediately for Worcestershire with Christian Seaton and Lord Maystone, their intention to liberate the latter's grandson from the home of Lady Francesca's half brother.

But not before it had been discussed and decided

that Bea should remain here with her real guardian, Sir Walter, while the other gentlemen were gone. She would far rather have accompanied them on their rescue mission, but had accepted that she would only have slowed them down, and no doubt have been in the way too.

Plus someone had to remain and offer some comfort to Sir Walter. The poor man was devastated, both by the revelations of his wife's affair with Griffin's wife, and by Lady Francesca's treasonous actions, and her subsequent arrest. Bea felt that she might at least be of some help to him by remaining here.

That had indeed proved to be the case, the two of them spending much time together as Sir Walter adjusted and accepted that his wife now faced many charges, including kidnapping and treason.

But he was a pragmatic man, and, having also learnt of his wife's sexual relations with another woman, seemed to have hardened his heart to her fate. Indeed, he was currently out riding his new hunter, having resumed his normal activities several days ago.

They had received word from Griffin after the rescue of Michael, Lord Maystone's grandson, had been as successful as they had hoped. Sir Rupert Colville was also now in custody, and the other three gentlemen had been on their way to London to reunite the little boy with his parents.

Bea had resigned herself to not seeing Griffin again now that he was returned to London.

'His Grace asked for you specifically, My Lady,' the butler now assured her.

'Then you may show him in, Shaw.' Bea nodded.

She turned to quickly check her appearance in the mirror, her mouth having gone dry at thoughts of seeing Griffin again.

At thoughts of the heartache of the two of them meeting and greeting each other as if they were polite strangers.

When that was the last thing they were.

Or ever could be, as far as Bea was concerned.

Her heart almost jumped completely out of her chest as Griffin strode purposefully into the room, not pausing at the doorway but heading straight over to where Bea still stood near the window.

He looked so dark and handsome in his perfectly tailored black superfine, worn with a grey waistcoat and grey pantaloons, his black Hessians gleaming.

So dearly beloved.

'Your Grace.' Bea affected a curtsy, head bent so that Griffin should not see the tears of happiness glistening in her eyes just at the sight of him.

'Bea?' Griffin gave a dark frown as he reached out to place a hand beneath the softness of her chin and raise her face so that he might better see her expression.

These past ten days had been both very successful and equally frustrating.

Maystone's grandson was reunited with his ecstatic family.

Several more of the conspirators to liberate Bonaparte were also now in custody.

The Corsican was well on his way to his remote place of exile.

The English Crown and its people could breathe easily again, for a time at least.

Griffin had also informed Maystone that he had carried out his last mission for the Crown, and intended to retire to his estate in Lancashire.

All of those things had been positive.

The negative had been Griffin's own enforced separation from Bea. Days and days when he had not so much as been able to set sight on her.

Days when she would no doubt have been left to her own thoughts for hours at a time, and have decided that Griffin Stone, the gruff Duke of Rotherham, had no place in the life she now led in quiet solitude with her guardian.

Griffin's own newfound freedom, from believing that the unhappiness of his marriage had been his fault, and that he was also responsible for Felicity's suicide, now sat light as a bird upon his shoulders. Most of all, he now accepted that he could never have made someone like Felicity happy.

The knowledge that Michael had not been the love

of Bea's life after all, but Maystone's grandson, had come as even more welcome news. Michael had become a spectre in Bea's dreams only because of the warmth of her heart, her concern for a little boy she had believed to be orphaned, like herself.

That knowledge was the only thing that had kept Griffin sane as he'd dealt with all the other matters in need of his attention before he was free to return to Lancashire.

To return to Bea.

She looked so very beautiful. She was wearing a gown he had never seen before. No doubt one of her own, which had now been delivered from the house in Worcestershire. A gown of the palest blue silk that made her skin appear both pale and luminescent.

Her face appeared a little thinner than Griffin remembered, but that was surely to be expected after the upset of the previous weeks. And the added knowledge that it was her own aunt who was responsible for her abduction and the beatings she had received while held prisoner in the filthy woodcutters' shed.

One of Griffin's last instructions, before he'd departed Stonehurst Park in the company of Christian and Maystone ten long days ago, had been for that shed to be burnt to the ground. That not a single sliver of wood was to remain.

And now here was Bea, looking more beautiful to him than ever.

But with a new wariness in those deep blue eyes as she looked up at him questioningly.

Griffin did his best to gentle his own expression, when what he really wanted to do was take Bea in his arms and kiss her until they were both senseless. A move guaranteed, he suspected, to increase rather than lessen that look of apprehension!

'Are you well, Bea?' he enquired guardedly.

Bea had managed to blink away her tears, and she now offered Griffin a reassuring smile. 'I am perfectly well, thank you. Sir Walter has proved to be an amiable companion these past ten days.'

Griffin removed his fingers from beneath her chin but still studied her intently. 'You are comfortable here, then?'

She moistened her lips before speaking. 'Sir Walter is my guardian. Where else should I go?'

'You seemed to enjoy living at Stonehurst Park.'

Bea gave him a quick glance before turning away to look out of the window facing out towards the gardens at the side of the house. 'I take it you will not be remaining there for long yourself, now that your other business is resolved?' Indeed, she had no idea why Griffin had come back to Stonehurst at all, when there must be so much to do in London now.

Although she was not disappointed that he had; just to see him again, to be with him, to *smell* that unique smell that was Griffin—a combination of lemon, sandalwood and a healthy man in his prime—

was enough to make her pulse beat faster. In fact, she would be surprised if Griffin could not hear the loud beating of her heart caused just by being near him again.

But it would be foolish of her to read any more into his visit to Latham Manor this morning than a courtesy call. To ensure that Bea was happy with her new guardian.

'I have stepped down from my work for the Crown, Bea.'

She was frowning slightly as she turned her head to look over her shoulder at him. 'You are perhaps tired of the intrigue and danger?'

Griffin gave a smile. 'I believe I would describe it more that I have found a reason to live.'

Bea's expression softened. 'I am so sorry for the things you have learnt about your late wife. It must have been such a shock to you.' She gave a shake of her head. 'I cannot imagine—'

'It was a relief, Bea,' he cut in firmly. 'Such a blessed relief,' he breathed thankfully. 'For years now I have blamed myself for the failure of my marriage, for not loving Felicity, or she me, so much so that she had preferred to take her own life rather than suffer to live with me another day. To finally know, even in such a way as I learnt the truth, that I was not responsible has caused me to hope—to dare to hope…'

Bea turned fully to face him, her gaze searching on his face as it now seemed to her that Griffin looked at her with hope in his expressive grey eyes. 'What is it you hope for, Griffin?' she prompted huskily.

His smile became rueful. 'What every man hopes for, I suspect. To be happy with the woman he loves.'

Bea's heart leapt once again in her chest. 'And do you already have such a woman in your life?'

Griffin drew in a sharp breath, knowing he still had much he needed to say before he went any further with this conversation. 'There are things I should tell you about myself, Bea. Things I have not shared, until very recently, with anyone beyond my closest friends. My father's indifference to me during my childhood being one of them.'

'You must try not to blame your father too much for that, Griffin,' she put in quickly. 'Christian told me a little of that situation,' she explained guiltily as Griffin raised questioning brows. 'He did not mean to break any confidences, he was merely trying to explain—to explain—'

'The reason for some of my gruffness of nature, no doubt,' Griffin guessed dryly.

'I do not find you in the least taciturn, Griffin,' she reproved primly.

'No?'

'You are everything that is amiable as far as I am concerned,' she insisted.

'Thank you,' Griffin murmured huskily. 'But we

digress.' He straightened. 'Something else I never talked of was the utter failure of my marriage.' He sighed. 'I realise the reason for that now. I accept it. But for those two reasons I have for years believed myself to be unlovable rather than just unloved.'

'Your friends all love you dearly,' she told him.

'Yes, I believe they do,' he acknowledged softly. 'But I had believed myself too dour, too austere, too physically overbearing, to deserve the love of any decent woman. I have lived my life accordingly, never wanting, never expecting, never *asking* for more than I had.'

The slenderness of Bea's throat moved as she swallowed. 'And that has now changed?'

'Completely,' Griffin stated without hesitation. 'Now I want it all. The wife. The children. The happy home. The love of the woman whom I love in return. My homes filled with vases of flowers,' he added ruefully.

Bea could barely breathe, so great was her own hope now that Griffin was talking to her of these things for a reason. 'And have you come here so that I might wish you well on this venture?'

'I want so much more from you than that, Bea,' he assured her firmly. 'I want, one day, for you to be my wife, the mother of my children, the mistress of my happy home, the woman who might love me as I have loved and continue to love you, and who will fill our homes with vases of flowers. I am more than happy to be patient, of course, to woo you, to court you, as you deserve to be—'

'But—I overheard you tell Seaton that our love-making was a mistake.'

'Because I believed you to be in love with the man you called out for in your sleep. A man called Michael.'

'Lord Maystone's grandson?'

'I did not know that at the time, Bea. I believed that by loving you, by making love with you, I was encouraging you to be unfaithful to the man you loved. It was only when Maystone finally referred to his grandson as Michael that I realised the truth.' Griffin was prevented from saying more as Bea launched herself into his arms. 'Bea?' he groaned even as his arms closed tightly about her and he crushed her against his much harder body.

Bea beamed up at him, eyes glowing. 'I find I am not patient at all, Griffin. I want all of those things you described *now.* I want *you* now,' she added shyly.

'Bea?' Griffin still looked down at her uncertainly.

She reached up to curve her hands about the hardness of his cheeks as she smiled up at him. 'I already love you, Griffin,' she told him firmly. 'I believe I have loved you almost since the moment I first opened my eyes and saw you seated beside my bed acting as my protector. And that love has only continued to grow every moment of every day since. I *love* you, Griffin,' she repeated emotionally.

He looked uncertain, confused, two emotions Bea had never associated with this strong and decisive man. 'Are you sure you are not confusing gratitude with love?'

'Of course, I am grateful for your having rescued me, and caring for me even though you had no idea who I was or where I came from; what sort of woman would I be if I were not?' she dismissed indulgently. 'I am grateful for all that, but it is you that I love, Griffin. The man, the lover, not the rescuer. These last few days, of not knowing if I would ever see you again, have passed in a haze of agony for me,' she acknowledged huskily. 'I love you so much, Griffin, I cannot bear to be apart from you, even for a moment.'

It was so much how Griffin felt in regard to Bea. 'Will you marry me, Bea, and be my duchess?'

'I will marry you, and gladly, but so that we need never be separated again, not to become your duchess,' she answered him without hesitation.

Griffin grinned and gave a heartfelt whoop of gladness before he claimed her lips with his own.

'If you do not mind, I believe the wedding must be soon, my love,' he murmured indulgently some time later, as the two of them sat together upon the sofa, Bea's head resting comfortably on his shoulder, his arms about her as he continued to hold her close. 'I find I want to make love to you again so very much, and I should not like our heir to make his appearance eight, or even seven, months after the wedding.'

Bea chuckled softly, so happy to be with Griffin again, to know that he loved her as much as she loved him, that they would never be parted ever again. 'I believe it should be possible for a Special Licence to be arranged for a man who has been so loyal to the Crown for so many years?'

Griffin chuckled softly. 'I believe you might be right, my love.'

'Sir Walter will give me away and Christian can stand up with you.'

'Christian is not in England at the moment,' he confided.

Bea looked up at him searchingly. 'Is he in danger?' she finally asked with concern.

Griffin felt a momentary twinge of that past jealousy before just as quickly dismissing it; Bea loved him. He had no doubt of it and he never would. 'Not that I am aware, no,' he answered dismissively. 'I am no longer privy to such knowledge, Bea, for Christian's sake, more than my own.'

'Of course you are not.' Bea once again settled herself on his shoulder. 'Then one of your other friends will have to stand up with you, for I find I do not wish to wait either.'

Which was reason enough for Griffin to begin kissing her all over again…

* * * * *

Don't miss the next book in Carole Mortimer's dazzling DANGEROUS DUKES *duet:*
CHRISTIAN SEATON: DUKE OF DANGER

CHRISTIAN
SEATON: DUKE
OF DANGER

To Peter, as always.

Chapter One

August 1815, Paris, France

'Touch one hair upon her head, *monsieur*, and you are destined to meet your maker sooner than you might wish!'

It took every ounce of his indomitable will for Christian Seaton, Fifteenth Duke of Sutherland, not to react or turn to face the person who had just spoken softly behind him.

Not because he was disturbed by the threat itself; his reputation as one of the finest shots in England was not exaggerated, and few gentlemen could best him with the sword either.

Nor was he concerned by the barrel of the small pistol he currently felt pressed against the top of his spine through his clothing.

Or that the person making the threat was a woman who, judging by her voice, was a woman of mature years.

It was the fact that the threat had been spoken in accented English which caused him such inner unease…

As an agent for the English Crown, Christian had arrived secretly in Paris from England by boat just two nights ago and, as had been planned, he had immediately taken up residence as the Comte de Saint-Cloud—an old and extinct title of his mother's French family—in one of the grander houses situated alongside the Seine.

Since his arrival Christian had been careful not to speak any other language but French, which he could claim to speak like a native, once again courtesy of his maternal *grandmère*.

He had been especially careful to maintain that facade in the Fleur de Lis, a noisy and crowded tavern situated in one of the less salubrious areas of Paris.

That he was now being addressed in English brought into question whether this pretence in his identity had somehow been compromised.

He continued to maintain his comfortable slouch at a corner table of the noisy tavern as he answered the woman in French. 'Would you care to repeat your comment, *madame*?' he replied fluently in that language. 'I understand English a little, but I am afraid I do not speak it at all.'

'No?'

'Non.' Christian calmly answered the scornful taunt, although that feeling of unease continued to prickle inside him. 'I am the Comte de Saint-Cloud—at your service, *madame*.'

There was the briefest of pauses, as if the woman were considering challenging him on that claim. 'My mistake, Comte,' she finally murmured, before repeating her earlier warning in French.

'Ah.' He nodded. 'In that case, I confess I have no idea which "she" you are referring to.'

A loud *hmph* sounded behind him. 'Do not play games with me, Comte,' the woman growled. 'You have had eyes for no one but Lisette since the moment you arrived.'

Lisette...

So that was the name of the beautiful young woman serving the tables situated on the other side of this crowded and noisy room.

Oh, yes, Christian knew exactly which 'she' this woman was referring to. Which of the serving wenches he had been unable to take his eyes off of for more than a minute or two since he had entered the tavern an hour ago.

And he was not alone in that interest, having noticed that several other well-dressed gentlemen in the room were also watching the young woman, if less openly than he.

The reason for those gentlemen's slyness now become apparent to Christian—obviously they knew better than to openly show their admiration for the red-haired beauty, for fear of having a pistol pressed against their own spine.

He gave another glance across the tavern to where the young woman had been kept busy all evening serving drinks to the raucous patrons. She was unlike any other tavern wench Christian had ever seen—tiny and slender, with pretty red curls, hidden for the main part beneath a black lace cap, she was also dressed more conservatively than the other serving wenches, in a long-sleeved and high-necked black gown.

A mourning gown…?

Whatever her reason for wearing black, it did not detract in the slightest from the girl's ethereal beauty. Rather it seemed to emphasise it; her hands and neck were slender, her heart-shaped face as pale and smooth as alabaster and dominated by huge long-lashed blue eyes.

She had also, Christian had observed with satisfaction, managed to neatly and cheerfully avoid any of the slyly groping male hands that had tried to take advantage of her as she placed jugs of ale down on the tables.

Unfortunately, Christian had not seen her until after he was already seated, his own table being served by a buxom and flirtatious brunette, and so preventing him from as yet finding opportunity to speak to the lovely Lisette.

A situation which Christian had intended changing before the night was over; a dalliance with one of the Fleur de Lis' serving wenches would be the perfect means by which he might visit this tavern often, without the regularity of those visits being remarked upon.

He gave a lazy shrug now, again without turning to look at the woman behind him. 'All of the ladies working here are very pretty, *madame*.' Once again he continued the conversation in French.

'But you have eyes for only one,' the woman rasped in the same language.

'Surely a gentleman is allowed to look, *madame*?'

'One such as you does not just look for long,' she said scornfully.

Christian was every inch the gentleman, known amongst English society for his charm and evenness of temper; indeed, he had long and deliberately nurtured that belief. But that was not to say that he did not have a temper, because he most certainly did; he simply chose to reveal it only to those who were deserving of it and on the occasions when it was most warranted.

But whether the French Comte de Saint-Cloud or the English Duke of Sutherland, he was obviously a gentleman, and this woman's insults and over-familiarity were deserving of such a set-down. 'I take exception to your remark, *madame*.' Christian's tone was icy-cold, something that those who knew him well would have known to beware of.

Whatever the woman standing behind him knew of him, she obviously did not know the nature of him at all.

At least it was to be hoped that she did not...

'One has only to look at the way you are dressed, at *you*, to know you are nothing but a rake and a libertine. *Coureur!*' she added disgustedly.

While it might be safer for this woman to believe Christian was a rake, and the 'womaniser' she had just spat at him, than for her to have any doubts as to his identity as the Comte de Saint-Cloud, he still took exception to the insult. 'On what grounds do you base such an accusation, *madame*?' His tone had grown even chillier.

'On the grounds that you have been undressing my...niece with your eyes for this past hour, *monsieur*!' she came back disgustedly.

Her *niece*?

The beautiful girl, Lisette, was the *niece* of the woman standing behind him with a pistol pressed against his spine? Surely that claim did not make sense unless—

Unless...?

Very aware of that pistol at his back, Christian carefully sat forward, his movements measured as he turned just as slowly to face his accuser. His brows rose slightly as he instantly recognised her as being none other than Helene Rousseau, the owner of this Parisian tavern.

The very same woman who was both the reason for his clandestine visit to Paris and for his presence in the Fleur de Lis tavern this evening.

Helene Rousseau was the older sister of André Rousseau, the man known to have been a French spy during the year he had spent in England as tutor to a young English gentleman.

A year during which André Rousseau had also gathered together a ring of treasonous co-conspirators amongst the servants of the English aristocracy, as well as some high-ranking members of that society itself. Their aim had been to assassinate England's Prince Regent, as well as the other heads of the Alliance, and so throw those countries into a state of chaos and confusion, allowing Napoleon, newly escaped from his incarceration on Elba, to march triumphantly back into Paris unopposed.

Christian had been one of the agents for the Crown who had managed to foil that assassination plot on Prinny. But not before André Rousseau lay dead in the street outside this very tavern, killed by the hand of one of Christian's closest friends.

Christian was in Paris now because it was suspected that Rousseau's sister had taken over as head of that resistance movement following the death of her brother. That she and her cohorts were still determined to undermine the English government, whilst working with those co-conspirators in England, by fair means or foul—and their methods had been very foul indeed—to find a way of releasing the Corsican upstart for a second time.

Indeed Christian, and several of his friends, had only days ago prevented news of the date and destination of Napoleon's second incarceration from being revealed, when it was believed that a second attempt would have been made to effect the Corsican's escape.

Nowhere in Christian's information on Helene Rousseau had there ever been mention of her having a niece.

The same young and beautiful woman whom Christian had been admiring for this past hour or more...

A young and beautiful woman who wore black because she was in mourning for her dead father, the French spy André Rousseau? As far as Christian was aware, Helene Rousseau had no other siblings.

His eyes narrowed on the Frenchwoman. Also dressed in black out of respect for her dead brother? 'I apologise if I have caused you any offence, *madame*.' He gave a courtly bow as he stood up. 'I assure you I meant none.'

Helene Rousseau was a woman of about forty, tall and voluptuous where her niece was tiny and slender, and the older woman had only a touch of red in her blonde hair; surely Christian could be forgiven for not having previously made the connection between an aunt and niece who were so different in appearance?

Especially as there had never been any information of André Rousseau having a daughter.

Hard blue eyes looked up at him scornfully as the female owner of the tavern continued to hold the small pistol at a level with his broad chest. 'A man such as you would not be in such a lowly tavern as this one, *monsieur*, if you were not looking to corrupt one of my girls.'

Christian raised a blond brow. 'Surely it is for those "girls" to decide for themselves as to whether or not they would see my attentions as corruption… or pleasure?'

'Not if your choice is to be Lisette.' Helene Rousseau looked at him with all the challenging hauteur of a duchess.

Christian bit back his impatience with this woman's temerity, knowing it would not serve his purpose to antagonise her further; his intention this evening, to be taken for just another gentleman bent on pleasure, had instead incurred this woman's notice as well as her wrath. Both of them he would rather have avoided at this stage of his mission. 'I have given my apology if I have caused you any offence—'

'I believe Claude wishes your presence in the kitchen, Helene,' a huskily soft voice interrupted them.

A huskily soft voice that, Christian discovered when his gaze moved to Helene Rousseau's side, belonged to none other than the beautiful Lisette herself...

Lisette had noticed the handsome gentleman with the lavender-coloured eyes the moment he entered the tavern earlier this evening; indeed, he was the sort of gentleman of whom any woman would take note.

He was exceedingly tall, with tousled overlong blond hair. The perfect fit of his black superfine coat over broad and muscled shoulders must surely be the work of the best tailors in Paris. As were the pantaloons tailored to his long and muscled legs. His black Hessians were so highly polished Lisette was sure she would be able to see her face in them if she cared to look.

But it was the hard masculine beauty of the man's face which drew the eye; a smooth, high brow, sharply etched cheekbones, his nose long and aristocratic, and a sensual and decadent mouth that was not too thin and yet not too full either, above a surprisingly hard and uncompromising jaw.

The man's most arresting feature by far was his eyes—Lisette did not believe she had ever seen eyes of such an unusual shade of lavender before—fringed by thick and curling lashes.

Eyes which she had sensed watching her this past hour, even as she went about the business of serving the many and increasingly inebriated customers...

The tavern was unusually crowded this evening, which was the only reason Helene had asked for Lisette's help; usually the older woman did not allow her anywhere near the men who patronised this bawdy tavern.

Lisette had not initially noticed Helene approaching or speaking with the lavender-eyed gentleman; it was only when she could no longer feel the intensity of his gaze upon her that she had glanced across the room and seen the two in conversation. Even across the width of the tavern Lisette had been able to sense the tension of that conversation, her eyes widening in alarm as the gentleman moved and she saw that Helene held a pistol in her hand, and that pistol was pointed at the gentleman's chest.

Quite what that gentleman had done to warrant such attention Lisette had no idea. As far as she was aware, he had not behaved in a rowdy or licentious manner, but remained quietly seated at his table without engaging with any of the tavern's other customers. Nor had he been overfamiliar with Brigitte on the occasions she had served him with one of the tavern's better wines.

'I am Christian Beaumont, the Comte de Saint-Cloud, at your service, *mademoiselle*.' That gentleman now gave her a polite bow.

Just as if Helene were not still pointing a gun at the broad elegance of his chest!

'Lisette Duprée.' She gave an abrupt curtsy, unable, now that she was standing so close to the gentleman, to look away from the intensity of that beautiful lavender gaze.

Christian repressed his smile of satisfaction at Helene Rousseau herself having effectively made the formal introductions possible. A formality that would allow him to more easily approach and speak to the lovely Lisette in future.

His gaze narrowed as he turned to look at the older woman. 'Please do not let us delay you any further when you are so obviously needed in the kitchen, *madame*.'

Helene Rousseau's mouth tightened even as she deftly stowed the pistol away in the folds of her gown. 'You will remember all that I have said to you tonight, my lord.' It was a warning, not a question.

Christian had every intention of remembering each and every word this woman spoke to him. Of dissecting it. Analysing it. In readiness for the report he would eventually take back with him to England.

And if it should transpire that Helene Rousseau was indeed behind the recent kidnapping of an innocent child, and the abduction and ill treatment of an equally innocent young lady, in order to try to blackmail information from the English government in the former, and repress information in the latter, then he feared there could be only one outcome to Helene Rousseau's future.

An outcome that would result in the lovely Lisette being in mourning for both her aunt and her father.

'I assure you, *madame*, my memory is impeccable,' Christian answered Helene Rousseau softly.

The older woman gave him a long and warning stare before turning to Lisette, the hardness of her features softening slightly as she looked at the younger woman. 'You must not linger here, Lisette, when there are customers needing to be served.'

'As you say, Helene.' Lisette's dark auburn lashes were lowered demurely as her aunt gave Christian one last warning glance before departing with a swish of her skirts. In the direction of the kitchen, it was to be hoped.

Christian found it curious that the younger woman addressed the older one by her first name rather than as her *tante*. Adding to the mystery of this relationship, that no amount of watching and spying on both André Rousseau before the man's death, and Helene Rousseau in the months since, had managed to discover, let alone explain.

'Would you care to sit down and join me, *made-*

moiselle?' Christian held back one of the chairs at his table.

Lisette eyed him curiously. 'I am at work, Comte, not leisure.' And she would not have frequented a tavern such as this one even if she were.

Until just a few months ago, Lisette had lived all of her nineteen years in the French countryside, far away from any city, let alone Paris. It had been a shock for her to suddenly find herself living in such a place as this tavern, after the death of the couple she had believed to be her parents.

Believed to be her parents…

The truth of the matter had only emerged on the day of their funeral, when a carriage had arrived at their farm late that afternoon and a tall and haughty blonde woman had stepped down, a look of complete disdain on her face as she stepped carefully across the farmyard to the house.

Learning that this woman was actually her mother had been even more of a shock to Lisette than losing the couple she had believed to be her parents.

Helene Rousseau claimed Lisette had been fostered with the Duprées since she was a very young baby, and that they had been sent money every month for her upkeep.

Having never so much as set eyes on this woman before that day, Lisette had been disinclined to believe her at first. Although she could think of no reason why anyone would want to make such a false claim; Lisette was not rich, and even the Duprées' farm had been left to their nephew rather than Lisette.

The reason for which had become obvious with the arrival of Helene Rousseau.

The older woman had clearly been prepared for Lisette's disbelief and had brought letters with her that she had received every month from the Duprées, in relation to Lisette's health and well-being.

It was the non-appearance of this month's letter that had alerted Helene Rousseau to the fact that something was amiss on the Duprée farm; enquiries had informed her that both of the Duprées had died when a tree had fallen during a storm and landed on that part of the farmhouse where the Duprées' bed-chamber was situated.

Lisette had only needed to read three of those letters sent by the Duprées to Helene Rousseau to know that the older woman was telling the truth; Lisette was indeed the other woman's illegitimate daughter.

What had followed still seemed like something of a dream to Lisette—or perhaps it might better be described as a nightmare?

Her belongings had all been quickly packed into a trunk—Helene Rousseau had disdained the idea of spending so much as a single night at the farm—after which Lisette had been bundled into the coach with the other woman before then travelling through the night to Paris.

If Helene Rousseau had found the sight and sounds of the farmyard unacceptable, then Lisette had been rendered numb by the noise and dirt of Paris as the carriage drove through the early morning streets.

Tradesmen were already about, hawking their wares amongst the people lying drunk in shop doors and alleyways, several overpainted and scantily dressed ladies slinking off into those same alleyways as the carriage passed by them.

The tavern Helene Rousseau owned and ran had been even more of a shock, situated as it was in one of the poorer areas of the city, with patrons to match.

It had been no hardship at all for Lisette to remain apart from such surroundings. To keep mainly in the bedchamber assigned to her by Helene—even all these weeks later Lisette could not think of the older woman as anything more than the woman who had given birth to her before then abandoning her for the next nineteen years. As far as Lisette was concerned, sending money for her daughter's upkeep did not equate to love on Helene Rousseau's part, only a sense of responsibility; the other woman had made no attempt in all of those years to actually see or speak with her daughter.

Given a choice, Lisette would not have travelled to Paris with Helene Rousseau at all. But she did not have a choice. How could she, when she had no money of her own, her foster parents were both dead and their nephew had made it clear that she could not continue to live on the farm once he had moved there with his wife and large family?

But within days of arriving in Paris, Lisette had come to hate it with a vengeance. It was smelly and dirty, and the people she occasionally met out in the streets or the tavern were not much better. And Helene Rousseau proved to be a cold and distant woman with whom Lisette had nothing in common but her birth.

There was also deep unrest still amongst the Parisian people, who had first had a king, then an emperor, then a king again, and then again an emperor, only for that emperor to then once again be deposed and their king returned to them.

Such things had not affected Lisette when she'd lived on the farm with the Duprées. There they had only been concerned with caring for the animals, and the setting of and then bringing in of the harvest each year.

But political intrigues seemed to abound in Paris, with neighbour speaking out against neighbour, often with dire consequences.

Lisette also strongly suspected there were meetings held in one of the private rooms above the tavern, in which that political unrest was avidly and passionately discussed. Meetings over which Helene Rousseau presided…

'Then perhaps you might meet with me outside and join me for a late supper at my home when you have finished your work for the night…?'

Lisette's eyes widened in shock as she looked up at the handsome gentleman who did not seem as if he should be in such a place as this lowly tavern at all, let alone asking one of the serving women if she would meet him for supper.

No doubt he was one of those gentlemen the Duprées had warned her of when she'd reached her sixteenth birthday and had shown signs of developing a womanly figure. Gentlemen who gave not a care if they disgraced an innocent, before continuing merrily on their way.

'I am afraid that will not be possible, Monsieur la Comte—' She broke off as the lavender-eyed Comte stepped forward to prevent her from leaving. 'I must return to my work, *monsieur*,' she insisted firmly.

Christian found that he had no wish for Lisette to return to her work. Indeed, he discovered he was not favourably inclined to this young and beautiful woman working in this tavern at all.

It was a lowly, bawdy place, where he had just observed a man thrusting his hand down the low-cut bodice of a barmaid's gown, before popping that breast out completely so that he might fondle and suckle a rosy nipple. Where in another shadowy corner of the tavern he could see another couple, the woman's skirts pushed up to her waist, the man's breeches unfastened, as the two of them actually fornicated in front of all who cared to watch.

Christian, for all his previous sins, most certainly did not care to view so unpleasant a sight.

Indeed, he had begun to find the whole atmosphere of this tavern to be overly lewd and oppressive.

And this delicate woman certainly did not belong

in such a place, no matter what her biological connection to the patroness might be.

He curled his fingers lightly about the slenderness of Lisette's arm. 'I will be waiting outside in my carriage for you to join me from midnight onwards—'

'I cannot, *monsieur.*' Her eyes had filled with alarm. 'Tonight or any other night.'

'I mean you no harm, Lisette.' Christian sighed his frustration with her obvious distrust. 'You must know that you do not belong here?'

Tears now swam in those exquisite blue eyes. 'I have nowhere else to go, *monsieur.*'

Rescuing an obvious damsel in distress was not part of Christian's mission. Indeed, his superiors in government would say it was the opposite of his purpose here. Most especially when that damsel was the niece of the woman—and quite possibly the daughter of the rabble-rouser André Rousseau?—he had come here to observe.

He released her arm reluctantly. 'I will be waiting outside for you in my carriage from midnight anyway, just in case you should change your mind...'

'I cannot, *monsieur.*' She cast a furtive glance towards the kitchen as the door swung open and Helene Rousseau strode back into the noisy tavern, her shrewd eyes narrowing as she saw Christian and Lisette were still standing together in conversation. 'I must go.' Lisette stepped hastily away from him. 'For your own sake, *monsieur,* I advise you do not come here again,' she added in a whisper.

Christian considered that warning some minutes

later as he sat in his carriage on the way back to his house beside the Seine, and he could come to only one conclusion.

That the lovely Lisette was frightened of her aunt...

Chapter Two

Lisette went about the rest of her work in a daze following the Comte's departure just minutes after their conversation came to an abrupt end.

In response to her warning, she hoped.

Although he had not appeared to be the sort of gentleman who would frighten easily.

As she was frightened.

The Comte de Saint-Cloud was perfectly correct in his concern for her well-being here, with the drunkards and bawds. Much as Helene might try to protect her.

But what else did the Comte have to offer her, besides supper and no doubt a seduction within his home; he might be wealthier and more highly born than the usual patrons of the Fleur de Lis, but he was no more to be trusted than the other men who came here, who would all willingly throw up her skirts and take her innocence, given the opportunity and the chance to escape from Helene's sharp-eyed gaze.

The Comte might do it more gracefully, and no doubt in pleasanter surroundings, but he would still take what Lisette did not wish to give. Before walking away unconcernedly to rejoin others of his class and forgetting completely the young woman whom he had seduced. And ruined.

The fact that he had frequented such a tavern as this at all was suspect. And surely indication of his intention to find a woman he might take to bed for the night, before having one of his servants show her the door in the morning, when he had no further use for her?

Lisette knew that could be the only possible reason for such a fine and titled gentleman to so much as enter a lowly tavern such as this one.

And yet for just a few moments, a minute perhaps, something had burgeoned inside her chest—a temptation to accept his offer of joining him for a late supper—in the hope that he might offer to take her away from this lowly place, which she hated to her very soul.

'You might as well stop mooning over the Comte,' Helene sneered several hours later, after having thrown out the last of her drunken customers into the alleyway at the back of the tavern, before locking the door behind her. 'He will not be returning here.'

Lisette looked at the older woman searchingly, easily noting the satisfaction in Helene's expression. 'How can you be so sure...?'

Hard blue eyes flashed a warning. 'You will not question me as to my…methods, Lisette.'

Her alarm deepened. 'I am sure Monsieur le Comte meant no harm when he spoke to me earlier.'

'I believe it is past time you retired to your bed-chamber, Lisette,' Helene dismissed. 'You have been most helpful this evening, but I do not think we will repeat the experience.'

'But—'

'Go to bed now, Lisette.' The older woman snapped her impatience as a knock now sounded softly on the closed back door of the tavern.

Lisette bit back her next comment, that discreet knock on the door warning her that this was one of those nights when Helene was to have another of her meetings.

Clandestine meetings, with men—and women?— who either did not want to be seen frequenting the tavern or openly associating with Helene Rousseau. Or perhaps both? The Fleur de Lis and its custom-ers were certainly not for the faint-hearted, or those members of society who should not even know such a woman as Helene Rousseau existed, let alone be calling upon her in the dark of night.

None of which helped to dispel Lisette's concerns for the welfare of the Comte de Saint-Cloud.

She had learned these past weeks that Helene was a powerful woman in these shadowed alleyways of Paris, with a knowledge of most, if not all, of the thieves and murderers that frequented them. It would be the simplest thing in the world for the older woman to request the assistance—after silver had exchanged hands, of course—of any one of those cut-throats in her desire to ensure the Comte de Saint-Cloud did not return.

Could not return.

'Certainly, Helene.' She made a curtsy before taking a lit candle and hurrying up the stairs to her bedchamber, only to then pace the small room restlessly as she tried to decide what she should do next.

She really could not allow the Comte de Saint-Cloud to come to harm just because he had dared to speak with her.

She had heard the murmur of voices in the hallway outside some minutes ago, followed by a door closing, which meant that Helene would now be kept occupied with her late night callers. If Lisette was very quiet, she could move softly along the hallway and down the stairs, leave a window open downstairs at the back of the tavern ready for her to climb into upon her return, and then—

And then what?

The Comte had said his house was situated by the river, but just the thought of being out alone at night in Paris was enough to cause a quiver of fear to run the length of Lisette's spine. These streets were unsafe for a lone woman in the daytime; at night she would be an easy target for much more than the thieves and bawds.

And the Comte de Saint-Cloud?

Her thoughts always came back to him, and the look of determination on Helene's face when she had said he would not be returning to the tavern. Such certainty of purpose could surely mean only one thing? Nor did Lisette make the mistake of underestimating Helene's ability to carry through with that purpose; many of the men who frequented the tavern, hard and callous men, were obviously in awe of the Fleur de Lis' patroness.

Lisette could not bear to think of the handsome Comte's lavender-coloured eyes closing forever.

Just as she could not continue to stay here in her bedchamber, acting the coward, when even now Helene's cut-throats might be closing in for the kill.

Lisette's spine straightened with a resolve she could not allow to waver as she pulled on her black bonnet and gathered up her black cloak—mourning clothes for the uncle she had never met—before quietly opening the door to her bedchamber and peering out to ensure that the hallway was empty. Assured it was so, she quietly slipped from the room and down the stairs. With any luck she would be able to find and visit the Comte's home, issue a warning and return to the tavern before Helene was any the wiser.

If not…

Lisette did not care to think of what might happen if she was too late to warn Monsieur le Comte.

Or of Helene's fury if Lisette did not return to the tavern before her absence was discovered.

Christian stood in the shadows of a doorway, a safe enough distance from the Fleur de Lis, but close enough that he was able to see the dozen or so gentlemen and two ladies, who had entered through the back door of that establishment during the past half an hour.

He was under no illusions as to the reason for their clandestine visit, knew that he must have stumbled upon one of the secret meetings of Helene Rousseau and her co-conspirators.

Stumbled, because Helene Rousseau was not the reason Christian had come back to the tavern tonight.

He had returned briefly to his house by the Seine after leaving the tavern earlier, going inside to his bedchamber so that he might change into dark clothing, before going out again. He had ordered his groom to wait with the carriage several streets away from the Fleur de Lis, before wrapping his dark cloak about him to move stealthily through the pungent and filthy alleyways to the doorway across and down the street from the tavern.

The tavern was in darkness apart from a single candle burning in one of the bedchambers above, which, from the slightness of the silhouette of a person he could see pacing back and forth past the curtained window, might possibly be the bedchamber of the lovely Lisette.

When even that candle was extinguished just minutes later, the tavern was left in complete darkness.

And Christian with a feeling of disappointment.

It had been too much to hope for, of course, that Lisette would change her mind and join him for a late supper. She did not know him, nor did she seem the type of young lady who would sneak out of her aunt's home in the middle of the night with the intention of dining alone with a gentleman. Even without her eagle-eyed aunt acting as her protector.

That look of innocence, and the tears that had shone in those huge blue eyes earlier when Lisette had told him she had 'nowhere else to go', could all be an act, of course. Nothing more than the clever machinations of an innocent-looking whore in search of a rich protector. Christian was sure he would not be the first gentleman to fall for such an act.

Yet there had been a sincerity to Lisette Duprée. An indication, perhaps, that her innocence might be genuine.

And Christian could just be the biggest fool in Paris for giving that young woman so much as a second thought. Indeed, Helene Rousseau's warning earlier, in regard to his staying away from her niece, might all be part of the ruse to pique and hold his interest, rather than the opposite.

There was also that disturbing moment to consider when Helene Rousseau had initially spoken to him in English. A test, perhaps, to see if he would respond in kind? Or possibly because she already knew he was not the Comte de Saint-Cloud?

If that was the case, then Christian's presence in Paris was a complete waste of time, and he would learn nothing. Except perhaps to feel the sharp end of a blade piercing his back when he least expected it.

Even more reason for Christian to concentrate on the meeting now taking place within the tavern, and the identity of the people present.

Rather than, as he had been doing, imagining how Lisette would look as she lay in her bed...

Would she be dressed demurely in a night-rail, or did she sleep naked?

Would her breasts be tipped by rosy nipples or darker plum-coloured ones?

And would the silky thatch between her thighs be as vibrant a red as the curls—?

'Monsieur le Comte...?'

It would be an understatement, considering the direction of his thoughts, to say that Christian was startled to hear the sound of Lisette's soft and huskily enquiring voice beside him.

Startled and not a little annoyed with himself for being so distracted by thoughts of this beautiful young woman that he had not even noticed her leaving the tavern, let alone approaching him. Such inattentiveness could easily get a man killed.

Christian gathered his thoughts as he turned to face her, approving of the fact that she at least wore dark clothing, as he did, the hood of her cloak pulled up over her bonnet, hiding the brightness of her hair. 'I am gratified to see you have changed your mind about joining me for supper, *mademoiselle*,' he answered her flirtatiously.

'We cannot stay here, where we might be seen at any moment, *monsieur*,' she came back urgently.

'No, of course not,' Christian readily accepted as he took a firm hold of her arm. He might now have to abandon his interest in the identity of the people who had so recently entered the tavern so surreptitiously but he had the next best thing: Helene Rousseau's niece. 'My carriage is waiting for us—'

'Oh, no, *monsieur*, I cannot come with you. I wished only to—'

'Hush!' Christian warned sharply as he pulled her into his arms and pressed her back into the shadows of the doorway, having noticed that several cloaked figures were now leaving the tavern.

'Monsieur!' Lisette protested indignantly.

'Hush—'

'Monsieur, I must protest—'

Christian could think of only one way he might prevent Lisette from alerting others to their presence here with her verbal indignation at his manhandling of her.

He took it.

Lisette's protests died in her throat, to be replaced by surprise and then pleasure, as the Comte took masterful possession of her lips with his own.

She had never been kissed before, nor had she ever dreamed that her first kiss would be with such a man as the handsome Comte de Saint-Cloud.

That he was an expert in such things came as no surprise to her; he was at least a dozen years her senior, and there was about him an air of ease and sophistication that spoke of his knowledge of women.

Even knowing that, Lisette was immediately lost to everything but the wonder of Christian Beaumont's mouth on hers. His arms were firm about her as he held her against the hardness of his body, and the warmth of his tongue dared a caress across her lips to part them and deepen the kiss.

Heart pounding, Lisette's hands moved to cling to the folds of his evening cloak, as she felt herself completely overwhelmed by the emotions coursing through her body: excitement and pleasure. The latter manifested itself in the tightening of the bodice of her gown, as if her breasts were swelling, the rosy tips tingling, and there was an unfamiliar but not unpleasant warmth blossoming between her thighs.

It was singularly the most wonderful experience of her short lifetime, beyond any imagining, beyond—

The Comte brought the kiss to an abrupt end as he lifted his mouth from hers. 'Do not speak, Lisette,' he warned softly against her ear. 'Whatever happens, do not speak.'

Whatever happens...?

Lisette felt too dazed still to understand what he meant by that. What did he imagine was going to happen? A kiss was a kiss, but anything more than that was unthinkable. And if the Comte thought— If he imagined for one moment—

'Feel like sharing, *mon ami*?'

'For the price I paid for her? *Non*.' The Comte turned his head to answer the intruder with a dismissive laugh, at the same time as the bulk of his body managed to keep Lisette shielded from any gaze that might try to pry any further into the doorway. 'I intend to take my money's worth and more!'

'Bon chance!' another man called out laughingly as the two continued on their way.

Lisette's face paled as she listened to the exchange between the three men, shocked by the earthiness of the conversation but also realising the Comte must have been protecting her from the attentions of the other men when he pushed her into the doorway.

At the same time she felt disappointed to realise that the Comte had kissed her for the same reason. It was a little humiliating to realise how much she had enjoyed the kiss when, to the Comte, it had only been a means of silencing her.

She pushed determinedly against the muscled chest pinning her in the doorway. 'I believe we are alone again now, *monsieur*. You may release me,' she instructed sharply as she failed to shift him by so much as an inch.

Christian had no desire to 'release' Lisette. Indeed, the opposite. He wanted to kiss her again, this time without the distraction of the approach of the two gentlemen he had noted leaving the tavern; Helene Rousseau's meeting was obviously over for tonight. Which meant that more of the co-conspirators would shortly be leaving the tavern too.

'We need to leave here, Lisette.'

'I came only to warn you—'

'Warn me?' Christian questioned sharply as he stepped back slightly to look down at her. Not that he could see very much; the streets were dark, and the doorway even darker.

'My—Helene did not take kindly to your attentions to me earlier this evening, *monsieur*—'

'Christian. Call me Christian,' he instructed shortly, having duly noted Lisette's slight hesitation after 'my'.

'It is not permissible—'

'I just kissed you, Lisette,' he drawled. 'I believe that now makes many things between the two of us "permissible".'

She drew in a soft gasp. 'It is ungentlemanly of you to talk of such things.'

Christian wanted to do more than talk about them; the throb of his arousal told him he wanted to kiss Lisette again, and keep on kissing every inch of her as he made full and pleasurable love to her. Which, given their circumstances, was beyond reckless of him.

Not only were they in a precarious position out here where they might be seen together, but also he still did not know whether Lisette was all that she appeared to be, or if she was working in cahoots with her aunt. Until he did know he would be wise to treat her, and anything she said to him, with suspicion.

Which would be easier for him to do if only she did not have those deep blue eyes he wanted to drown in, and those soft and delectable lips he wished to kiss and keep on kissing…

'We cannot stay here, Lisette.' Christian took a firm hold of her arm to pull her along at his side as he stepped out of the doorway and began to walk quickly away from the tavern. 'My carriage is but a short distance away. We will talk again once we are inside and well away from prying eyes and ears.'

'Please—I must return to the tavern before I am missed,' Lisette protested as she almost had to run to keep up with the Comte's much longer strides or risk falling over onto the dirty cobbles beneath her feet.

The Comte either did not hear her or chose to ignore her as he continued to stride purposefully, and knowledgeably, down several alleyways Lisette had not even known were there, despite having lived in Paris for some weeks now.

A carriage waited in the shadows of one of the streets, and it was towards this vehicle that the Comte now guided her as a groom jumped quickly down to hold the door open for them both to get inside.

Lisette held back from entering the carriage. 'It is impossible for me to go with you, *monsieur—Umph!*' The rest of Lisette's protest was cut off as the Comte de Saint-Cloud unceremoniously picked her up in his arms and deposited her inside the carriage before tersely instructing the groom to move on as he joined her and the door was firmly closed behind him.

A lantern lit the inside of the heavily curtained carriage—which was perhaps the reason Lisette had not been able to see the light before now?—allowing her to appreciate the plushness of the interior.

And the man now seated opposite her...

His hair shone like burnished gold in the lamplight, those lavender eyes narrowed in a face that was far too handsome for any woman's comfort. Especially so, when he had kissed that woman a short time ago and she was now alone with him in his carriage.

'You take liberties, *monsieur*.' Lisette glared across at the Comte as she now straightened her bonnet from where it had been knocked askew when he had picked her up and thrust her inside the carriage.

Some of the Comte's tension seemed to ease and he relaxed back against the upholstery as the carriage began to move forward. 'You are the one who came looking for me, Lisette, remember.'

She did remember. And she now regretted it. For surely this man had demonstrated in the past few minutes that he was perfectly capable of taking care of himself. Even against such men as Helene might send to accost him? Yes, Lisette believed that might be the case.

That air of easy charm he had affected in the tavern earlier this evening had now been replaced by a narrow-eyed watchfulness. Which Lisette sensed could be as dangerous as Helene's implied threats against him had been such a short time ago. Leading Lisette to believe she had wasted her time, and put herself in danger of incurring Helene's wrath, by leaving the tavern to seek out and warn such a self-assured gentleman.

Her chin rose. 'You were the one waiting outside the tavern in the hope I might join you.'

Christian could hardly argue with the logic of that comment. Unless he also wished to confess to Lisette that she had not been his only reason for skulking about in that doorway tonight.

As he still had no idea yet whether she was the innocent she seemed or an accomplished actress, he would be wiser to allow her to continue with her assumption that his intentions were dishonourable.

Especially as he was unsure if that might not be the case…

Her kiss had seemed to lack experience, but that could have been part of an act. Innocence was not a trait that usually appealed to him in a woman, but it had succeeded in arousing him in Lisette's case.

He was still aroused.

He shifted slightly forward on his seat so that his arousal was not noticeable. 'Are you sorry that I did?' he prompted softly as he took both her gloved hands in his much larger ones and continued to act the *roué* Comte de Saint-Cloud.

She blinked long lashes over those huge blue eyes. 'I—' she moistened plump lips '—I came only to warn you, *mon*—Christian,' she corrected huskily as he gave her a reproving smile.

Christian forced himself not to tense at her comment. 'To warn me of what, *mon ange*?'

It had been so long since anyone had spoken to Lisette with such gentleness, such kindness, that she felt the sting of tears in her eyes.

Helene had provided her with all the necessary comforts—a home, a bed, clothes to wear—but there was no softness in the woman who claimed to have given birth to her. Helene possessed none of the

Duprée warmth and easy affection. Indeed, Lisette found it difficult to believe that the older woman could ever have felt passionately enough about a man to have made a child with him.

Until this moment, when the Comte spoke to her so gently, she had been battling so valiantly to adapt to her new life that she had not realised how much she had missed the warmth of another human being.

Even one as dangerously attractive as the Comte de Saint-Cloud.

And he was dangerous. He had flirted with her earlier. Invited her to supper at his home—and goodness knew what else he intended. And he had kissed her a short time ago. A kiss such as Lisette had never imagined receiving from any man. A kiss that had warmed her from her head to her toes, and caused sensations within her body she had never felt before, nor could explain.

She straightened determinedly. 'I came to warn you that Helene is most displeased by the attentions you showed me tonight. So displeased that I believe she might mean to ask some of her…friends to cause you actual physical harm.'

There, she had now done what she intended to do, and given this man fair warning. It was now up to the Comte whether or not he acted upon that warning.

'If you would stop the carriage now?' Lisette requested. 'I believe I might be able to walk back to the tavern from here.' Although she could not say she relished the idea; Helene had warned her that pickpockets—and worse—lurked upon these streets after dark, in search of the unwary and the drink-sodden, and they did not return to their lairs until daybreak. The thought of being accosted by such people as she walked back to the tavern was enough to cause her to tremble.

Christian suspected that there was more about him that 'displeased' Helene Rousseau than his overt flirtation with her young niece.

As for his allowing Lisette to depart his carriage now… 'We will return to my home first, where we can sit and talk in warmth and comfort—'

'Oh, but—'

'If you still wish to return home afterwards—' he talked over what he knew was going to be Lisette's protest '—I will bring you back in my carriage.'

'There is no "if" about it, *monsieur*,' she assured him firmly. 'Nor do I wish to go to your home; an unmarried lady does not enter the house of an unmarried gentleman without causing severe damage to her reputation.'

The fact that Lisette currently lived in a lowly tavern with a woman such as Helene Rousseau was surely already damage enough to her reputation?

As if aware of his thoughts, a blush now appeared in Lisette's cheeks. 'I did not always live in a tavern, *monsieur*,' she informed him stiffly. 'Until just two months ago I lived on a farm in the country with my…with relatives.'

Very curious…

Although it would explain why there had never been any mention of Lisette in the reports made by other agents for the Crown, in connection to Helene or André Rousseau.

'I, for one, am grateful that your aunt brought you to live with her in Paris,' he drawled.

'My aunt?' Lisette repeated sharply.

'Mademoiselle Rousseau,' Christian supplied slowly even as he looked at Lisette searchingly; she seemed surprised—shocked?—by his knowledge of her relationship to the older woman. 'She explained your connection to me earlier this evening,' he added gently.

Lisette moistened her lips with the tip of her tongue. 'Yes, of course...my aunt,' she rallied slightly, even tried to smile a little.

Christian was not fooled for a moment by Lisette's attempt to cover her confusion.

He just had no idea as to the reason for that confusion...

Chapter Three

Lisette was so taken aback by the Comte de Saint-Cloud's comment regarding her relationship to Helene that she could think of nothing more to add to the conversation.

Of course she accepted that it would have been awkward for Helene to suddenly produce a fully grown daughter.

But surely no more awkward than it was for that fully grown daughter to suddenly discover that the couple she had thought were her parents were not even related to her, and that instead the cold and haughty Helene Rousseau was actually her mother?

Even so, Lisette had not realised until now that Helene had not publicly claimed her as her daughter at all, but instead only as her niece.

She was not sure how she felt about that.

'Lisette…?'

She had been so deeply in thought that she had not realised the carriage had come to a halt, and that a groom now stood beside the open door waiting for her and the Comte to alight.

Which must mean, whilst she had been lost in thought, they had arrived at the Comte de Saint-Cloud's home.

She gave a firm shake of her head. 'I wish to return to the tavern now, *monsieur.*'

'Why?'

'Why? Because…well, because—'

'What so urgently awaits you there, Lisette, that you cannot spare a few minutes to sit and share a glass of wine with me?' the Comte teased softly.

It was not her time that concerned Lisette, but her reputation.

At the same time she felt slightly rebellious after learning that Helene chose to claim her only as her niece—that relationship implying she was the daughter of a man, Helene's brother André, who was now dead.

Also, Lisette did not think that the Comte had taken her at all seriously when she had tried to warn him of the possible danger he was in from Helene Rousseau.

'Very well, *monsieur*, but a few minutes only.' She nodded as she moved forward to step down from the carriage onto the cobbled street, her eyes widening as she looked up at the huge and imposing four-storey house before her. The Comte de Saint-Cloud's Paris home?

Lisette had never seen such a grand house as this, let alone been inside one. She only did so now because the Comte, having ordered the coachman to wait, now took a firm hold of her arm to walk up the steps to the huge front door now being held open by a man dressed in full livery.

The candlelit and cavernous entrance hall took her breath away, with its pale blue walls with gold-inlaid panels, ornate statues and the wide and sweeping staircase to the gallery, a huge crystal chandelier suspended from the high ceiling above.

Lisette felt small, and totally insignificant, amongst such grandeur.

'Brandy and wine in the library, François,' Christian instructed as he handed his coat and cloak to the other man before picking up a candelabrum to light their way through the entrance hall, on his way to the only room in the house he could tolerate for any length of time. The previous owner had possessed an air for the dramatic and ornate in regard to decor, one that did not suit Christian's more elegantly subdued tastes at all.

He could see at a glance that their surroundings had made Lisette shrink back into herself, her face appearing very pale beneath the rim of her black bonnet. Or perhaps that was through nerves at her own temerity in entering the home of a single gentleman? Whichever of those things it was, Christian did not enjoy seeing her so discomfited.

'Sit down in a chair by the fire,' he bade lightly once they had entered the book-lined library, the warmth of a fire crackling in the grate. Hopefully, the heat would bring some colour back into Lisette's cheeks.

'Just for a moment.' Lisette looked so tiny, defenceless, as she sat in the huge wingback armchair, her feet barely touching the ground as she held her gloved hands out towards the flames.

'*Merci*, François, that will be all for tonight.' Christian continued to watch Lisette as he spoke to the other man distractedly, the butler placing the silver tray with the drinks on down onto a side table before departing.

Christian still wondered if Lisette's air of innocence, her reluctance to enter the house with him, could all be an act for his benefit, as he turned his attention to pouring the brandy and wine into two glasses. There was only one way to find out.

But first…

'Your wine, Lisette.' He held the crystal glass out to her.

'*Merci*.'

Christian gave a rueful smile as she took care for her gloved fingers not to come into contact with his own as she took the glass from him. 'What shall we drink to?' he mused. 'Our continued…friendship, perhaps?'

Lisette felt slightly disconcerted by the Comte's close proximity as he made no effort to step away from where she sat after handing her the glass of wine.

He was just so—overpoweringly immediate in these more intimate surroundings. Seemed so much bigger, more imposing even than he had been in the tavern earlier or in his carriage on the journey here.

His shoulders were so wide—and dependable?— his chest and arms muscled beneath the fine cut of his coat, as if he spent much of his time pursuing the gentlemanly sports, such as fencing and swordplay, rather than in the drinking salons, and taverns such as the Fleur de Lis.

His fashionably overlong hair shone a pure gold in the candlelight and was rakishly tousled. As for the effect of those long-lashed lavender-coloured eyes in that harshly handsome and lightly tanned face; Lisette truly had never seen such beautiful eyes before, on a man or a woman.

She was very aware that the two of them were very much alone here now that he had dismissed his manservant for the night.

Her gaze dropped from meeting that mesmerising lavender one. 'We can drink only to the present, Comte.'

'The present,' he echoed as he gave a mocking inclination of his head before taking a sip of his brandy, 'is very much to my liking,' he added gruffly.

A blush warmed Lisette's cheeks even as she took a sip of her red wine. It was a very good red wine, not at all like the rough vintage Helene served at the tavern. And further emphasising the fact that the Comte de Saint-Cloud inhabited a very different world from the one in which Lisette currently found herself. Even as the daughter of the Duprées she would have been completely out of her element with a man such as this one.

She carefully placed her glass down on the small table beside the chair. 'I do not believe you took my warning seriously earlier, Comte.' She looked up at him earnestly. 'My…my aunt has many associates who are not particularly pleasant, and who I believe would slit your throat for the price of a few pennies if asked to do so.'

'And has your aunt asked them to do so?' Christian arched mocking brows, again noting Lisette's slight hesitation when stating that Helene Rousseau was her aunt. But if not the girl's aunt, then who or what was she to Lisette?

Her madam, perhaps, with Lisette as the innocent prize to be won?

That explanation would certainly be in accordance with Lisette's behaviour tonight. The 'helpless innocent' come to warn him of danger was the sort of behaviour designed to tighten the net about an infatuated victim.

Or Lisette could simply have been sent here to him this evening in order to confirm or deny, by whatever means necessary, Helene Rousseau's suspicions regarding him.

'I believe she has, yes,' Lisette answered him worriedly.

'And why do you think that?' Christian moved to sit in the chair opposite her, his posture one of outward relaxation and unconcern; inwardly it was a different matter.

The title of Comte de Saint-Cloud might be his own to use if he so wished, but nevertheless he was alone in a country that was not his own and amongst people he could not trust.

Not even the lovely Lisette.

Perhaps especially the lovely Lisette.

'She assured me earlier that I would not be seeing you at the tavern again after this evening.' Lisette frowned.

Christian raised his brows. 'That was very... precipitate of her.'

'I believe it was because she already has plans afoot to ensure you are unable to return, *monsieur*,' Lisette pressed urgently.

'Christian.'

She gave him an impatient glance. 'What does it matter in what manner I address you, if you are not alive to hear it?'

Christian gave a lazy smile. 'I am not that easy to kill, lovely Lisette. Besides,' he continued lightly as she would have protested, 'I am alive here and now, and we are together, which is all that is important, is it not?'

'No, it most certainly is not all that is important!' She eyed him exasperatedly.

'I find your concern for me most charming, Lisette,' he drawled flirtatiously. 'But you really need not concern yourself on my account—'

'How can I not concern myself?' She rose agitatedly to her feet. 'When I am the reason you are in danger?'

Christian sincerely doubted that; he was becoming more and more convinced by the moment that Helene Rousseau did suspect him and his reason for being in Paris. To a degree where it was no longer safe for him to continue to remain here posing as the Comte de Saint-Cloud?

That would be a pity, considering all the work and planning that had gone into establishing that identity before his arrival in France.

It also meant that tonight might be the only time he had left in Paris.

A night he might spend with Lisette?

He placed his brandy glass down on the side table before rising lazily to his feet. 'I am sure you would feel more comfortable if you were to remove your bonnet and cloak.'

'I do not wish to feel more comfortable—'

'Of course you do.' Christian crossed the distance that separated them before unfastening her bonnet himself and removing it, ignoring her efforts to stop him as he then untied the cloak at her throat before placing them both down on the armchair and turning back to her. 'Much better,' he noted with satisfaction as he took both of her gloved hands in one of his.

He did not particularly care for the plain black gown Lisette was wearing, would much rather see her in bright colours that would flatter rather than detract from her delicate complexion. But her hair gleamed like copper in the firelight, and the warmth of the fire had indeed brought back a little of the colour to her cheeks.

She looked slightly bewildered at his deft removal of her bonnet and cloak. 'I told you I cannot stay above a minute or two—'

'You really must not distress yourself, my dear Lisette,' Christian soothed softly. 'As I have said, we have tonight together...' He held her now startled gaze as he slowly lowered his head towards her.

Lisette's head began to spin as she knew this completely compelling man, Christian Beaumont, Comte de Saint-Cloud, was about to kiss her again.

She couldn't move, was held completely mesmerised by those lavender eyes gazing down into her own as the Comte's lips brushed gently against hers.

Her hands were still held captive in his much larger one as his other arm moved about her waist and pulled her in tightly against him. Instantly making Lisette aware of his strength and the hardness of his muscled chest.

Until tonight she had never been kissed before, but she was sure that if she had it would not have made her feel the way that Christian's kisses did: as if she were floating on air and Christian's arm about her waist was the only thing keeping her feet on the ground.

Her life had been so miserable since coming to Paris, everything strange and uncomfortable to her, and this—being held by Christian, being kissed by him—was so overwhelmingly *pleasurable* after so many weeks of unhappiness and uncertainty and feeling that she no longer belonged anywhere.

For this moment, for here and for now, surely she

could just forget all of that and enjoy being in this man's arms.

Lisette pulled her hands free of his to glide them up the length of his muscled chest before resting them on his shoulders, as she stood on tiptoe and returned the kiss. Not expertly, she was sure, but she hoped that what she lacked in experience she more than made up for in her obvious enjoyment and enthusiasm.

Better—much, much better, Christian acknowledged with inner satisfaction as he deepened the kiss by running his tongue lightly, questioningly, along the line of Lisette's closed lips. He felt her brief hesitation before those softly pouting lips parted, allowing him access as his tongue now glided inside the moist and welcoming heat of her mouth.

He groaned softly as he felt the stroke of her tongue along his, hesitant at first and then more assuredly. His body instantly responded to the intimacy, engorging, and lengthening impatiently inside his pantaloons.

Christian pressed his body intimately into Lisette's as he kissed her harder, deeper. Hearing her responding groan as his tongue now explored the sweetness of her mouth, at the same time as his hands moved restlessly up and down the length of her spine.

His fingers brushed against the tiny buttons fastening the back of her gown, and he continued to kiss her as he unfastened enough of those buttons to slip one of his hands inside and touch the softness of her bare skin.

She felt like silk beneath his fingertips. Warm, soft silk that seemed to heat to the touch of his caressing hands.

It was not enough. Christian needed to see all of her. To touch her. To caress and pleasure her—

'No!' Lisette had wrenched her mouth away from Christian's to protest, eyes wide as she stared up at him in what looked like a mixture of fascination and shock.

The first emotion Christian could understand; he was experienced enough to know when a woman found pleasure in his kisses. And he had no doubt Lisette had enjoyed their kisses as much as he had.

The shock appeared to have occurred because he had unfastened her gown and touched her bared skin...

Her dilated pupils, and the quick rise and fall of her breasts as she breathed deeply, told him that Lisette's shock was completely genuine.

Not a whore, then.

The mystery that surrounded this young woman deepened every second they were together.

She pushed determinedly against his chest now in an effort to escape his imprisoning arms. 'You must release me, Christian. Please!' Her eyes met his in appeal when her efforts to free herself proved unsuccessful.

He looked down at her searchingly. 'You did not enjoy being kissed?'

'No! Well. Yes.' A blush heated her cheeks. 'Of course I enjoyed being kissed—'

'Then why have you stopped me?'

Why had she stopped him?

For the same reason she knew that she could not remain here alone in this room with this man a moment longer.

Because she had enjoyed his kisses too much. Had wanted his hands upon her bared flesh too much.

Because she had wanted so much more than just his kisses.

For just a brief time, a few moments, Lisette had wanted to lose herself in Christian's kisses and caresses, to forget the unhappiness of these past months, along with the uncertainty of no longer knowing who or what she was.

For this time, here with Christian, she had wanted to just be herself. The Lisette Duprée who had been loved and cherished by the couple she had believed were her parents, and not the illegitimate daughter of a woman who seemed to care nothing for her, who owned and ran a lowly Parisian tavern frequented by criminals and whores.

That same woman who Lisette now knew had not even claimed her as being her daughter.

Except it really would not do.

The brief pleasure Lisette might know in Christian Beaumont's arms would not, could not, drive away the otherwise unhappiness of her life for more than a few minutes, at the most hours.

Whereas the reality of the life she now led would last for her lifetime.

'I have to go.' She avoided meeting Christian's

gaze as she stepped away from him. 'I must return to the tavern before I am missed—'

'Perhaps you have already been missed...?'

Her heart leaped apprehensively in her chest. 'Do not say that, Christian, even in jest.'

Christian frowned. He saw how pale her face was in the firelight. 'Do you fear retribution from your aunt?'

'No.' Her gaze avoided meeting his. 'No, of course I do not.'

Her denial came too quickly for Christian's liking. 'Come away with me, Lisette.' The offer was completely spontaneous and as much of a surprise to Christian as it appeared to be to Lisette. 'We could go to my country estate—' the Saint-Cloud family still had one somewhere in Brittany '—or...the war is over now and I have relatives in England. I could take you there if you would rather leave France altogether?'

'Leave France?' she echoed faintly, as if the idea both thrilled and terrified her.

Christian regretted his offer as soon as the words left his mouth. The idea of taking Lisette back to England with him was ridiculous; what would he possibly do with the niece of Helene Rousseau once they were back in England?

For one thing, once in England, Lisette would quickly realise that he was not Christian Beaumont, the Comte de Saint-Cloud, at all, but in actual fact Christian Seaton, the Duke of Sutherland.

But perhaps, as he suspected in regard to her aunt,

Lisette already knew that, and returning to England with him had been her plan all along?

Admittedly, she had looked shocked at the idea, but Christian still had no proof, either way, whether Lisette was all that she seemed to be.

Indeed, he was more unsure than ever as to what she *seemed*.

The niece Helene Rousseau claimed her to be? A description which had seemed to startle Lisette when he'd called her such earlier.

Or something else completely?

No doubt Lord Aubrey Maystone, his immediate superior in his work for the Crown, would be more than happy to have the niece of Helene Rousseau in his clutches, after the kidnapping of his young grandson.

What might happen to Lisette once Christian had delivered her into the older man's hands did not bear thinking about; Christian's first loyalty might be to the Crown, but he had no evidence that Lisette was guilty of anything, other than the misfortune of being related to Helene Rousseau. Which would make her an innocent pawn, as Aubrey Maystone's grandson had been.

It was not a risk Christian was willing to take.

'A ridiculous idea, is it not, when I have only just arrived in Paris and there is still so much for me to enjoy?' he dismissed lightly.

Lisette blinked at the Comte's about-turn when, just for a moment, a brief euphoric moment, she had dreamed of escaping Paris, the tavern and her association with Helene Rousseau. To leave France completely and begin again somewhere new, where no one knew her or the shameful secret of her birth she carried with her every moment of every day.

But the Comte was perfectly correct; it would not do, and it was ridiculous of her to have even contemplated the possibility.

She frowned up at him. 'It is your intention to remain in Paris, even after the things I have told you?'

The Comte gave an indifferent shrug. 'I thank you for your concern, of course. But I am sure your worries are unfounded and Madame Rousseau will have forgotten all about my flirtation with you by tomorrow.'

Lisette wished she could feel as confident of that. Unfortunately, she could not.

But she had done what she intended tonight, and if the Comte would not take her warning seriously, then there was nothing more she could do. 'If I might prevail upon your generosity for the use of your carriage to take me back to the Fleur de Lis?' She really could not bear the thought of travelling back by foot along the streets to the tavern.

'But of course.' The Comte gave a charming bow. 'I will accompany you, of course—'

'I would rather you did not.' Lisette replaced and retied her bonnet before reaching for her cloak. 'I will instruct your coachman to stop a street or two away from the tavern and make my own way back from there.'

Christian scowled his displeasure. 'That is too dangerous—'

'Nevertheless, it is what I shall do,' she stated determinedly.

Not what she 'intended' to do, Christian noted with wry amusement, but what she would do. Lisette Duprée might be young in years, but she had a very determined and definite mind of her own.

No more so than he, admittedly, and if she thought he really intended to allow her to walk the Paris streets alone at this time of night, even for a short distance, then she was mistaken.

'It is far too early for me to retire as yet,' he informed her airily. 'I can see you safely returned to the tavern on my way to other entertainments.'

Lisette looked up from refastening her cloak. 'You are going out again…?'

'But of course.' The Comte waved a hand unconcernedly. 'The gaming hells and…other clubs will only now be becoming interesting.'

Of course they would, Lisette acknowledged heavily. And no doubt the Comte would be luckier with the ladies in those clubs, as well as the cards, now that she had refused to entertain him for the rest of the night.

She had behaved the fool, she realised. A stupid, naive fool, to have believed for one moment that the Comte had any more than a passing interest in her— an interest that had obviously 'passed' now that she had made it clear she did not intend to spend the night here with him.

She raised her chin. 'I am ready to leave now.'

Christian knew by the stiffness of Lisette's demeanour that he had thoroughly succeeded in alienating her when he'd informed her that he intended to go out again. As had been his intention. His mission in Paris had been clear: to watch Helene Rousseau and make note of the comings and goings of the Fleur de Lis.

It had occurred to him earlier to use an interest in one of the tavern's serving girls to enable him to observe Helene Rousseau and the movements of her co-conspirators. Unfortunately, his choice of Lisette as the focus for that interest seemed only to have antagonised the older woman, so bringing more attention to himself.

Helene Rousseau's threats towards him, because of the interest he had shown in Lisette, now meant that his time in Paris was in all probability limited, if he did not want to end up dead in a filthy alley one night.

Chapter Four

'Where have you been?'

Lisette, having just closed and locked the window behind her, after climbing back into the storeroom at the back of the tavern, now gave a gasp of shock as she turned to face her accuser.

Helene stood in the doorway in her night robe, her tall frame silhouetted by the candle left burning outside in the hallway, her hair loose about her shoulders, eyes glittering with her displeasure. 'I asked where you have been,' she repeated harshly.

Lisette swallowed, her lips having gone dry. 'I could not sleep— I went— I thought to—' She faltered as she realised that nothing she said was going to excuse the fact that she had obviously left the tavern sometime earlier tonight and was now sneaking back in again. Or change the fact that Helene had somehow discovered her disappearance. 'I went for a walk.' Her chin rose in challenge.

Helene reached for the candle in the hallway,

bringing the light into the room to illuminate the stored barrels and sacks, as well as a defiant and no doubt dishevelled Lisette; how could she be any other when she had been climbing in and out of a window?

'You went to Saint-Cloud.' Helene's nostrils flared with distaste. 'Do not attempt to deny it; I saw you arrive back just now in his carriage.'

Lisette's heart sank. She had told Monsieur le Comte, had in fact pleaded with him to let her depart the carriage in the street adjoining this one, but he would have none of it. Had instead insisted on bringing her to the back door of the tavern and waiting in his carriage until he was sure she had climbed safely back inside. She had seen his carriage depart as she closed and locked the window.

Well, the Comte was now gone, she was 'back inside', but the fury in Helene's expression did not augur well for it being 'safely'.

Helene carefully placed the lit candle down on top of one of the barrels. 'I told you earlier that I did not approve of you associating any further with the Comte.'

'I do not believe you actually told me not to—'

'Do not contradict me, Lisette.' The woman who was her mother glared at her furiously. 'The Comte is a dangerous man.'

'He has always behaved the gentleman towards me,' Lisette defended, her cheeks burning as she knew that was not strictly true; after all, he had kissed her, not once, but twice.

Helene gave an impatient shake of her head at that telling blush. 'You have not only openly defied me by meeting secretly with the Comte, but defiled your own reputation at the same time—'

'I have done nothing wrong!' she asserted heatedly.

'I do not believe you.'

'I do not care—' She broke off with a pained gasp as Helene's hand struck out at her face. Hard.

Lisette raised a shocked hand as she felt the sting of pain and then the flow of blood on her bottom lip, her fingers covered with the sticky redness when she looked down at them through tear-filled eyes.

No one had ever struck her before this. Not for any reason.

She kept her hand pressed against her bleeding lip as she glared her defiance at the older woman. 'That was truly unforgivable!'

'No more so than your own behaviour has been tonight.' Helene looked at her coldly, unrepentantly. 'I did not bring you to Paris so that you could whore yourself for the first titled gentleman to show you attention.'

'Then why did you bring me here?' Lisette challenged, chin held high. 'You do not care for me. You do not even acknowledge me as your daughter,' she added scornfully as she remembered what the Comte had said to her earlier. 'What am I even doing here?'

Helene gave a snort. 'What else was I supposed to do with you once I learned the Duprées were both dead?'

Lisette felt a fresh sting of tears in her eyes at this woman's total lack of feeling for her.

If she had needed any confirmation of that, after Helene had just struck her without warning or sign of regret.

She straightened her spine. 'In that case, it will be no hardship to you if I remove myself from here tomorrow.'

'To go where?' the older woman derided. 'To your titled lover, perhaps? As if the Comte would have you! To a man such as he, you will either have been no more than a source of information about me—'

'You flatter yourself, *madame*!'

'—or a willing female body in his bed. If it was the latter, then I have no doubt he has already forgotten you!'

Lisette could not deny the truth of this last comment; that the Comte had gone out for further entertainment, after bringing her back to the tavern, proved that the kisses they had shared had meant nothing to him. As she meant nothing to him.

'Do not assume everyone to have the same morals as yourself, *madame*,' she hit back in her humiliation.

'Why, you little—'

'If you hit me again, then I shall be forced to retaliate!' Lisette warned, her hands now clenched into fists at her sides as she faced the taller woman challengingly.

Helene fell back a step as grudging respect dawned in those icy blue eyes. 'This is the first occasion when I have seen any visible sign that you are my daughter.'

'And it will be the last!' Lisette assured her scornfully. 'I intend to pack my bags, such as they are, and leave here in the morning.'

'As I asked before—to go where?' The older woman looked at her coldly. 'You have only the few francs I have given you since you arrived here; have no other money of your own. You do not own anything that I have not given you. You *have* nowhere else to go, Lisette.'

Another indisputable truth.

The very same truth Lisette had told Christian Beaumont earlier this evening...

'If you choose to leave here, you will have no choice but to become a whore or to starve,' Helene added cruelly.

'Then I will starve, *madame*,' she replied with dignity.

'You are behaving like a child, Lisette,' the other woman bit out impatiently.

No, what Lisette was doing inwardly was shaking in reaction to this unpleasant conversation, and her bottom lip now felt sore and swollen from the painful slap she had received from Helene Rousseau. Something Lisette still found difficult to believe had happened at all, when the Duprées, of no relationship to her at all, had shown her nothing but love and kindness for the past nineteen years.

Although that slap certainly made it easier for Lisette to accept her own lack of softer feelings towards Helene. Something she had felt guilty about until this moment. But no longer. Helene Rousseau was a cold and unemotional woman, and one Lisette found it impossible to feel affection for, let alone love. Now that she had decided to leave she did not need to bother trying to do that any more.

Helene was right, of course, in that Lisette did not have anywhere else to go, nor did she have more than a few francs to her name, but her pride dictated she could not allow that to sway her in her decision. She did not belong here. Not in the sprawling city that was Paris. And definitely not in this lowly tavern.

'But not *your* child,' she came back scornfully. 'You do not claim me as such, nor do you have any right to do so after your behaviour tonight,' she added as the other woman would have spoken. 'If you permit it, I will stay here for what is left of the night and leave first thing in the morning.' She gathered her cloak protectively about her.

Helene sighed wearily. 'Lisette…'

'Did you even bother to name me yourself before handing me over to the Duprées?' Lisette challenged derisively. 'Or did you leave even the naming of your child to strangers?' She knew by the angry flush that appeared in the older woman's cheeks that it had been the latter.

'Surely you realise I could not have kept you here with me, Lisette—'

'Could not? Or maybe you did not want to tarnish what is left of your own reputation by acknowledging me as your bastard child?'

Helene sighed heavily. 'It is far too late at night for this conversation—'

'It is too late altogether, *madame*.' Lisette gave a disgusted shake of her head. 'Would that you had left me in ignorance in the country.'

'To do what? Live off turnips and marry a local peasant?' The older woman's lip curled.

'Far better I had done that than live in this place!' Lisette retorted. 'I will leave here as soon as I am able,' she repeated wearily as she brushed past the other woman to gather up a candle and light it before walking proudly down the hallway and going up the stairs.

She made it all the way to her bedchamber before giving in to the tears that had been threatening to fall since she had received that slap on her face.

Tears that were long overdue, as she placed the candle carefully on the bedside table before throwing herself down on the bed and sobbing in earnest; for the loss of the Duprées and the life she had known with them, for the shock of discovering Helene Rousseau was her mother, for her unhappiness since coming to Paris, for the lack of prospects ahead of her once she had left this place.

For the knowledge that the lavender-eyed Comte *had* in all probability already forgotten her existence.

Christian had instructed his coachman to drive around and park the carriage a short distance from the front entrance of the Fleur de Lis, once he was assured Lisette had climbed safely into one of the downstairs windows of the tavern. He was deter-

mined, before leaving the area completely, to see
that Lisette reached her bedchamber safely.

He had been lying, of course, when he told Lisette
he intended to go on to further entertainment. Helene
Rousseau, and the clandestine comings and goings
to her tavern, was his only reason for being in Paris.

At least it had been.

The puzzle that was Lisette Duprée had changed
that somewhat.

There was a mystery there he did not understand.
Helene Rousseau had been so overprotective of Lisette earlier in the tavern when she held a gun to his
back, and yet at the same time there was an obvious lack of familial feeling between the two women.
A disconnection that surely should not have been
there—

Ah, he had just seen candlelight behind the curtains in the bedchamber he believed to be Lisette's,
instantly reassuring him as to her safe return.

'Drive on,' Christian instructed his coachman before settling back against the plush upholstery, his
mind still occupied with the relationship between
Helene Rousseau and Lisette.

There had never been mention of André Rousseau having a daughter, and surely the other man
could not have been old enough to have a daughter
of Lisette's age? And yet, to Christian's knowledge,
Helene Rousseau had no other siblings.

In any case, the discovery of Lisette was an unexpected vulnerability in regard to Helene Rousseau.
One that Christian felt sure Aubrey Maystone would

not hesitate to use against that lady. As the French-woman had been involved in using other innocents as pawns in her own wicked games.

Christian frowned at the very idea of using Lisette in that way.

Another reason for not taking her back to England with him?

He found the whole concept of using her as a pawn in a game to be totally repugnant. Complete anathema to his code as a gentleman.

And yet there was no place for a gentlemanly code when it came to the defence of the Crown.

But to use Lisette in that way, no matter whether she was the innocent she appeared to be or something more, did not sit well with Christian—

'We have company, milord!' his coachman had time to call out grimly seconds before the carriage came to a lurching halt and the door beside Christian was wrenched open, a masked man appearing in that open doorway, a raised pistol in his hand.

Lisette's earlier warning barely had time to register before there was a flash in the darkness and the sound of a pistol being fired.

Lisette sat up with a start, her tears ceasing as she heard the sound of an explosion of some kind ringing through the stillness of the night, followed by the sound of raised voices.

She rose quickly to her feet before hurrying across the bedchamber to look out of the window.

The street was poorly lit, of course, but she could

see a carriage a short way down, and it appeared to be surrounded by a group of darkly clothed men. A carriage that seemed all too familiar to her, considering she had been driven back to the tavern in it just a short time ago.

The Comte de Saint-Cloud's carriage!

Lisette gave no thought to her own safety as she ran across the bedchamber and threw open the door before running down the hallway to descend the stairs. She heard the sound of a second shot being fired and then a third, causing her fingers to fumble with the bolts and key as she quickly unlocked the front door of the tavern before throwing it open and running out into the street.

The carriage was still parked a short distance away, but there were no longer any dark-clothed men surrounding it, the street quiet apart from the horses snorting and stamping their shod feet on the cobbled road in their obvious distress.

Lisette stilled her mad flight at the sound of that deathly silence, her steps becoming hesitant as she approached the carriage, its door flung open and swinging slightly in the breeze.

In keeping with this lowly neighbourhood, no one else had emerged from any of the buildings in response to hearing those three shots being fired, and Lisette herself feared what she might find once she had reached and looked inside that eerily silent carriage.

She raised a shocked hand to her mouth as she drew nearer and saw a body lying on the cobbles beside the carriage, recognising the groom who had opened the door for her earlier tonight lying so still and unmoving, a bloom of red having appeared on the chest of his grey livery.

Which surely meant that the Comte de Saint-Cloud was inside the carriage still; otherwise Lisette had no doubt he would be out here now tending to his groom. Or perhaps, having discovered the man dead, he was off chasing the men who had attacked them.

She ceased breathing and her heart seemed to stop beating altogether as she apprehensively approached the open door of the carriage, so very afraid of what she was going to find when she looked inside.

In all possibility, the Comte, as dead as his groom appeared to be?

Her heart stuttered and then stopped again as she heard the sound of a groan from inside the depths of the carriage. Indication that at least the Comte was alive, if obviously injured?

'Christian!' Lisette called out frantically as she no longer hesitated but hurriedly ascended the steps.

'Lisette?' The Comte groaned uncomprehendingly, the lantern inside the carriage showing him lying back against the cushions, his face deathly white, a bloom of red showing, and growing larger by the second, on the left thigh of his pale-coloured pantaloons. 'You should not be here,' he protested as he attempted to sit up.

'Do not move!' Lisette instructed sternly as she stepped fully into the carriage to fall to her knees beside him and began to inspect the wound to his thigh.

'They might come back—'

'I doubt it,' she snorted disgustedly. 'Cowards. Half a dozen men against two—'

'You saw them?' Christian, grateful that he had the foresight to speak to Lisette in French, had now managed to ease himself back into an upright position, although his thigh hurt like the very devil with every movement.

Lisette nodded distractedly, her face a pale oval in the lamplight. 'From the window of my bedchamber. At least half a dozen men. Are you hurt very badly?' She looked at his thigh but did not attempt to touch him.

Christian's jaw was clenched against the pain. 'I believe the bullet has gone through the soft tissue and out the other side.'

Lisette's face seemed to pale even more. 'We should call for law enforcement, and you need a doctor—'

'No—no doctor,' he refused grimly.

'You are bleeding badly—'

'No, Lisette,' he repeated determinedly. 'My groom?'

Her gaze dropped from meeting his. 'I fear— He does not appear to be—'

'Damn it, they have killed him!' Christian struggled to sit forward, intent on seeing his groom for himself. 'Please move aside, Lisette, so that I can go to him.'

'You must not move, Christian—'

'Indeed I must, Lisette.' He gritted his teeth as that movement caused his leg to throb and the blood to flow more freely over the fingers he had pressed to his flesh to staunch the wound. He looked at Lisette as she now sat on the other side of the carriage, a bewildered look upon her face. 'I am afraid I shall need your help to get Pierre into the carriage.'

Her face lost any remaining colour at the mere idea of touching a dead body. Christian nodded approvingly as she nonetheless moved valiantly forward to follow as he stepped awkwardly down from the carriage, before limping over and going down on one knee beside his groom lying unmoving on the cobbles.

'Not dead, and I think the shot has pierced his shoulder rather than his chest,' Christian said thankfully after placing his bloody fingers against the other man's wrist and feeling a pulse. 'Help me lift him inside the carriage, would you?'

'I— But— What are you going to do with him then?'

'Return to my home, of course.'

Lisette felt totally perplexed by the Comte's behaviour. Surely a doctor, at least, should be called for, even if Christian did not feel inclined to ask for the help of the police enforcement that had been established in Paris just five years ago.

The dissolute rake he had appeared earlier this evening was completely gone, Christian Beaumont's eyes now sharp with intelligence and determination as the two of them struggled to lift the groom and place him inside the carriage.

Not an easy task when the Comte was injured and Lisette was so slight in stature.

It seemed to take forever as they struggled to get Pierre inside the carriage and lying on one of the bench seats, but was in fact probably only a few minutes. Both of them were smeared with the other man's blood by that time, and Christian Beaumont's own wound seemed to be bleeding more profusely too.

Lisette gave a dismayed gasp at how deathly pale his face was as he straightened. 'I really must insist you are attended by a doctor—'

'I shall consider it once we are returned to my home and I have been able to inspect Pierre's wound more thoroughly.' He nodded grimly even as he placed a hand against the carriage for support.

Lisette frowned her disapproval. 'And exactly how do you intend doing that, when both your groom and yourself have been shot?'

A touch of humour tilted the Comte's lips. 'Did you ever drive a horse and cart on that farm you once lived on, Lisette?'

She gave him a startled look. 'You are not suggesting that *I* should drive your carriage...?'

He gave a pointed look about the empty street. 'I do not see anyone else I can ask, do you?'

'But— Christian!' Lisette stepped forward to put her arm about the leanness of his waist and the support of her shoulder beneath his arm as he appeared to sway precariously.

'And I suggest that you do it soon, Lisette,' he

muttered faintly. 'Whilst I am still conscious to direct you.'

She had never heard of anything so ridiculous as
to expect her to drive the Comte's carriage; it was
nothing like the old cart they'd had on the farm, nor
were the four horses pulling this elegant carriage in
the least like the elderly and plodding mare owned
by the Duprées. Indeed, these high-stepping animals
might have been a different breed altogether from
the docile Marguerite.

Lisette eyed the four black horses doubtfully as
they still snorted and stamped their displeasure. 'You
are asking too much, Christian.' She gave a shake
of her head.

He nodded. 'I would not ask at all if it were not
important.'

Lisette looked up at him searchingly. 'I do not understand,' she finally murmured slowly.

'And I do not have the time, or indeed the strength,
to explain the situation to you right now.' He sighed
weakly.

Lisette glanced down to where his thigh was still
bleeding freely, front and back. 'Something needs to
be tied about your thigh in order to slow the bleeding...'

'Lisette...?' Christian's eyes widened as she did
not hesitate to lift her gown before efficiently ripping a strip from the bottom of her petticoat, and then
proceeded to crouch down in front of him to wrap
and tie that strip tightly about the top of his thigh.

It was perhaps as well that there was no one on

the street to observe them because Lisette, crouched in that position, looked very—risqué, if one did not realise she was merely applying a tourniquet to his thigh.

'There.' She gave a nod of satisfaction as she straightened, seemingly completely unaware of the picture of debauchery she had just presented to the world. 'I shall need your instruction to drive the carriage, Christian. Do you feel strong enough to be helped up into the driving area?'

He determinedly dragged his thoughts back from the lewdly suggestive delights that having Lisette kneeling in front of him had evoked.

It looked a very long way up to where his groom drove the carriage, when he was feeling less than agile, the loss of blood having also made him feel slightly light-headed.

He set his jaw grimly. 'I shall manage with your help, yes.' He was determined to do so, knew that he and Lisette must now get themselves away from here as soon as was possible, that they had delayed long enough.

He had no doubt that the men who had accosted and then shot him and Pierre were the cut-throats Lisette had warned him Helene Rousseau had intended sending to dispose of him. That at any moment they might return and finish the job.

There was no sign of life or candlelight inside the Fleur de Lis itself, but that did not mean that Helene Rousseau was not observing the two of them right now. And no doubt filled with fresh resolve now that she had seen he was not only still alive but also mobile enough to struggle up onto the carriage with Lisette's help.

That resolve would no doubt deepen, and Helene Rousseau herself be filled with renewed rage, when she saw her niece drive away with him in his carriage.

'Perhaps you should not accompany me, after all.' Christian frowned as Lisette climbed up beside him. 'Your aunt will no doubt make her disapproval known—'

'I have already told Helene that I shall be leaving the Fleur de Lis in the morning.' She shrugged.

'The two of you have argued?'

'That is one way of describing it.' Lisette's hand moved up to touch her mouth.

Christian's eyes darkened as he saw her bottom lip was slightly swollen. 'She struck you?'

'Yes.'

'Because of me?'

'The reason is unimportant.' Her expression was grim as she picked up the reins, ready for departing. 'And she is not my aunt.'

'Not your aunt...?' Christian echoed softly, the effort of climbing up into the carriage having taken the last of his strength.

'No.' Lisette's jaw was clenched.

Well, that at least explained Lisette's hesitation every time he referred to her as such. It did not, however—

'Madame Rousseau is my mother, not my aunt,' she continued scathingly. 'And I do not care what her opinion might be on any of my actions after the way she has behaved this night!'

Christian dropped back weakly against the seat, knowing that this revelation now gave him no choice where Lisette was concerned.

Leaving Helene Rousseau's niece behind in Paris might have been explained away—just—but the daughter of Helene Rousseau *must* return with him to England.

Chapter Five

The journey was a long and painful one, as each rumble of the carriage wheels over the cobbled streets caused renewed pain to spear up through Christian's thigh, and it took every effort of will on his part to stay conscious long enough to direct Lisette in the initial driving of the carriage. Luckily, she was an intelligent as well as capable young lady, and had mastered the horses and the carriage within a few minutes.

Leaving Christian to contemplate the leaden weight in his chest at the knowledge that the young woman sitting beside him was the daughter of a woman believed responsible for attempting to free the Corsican usurper by causing actual physical harm to people he cared about.

A belief Christian was even more convinced of after the attack on him tonight. An attack Lisette believed to have happened because of his attentions towards her earlier this evening, but which Christian believed to have been for a different reason entirely; Helene Rousseau not only knew *who* he was, but also the reason for his currently being in Paris.

And if she knew that, then there was every chance that she would try to have him killed a second time, if he remained here. More than a chance, now that he had her daughter with him.

Once returned to his temporary home he would have to make immediate arrangements for both himself and Lisette to take ship to England. Without, he acknowledged heavily, telling Lisette exactly why he was taking her with him. He doubted she would come with him to England at all if she knew who he was and the reason he had been in Paris, much less that he now had no choice but to deliver Helene Rousseau's daughter to Aubrey Maystone.

No, much as it pained him, he could not tell Lisette any of those things just yet.

Better by far that he at least waited until they were on the ship bound for England, when it was too late for Lisette to do anything else but complete the voyage. That she would dislike him intensely afterwards could not be avoided.

Lisette had been keeping half an eye on the Comte as she carefully guided the carriage through the deserted Paris streets, and so she knew the exact moment that he lost consciousness. Either from loss of too much blood or from the pain he was suffering. The latter, she hoped, otherwise there was a serious possibility that he might die before she was able to get him to help.

A part of her still wanted to take him to the home

of the nearest doctor—if she had known where that was, which she did not—but the Comte had been adamant in his refusal of medical assistance, and Lisette did not wish to make this situation any worse than it already was by going against his wishes.

If that was possible.

At the moment she had two unconscious men in the carriage with her, one seated beside her, the other inside the carriage. Both of them clearly suffering wounds from a pistol shot. And she herself was covered in blood from both those gentlemen, on her hands and her gown. If she was stopped by the authorities—

Hysteria could come later, Lisette told herself sternly. Once they had safely reached the Comte's home. She did not have the time or thought enough to spare for such things when she was so concentrated on driving the Comte's carriage.

She breathed a sigh of relief when she recognised the Comte's house just a short distance away, her shoulders and back aching from controlling such spirited horses, and her hands sore from grasping the reins so tightly.

She almost cried with relief when she finally drew the carriage to a halt in front of the house, François's politely bland expression as he opened the door changing to one of alarm as he ran down the steps to grab hold of the bridle of one of the front horses.

'The Comte and his groom have both been shot, François,' Lisette explained economically as she hitched up the skirt of her gown to quickly climb down from the carriage.

It was testament to the man's character that he wasted no time asking for explanations but instead instantly called up to a hovering footman for reinforcements. Several other footmen now appeared from inside the house, followed by a couple of grooms from the back of the house.

Between them they managed to lift the still unconscious Comte and the groom from the carriage before carrying them inside. Lisette insisted that the groom must also be carried up to one of the guest bedchambers. If Christian would not allow a doctor to be called for, then she would have to do the best she could to doctor the two men herself, and it would be far easier for her if they were within feet of each other.

Again, François showed his character by not so much as batting an eyelid at her request, but instead continued the directing of the two wounded men after sending one of the footmen off to the kitchen to acquire the supplies Lisette said she would need to clean and then dress their wounds.

If either man still had a bullet inside one of those wounds then she would have no choice but to send for a doctor, despite Christian's instructions to the contrary. A bullet, left inside the wound, would surely fill with pus and possibly result in the man dying.

There was no doubt in Lisette's mind that if he were awake Christian would have insisted she attend to the groom first, but as he was not…

François proved to be her rock during the next hour, helping her to remove the Comte's boots, pantaloons and undergarments—a moment when Lisette had discreetly looked the other way—and acting as her assistant as she inspected and then cleaned both the entry and exit wounds in Christian's thigh; he was proved correct, in that the bullet had gone straight through the soft tissue of his thigh and then out again.

Nevertheless, once her makeshift tourniquet had been removed both wounds bled profusely and she was grateful that Christian continued to remain unconscious throughout. He looked so pale and still once she had bound his wound tightly to allow the skin to knit back together—he should perhaps have had stitches applied, but again Lisette did not feel qualified to do so, and so they had just made him as comfortable as they could beneath the bedclothes once she had applied the bandages.

Which was when the enormity of what she had just done bore down upon Lisette. Not only had she dressed the Comte's bloody wounds, but he had been half-naked as she did so. Admittedly François had draped the sheet across Christian's groin to protect his modesty, but that did not alter the fact that he had been completely naked beneath that sheet.

'Would you care for some brandy before we go to Pierre, *mademoiselle*?' François offered as he looked at her concernedly.

She smiled her gratitude for that concern. 'Perhaps afterwards, thank you, François. It would perhaps be as well if I continue to have a steady hand until after I have seen to Pierre!' she added ruefully.

François was the one to once again undress the man lying injured on the bed while they waited for one of the footmen to bring up fresh hot water and bandages. Allowing them to see that the groom's wound was in the shoulder, as Christian had surmised it might be, but more complicated, in that the bullet was obviously still embedded in his flesh.

'It will have to come out, *mademoiselle*,' François said with a frown.

Lisette swayed slightly on her feet, both from the gory work of this past hour and the deep fatigue she felt after such a long and exhausting day.

It seemed far longer than the six, or possibly seven, hours since she had first met the Comte de Saint-Cloud at the Fleur de Lis. Six or seven hours when her life had been completely turned about, to the point that she now had no home, and no family to speak of.

Self-pity was not permissible now, Lisette told herself firmly, any more than it had been when the Duprées both perished. She might not have a home or a family, but the Comte had been shot because of his association with her, and the outcome of his wound was still questionable.

As was poor Pierre's...

She straightened her shoulders determinedly. 'I will need something with which to remove the bullet, François. And your assistance for a little longer, if you please.'

'As long as it takes, *mademoiselle*,' he assured her gravely.

Lisette gave him a grateful smile before she turned her attention to the now ashen-faced groom.

Christian awakened with a groan of pain, feeling as if he had been kicked by a horse and then his leg trampled upon by that same horse.

Every part of him seemed to hurt, but it pained him the most in his left thigh. He had no idea—

'Do not attempt to move, Your Grace,' a voice advised urgently in English.

Christian had no strength to struggle against the hand now pressing against his shoulder, and so instead he opened heavy lids to look up at a dishevelled François, the weak sunlight shining in through the window of his bedchamber showing him that the man's coat was unfastened over a bloody shirt, his wig slightly askew on his bald head, and there were dark shadows under his eyes. A testament to lack of sleep?

'I believe we must keep to Monsieur le Comte,' Christian murmured weakly in French.

'Of course.' François nodded as he answered in the same language. 'Do you remember being shot, *monsieur*?' The butler looked down at him quizzically.

Christian frowned in concentration, trying to recall— Dear Lord, yes, he remembered now. His groom's warning, followed by the sound of a shot being fired, the carriage coming to a halt and the door being thrown open, another two shots being fired, the arrival of the red-haired angel—

No, that last part was not right. It had not been an angel, but Lisette who had entered the carriage, before helping him outside so that they might both check on his groom, lying unconscious on the cobbled road.

'Pierre?' he prompted sharply.

François's eyes avoided meeting his. 'He is…not doing so well as you, *monsieur*, but Mademoiselle Lisette is doing all that she can for him.'

'Lisette…?'

'She is with Pierre now, Your Grace.' François grimaced. 'Once she had attended to you, she turned her attention to Pierre and has remained with him all night. In fact, she has refused to leave his bedside.'

Christian could hear the admiration for Lisette in the older man's voice. Admiration fully deserved, if he was to understand the situation correctly; Lisette had not only doctored him last night but also Pierre. A task that would have sent most women of Christian's acquaintance running in the other direction. With the exception of his sister and the wives of his closest friends, of course. But every other woman Christian knew in society would have shrunk away from being asked to perform such a gory task.

A task he realised he was responsible for asking of her, as he recalled that he had refused to allow a doctor to be called for to attend either him or Pierre.

He had his reasons for that, of course. But Lisette

was not privy to those reasons and had simply acted as he requested without explanation.

There was also the matter of her revelation that she was Helene Rousseau's daughter and not her niece to consider. Lisette's earlier claim, of having lived on a farm with relatives until just weeks ago, would explain why no one had known of the existence of Helene Rousseau's daughter before now.

A daughter Aubrey Maystone would have much interest in learning about.

'Take me to her.' Christian attempted to sit up.

'You will remain exactly where you are, Christian, and not undo all my good work of last night, unless you wish to feel the sharp lash of my tongue,' an imperious voice informed him firmly as Lisette stepped into the bedchamber.

Her own appearance was as dishevelled, if not more so than François's: her hair had escaped its pins and was falling down about her shoulders in untidy wisps; there were smears of blood on her cheek and throat, her black gown showing several darker stains which were almost certainly more blood. Her face was also deathly white, no doubt from spending a sleepless night attending to first Christian and then his groom, and her bottom lip was still slightly swollen from where Helene Rousseau had struck her.

And this was the young woman Christian intended to take back to England with him with the intention of handing her over to Aubrey Maystone.

Shame washed over Christian at the betrayal of such an act in the face of Lisette's selflessness last night. Not only had she brought them all home by driving the carriage then tended to both men's wounds all night, but by doing so she must also have known that she would be further incurring her mother's wrath, not only for having done those things but also by remaining out all night.

'Pierre?' he questioned softly.

She nodded. 'He has a slight fever, but I do not believe he will become any worse.' She placed a bowl of water and fresh bandages down on the bed-side table.

'God be thanked,' Christian muttered gratefully; he already had enough on his conscience without the death of this innocent French groom.

All of the household staff were aware of his true identity, of course, were all loyal to the French Crown and aware of the danger they placed themselves in by working with him. But that did not mean that Christian wished to be responsible for the death of one of them.

'You, on the other hand, will remain in bed for the remainder of the day.' Lisette spoke firmly again. 'And tomorrow too, unless you wish for me to send for the doctor you refused to have attend you last night?'

Christian did not remember the last time a woman had spoken to him in so imperious a tone as this; his *grandmère*, before her death, and his sister Julianna tried to do the same, but Christian had grown adept at avoiding confrontation by meeting those dictates with a charming disregard for their content.

The determined expression on Lisette's face told him that the events of the night had stripped away all social politeness, and that she had no intention of being ignored nor charmed.

Besides, how could he possibly argue with the woman who was probably responsible for not only saving his own life but also that of the young French groom?

The young and handsome French groom, Christian recalled with a displeased frown, with whom Lisette had sat up most of the night.

Which was utterly ridiculous of him in the circumstances.

His own clandestine presence in Paris was responsible for Pierre's injuries as well as his own, and also for Lisette's present exhaustion from doctoring them both. How could he possibly now feel jealous of the attention Lisette had necessarily shown the groom?

There was no logic or reason to it; it was just there, inside him. And, unlike the wound in his thigh, it felt as if it might be festering.

He smiled up at her. 'I have no intention of "going against doctor's orders" and getting out of bed, now that I can see for myself that you have come to no harm. I do, however, believe that you have done enough for both Pierre and myself for now and need to take your own rest.'

Lisette was well aware of how bedraggled she must look, after a night spent tending to Christian and his groom, and she certainly did not need him to remind her of it. 'It is my intention to break my fast before then returning to the Fleur de Lis to collect my things.'

'You are still intent on leaving there?'

'I cannot stay.' She shook her head. 'But first I will check your wound.' She indicated the bowl of water and fresh bandages.

'Is that necessary?'

'My— When I lived on the farm with the Duprées, we found that if a wound was kept clean, with fresh bandages applied often, there was less chance of it becoming inflamed.'

'I am sure François will be only too happy to do that for me.'

'It is a little late for modesty now, *monsieur.*' Lisette eyed him impatiently as her attempts to pull back the bedclothes were met with resistance. 'I assure you, François and I have already seen all,' she now added drily.

In truth, she was no more comfortable with inspecting Christian's wound than he was in allowing her to do it now that he was fully conscious and aware of the intimacy. But she really had no choice in the matter. The wound must be looked at, and redressed if necessary.

The Comte's jaw tightened even as he slowly released the bedclothes. 'I believe you are enjoying my discomfort far too much, Lisette!'

Was she? Perhaps. It had been a long and eventful twenty-four hours, and she really had no patience, or strength, left to fight such a silly battle as this one.

Of the two, she was perhaps the most embarrassed

as she and François carefully removed the bandage she had applied last night, Lisette's cheeks feeling hot with that embarrassment as she inadvertently touched the warmth of Christian's other inner thigh.

'I am sorry,' she muttered awkwardly as her hand instinctively pulled away, taking the bandage with it, which unfortunately was stuck to the wound at the front of his thigh. She winced as she saw a well of fresh blood instantly appear at the wound's surface.

It looked clean enough though, and there was no redness about it, so hopefully there would be no inflammation if she kept applying clean bandages; her foster mother had sworn by this method of avoiding inflammation to a cut or wound.

Tears filled her eyes as she now thought of the couple who had brought her up as if she were their own, and these horrible weeks since Helene Rousseau had brought her back to Paris with her.

No doubt this weakness of emotion was brought about by her tiredness and exhaustion, but that did not stop the emotion from being real. She missed the Duprées, and the quiet and simple life she had led with them, more than she could say.

'Lisette…?'

She brought herself back to her surroundings with a start—indeed, she was not sure how she could possibly have allowed her thoughts to stray in the first place, when she had a half-naked Christian Beaumont lying on the bed in front of her!

'I am very tired, *monsieur.*' She straightened. 'Perhaps, for your own safety, François should finish applying the rest of this clean bandage?' She looked questioningly at the butler, although he looked almost as tired as she did.

Christian frowned as he easily saw the signs of Lisette's exhaustion, in the paleness of her face and the slightly glazed look in her eyes. Her hands were also shaking slightly.

He turned to his butler. 'François, arrange for breakfast to be brought up to Mademoiselle Lisette in the blue bedchamber, followed by a hot bath, after which she is not to be disturbed for the rest of the day.' He had no doubt Lisette had already incited the wrath of her mother again by not returning to the tavern last night, so he couldn't see what further harm it could do if she did not return there for another day.

Her auburn brows rose. 'I see you are back to being your usual dictatorial self, *monsieur.*'

'Did I ever stop?' He eyed her ruefully.

She seemed to give the matter some thought before answering. 'No, I cannot say that you did.'

'And I see that you have developed a sharp tongue overnight,' Christian drawled.

'I am too tired to be any other way,' she admitted wryly.

'François will now take you to the blue bedchamber, arrange for breakfast and a bath to be brought up to you,' he decided briskly. 'And then both of you are to go away and get some sleep. The household can run without you for one day, François, a maid or footman can see to Pierre, and I am quite capable of wrapping a fresh bandage about my own leg—'

'Oh, but—'

'You will go with François now, Lisette,' Christian added firmly. 'Eat, bathe, rest.'

'If you undo all my good work—'

'Then I can expect to feel a further lashing of your tongue.' When he would much rather feel the soft caressing stroke of her hot, moist little tongue against any part of his anatomy.

Obviously, being shot in the thigh had not lessened his desire for this young woman in the slightest, Christian acknowledged self-derisively.

She nodded. 'That is exactly what you will feel, yes.'

Christian gave a throaty chuckle. 'Go, Lisette, and do not come back until you are completely rested and refreshed.'

Lisette really was too tired to argue any further as she followed François from Christian's bedchamber a short distance along the hallway to the 'blue bedchamber', a room so luxurious, with its white ornate furniture and blue carpets and blue satin drapes, both at the windows and about the huge four-poster bed, that she felt positively overwhelmed.

She turned to François. 'I do not need the use of such a lovely bedchamber as this—'

'The Comte believes you do. And so do I,' the butler added softly.

Lisette's cheeks warmed at the compliment. 'I do believe I might sleep for a week in such a comfortable-looking bed!' It certainly looked nicer than the slender cot she had been sleeping on at the tavern these past weeks.

François smiled. 'But first you must eat and bathe.'

Lisette looked at the dishevelled butler and then down at her own less than pristine appearance. 'We are a sorry-looking pair, are we not, François!'

He gave a boyish grin. 'We are merely battle-worn, Mademoiselle Lisette.'

Yes, 'battle-worn' correctly described how Lisette felt as she sank weakly down onto the stool in front of the dressing table once François had left to give instructions in regard to her breakfast.

She really had never seen such finery as the satins and velvets in this bedchamber, let alone thought she would ever sleep in such luxury.

But she had no doubt that, by leaving the tavern in the hurried way that she had last night, repugnant as returning to the Fleur de Lis was to her, if she did not go back to collect the few belongings she had, she now literally owned no more than the clothes she stood in—sat down in.

Chapter Six

'I— But just yesterday, you said you had no plans to leave Paris as yet...'

Christian, having just told Lisette when she came to his bedchamber that evening that he had arranged passage for them both to go to England later tonight, could well understand her surprise.

He had kept his promise not to stir from his bed, but otherwise he had not been idle during the hours Lisette slept. Besides receiving continual updates on Pierre's condition—which seemed to be improving, thank God—and arranging passage to England for himself and Lisette, Christian had also sent out for several gowns and other female apparel for her.

She had protested, of course, but Christian had then pointed out that she could not continue to wear the soiled black gown. He was, after all, the reason she did not have anything but that soiled—and un-attractive—black gown to wear.

The ordering of three new gowns had also al-lowed Christian to choose colours for her other than black. The deep purple gown she now wore and the pale and dark grey of the other two gowns were also mourning colours, but so much less sombre than that funereal black.

A mourning which he now knew to be for her uncle, the French spy André Rousseau.

Much as he might wish it, Christian knew he could not ignore or forget that fact.

His mouth firmed. 'You must know as well as I that the events of last night have necessitated changing my plans somewhat. As well as your own,' he continued softly. 'You already told me you intended leaving the tavern today anyway and it would perhaps be as well if you did not go back there at all. Unless there are things of your own there you cannot bear to be parted from?'

She grimaced. 'I have very few personal possessions...'

'Then leave them for now. There is no reason why you cannot claim them at a later date,' Christian added as she still hesitated.

She frowned. 'Even so, that does not mean I have any intention of travelling to England with you.'

Christian would much rather that Lisette came with him willingly; after all that she had done for him, he did not relish the idea of forcing her into accompanying him.

He wished he did not have to take her to England with him at all, knowing what fate awaited her there. But after last night he could not see a future for her here in Paris either. And if Lisette was as innocent as he believed her to be, then surely, once Aubrey Maystone had questioned her and realised her innocence for himself, Christian might be able to find a place for her in an English household, as a companion or governess, perhaps?

Perhaps his sister Julianna, expecting her first child in a few months' time, might even be persuaded into engaging Lisette as a nanny for the child?

'Parlez-vous anglais?' Christian asked her, to which she gave a firm shake of her head. 'Then I shall have someone teach you the rudiments of the language once we are in England.'

'Why?'

'You cannot live in another country and not speak the language.' He eyed her frustratedly.

Whilst Lisette looked totally refreshed after her rest, and the purple gown was most becoming to her creamy complexion and tidily upswept red hair, Christian was feeling decidedly tired and not a little bad-tempered after his busy day making the necessary arrangements for their departure from Paris. It was now early in the evening and his thigh throbbed like the very devil from his daytime exertions.

Lisette's eyes widened. 'Even if I were to agree to accompany you now, I would not remain in England longer than it takes to see you are safely returned.'

'I doubt your mother will welcome you back when, to all intents and purposes, you spent the night here with me, before then travelling to England with me,' Christian pointed out gently.

'She is not my mother! Biologically, perhaps,' Lisette conceded reluctantly as Christian raised surprised brows. 'But I do not know her, had never even met her or knew of her existence until two months ago.'

'That is…hard to believe,' he murmured cautiously.

'Why is it?' Lisette stood up restlessly.

She now felt refreshed from her hours of sleep. Enough so that she had given thought to her present dilemma, and although she might accept that going to England with the Comte seemed the logical choice—the safest choice—for the moment, she could not think of remaining there. She was French, knew no other life than the one she had led with the Duprées, and briefly with Helene Rousseau here in Paris. One life was closed off to her, the other she had no wish to re-enter.

Even so, Lisette knew nothing of England or the English, apart from the fact they had been at war with France, under Napoleon's rule, for so many years.

She gave a shake of her head. 'I am sure I cannot be the first bastard child you have ever heard to have been fostered with strangers.'

'Unfortunately not,' he acknowledged tightly. 'But it is usual for that child to be aware they are being fostered. And who their real mother is.'

Was Lisette imagining the question in Christian's voice as he made that last comment? Did he doubt her claim of knowing nothing of Helene Rousseau's existence until just weeks ago?

'I assure you I did not,' she answered him tartly. 'Nor do I have any idea who my father is.'

'Madame Rousseau has not confided in you?'

'No.' Lisette stood in front of the window, the slowly flowing Seine glittering like silver in the moonlight. 'I am not sure I wish to know either, considering the...the type of man I know frequents the Fleur de Lis.' She repressed a shudder of distaste at the thought of one of the loutish and lowly men she had encountered there these past few weeks being her father.

Christian could totally sympathise with this sentiment after his visit to that establishment the evening before.

'Which brings me to another point, *mon*— Christian,' she corrected at his frowning glance. 'Whatever you may have assumed to the contrary, I am nothing like Helene Rousseau. I have not, nor do I intend to take a lover or series of lovers.' Embarrassed colour glowed in her cheeks.

No doubt from thinking of the kisses the two of them had shared the night before. Far from innocent kisses, which could so easily have led to something deeper.

Christian's mouth twisted into a smile. 'I believe you will find I am somewhat...incapacitated, in any case, in that regard at present!'

'I am glad you find me so amusing, Christian.' She shot him an irritated glance for this show of levity. 'But your wounds will eventually heal.'

'You then expect I shall proposition you into

agreeing to become my mistress?' Christian was finding this conversation less and less amusing by the minute.

Her cheeks flushed prettily. 'I can think of no other reason why you might take me to England with you.'

Christian wished that were the case! 'And if I were to make you a promise that I shall attempt not to do so?'

She blinked. 'Are you making me such a promise?'

Christian's jaw tightened. 'That I will promise not to attempt to do so, yes.'

She gave a typically Gallic sniff. 'Then I suppose that will have to do. But I still maintain that you cannot seriously expect to be able to travel back to England tonight. You will need to rest for several more days before even contemplating such a journey.'

'Whilst I have every confidence in François and my other employees here,' Christian bit out, 'I do not wish to put any of them in further danger by remaining in Paris longer than is necessary. I am well enough to travel to the ship later this evening,' he continued as she would have spoken. 'After which time I will retire to my cabin and, with your assistance, continue to rest for the remainder of the journey ho—to my estates in England.' He inwardly cursed himself for almost slipping up and calling England 'home'.

He knew he would have to reveal the truth of his identity before they docked in England. He had already sent on ahead for his ducal coach to be waiting for them at the quayside when they arrived. But, as he'd already decided, he would not do so until the ship was well under way and Lisette had no choice but to accompany him.

His appeal for her assistance on the journey, of playing upon the softness of her heart, was his way of ensuring she accompanied him.

Christian deplored even that subterfuge in regard to this young woman who had surely saved his life the previous night. And he fully intended to make his feelings on the subject known to Aubrey Maystone when he made his report to the older man; Lisette was not to come to any harm or Maystone would answer directly to him. But, powerful as the Duchy of Sutherland undoubtedly was, Christian knew that would still be no guarantee in regard to Lisette's future safety.

'I suppose that will have to do, if you are set on the idea...'

'I am,' Christian confirmed tautly. 'To that end, François has already arranged for my bags to be packed and the coach to be ready to leave for the docks in one hour's time.' And on this occasion Christian would ensure that the groom and driver accompanying them would be armed and ready to fight off anyone who tried to stop them from reaching the dockside.

Lisette realised, by the determined set of the Comte's jaw, that nothing she had to say would succeed in persuading him into altering those plans.

Having only just removed and hung up her new gowns and put away the pretty undergarments, Lisette now realised she would have to repack them all; grateful as she was for the new clothes, she still blushed to think of the intimacy of having Christian Beaumont order such things for her. No matter what he said to the contrary, it had the definite feel of a *patron* bestowing largesse upon his mistress.

Perhaps once she was in England, she would be able to find respectable employment for a time, and in that way repay him for the purchase of the new gowns and undergarments?

If so, Christian was right; she would need to learn and speak English. 'Very well, *monsieur*.' This time Lisette ignored his frown of disapproval; if they were to travel to England together, then the formalities must be maintained in order to keep a distance between the two of them. A distance that had already been breached. Several times… 'I will return to my bedchamber and pack my own things now, and be ready to leave within the hour.'

Christian nodded his approval; he could not abide a woman who fussed and flounced and generally made a hullaballoo when it came to doing anything asked of her. Not that he had expected that of Lisette; she had already shown, time and time again, that she was made of much sterner stuff than to throw a tantrum because her plans had taken a sudden turn.

And he would protect her once they were in England, he vowed fiercely.

Against all and anyone who tried to harm her.

* * *

'I had no idea that sailing could be so invigorating as this!' Lisette smiled her happiness as she swept into Christian's cabin aboard the elegant sloop the following morning.

Any doubts that Christian might have had in regard to Lisette being a 'good sailor' had been dispelled the night before when, once on board the fast sloop, she had stayed up on deck conversing with the captain, who could speak and understand a rudimentary smattering of French—despite Christian's urgings for her to stay below deck—during the whole process of the ship setting sail and leaving the harbour.

This morning she looked even more bright-eyed and happily flushed in the cheeks.

Whereas Christian was in great discomfort from the wound to his thigh. Indeed, he had only managed to remove his boots the previous night before collapsing onto the bunk bed in which he now lay. He had then tossed and turned for most of the night, the swaying of the ship not helping in the slightest.

'At least one of us is pleased with the arrangement,' he snapped in disgruntlement.

Lisette's eyes widened at this show of bad temper from Christian; he had always seemed to be so calm and unruffled in their acquaintance to date. Even when he had been shot.

She studied his appearance more closely; his boots had been removed, but otherwise he seemed to have slept in his clothes—possibly because he had been unable to undress completely without assistance?

Assistance Lisette was ashamed to admit she had not thought to offer the previous night, in her enchantment with remaining on deck to watch as they set sail for England.

Christian's hair was also tousled and unkempt, there were dark shadows beneath those lavender-coloured eyes and his face had a greyish cast to it. Not a particularly good sign, but far better that he be pale in the face than flushed with a fever.

'I believe you will need to undress, so that I might look at your wound again,' she announced lightly—in an effort to hide the embarrassment she felt at the thought of the two of them being alone here when she helped Christian to remove his clothes.

She had not considered that, in her relief on discovering they had been given separate cabins aboard the ship, she would find herself completely alone with Christian when she came to his cabin; François had always been present when she had dressed Christian's wound whilst they were in Paris.

Christian scowled up at her. 'Do I look as if I am capable of undressing?'

Yes, the Comte was decidedly out of sorts this morning. 'I meant with my assistance, of course,' she came back pleasantly.

'Are you sure?' He quirked an impatient eyebrow. 'I would not wish to keep you from going up on deck and enjoying the rest of the voyage or to "damage your reputation"!'

Lisette ignored the jibe. Not only was it unworthy of the man she had come to know, but they must both be aware, even occupying separate cabins as they were, that her reputation would be 'damaged' forever, just from her having travelled alone with him to England.

Lisette had considered at the time, and still did, that it was a small price to pay in exchange for escaping, even only for a while, the life she had been forced to lead in Paris.

'I will help you to undress,' she repeated briskly. 'And then go and beg some hot water from the ship's cook to first help you wash and then to cleanse your wound. I will also need to acquire something I can use for clean dressings.'

'No doubt you are now on speaking terms with all the crew!' the Comte snapped accusingly as she crooked an arm beneath his to help him sit up higher against the pillows.

Yes, definitely out of sorts—and rude with it. 'The Captain was kind enough to introduce me to his officers and the men in the galley last night, yes,' Lisette answered distractedly, her expression deliberately neutral as she peeled the fitted jacket from him, before untying and removing his cravat and unfastening the buttons on his shirt.

Some of which she was sure Christian could have done for himself last night, but had perhaps been too tired or irritable to do so, after struggling to remove his boots. Men, her *maman* had once warned her, did not make good patients—mainly because they had no *patience* with their own weakness in having become sick in the first place. Although that could not be said of Christian's current predicament, when he had come by his present injury through no fault of his own.

Except in showing a marked interest in her.

Her own guilt over that was enough to cause Lisette to hold her tongue in regard to Christian's uncharacteristic bad temper as she lifted and then removed the shirt from his body.

Her breath caught in her throat when she turned back from depositing the soiled shirt on the floor and found herself looking at Christian's completely bared chest.

And what a chest it was—lightly tanned, with tautly defined muscles and just a light dusting of blond hair in the centre of his chest and tapering down to the waistband of his pantaloons.

Pantaloons Lisette now had to remove if she was to inspect and re-dress the wound on his thigh.

Christian inwardly acknowledged he was being less than gracious, let alone gentlemanly, this morning and, sensing Lisette's reluctance when it came to the unfastening of his pantaloons, he deftly released the buttons himself. But there was little he could do to help in regard to removing them; his leg now felt so stiff and sore he could barely move it.

Lisette's slightness of stature, and the height of the bunk bed upon which Christian lay, meant that her breasts were almost on a level with his chest, allowing soft wisps of her silky hair to brush across the bareness of his skin as she bent over the bed and struggled to peel back the pantaloons.

His manhood, in complete rebellion with how debilitated the rest of his body felt, instantly sprang to attention. Noticeably so, as Christian finally lay back weakly against the pillows wearing only his drawers.

That weakness was no doubt being increased because all the available blood seemed to have now gathered in his engorged member!

Had he ever suffered such an embarrassing moment as this before? Not that Christian could recall, no.

'I will go and collect some hot water from the galley.' Lisette was obviously aware of his physical response, her cheeks having flushed a becoming pink as she deliberately kept her gaze above the waistline of his drawers before she turned away and hurried from the cabin.

Christian stared up at the ceiling as he cursed the physical evidence of his arousal and wondered how he could possibly feel desire at a time like this. Admittedly, Lisette looked beautiful this morning, in her gown of pale grey and her face aglow with good health and humour, but that really was no excuse for such an ungentlemanly display of visible arousal. Not that he had any control over the matter, but still…

As a consequence, he was not in the least surprised to see Lisette was accompanied by a young man when she bustled back into his cabin several minutes later.

'Davy is Cook's galley assistant,' Lisette introduced in an offhand manner as she stood aside to put on an apron the cook had also given her, whilst Davy placed the bowl of water down upon the chest of drawers beside the bunk on which the Comte reclined, a sheet now covering his lower body.

She could not quite bring herself to look directly at Christian as she laid down the clean towels and the cloths she had brought with her to use as a dressing, her cheeks having warmed the moment she re-entered the cabin, at the memory of his physical arousal. She had been more than happy to accept Cook's offer of having his young assistant return to the cabin with her.

She was more grateful than ever for Davy's presence, having thrown back that covering sheet—and just as quickly replacing it again—after discovering that Christian had managed to remove his drawers in her absence and was now completely naked beneath that flimsy sheet.

Lisette pressed her lips together to stop herself from gasping out loud. Which in no way helped to eliminate the image now firmly imprinted in the forefront of her brain.

She had been too tired, whilst attending to Christian's wound through the night at his home in Paris, to be overly concerned by the dangerously predatory man himself.

A night of deep, restful sleep and the exhilaration of sailing to England, and Lisette found it far less easy to dismiss the raw masculine beauty of the man—flat and muscled abdomen, lean hips and long elegant legs, with dark blond curls surrounding his still semi-erect member.

The same man who just minutes ago had physically responded so visibly merely to her proximity.

As she now felt her own body responding to him…

Since meeting Christian, and being kissed by him, Lisette now recognised these signs of arousal in her own body for exactly what they were—the warmth in her cheeks, the tightness of her breasts, the tips sensitive and tingling, and the sudden damp heat between her thighs.

She sensed lavender-coloured eyes upon her as she arranged the sheet over Christian in such a way as to save them both further embarrassment, her movements deliberately brisk as she had Davy assist her in removing the soiled bandage. 'The Captain says we have made good time, the tide and winds having been kind to us, and so should be arriving in Portsmouth within the hour,' she remarked conversationally after folding back the bandage and looking at Christian's wound.

It looked raw and uncomfortable, but there did not appear to be any unusual sign of redness or pus, either back or front of that muscled thigh. No doubt Christian's discomfort was mainly caused by the exertions created by his having insisted they set sail last night, rather than remain in Paris to rest his leg and allowing the wound to heal, as she had advised he should.

Not that she was about to rebuke Christian for that

again; he did not appear to be in the sort of mood today to tolerate any such chastisement, from her or anyone else.

Although she very much doubted he would be well enough to continue with their journey on to London by coach once they had reached Portsmouth; just the thought of his being jostled and bounced about inside a coach for hours was enough to make her wince.

'Cook has given me a salve to apply to your wound.' Lisette looked down dubiously into the stone jar before lifting it to her nose and sniffing at the contents. The mixture was a rather unattractive shade of pale brown, and she thought she could also detect the smell of lavender and cinnamon, no doubt in an attempt to override the strong smell of goose fat. 'Perhaps once I have cleansed the wound it would be as well not to tamper with the body's own healing qualities.' She quickly placed the stone jar back on the bedside cabinet before wiping her hands on her apron.

Christian's discomfort had eased since the bandage and soiled dressing had been removed, and he now held back a smile as he saw Lisette's obvious distaste for the cook's salve. 'Perhaps that would be as well,' he conceded drily.

Of course his tension might have been eased simply because he now knew he would be back on English soil within the next hour. In truth, the swaying and pitching of the sloop had almost certainly added to his suffering during the night. Just the thought of being able to depart this infernal swaying boat was enough to lift his spirits somewhat.

Enough so that he grinned at Lisette as she carefully used a pristine white cloth dipped in warm water to clean his wound; if he was not mistaken, it was one of the linen squares no doubt used in the dining room by the officers of the sloop. 'I really must commend your "bedside manner" as being as near perfection as I have ever known, Lisette,' he drawled just for the pleasure of seeing the blush that instantly warmed her cheeks at his deliberate double entendre.

A double entendre he doubted that Davy would understand, considering he and Lisette were talking in French and all the crew aboard the sloop were English. A fact Lisette had not yet remarked upon but which he was sure, with her quickness of mind, she must be well aware of and would no doubt question him on once they were safely on English soil.

'Perhaps you should reserve judgement, Monsieur le Comte, until after you have been attended by a physician and he is certain there is no need to have the leg amputated?' she retorted sweetly.

The little *chat* continued to flex her newly discovered claws, Christian acknowledged appreciatively as he settled back more comfortably against the pillows. 'It is unkind of you to punish me in that way, Lisette, even teasingly.'

She glanced up at him. 'If your wound does not become inflamed and full of pus, then it will not be because of anything you have done to prevent it!'

Ah, the lovely Lisette was still put out because

he had chosen to ignore her words of caution the night before. 'It is not attractive in a woman to bear a grudge, Lisette,' he responded drily.

'And it is not attractive in a man to behave so *tête de cochon*,' she came back pertly.

Christian chuckled softly at hearing himself described as being 'pig-headed'. He preferred to think of himself as determined or strong-willed, but obviously Lisette saw it differently. 'I promise you that once we are back on English soil I will do everything within my power to facilitate my complete recovery.' He placed a hand over his heart as part of that pledge.

'Indeed.' Lisette eyed him mockingly as she finished cleansing his wound, believing in that moment that this man's arrogance alone was enough to prevent the wound from becoming inflamed.

He grinned at her unabashedly. 'I feel better already just knowing I will very soon be stepping off this constantly rocking boat onto terra firma!'

'I doubt you will be "stepping" anywhere with any degree of comfort or balance.' She began to apply the clean bandage. 'As I also doubt that you will be well enough for several more days to continue the journey on to London.'

Christian had already thought of that and, much as it irked him to admit it, he knew that a long journey by coach was not something he could contemplate right now. It would have to be enough, for the moment, that he was back in England. The delay would necessitate that he, and consequently Lisette, must tarry for a day or so in one of Portsmouth's more comfortable inns. An inn Christian had frequented many times before on his illicit travels to and from France, and of a kind only found away from the dockside. But there was no reason, whilst he languished there, that he could not send word to Aubrey Maystone, and the other Dangerous Dukes, of his safe return.

A frown creased his brow at the thought of Maystone's reaction to news of Lisette's presence in England. The last thing he wanted was for the other man to come to Portsmouth and take charge of the situation—of Lisette—whilst Christian was too incapacitated to stop him or defend her. No, perhaps he would wait awhile longer before apprising Maystone of the fact he was now back in England.

'Am I causing you discomfort?' Lisette prompted with concern as she saw the frown on Christian's brow.

'No more than usual,' he drawled as that frown lifted, lavender eyes now glittering with devilment.

The warmth in Lisette's cheeks seemed to have become a permanent fixture, and she glanced at Christian impatiently, knowing he meant to deliberately disarm her. That he was actually enjoying himself now at her expense.

Obviously, he was feeling slightly better, in temper as well as in physical comfort.

'Pity,' she snapped as she tightened and secured the bandage and saw him wince before she stepped away from the bunk bed. 'I will leave Davy to help you dress now, whilst I go to my own cabin and prepare for when we disembark.'

Christian's disappointed gaze followed her as she crossed the cabin before leaving; he was becoming too accustomed, he realised, to like and appreciate too much these scintillating conversations with Lisette.

'Ya ward's a pretty one, me lord.'

That scowl once again creased Christian's brow at Davy's shyly voiced praise for Lisette; indeed, if he was not careful, those lines between his eyes would be there to stay! Brought about, he had no doubt, by the advent of Lisette into his life.

And what was this nonsense of Lisette being his 'ward'?

An assumption by the crew, in view of their separate cabins? Or something that Lisette had told them in an effort to maintain some of the proprieties?

It made a certain sense, if he considered it. His absence and incapacity below decks would have placed Lisette in a vulnerable position aboard the sloop inhabited only by men, and consequently she had perhaps considered it to be the wisest explanation for their travelling to England alone together. It was rather enterprising of her, in fact, and perhaps something Christian should have thought of himself.

Although he could not say he altogether cared for the way it placed him in the position of being a paternal figure to her in the eyes of others. Such as the fresh-faced Davy, now assisting him in dressing. A presentable and handsome young man who was of a similar age to Lisette.

Was Christian feeling the unfamiliar pangs of *jealousy* again?

He did not wish to answer that question.

But one thing he knew for certain—he did not appreciate Davy's obvious admiration for Lisette.

Chapter Seven

'*The Duke of Sutherland?*'

Christian gave a wince at the accusation he could hear in Lisette's voice as she glared at him across the best bedchamber at The Dog and Rabbit Inn in Portsmouth.

He had intended to talk to her, tell her of his title, before they arrived at the inn. But in truth, he had been so discomfited by the time he departed the sloop, having also had to stand by as witness to Lisette bidding a fond farewell to the Captain before they could enter the waiting carriage, each jolt of that vehicle on the way here causing him immeasurable pain, that it had been all he could do to remain conscious.

Unfortunately, the landlord at the inn knew him only as the Duke of Sutherland and had greeted him as such, along with much bowing and scraping, as he accompanied the two of them up to the luxurious suite of rooms where Christian now gratefully reclined upon the bed in the main bedchamber.

He gave a dismissive shrug. 'It is merely another one of my titles.'

'The Duke of Sutherland is not "merely" another anything.' Lisette was now staring at him as if he were a creature come from another planet. 'Dukes are very important men in England, are they not? The elite of the aristocracy?'

Christian grimaced. 'I am not sure that "elite" quite—'

'Do not play games with me, Monsieur le Duc.' Lisette had hardly been able to believe her own ears when she heard the landlord of this fashionable inn address Christian so formally. A duke! She had felt completely out of her depth knowing he was the French aristocrat the Comte de Saint-Cloud, but this—an English duke—was beyond her comprehension.

Perhaps...

Lisette narrowed her eyes. 'You are not at all what you pretend to be, are you...?' It had just occurred to her that an English duke would not have frequented a lowly Parisian tavern such as the Fleur de Lis.

'I do not pretend to be anything, Lisette,' Christian answered her firmly. 'I have every right to use the title of Comte de Saint-Cloud, as well as that of the Duke of Sutherland. I merely prefer, when I am in France and in such places as the Fleur de Lis, not to flaunt the English title.'

It made a certain sense, Lisette conceded reluctantly; the war between France and England might be over, but in some quarters of France it would still be painting a target upon any man's back for him to admit to being English. In a lowly French tavern such as the Fleur de Lis, it could have been lethal.

It might also be, she acknowledged grudgingly, that the Duke of Sutherland would not wish English *société* to know of his visit to such a bawdy establishment.

And yet...

Christian Beaumont—if that was even his true name—had never seemed to her the type of man who would come to the tavern in search of a willing woman to share his bed. Or possibly a man—since arriving at the tavern, Lisette had become aware of such relationships.

This man had drunk his share of wine that first evening, yes, and flirted a little with Brigitte and also with her, but it had not been an overt or predatory flirtation such as she had witnessed in the past of members of the aristocracy in search of a night's bawdy entertainment.

Her mouth thinned. 'You are English, then, rather than French?'

Another grimace. 'I am, yes.'

'Did Helene know this?' Lisette now eyed him speculatively. 'Is that the reason she pressed a pistol to your back that first evening?'

Christian would have much preferred to have had this conversation when he was not feeling at such a physical disadvantage. Although he acknowledged that might not be for some time, and Lisette was certainly entitled to some sort of explanation from him. An explanation he doubted she would take too kindly to.

'I believe the lady to have stated at the time that her reason for doing so was as a warning for me to stay away from you,' he answered mildly.

Lisette's eyes widened before narrowing again. 'You did not answer my question, Monsieur le Duc. Did Helene know who you were that night?'

Christian could have continued to avoid answering the question directly, but he knew by the angry glitter in Lisette's eyes and the same flush of anger in her cheeks that it would not be wise for him to do so. Lisette might bear no physical resemblance to the woman who was her mother, but he now knew she most certainly shared the older woman's fiery temperament. He might just find himself at the receiving end of another pistol if he continued to fob Lisette off with half-truths and lies.

He sighed deeply. 'Following events would appear to indicate that as being the case, yes.'

'Following—? *Mon Dieu*, Helene's reason for sending her attackers against you had nothing to do with the attention you showed towards me,' Lisette gasped in realisation, 'and everything to do with her knowing you are an English *spy*?'

Christian shifted uncomfortably. 'I do not believe I have admitted to being any such thing—'

'You do not need to do so,' Lisette interrupted in disgust as she began to pace the bedchamber restlessly. It all made so much sense to her now.

Helene's warnings that night regarding associating with the Comte de Saint-Cloud.

Helene's desire to have the Comte killed.

The fact that Lisette had found Christian lurking in a doorway across from the tavern later that evening.

He had not been waiting there for her, but spying on Helene and the people who entered the tavern after it had closed for the night.

Just as Helene had not been concerned for her welfare but instead attempting to keep her away from a man she knew to be spying on her and her associates.

It also explained the attempt of Helene's cutthroats to kill *le Duc* in the middle of the street.

And their flight to England the following night.

It all made such sense to Lisette now.

Perfect—and humiliating—sense. She had thought—believed—that he had enjoyed and been as aroused by their kisses as she had, and all the time—

Christian winced as he had difficulty keeping up with—translating—the tirade in French that now followed his admission, Lisette's accusations and insults flowing forth without pause from that highly kissable mouth. Obviously, not all of Lisette's time at the French tavern had been wasted.

English bastard he understood. Followed by such a barrage of other insults and names he had no chance of deciphering one from the other.

Instead, he decided to lie back against the pillows and allow Lisette to give vent to her anger. He might not be able to keep up with those insults, but he did know he deserved everything she might accuse him of being.

Lisette's shock and outrage were also further proof, if he should need it, that she really was everything she appeared to be—a young innocent caught in the middle of a dangerous game she did not know of or comprehend.

Now all Christian had to do was convince Maystone of the same.

All?

Following the abduction and kidnapping of his grandson, even if he was eventually safely returned, Aubrey Maystone was not currently in a forgiving or tolerant mood. It would take more than Christian's opinion on the matter to persuade that gentleman into accepting Lisette's innocence. Especially if the other man should realise Christian's opinion was not impartial where Lisette was concerned.

As he had demonstrated only too clearly these past few days, a man could not hope to hide his physical response to a woman. And Aubrey Maystone was nothing if not astute.

Which meant that Christian—

'Are you even listening to me?' Lisette challenged, becoming even more outraged as she noted his distraction. 'Of course you are not. Why should a *duc* care for the opinion of a woman he knows to be Helene Rousseau's daughter, and no doubt considers to be nothing more than a French *putain*—?'

'You go too far, Lisette!' Christian's voice was

a low and dangerous growl, a warning that all who knew him would most certainly have taken heed of.

But not Lisette. 'I will go as far as I wish, *Your Grace*—' she somehow managed to make the formal title sound every bit as insulting as the word *putain* '—when you obviously misled me from the very first words you ever spoke to me!'

As those 'very first words' had been his false surname and title, Christian could not deny the accusation. 'I am Christian Algernon Augustus Seaton, Fifteenth Duke of Sutherland, as well as numerous other titles, at your service, *mademoiselle*. I trust you will forgive me if I do not get up and present a formal bow?' he added with self-derision for his recumbent and incapacitated figure on the bed.

Lisette's present feelings of humiliation were such that she could forgive this—this *duc* nothing. Helene's treatment of her had been hard enough to bear, but to realise, to now know, that Christian *Seaton* had only been using her to get close to Helene, and in the process play Lisette for the fool, was beyond forgiveness.

She straightened, her spine rigid with the anger she felt. 'No, I do not forgive you, Your Grace. Nor do I intend remaining in your company, or your vicinity, a moment longer—'

'You cannot leave, Lisette—'

'I do not believe you are in any condition to prevent me from doing exactly as I wish!' She eyed him scornfully as he sank back weakly against the pillows after having sat up abruptly, obviously with the intention of standing up, until the pain of the movement became too much for him. 'I am not completely heartless, and will arrange for a doctor to be sent to attend you before I leave, but—'

'The landlord here believes you to be my ward—'

'—be assured, I do not intend— Why would you claim such a thing, now that we are back in England?' Lisette frowned across at him.

Irritation creased Christian Seaton's brow. 'I felt compelled, as you did aboard the sloop,' he added pointedly, 'to give some explanation for our travelling together without benefit of a valet or maid.' He grimaced. 'I felt it best for all concerned, now that we have arrived in England, to continue with that pretence.'

'I do not believe you *felt* anything or gave the matter a moment's consideration, where I am concerned, Monsieur le Duc.' Lisette glared her anger at him. 'You had no thought other than your own need to avert a scandal.' She turned on her heel and marched to the door of the bedchamber. 'I only agreed to accompany you to England because of concern for your injury, but now that you are arrived safely I have no intention of remaining here with you a moment longer—'

'I cannot allow you to leave, Lisette.'

'You cannot *allow*?' She spun back to face him, her cheeks warm with temper and the need to hold back the tears now stinging her eyes; she would not cry in front of this man.

Since the Duprées had died so suddenly, Lisette

had been plunged into a life such as she had never imagined possible. That she now found herself in England, an outcast from her own people and country, and completely at the mercy of the false-faced Christian Seaton's whims and fancies, was beyond enduring.

'I shall go when and where I please, *monsieur*,' she informed him stiffly. 'And neither you nor anyone else shall stop me.'

'You are a woman alone, without funds, and as such you are vulnerable—'

'I am more aware of what that means than you are, I assure you,' Lisette said scornfully. 'But I would rather sell my soul to the devil than be beholden to you for a moment longer!'

A nerve pulsed beside Christian's thinned lips, his jaw clenched as he attempted to maintain a hold on his own temper. 'Believe me, alone in a foreign land and without money, it is not your soul you would have to sell in order to survive.'

Her face paled, even those pouting lips having become a pale rose colour, her eyes dark and haunted. 'I despise you utterly.'

If she had said those words with venom, with any trace of emotion at all, Christian might have known what to say in return. As it was, he could only feel the cut of that emotionless statement from the top of his head to the toe of his boots.

'I do not feel the same way about you, Lisette,' he told her huskily. 'Far from it, in fact,' he added drily for the evidence she had seen just that morning regarding his body's reaction to her.

She eyed him scathingly. 'Then that is your misfortune, *monsieur*, because I most assuredly now despise you.'

Christian could see that emotion burning fiercely in her eyes. And she was only going to hate him more once she met Maystone and knew of Christian's real motivation in bringing her to England with him. 'But you will stay anyway.' It was a statement, not a question.

Lisette drew in a ragged breath. 'And what happens when your "ward" suddenly disappears? When I have returned to France? What lies will you tell about me then?'

The truth was Christian had no idea what the future held for Lisette.

He only knew his own need to protect her as much as he could. And publicly claiming her as his ward now he was back in England was the only way he knew to do that.

'As you are now acknowledged as being my ward, I will be perfectly within my rights to hunt you down and bring you back if you should attempt to run away from me,' he stated evenly.

'You—'

'Just as, as your guardian, I would also be perfectly within my rights to hunt down anyone who attempted to hurt you,' he added softly, understanding now why his close friend Griffin Stone, the Duke of Rotherham, had once felt pressed to claim his now wife as his ward. As he had also discovered, for a single gentleman it was the only way in which to protect an unprotected female who had no one else to care what happened to her.

And Christian did care what happened to Lisette. Very much so.

'—are an arrogant—' Lisette stared at him suspiciously. 'Why should anyone attempt to hurt me? I do not know anyone in England. Or they me.' She looked puzzled.

The time for truth, Christian acknowledged with an inner wince. 'Unfortunately, that is not true of your mother—'

'Helene?' Lisette looked even more mystified. 'As far as I am aware, she does not know anyone here either—' She broke off to look at him searchingly. 'This has something to do with the fact that you were in Paris spying upon her, doesn't it?'

'Did you know your uncle, André Rousseau?'

Lisette stilled. 'I believe I told you that he died before I arrived in Paris...'

'I believe you did too.'

'And?'

Christian Seaton grimaced. 'And I have no way of confirming whether that is the truth.'

Lisette's chin tilted challengingly. 'Unlike you, Your Grace, I do not lie.'

His mouth thinned at the rebuke. 'I did not start out with the intention of lying to you, Lisette.'

'That may be true,' she allowed grudgingly. 'But you are certainly responsible for continuing to do so.'

He grimaced. 'I had no way of knowing if you were to be trusted with the truth.'

Lisette gave what she knew to be a humourless smile. 'You still do not.'

'True,' the Duke conceded. 'But we are on English soil now.'

They were, yes, and, despite Lisette's outward show of bravado, she was more than a little unnerved by being in a strange country where she knew no one. Except the man who had been lying to her from the moment they first met. A man whose reason for being in Paris had been to spy on Helene Rousseau.

'What did you hope to learn by watching Helene?' she prompted cautiously; she knew that the woman who was her mother had been plotting and planning—even if Lisette had no idea of the details of those plots and plans—during those late night and secret meetings in a room above the tavern. But she had no way of knowing how much Christian Seaton knew of those meetings, or indeed Helene herself.

In the circumstances, sadly perhaps more than Lisette knew herself, in regard to the latter.

'How much do you know of her…nocturnal activities?'

Lisette blinked. 'I am uncertain of your meaning,' she came back cautiously.

Christian could not help but smile ruefully at Lisette's guarded response to his question. No, there might not be any physical similarities between Lisette and her mother, but the intelligence was most certainly there.

'Oh, I believe you understand me perfectly.' He nodded. 'That you are well aware your mother is a Parisian who has no affection for her own King.' He paused but Lisette offered no reply. 'Your uncle, André Rousseau, was another. He came to England two years ago under an assumed name, to work as tutor to the son and heir of an English earl. During the year he spent here he set up a network of spies, within the homes of many members of society as well as the English government,' he continued evenly. 'Their ultimate intention was to assassinate the Prince Regent, as well as the other leaders in the coalition, and thus cause chaos within those countries which would allow the newly escaped Bonaparte to march on Paris and resume his place as Emperor of France.'

Lisette was so shocked by what Christian was telling her that her legs felt so weak she now stumbled her way across the bedchamber to drop down onto the chair beside the window before answering him. 'That is incredible.'

'But nevertheless true.'

She swallowed with difficulty, her mouth having suddenly become very dry.

'To achieve their goal they kidnapped the young grandson of a powerful man behind the English government, threatening to kill the boy if that gentleman did not hand over certain information regarding the date and locality of Bonaparte's second incarceration,' the Duke continued remorselessly.

'No...!' Lisette felt her face pale.

'Yes,' he confirmed grimly. 'Luckily, we were

able to rescue the boy in time, without that necessity, and so prevent Bonaparte from escaping a second time.'

'And you believe—you are of the opinion Helene was involved in this plot?' Lisette felt sick at the thought.

Although why she should be she had no idea; Helene had already demonstrated, by not so much as bothering to see or visit her own child once during the first nineteen years of that child's life, that she was not in the least maternal. Nor, apparently, was she afflicted with any softer feelings in regard to a child's life.

'Your uncle, André Rousseau, was instrumental in setting these plans in motion, but I believe that it was your mother, Helene Rousseau, who was responsible for seeing that those plans were carried out after his death.' He nodded tersely.

Lisette moistened the dryness of her lips before speaking. 'I had no idea...'

Christian so much wanted to believe that. He *did* believe that. Convincing Maystone of the same was the stumbling block.

His discomfort now owed nothing to his wounded thigh and everything to do with what he had to say next. 'There are...people in England who will wish to speak with you, Lisette.'

'Me?' She looked shocked at the idea.

He grimaced. 'You are as close to Helene Rousseau as we are likely to get—'

'I am not close to her at all!' Lisette protested. 'I hardly know her.'

'Nevertheless, you are her daughter.'

Lisette took in the full import of Christian's words. 'You are hoping to use me in some way in order to influence Helene's future actions.'

A nerve pulsed in Christian's clenched jaw. '*I* am hoping to protect you; others may wish to do otherwise.'

Lisette no longer knew what to think.

That Helene could be involved in something so monstrous as kidnapping a child was abhorrent to her.

That *she* would be used as a similar weapon against Helene was also obvious.

She gave a shake of her head. 'Helene will not be swayed by any threats that are made towards me.'

Unfortunately, Christian also believed that to be the truth; fanatics such as Helene and her brother André were not people who allowed personal emotions to enter into their bigger plans. Something else he would need to convince Maystone of.

In the meantime, as he had suspected, he had now succeeded in frightening Lisette with the truth. 'I will not allow anyone to hurt you—'

'And how will you stop them?' Lisette rose abruptly to her feet as she looked at him coldly. 'I should have known that your interest was never in me, that I was merely a convenient pawn for you to use in the continued war against Napoleon!'

'That is not true—'

'It is true, and you know that it is!' Tears glistened in those beautiful blue eyes. 'I cannot believe, after I helped to save you from your attackers, and then nursed you through the night and on the voyage to England, that you were all the time being so deceitful!' She turned on her heel and ran to the door.

'Lisette—!' Christian once again attempted to sit up and swing his legs to the side of the bed with the intention of rising to his feet, ignoring the pain as he pushed up unsteadily onto his feet, wanting only to reach Lisette, to prevent her from leaving, to reassure her—

'Well, well, well, and what have we here?' drawled an all too familiar voice.

Christian felt himself toppling and then falling back onto the bed as he looked up and saw his brother-in-law Marcus Wilding, the Duke of Worthing, standing in the doorway with Lisette an unwilling prisoner in his arms.

Chapter Eight

'Can you manage, Christian, or shall I release this beauty in order to assist you?'

Christian glared across the bedchamber at his brother-in-law as he carefully sat up on the bed; Marcus was one of his best friends as well as his brother-in-law, but that did not change the fact that he also had an infuriating knack for the understatement.

'Ah, I see you have decided to manage on your own.' Marcus's green eyes were alight with curiosity. 'Perhaps you would care to make the introductions?' He arched a pointed black brow at the young woman whose wrist he now held securely in order to prevent her from leaving.

Christian's glare turned to a scowl. 'What are you doing here, Marcus?'

The other man looked completely unruffled, by Christian's taciturn tone and Lisette's continued efforts to release herself.

'I am here to see you, of— Ouch!' Marcus looked down in surprise as one of Lisette's tiny booted feet came down painfully on his instep. 'A hellion, by God!' he murmured admiringly.

Christian *would* have warned the other man, in regard to Lisette's temper, if he was not feeling quite so out of sorts with Marcus himself.

Having sent word ahead for his coach to arrive in Portsmouth, he should perhaps have realised that his overprotective sister, and consequently his totally besotted brother-in-law, would keep themselves apprised of his movements.

'Just so,' he confirmed drily as he settled himself more comfortably on the side of the bed. 'Lisette, the man you just assaulted is Marcus Wilding, the Duke of Worthing, and married to my sister Julianna.'

Lisette ceased her struggles instantly to instead look up at the devilishly handsome man holding her prisoner; green eyes were dancing merrily down at her as he met what was no doubt her shocked gaze.

Of course she was surprised at meeting yet another duke; indeed, she seemed to be meeting more than her fair share of them recently.

'And you are...?' this new duke queried pointedly.

'I am—'

'Lisette Duprée, my ward,' Christian Seaton answered the other man challengingly, or so it seemed to Lisette.

And no doubt it was; if this was Christian Seaton's brother-in-law, then he must know that the other man did not have a ward. Or, at the very least, he had not done so the last time the two of them had met.

'My ward,' Christian repeated firmly.

'Your *French* ward?' The Duke of Worthing arched questioning brows.

'As I said.' The other man nodded stiffly.

Lisette now found herself the focus of Marcus Wilding's narrowed gaze as he obviously tried to make sense of Christian's announcement. 'I am—I was—I am travelling to visit my relatives in England, *monsieur*, and His Grace was kind enough to offer to act as my guardian for the duration of the voyage.' A guilty blush coloured her cheeks even as she spoke the lie.

'Really?' Those dark brows arched even higher. 'She speaks no English at all, Christian?' He addressed the other man in that language.

Christian's jaw tightened at the almost accusatory tone he could hear in his brother-in-law's voice. 'I will explain all later, Marcus.'

'I am not the one you will need to explain yourself to,' the other man assured him ruefully.

'Maystone—'

'I was thinking more of Julianna, actually,' Marcus drawled mockingly. 'Although I am sure Maystone will be interested in this…development too.'

Christian frowned at thoughts of both Julianna and Maystone. But the die had been cast now, his claim made, and he had no intention of abandoning Lisette to interrogation by either Maystone or Julianna.

'Care to explain the reason why you're currently… incapacitated?' His brother-in-law indicated his injured thigh.

'Again, not now,' Christian answered tightly.

Amusement darkened Marcus's eyes. 'The hellion did not shoot you, did she?'

Christian's eyes narrowed. 'No.'

'Then perhaps one of her outraged relatives?'

That question was far too close to the truth for Christian's liking. 'Stop enjoying yourself at my expense, Marcus, and tell me—is Julianna well?' He was fully aware this was the easiest way in which to divert Marcus; the other man enjoyed nothing more than talking of the wife he adored.

'Very.' Marcus instantly beamed.

'My sister is *enceinte*, Lisette.' Christian included her in the conversation as she looked at them both curiously.

'Mon félicitations, monsieur,' she offered warmly.

'Merci, madamoiselle. You really must do something about this only speaking French, Christian.' Marcus frowned. 'It will not go down well in some quarters.'

'I intend to do so.' In truth, it seemed that Lisette had already acquired a smattering of English; several of the names she had called him earlier—in heavily accented English—were worthy of a dockside sailor. Which, no doubt, was exactly from whom she had heard them!

'The two of you seemed to be having…some sort of disagreement when I arrived?' Marcus glanced at him questioningly.

'A difference of opinion, that is all,' Christian dismissed.

Marcus's brows rose. 'Sounded a bit more than that to me, old chap.'

'Well, no doubt as a married man you would know more about such differences of opinion than I!' Christian came back tersely.

'Not so, Christian. Julianna and I rarely, if ever, differ in opinion,' the other man dismissed loftily.

'That is because Julianna thinks you are a conceited ass and you know that you are!'

'Something like that.' Marcus grinned unabashedly before sobering. 'You realise Maystone will have to be informed of both your return and your injury.'

'But not immediately.' He would much prefer it if he was not at a disadvantage, caused by his wound, when he spoke with the older man.

Marcus shrugged. 'Not sure how that's going to be possible, Christian. We were not the only ones awaiting word of your return, and the moment he learned you had sent for your carriage, Maystone dispatched me here to meet you and accompany you back to London. He wishes you to report to him immediately as to your findings.'

Christian deeply regretted having sent for his carriage at all, if that was the case. 'That is obviously not possible in my present condition.' He grimaced.

'Obviously.' His friend nodded. 'What do you want me to tell Maystone when I return to London later today?'

Christian felt no surprise at hearing Marcus intended to return to the capital today, with or without him. Previously a profligate rake, Marcus was now totally devoted to Julianna and the baby they were expecting; no doubt he could not bear the thought of being separated from her, even for a single night. It pleased Christian that his sister and his friend had found such happiness together.

At the same time it in no way helped him to find a solution to this present dilemma. 'You could always tell Maystone I have not arrived as yet?'

The other man grimaced. 'In which case, he will have expected me to linger in Portsmouth until you do.'

Damnation.

'Perhaps, Your Grace,' Lisette was the one to put in softly, 'you might tell this gentleman, of whom you both speak so respectfully, the truth? That Christian was injured whilst involved in the work for which the gentleman named Maystone no doubt sent him to Paris?'

Both men turned to look at her in astonishment. Rightly so; it might have been rude of them to do so, but their conversation had all taken place in English.

Lisette steadily returned their shocked gazes. 'I said I did not speak English, Your Grace, not that I did not understand it.'

Hell and damnation!

Christian had been under the misapprehension all this time that Lisette did not understand any conversation spoken in English. To now learn that she had knowledge of the language made him question any and all of those conversations unguardedly spoken in front of her.

Could it be that she *was* indeed a spy for her mother, Helene Rousseau?

Until a few moments ago Christian would have staked his life on that not being the case. The revelation that Lisette understood English, even if she did not speak it, meant he was now less certain. A *lot* less certain. Especially as he and Marcus had not exactly been discreet in their own conversation.

Christian felt sick at the very thought of travelling to London today. But did he really have a choice? Marcus would return to London today regardless, and with Christian unable to move from his bed, Lisette would then be free to roam Portsmouth. With the idea of making contact with one of her mother's cohorts? Christian knew that he could no longer trust his own judgement in regard to Lisette.

He breathed deeply in resignation. 'If you will allow me to rest for a few hours, Marcus, Lisette and I will accompany you back to London later today—'

'I am not going to London—'

'I think that might be for the best, Christian.'

Lisette and the Duke of Worthing spoke at the same time, the one to protest the idea, the other to agree to it.

Lisette gave the Duke of Worthing a disapproving frown before stepping back into the bedchamber to glare at Christian Seaton. 'I do not wish to go to London, and you cannot travel anywhere in your present condition!'

He gave a weary shrug. 'I believe I must.'

'You will undo all of my efforts to prevent your wound from becoming inflamed if you attempt to do so,' Lisette maintained stubbornly as she came to stand beside the bed.

Christian looked up at her ruefully. 'I would have thought such discomfort might please you, considering the names you called me a short time ago?'

Lisette blushed at the memory of some of the names she had called him in temper. Not wholly undeserved, but still…

She raised her chin. 'You have deceived me,' she stated. 'Nor does your duplicity have anything to do with this present conversation.'

'No?'

'No!' she snapped impatiently. 'I have spent the past twenty-four hours ensuring that you have every opportunity to recover from your wound.'

'And, if I am not mistaken, just minutes ago you consigned me to the devil—'

'Much as I am enjoying this exchange,' Marcus Wilding cut in drily, 'I do not see that it is achieving much.'

'Oh, do be quiet, Marcus!'

Lisette continued to glare at the Duke of Worthing. 'Christian—His Grace, received a bullet wound to his thigh only two nights ago. The voyage to England was madness, this—travelling to London today—would be even more so.'

Christian felt Marcus's gaze on him as Lisette spoke. 'You really were shot…?'

He grimaced. 'A trifle—'

'The bullet passed straight through the flesh of your thigh,' Lisette contradicted impatiently.

'Julianna is going to be most displeased.' Marcus gave a wince. 'I assured her you would be in no danger during your visit to France.'

'That was rather reckless of you, Marcus,' Christian Seaton drawled.

The other man shrugged. 'I did not want her to worry in her condition.'

'Even so…'

'When you two gentlemen have quite finished!' Lisette frowned her frustration at them both. 'Thank you,' she bit out when she once again had the attention of both gentlemen. 'You are not going anywhere today,' she informed Christian. 'And neither are you,' she instructed the other man. 'If Christian must go to London, then it will have to be tomorrow, after he has rested today and had a night's sleep, and *you* will have to accompany him. I am sure, for the sake of her brother's health, that your duchess will not mind your absence for one night.'

'Oh, I don't know about that—'

'I should give it up, if I were you, Marcus,' Christian advised as he saw the implacability of Lisette's expression. 'When Mademoiselle Lisette takes on that particular mutinous expression, I have found it is in everyone's interest not to argue with her!'

Marcus's eyebrows shot up into his hairline.

Not surprisingly; Marcus was well aware that Christian's outwardly charming disposition hid a will of steel. It must be something of a surprise to the other man to learn that Christian appeared to have more than met his match in 'Mademoiselle Lisette'.

It had come as something of a surprise to Christian, after his assumption that first evening that she was a shy innocent.

'And while I am "resting and sleeping", what will you be doing…?' He now eyed Lisette guardedly.

'I will be out seeking employment and somewhere to stay whilst I earn the money to pay for my passage back to France,' she informed him pertly.

'Absolutely not.' Christian spoke firmly.

Those blue eyes sparkled with rebellion. 'You are a…' She trailed off, obviously not finding a word that adequately expressed her frustration. 'You do not have the right to tell me what I may or may not do— You find something amusing, Your Grace?' Lisette looked challengingly at Marcus Wilding as he began to chuckle.

This added challenge only seemed to increase the other man's humour rather than quell it, Marcus now consumed with laughter as he placed an arm about his waist before bending over slightly.

Christian allowed his friend his few moments of amusement at his expense, only too well aware of the reason for it; Christian Seaton, the Duke of Sutherland, was a man that few dared cross let alone berate and rebuke. Lisette had just done both.

'Oh, good Lord!' Marcus was wiping tears of laughter from his cheeks when he finally straightened. 'Never thought I would see the day!' He continued to chuckle. 'Wait until the other Dangerous Dukes hear about this.'

'Dangerous Dukes?' Lisette echoed guardedly.

'I will explain another time.' Christian dismissed her question with a pointed frown at Marcus; the six friends, the Dangerous Dukes, had earned that title because of their exploits in the bedchamber as much as their work for the Crown. Lisette already had enough of a bad opinion of him at the moment, without adding to it. 'I suggest, whilst I rest, that Marcus accompanies you down to luncheon. You have to eat, Lisette,' he added cajolingly as she looked set to refuse the suggestion.

It had been several hours since Lisette enjoyed a breakfast of fruit and bread aboard the sloop. Besides, she had no money as yet to be able to buy her own lunch. There was a time for pride and a time for practicality, and her empty stomach decided that luncheon fell into the latter category. 'If Monsieur le Duc is agreeable.' She gave the other man a polite smile.

'As if butter would not melt in her mouth,' Marcus noted admiringly.

'Monsieur?' Lisette looked at him in innocent enquiry.

'Never mind.' The Duke of Worthing ruefully shook his head before turning to Christian, who gave a pained groan as he attempted to once again lie down upon the bed. 'Do you think you will be well enough to travel to London tomorrow?' He frowned his concern. 'Perhaps we should call a doctor—'

'Le Duc has refused to have a doctor attend him.' Lisette shrugged her shoulders.

Christian completed his struggle to lie prone on the bed before answering her. 'Why call for a doctor when I have you to care for me, my dear Lisette?' He gave her a sweetly insincere smile.

Lisette was still angry with him, had no wish to find this man in the least amusing, nor did she wish to smile at his sarcasm, and yet she did not seem able to stop herself. 'I will not be here to attend to you after tomorrow,' she conceded exasperatedly; one more night, spent in the comfort of this inn, would not make too much difference to her ultimate plan to leave the company of Christian Seaton. 'Come, Monsieur le Duc, let us go and eat luncheon together.' She rested her gloved hand in the crook of Marcus Wilding's arm.

Christian scowled as Marcus shot him a mocking glance over his shoulder as he and Lisette departed the bedchamber together in search of the dining room downstairs.

Not that he was in the least troubled by thoughts of Marcus charming Lisette—as the other man had charmed so many other ladies before his marriage to Julianna. No, Christian had no such fears where his friend was concerned, knew of his complete devotion to Julianna; it was the fact that he was giving the matter any thought at all that he found so disturbing.

As he found the idea of Lisette remaining in Portsmouth disturbing.

And equally impossible.

Somehow, in some way, he knew he had to persuade Lisette into accepting that she had no choice but to accompany the two men to London.

When he would have to pass her over to the tender mercies of Aubrey Maystone's interrogation?

Not if he had anything to say about it!

And he would...

'Perhaps if you were to sit here beside me it would help to prevent my being jostled about so much...?' Christian looked persuasively across the carriage at Lisette.

She made no reply as she coldly returned that look; the two of them had not so much as spoken a word to each other since Christian's carriage departed Portsmouth earlier that morning.

Christian had tried the previous evening, in every way he could, to persuade Lisette that going to London with them, talking to Maystone herself, convincing that gentleman of her innocence, was by far the best course of action.

Marcus, apparently tired of the arguments, had decided to take the matter into his own hands this morning—no doubt feeling disgruntled after a night spent away from Julianna and their bed—and simply picked Lisette up in his arms and deposited her in Christian's coach, before instructing the groom to drive on.

Not an auspicious beginning to their journey!

Not that Marcus was the one who had to bear the

brunt of Lisette's stony silence, that gentleman having chosen to ride ahead on his horse.

Lisette had not been silent either initially, of course, as she had once again reviled Christian with a list of insults that would have made a fishwife blush. After which she had fallen into this icy silence that was, quite frankly, causing Christian far more discomfort than his thigh.

Indeed, his thigh felt a little easier today, after the long rest yesterday and a night's sleep, and he had even managed to dress himself this morning, with Marcus's help, and eat a little of the breakfast brought up to his bedchamber.

Food that seemed to have settled uncomfortably in his stomach as the icy silence continued between himself and Lisette. 'I am not the one who picked you up and placed you—'

'Only because you are not yet well enough!' Her eyes flashed with anger. 'If you had been, I have no doubt you would have manhandled me as uncivilly as did Le Duc de Worthing.'

Christian gave a wince. 'Please come and sit beside me, Lisette.'

'Why?'

Because Christian badly needed to hold her in his arms. In truth, he had thought of doing little else since she had retired early to her own bedchamber the previous evening. No doubt with the intention of plotting and planning a way in which she might leave the inn and so avoid being made to accompany him and Marcus to London today.

When he had voiced that concern to Marcus, the other man had assured him that he had placed one of the inn's servants outside the door of Lisette's bedchamber to prevent such an occurrence.

'Please, Lisette.' Christian now patted the upholstered seat beside him. 'Or I shall be forced to come to you,' he added softly; after all, there was only so much space for Lisette to retreat inside his ducal carriage.

'You will do no such thing!' Lisette frowned at him. 'I may not like you or your friend very much at the moment, but neither do I wish you any further harm,' she acknowledged begrudgingly, having spent many wakeful hours of the night considering her position.

There was no doubting that Helene was indeed up to something nefarious during those late night clandestine meetings with her cohorts. Nor could Lisette change the fact that she was the other woman's daughter.

Consequently Christian could not know with any certainty that Lisette was not in cahoots with the older woman and had only accompanied him to England in order to gain information to further her mother's plot to undermine the English government and monarchy.

Which was not to say that Lisette in any way forgave Christian for deceiving her, only that she now understood it, in part.

Unfortunately for Christian, it was not the part of her that had been so attracted to this *Duc Dangereuse*.

Oh, yes, Lisette understood that sobriquet too

now, having charmed Marcus Wilding into confiding in her when they dined together the previous evening.

Nor was she as self-confident and self-contained as she wished to appear in front of Christian. She felt completely vulnerable in this strange country amongst people she did not know. She also feared what was going to happen to her when she arrived in London.

She set her lips firmly in an effort to stop them from trembling. 'What are your plans for me once we reach London, Monsieur le Duc? Am I to be locked up in chains until I reveal all to this man Maystone?' Considering she knew absolutely nothing about Helene Rousseau's plotting and planning, and so had nothing to reveal, that might possibly be for some considerable time.

'I did not—I will not allow anyone to "lock you up in chains", Lisette!' Christian huffed his impatience.

She gave a shrug of her shoulders. 'M'lord Maystone may have other ideas.'

Christian frowned his frustration for several moments, able to see the vulnerability in Lisette's eyes that she obviously thought to hide from him with the lashing of her tongue. Just as he recognised the stubborn set of her mouth for what it was—a determination on her part not to reveal that vulnerability.

He gave up any idea of having Lisette come to him and instead made the move to join her on the other side of the carriage. Movement, along with the jolting of the carriage, that caused him considerable pain but which he chose to ignore. He was more interested in Lisette's welfare than he was his own; he knew everything that had been revealed to her since they arrived in England must be more than a little frightening for her. Completely in character for the young woman he had come to know, she did not wish anyone to see that fear. Least of all, him.

Her eyes widened in alarm as she obviously guessed his intention. 'You must not—'

'I already am, my dear Lisette,' Christian assured her as he sank down gratefully onto the seat beside her before turning to take her in his arms. 'The "mountain" will happily come to you if you will not come to it,' he murmured ruefully. 'Lisette, *please*,' he cajoled as she struggled in his arms.

Lisette had no strength to remain immune to the plea in Christian's voice, her shoulders dropping their defensive stiffness as she stopped fighting him and instead sank down against him, her head resting on his shoulder and so allowing her to hear the steady beat of his heart. 'I have done nothing wrong, Christian,' she said huskily.

His arms tightened about her. 'I know.'

'Do you?' She looked up at him.

'Yes.'

'How do you know?'

He gave a regretful grimace. 'By the fact that you really did not wish to travel to England with me, but came only for my comfort. By the fact that you most certainly did not wish to travel to London today.'

'That is true.' Lisette eyed him guardedly. 'But you did not seem to think that yesterday.'

'I have had a great deal of time to think since yesterday.' He sighed. 'Lisette, could we perhaps make ourselves more comfortable?'

'More comfortable?' she echoed doubtfully; she was already seated beside him and held in his arms; how much more 'comfortable' could they get inside a moving carriage?

'If I sit back this way, thus.' Christian moved so that his back was against the side of the coach rather than the back of the seat. 'Then I am able to do this, thus.' He manoeuvred his injured leg so that it lay along the length of the seat. 'And you can now sit, thus.' He turned Lisette so that she now sat along the length of the seat between his legs, her back resting against his chest, her feet on the seat and her knees drawn up, his arms about her waist.

A position Lisette was not at all sure to be proper, with so much of their bodies now in such close contact, particularly her bottom nestled back against the intimate vee between Christian's thighs.

She moistened her lips nervously. 'Christian...?'

'Are you about to deny me this simple pleasure, Lisette?' His voice was husky and extremely close to her ear.

Lisette was only too well aware that she was incapable of denying this man anything. It was part of the reason she had been so defensive on the journey from France to England, and for the time they had spent at the inn together. The same reason she had been so against accompanying him to London today.

Christian Seaton was not only the most handsome man she had ever seen, but also a duke, and a man whose service was valued by the English Crown.

A man far and above her own lowly station in life—the bastard daughter of a woman who owned and ran a French tavern. The same woman Christian knew to be plotting against his own Prince Regent, and who might be—no, in all probability was!— connected to the kidnapping of this man Maystone's young grandson.

The two of them sitting together so cosily in this carriage was ludicrous in those circumstances.

And yet...

Lisette was no longer an innocent when it came to a man's body, and she could now feel the undeniable hardness of Christian's lengthy arousal pressing against her.

His arms about her waist held her tightly back against him, and his hands were resting dangerously close beneath the fullness of her breasts.

She moistened her lips. 'Christian, I do not think—'

'I do not want you to think, Lisette,' he groaned, his cheek now resting atop her head.

'But—'

'Shh,' he encouraged. 'We have been at odds with each other these past few days; let us now just sit here quietly and enjoy each other's company in silence.'

Lisette had no doubt that the now familiar tingling of her breasts and the almost uncomfortable warmth between her thighs was in direct response to Christian's close proximity. The hard arousal now pressing so insistently against the softness of her bottom was demonstration of Christian's response to that closeness.

Just as she had no doubt that it was not each other's 'company' they now wished to enjoy.

Chapter Nine

Christian gave a sigh of contentment as he held Lisette in his arms once again and breathed in the familiar perfume of the softness of her hair, a heady mixture of lemon and the light scent of flowers. A perfume he had missed these past two days. As he had missed holding the sweet curves of her body pressed against his own.

Marcus had warned of it being a dangerous attraction yesterday evening, as the two men talked quietly and enjoyed a brandy together before retiring for the night.

Dangerous, and as undeniable to Christian as his next breath.

'What are you doing...?'

Christian laughed huskily. 'I do believe I am placing my hands upon your breasts.' His hands now cupped beneath that delicious fullness, allowing him to feel the hardened nipples pressing against his palms. Evidence that, no matter what she might now say to the contrary, Lisette enjoyed having her breasts held and fondled as much as he enjoyed holding them.

'The windows, Christian,' she protested half-heartedly. 'Anyone might ride by and see—and see what we are doing.'

Christian felt heartened by the 'we' in that statement. 'Pull down the blinds if it bothers you,' he encouraged softly as his lips now tasted the creaminess of her throat.

'Of course it bothers me—'

'Why?'

'I am not an exhibit for people to gawk at!'

'Then pull the damned blinds!'

'You are not well enough for such exertion.'

'Certain parts of my body appear to have other ideas.' He gave another husky chuckle. 'Does anything else about my intentions bother you?'

'I— Well—it is full daylight outside—'

'Pull down the blinds and it will not seem to be.'

'We really cannot, Christian.'

Christian could hear the lack of conviction in her breathy voice. 'Do it, Lisette, and you will see how easily we *can*,' he prompted more insistently, filled with an urgency to do more than fondle those full and tempting breasts.

He must indeed be feeling better.

These past few days had been a torment to him. Not because of his injury but because he had disliked intensely the distance that now lay between Lisette and himself, both emotionally and physically.

Here and now he wanted to dispense with that distance, to bare Lisette's breasts completely, pull on those roused nipples until they were as red as ripe strawberries, before taking them into his mouth and suckling. Deep and hard.

He smiled his satisfaction as Lisette moved up onto her knees on the seat to pull down first one blind and then another. 'If Monsieur le Duc should return—'

'Then he will know by the lowered blinds not to intrude,' Christian assured her softly.

She turned to look at him, eyes glittering in the now semi-darkness of the coach. 'Is that how you usually signal to each other that you are...engaged in such pursuits?'

'Hardly, when Marcus is married to my sister!' Christian drawled.

'I was referring to before he married your sister—'

'I believe you are deliberately trying to annoy me, Lisette.' Christian looked at her sternly. 'But, just so that we are clear on the subject, I do not make love to women in coaches. Ever. Does that satisfy your outraged sensibilities?'

She raised her brows. 'You have made love to me in a coach.'

'I will be putting you over my knee and spanking your bottom in a coach if you continue with this delaying tactic!' How could one tiny woman incite such desire within him and yet annoy him equally at the same time?

'Tactics are your forte, Christian.' Lisette pulled down the last of the blinds before once again turn-

ing to face him, chin lifted challengingly. 'And if
you even attempt to spank my bottom, I will tell the
Duke of Worthing and your sister, if I should meet
her, what a brute you are!'

Christian gave an unconcerned grin.

He arched one blond brow. 'Unless I am mistaken,
you now sound more curious at the prospect than distressed, Lisette...?'

She was. There was no denying it.

Having a man—Christian—spank her bottom
sounded barbaric, and yet—

And yet...

If that was so, then why had the warm flush increased between her thighs and those already tingling buds that tipped her breasts become so hard
and aching?

Unfortunately, her knowledge of physical pleasure
was limited to these occasions with Christian, and
so she could not answer that question.

She looked up at Christian through her lashes.
'Would you lift up my gown and remove my...my
undergarments first, or spank me through my clothing?'

Just when Christian thought he might, for once,
have the upper hand in a conversation with Lisette,
she very neatly turned the tables on him in that totally disarming manner she had. 'Which do you
think you would prefer?'

She appeared to give the matter some thought,
arousing Christian even further. 'I do not believe
such punishment would be as effective if adminis-

tered through one's clothing. Do you?' she finally answered curiously.

Christian's lengthening manhood was now taking more than a passing interest in their conversation. 'Probably not,' he acknowledged gruffly. 'Perhaps we might carry out a little experiment on the matter…?'

Her eyes widened. 'Now?'

Unless he was mistaken, there was now an edge of anticipation in Lisette's tone. 'If that is what you would like?' He eyed her curiously.

He knew that some whores and courtesans enjoyed having their bottom spanked, as some gentlemen paid to administer such treatment. Behaviour which would no doubt have shocked their wives.

'Christian…?'

Lisette's eyes glowed a feverish blue in the semi-darkness of the carriage. With excitement? At the thought of Christian laying a hand on her bare bottom?

It was an intriguing and arousing thought.

'I believe I should enjoy…fondling your bare bottom rather than spanking it,' he ventured cautiously. He did not wish to misunderstand the situation; he knew better than most how heated Lisette's temper might be if he should proceed with a course of action she did not wish for.

His suggestion was answered with a slight lessening of that feverish glow in Lisette's eyes, but no less curiosity. 'Is that something that all men enjoy?'

The thought of any other man, singular or otherwise, touching any part of Lisette in pleasure or otherwise, was enough to cause Christian to want to forget the fondling and go straight to the spanking.

Besides which, he had no answer to her question; his own dealings with women these past fifteen years, in society or out of it, had been straightforward bed sport, enjoyable and satisfying, if not particularly memorable. Although he could not deny he had been tempted to put Lisette over his knee more than once for the rashness of her actions.

But surely it was the thin end of the wedge to indulge in such practices in bed?

You are not in a bed but a carriage, a little voice reminded inside his head.

Having started this conversation, was he not now duty-bound—?

Duty-bound be damned; having talked of the possibility, Christian now wanted Lisette over his knee, skirts thrown up, bottom bared, and once he had achieved that he could then decide what was best for the lady's pleasure as well as his own.

'Turn around so that I might unfasten and remove your gown.'

Lisette felt a delicious tremor of fear curl down the length of her spine as she heard the deep intensity of Christian's voice. At the same time she knew she had taken this conversation much further than she had intended.

At least she did not *think* she had intended it to go this far.

She had begun the conversation with the idea of

shocking, only to have that audacity immediately turned back on her.

Her actions since first meeting Christian Seaton had not been at all how she would normally behave. He seemed to bring some devilment out of her which, once released, she did not seem to be able to take back under her control.

Added to which, Christian did not appear to be either surprised or shocked by her conversation. Indeed, that glitter of interest in his eyes seemed to be the same excitement as Lisette was now feeling.

She ran the moistness of her tongue across the sensitivity of her lips. 'I meant our conversation to be in the abstract only, Your Grace.'

'Liar.'

She was a liar, Lisette acknowledged slightly breathlessly. What had been intended to shock had now become completely, intimately personal.

She gave a shake of her head. 'I do not think I should like being spanked after all, Your Grace.'

He gave a hard smile. 'And perhaps that is the very reason that you need to be?'

She eyed him warily. 'I do not understand.'

'Turn around.'

'I—'

'I said turn around, Lisette.'

She swallowed at the implacability of his tone. 'I believe this was not such a good idea—'

'I am afraid you are a little too late in making that decision.'

Her heart fluttered in her chest. 'Too late…?'

'Turn,' he instructed again harshly.

At some time in their conversation, Lisette realised, she had ceased being the antagonist and instead had become the hunted. And in a confined space such as this carriage, she had nowhere to run or hide.

Except, perhaps, behind her earlier anger and indignation?

'Do not even attempt it, Lisette,' the Duke growled in warning. 'I was quite prepared to pass the time pleasantly on this journey to London, but instead I was first subjected to another of your lengthy and wholly undeserved rebukes, when it was Marcus who lifted you and put you in the carriage, not I. That was followed by another of your icy silences. I now believe you have traversed along a path from which there is no turning back.'

As Lisette had feared might be the case. 'I am overly impetuous sometimes, Your Grace—'

'It would seem that you are overly impetuous all the time, Lisette,' he corrected impatiently. 'A habit that needs to be curbed if we are to progress together.'

Lisette had no idea what *that* meant; there could not be much further to go on this journey to London, after which she was to be handed over to this man Maystone. She had no idea what was to become of her after that.

'Turn around, Lisette!'

She tensed at Christian's increasingly uncompromising tone, realising that she had pushed him too far with her taunting and curiosity, that there really was no 'turning back'.

She quickly turned her back towards him. 'You will not hurt me, Christian…?' she ventured nervously as she felt those deft fingers unfastening the tiny buttons at the back of her gown.

'I have not decided as yet,' he answered her gruffly.

Lisette did not move as the unfastened bodice of her gown slid down her arms before falling about her knees as she still knelt on the seat between his parted thighs, leaving her dressed only in her chemise, drawers, stockings and slippers.

'Now turn and face me.'

Lisette felt like a marionette as she slowly turned, face blazing with heat as Christian openly enjoyed staring at her breasts, the pleasurably hard pebbles of her nipples no doubt visible through the thin material of her chemise.

She wrapped her arms about her protectively. 'I am cold—'

'You are aroused,' Christian corrected huskily, 'which is not the same thing at all. Lower your arms, Lisette.'

She wanted to deny him, to berate him with her ready temper, but something in his eyes, a dark and unrelenting intensity, prevented her from doing so as she slowly, oh-so-slowly, lowered her arms instead.

'Now slip the straps of your chemise off your shoulders.'

Lisette gasped, even as she felt her breasts swell and tingle in response to the instruction. 'This can-

not be at all correct, Christian— What is so funny?'
she demanded as he chuckled throatily.

He gave a shake of his head. 'I do not believe you
have done one "correct" thing since I first met you!
Seeking me out in the darkness and coming back to
my home with me. Running out into the street in the
middle of the night, without hat or cloak, when you
heard guns being fired.' His voice had hardened per-
ceptibly. 'Driving my carriage as if you were born
to it. Tending to not only my own wound but also
Pierre's. Sailing on a boat back to England with me
completely unchaperoned. Spending a night at an inn
with me under the same circumstances. And now
travelling in a coach alone with me—'

'That is most unfair!' Lisette protested. 'The circumstances under which we have so far been acquainted have not been conducive to—'

'I am known for my patience, Lisette—indeed, I
believe I am praised far and wide for it,' Christian
snapped impatiently. '*You*, however, have the ability
to make me forget how to be patient, let alone behave
the gentleman!' With this last comment he reached
out to grasp the flimsy material of the neckline of
her chemise and with one sharp pull ripped it from
top to bottom.

'*Christian!*' Lisette's shocked gasp was accompanied by her raising her hands and placing them over
her completely exposed breasts.

For once in their acquaintance Lisette was at
a loss for words. Whether as the Comte de Saint-

Cloud, the Duke of Sutherland or simply Christian, she did not appear to have any defences against this man.

'I can smell your arousal, Lisette,' he told her softly. 'Yes,' he insisted as she gasped in protest. 'Peaches, or perhaps apricots, mixed with a musky wholly feminine smell.'

'You would know of such things better than I!' she accused in an attempt to regain some of her lost dignity.

'Your insults do not bother me, Lisette,' Christian dismissed derisively. 'Not when I know they are made with the intention of annoying and distracting me.'

That *had* indeed been Lisette's intention. But this arrogant duke was obviously not going to allow himself to be distracted.

'Remove your hands, Lisette,' Christian bit out between his clenched teeth; he could not decide which was throbbing the most—his injured thigh because of these physical exertions, or the hardness of him. He did know that the heady smell of Lisette's arousal was causing him to fast lose all sense of control, let alone his usual veneer of civility. 'Now, Lisette!'

Her back straightened, her chin rising defensively. 'I am not a servant or a horse you may instruct to your will, Your Grace.'

'No—you are about to become my lover, which requires even more instruction from me, it seems!' Christian growled. 'And do not "Your Grace" me,

Lisette, when you obviously have little or no respect for the title.'

A frown creased her brow. 'It is not my intention to be disrespectful.'

Christian sighed. 'It is not my intention to behave with disrespect towards you either. I am simply a man pushed beyond his limits.'

She eyed him warily even as her hands slowly lowered back down to her sides.

Christian's eyes had now completely adjusted to the dim light of the carriage, allowing him to see the soft fullness of Lisette's naked breasts, tipped with fully engorged and pouting nipples, her waist incredibly slender before curving out to luscious hips. She wore white stockings held up by pretty white garters decorated with rosebuds the same deep fuchsia colour as her nipples.

'What do you *instruct* now, Christian?' She held herself proudly, shoulders back, breasts thrust forward.

He should never have started this, should not have allowed Lisette to challenge him so much that it was now almost too late for him to pull back from the brink— Damn it; it was too late! 'Help me to undress,' he encouraged huskily as he reached up and deftly removed the neck cloth from about his throat before unfastening his shirt.

Her throat moved as she swallowed. 'You intend to completely compromise me?'

He gave a hard, humourless grin. 'If that bothers

you then we can always say that it was you who compromised me.'

'We will not need to say anything at all if you stop
insisting upon this—this—'

'Lovemaking,' he supplied evenly.

'Lovemaking takes place between two people
when they are married.'

'To each other?'

Another tirade of French insults—ones that Christian decided were best not translated—followed this
remark.

'If not married, then at least in love with each
other,' Lisette finally added primly.

Christian looked up at her through narrowed lids.
'How do you feel when I touch you here?' He reached
out to push her ripped chemise completely aside before stroking his fingertips across the turgid tip of
her breast, nodding his satisfaction as Lisette drew
her breath in sharply, her back arching instinctively
into that caress. 'Or do this?' He took her now fully
erect nipple between his thumb and finger and gently
squeezed, the scent of Lisette's arousal now so strong
in the heaviness of the air Christian could almost
taste it.

He *intended* to taste it before they reached London.

'I— That is—' Lisette now moved restlessly at
the unfamiliar sensations coursing through her body.
Unfamiliar before she had met Christian, that was.

No matter how angry she became with him, how
uncertain she was about her future, this man only

had to touch her with intimacy to arouse her. Sometimes he did not need to even touch her!

'Pleasurable,' Christian purred as he now cupped both her breasts in his hands.

'Yes…'

'Sensual.' The soft pads of his thumbs stroked across the swollen tips.

'Oh, yes…'

'Arousing.' He now pinched both those ripe berries between his thumbs and fingers.

'*Dieu*, yes!'

Christian proceeded to stroke and pinch, again and again, encouraged by Lisette's rapidly increasing breathing and the way she could not help but arch into those pleasurable caresses.

'Oh…!' she gasped within minutes. 'Do not stop. Oh, please do not, Christian…!' She pressed even harder into those caresses.

'I have no intention of doing so.' Christian frowned in concentration as he gauged exactly what gave her the greatest pleasure, determined to bring her to full pleasure before progressing any further.

The lightest of strokes. A caress. A gentle pinch. A squeeze, just so.

He had always been a considerate lover, he hoped, but it had never mattered quite so much to him before that the woman he was with attained the greatest pleasure from their lovemaking. He wanted Lisette to enjoy, to savour everything they did together, in the same way that he now was.

Lisette was beyond speech, beyond anything but

the mindless pleasure flooding through her body, her breasts heavy and aching as Christian continued to stroke and squeeze. Between her thighs—*mon Dieu*, the swelling pleasurable sensation between her thighs was beyond anything she had ever experienced before.

'Let go, Lisette,' Christian encouraged fiercely, his face flushed, hair dishevelled.

'I do not under— Ooooh!' Something had burst free inside her, a huge explosion of such a myriad of pleasures, that overwhelming pulsing centred between her thighs, her core now contracting and releasing, throbbing as those waves of pleasure crashed over her again and again. 'Christian…!' she finally sobbed as she collapsed weakly forward against his chest.

Christian gathered Lisette into his arms, holding her close as he ran soothing hands up and down the length of her spine, allowing her to ride out the storm as she continued to softly gasp and sob in the aftershocks of her climax.

He felt such a swelling of emotions in his own chest as he continued to hold her, too many to be able to discern one from the other with any degree of certainty, but he knew he felt an increased tenderness, protectiveness towards the young woman he had just pleasured and now held in his arms. It was—

A sharp rap of knuckles sounded on one of the coach windows. 'We are almost arrived at Sutherland House, Christian.' Marcus's voice was slightly muffled through the glass but the words were discernible nonetheless.

Christian barely had time to absorb those words, to register the sounds of the city outside—street vendors shouting their wares, the sounds of other carriages and horses traversing the cobbled streets, the ringing of church bells to the hour of twelve—sounds he had been totally unaware of until now, as he focused all of his attention on pleasuring Lisette.

Lisette pushed against his chest and sat up abruptly, eyes dark. Her cheeks were also flushed, her bared breasts full and the nipples red and swollen from Christian's ministrations.

She quickly grasped the two sides of her ripped chemise to cover those breasts as she glared at him accusingly.

'Do not,' Christian advised wearily as she opened those delectable lips to deliver what, he had no doubt, would be another sound tongue-lashing for the liberties he had just taken with her person.

Much as it might be deserved, it was not at all the tongue-lashing he now ached for.

And so much for *tasting* Lisette.

For having her taste him.

Christian had not realised how close to London they were when they began their lovemaking—it seemed he barely knew what time of day it was when he was with Lisette!—and he was now left feeling even more physically frustrated and out of sorts than he had been when they began.

A discomfort he would now have to deal with

himself once he reached the privacy of his bedchamber at Sutherland House.

Speaking of which…

'You will need to dress, Lisette, if we are to arrive shortly—'

'How would you suggest I do that when my chemise is now ruined?' she came back agitatedly even as she moved along the seat before standing up, her crushed gown instantly falling to the carriage floor. 'Look at me!' She wailed her distress.

Christian *was* looking.

He could not seem to do anything else but look as Lisette bent over slightly beneath the roof of the carriage, her hair in complete disarray, face flushed and wearing only the tatters of her ripped chemise, her drawers and those white stockings held up by the pretty garters.

She had the appearance of a sensual woman who had been well and truly seduced.

Which she was and had.

Never in Christian's experience had he ever known a woman to attain her physical release just from having her breasts played with.

'Christian!'

He blinked, shaking his head to clear it of such thoughts, as he raised his gaze from those responsive breasts to look at Lisette's face.

A face that bore an expression of dismay now, rather than her previous satiation, followed by agitation. 'Best to remove the chemise completely and I will dispose of it later,' he instructed economically.

'Then put your gown back on, your cloak over the top of it, and no one will be able to tell that you are not wearing your undergarment.'

'Until I remove the cloak,' she pointed out irritably even as she did as he suggested and impatiently removed the chemise.

A move that played havoc with Christian's unsatisfied arousal as he gazed his fill of slender shoulders, those completely bared breasts, her curvaceous waist and hips. 'Then do not remove your cloak until after you have reached the privacy of your bedchamber,' he answered her distractedly, the throb of his manhood painful still in its intensity.

'My bedchamber?' Lisette stilled, seemingly unconcerned with her near nakedness.

Would that Christian felt the same disinterest!

He nodded tersely. 'You will be staying with me at Sutherland House until…until I have opportunity to speak with Lord Maystone.'

'After which I am no doubt to be held a prisoner in the Tower of London, where all traitors to England are incarcerated.' Lisette's stubborn little chin rose. 'Whether they be innocent, as I am, or guilty,' she added disgustedly even as she pulled her gown into place to cover her nakedness.

'How you do love the dramatic, Lisette.' Christian snapped his impatience with the trait as he sat up and gingerly swung his legs to the floor of the carriage, paying special attention to his injured thigh. 'No one is going to lock you up in a tower, now or in the future.'

Lisette looked at him anxiously. 'You promise?'

Christian's expression softened as he saw the fear had returned to her eyes. 'I promise.'

Although he was not quite so confident about being able to keep that promise when the first person he saw as he stepped down from his carriage with Marcus's help was Lord Aubrey Maystone...

Chapter Ten

What the devil—?

'My fault, I am afraid,' Marcus muttered after glancing at the older man coming down the steps towards them. 'I sent word ahead of the delay because of your having been shot, and to expect our arrival today. I also informed Maystone that you had not returned from France alone,' he added at Christian's scowl. 'I did not tell him that Lisette was Helene Rousseau's daughter—'

'I suppose I should be grateful for small mercies.' Christian continued to scowl his displeasure.

'I did so before I came to know Lisette for the charming girl she is,' he said defensively as Christian gave him a censorious frown.

'She is not a girl but a woman.'

'So it would seem.' Marcus gave a pointed glance towards the carriage. 'You obviously found her to be so on the journey here.'

'Marcus…' he growled in warning.

The other man shrugged. 'None of my business

how and with whom you choose to pass the time of day, old chap.'

'I am pleased to hear it.' Christian turned to assist Lisette down from the carriage. 'Do not be alarmed,' he assured her gently as her panicked gaze moved past him to the rapidly approaching Aubrey Maystone. 'All will be well, Lisette.' He kept a firm hold of her arm, just in case she should be tempted to turn on her booted feet and run.

He would not put it past her to attempt such a move; Lisette had shown these past few days that she could be an enterprising young lady when the situation warranted it. And, damn it, her present apprehension in regard to Aubrey Maystone showed all the signs of becoming such a situation.

Maystone was usually the most charming of men, shrewd to a fault, admittedly, but invariably polite to the ladies. Unfortunately, this business with his grandson had turned even that amiable gentleman into a man intent on vengeance against the person or persons responsible for ordering the kidnapping. The three people now held in custody had only been instrumental in carrying out those orders; they had not instigated them.

Christian was certain that he now held the daughter of the person guilty of that crime close to his side. So close that he could feel the slight trembling of Lisette's body as she pressed against him, as if for protection.

His mouth tightened determinedly as he turned to greet the older man. 'Maystone.'

'Sutherland.' The other man nodded distract-edly, his piercing gaze fixed on Lisette. 'Perhaps you would care to explain…?'

'I will make the introductions once we are in-side.' Christian spared no time in waiting to see if the other two gentlemen agreed or disagreed with his suggestion as he stepped towards the house and took Lisette with him.

Whilst he had every reason to trust the members of his own household, he had no intention of engag-ing in any sort of conversation in a public street.

'He looks a very fierce gentleman,' Lisette com-mented softly after giving an anxious glance back at the two men following close behind them.

'He has…been under a great deal of strain these past few weeks,' Christian excused.

'How old is his grandson?'

'Just eight.'

'Mon Dieu,' she breathed softly. 'If Helene is guilty of ordering his kidnapping—'

'I believe that she is, yes,' Christian confirmed grimly.

She sighed heavily. 'Then once Lord Maystone knows the truth, he cannot help but feel it only just that Helene's child should be made to pay for her crimes. The "sins of the father" or, in this case, mother,' she added with a grimace.

'You cannot believe that any more than I,' Chris-tian rebuked her.

She gave another of those Gallic shrugs. 'It is how I would feel if I were Lord Maystone.'

'Then I suggest you keep that opinion to your-self,' Christian came back with soft impatience as he turned to greet his butler. 'Miss Duprée would prefer to keep her cloak on for the moment, Evans,' he informed the elderly man as he reached to take the garment from her.

Lisette smiled her apology at the elderly butler even as her cheeks coloured a becoming pink.

No doubt at the memory of why she needed to continue to wear that cloak.

In truth, Christian felt slightly ashamed of his be-haviour towards her in his carriage. He was a man usually in complete control, of himself as well as others, but where Lisette was concerned, it seemed he constantly lost every shred of that control.

And he defied anyone, least of all himself, to at-tempt to put any control on the stubbornly deter-mined young lady he now knew Lisette to be...

'Refreshments in the library, if you please, Evans,' Christian instructed as he continued to limp his way into and through the cavernous entrance hall of his London residence.

Christian had chosen the library in which to talk, for two reasons.

Firstly, Lisette had found his house in France overwhelming and Sutherland House was even more so. The library was one of the less imposing rooms in the house, and the place where Christian usually spent his evenings at home relaxing by the fire, read-ing a book or dealing with correspondence.

His second reason—the library *was* his place of

business, and he preferred any conversation with Aubrey Maystone to be completely that.

Despite Lisette's earlier observation, Christian believed the older man looked less strained than he had before Christian left for France. No doubt because he had now had the chance to enjoy the safe return and company of his only grandson, even if that abduction still played heavily on his mind.

Now all Christian had to do, once he had revealed Lisette's true identity, was to convince Maystone that she had no knowledge of or involvement in that kidnapping!

The first he would do carefully, so as not to cause a reaction that would frighten Lisette any more. After which he would explain how Lisette had not even known Helene Rousseau was her mother until just a few short months ago.

Lisette waited only long enough for the butler to leave the room and close the door behind him before crossing to where Lord Maystone stood in front of the window looking out into the garden at the back of the house.

She drew in a deep breath, determined to have her say and not allow herself to be overwhelmed by this imposing house and its liveried servants. Or the three gentlemen with whom she shared the room. Although that was a little harder to do when two of them were dukes and the third a lord.

Lisette straightened her shoulders determinedly. 'I cannot tell you how sorry I am for all that you have endured, m'lord.' That gentleman's eyes widened in obvious surprise, no doubt because she spoke to him in French as she reached out and took both of his hands in her own. 'Your grandson has not suffered any lasting effects from his ordeal, I hope?' she prompted anxiously.

'Good Lord, Sutherland, she's French!' the older man gasped, obviously shocked.

'I have often remarked upon Maystone's powers of observation, have I not, Christian?' Marcus Wilding drawled from where he had made himself comfortable in a chair beside the lit fireplace.

'Now is not the time for levity, Marcus,' Christian warned.

'I am indeed French, m'lord, and my name is Lisette Duprée.' She gave a small curtsy as she continued to concentrate on the man before her rather than the conversation of the two gentlemen behind her. 'I am also—'

'My ward,' Christian put in hastily.

'Your ward…?' Lord Maystone echoed faintly, appearing totally bewildered by these introductions.

As no doubt he was. That explanation might have sufficed in a Portsmouth inn, but Lisette doubted very much that any in London would believe Christian's insistence in introducing her as such.

Her mouth firmed. 'I am also—'

'Lisette, no!' Christian attempted to forestall her. 'Let me—'

'—Helene Rousseau's illegitimate daughter.' Lisette refused to be silenced, having no intention of attempting to hide her identity or deceive the gentleman now standing before her.

'Good God...!' Lord Maystone stared at her in astonishment.

'I do not think God has, or ever had, any part in Helene Rousseau's actions.' Lisette wrinkled her nose disapprovingly. 'I can only offer my most sincere regret for any hurt or discomfort she may have caused to you or your family.'

Lisette's candour had completely overridden Christian's own intention, of approaching the subject of Lisette's identity as Helene Rousseau's daughter with caution. Indeed, he had been rendered momentarily speechless by Lisette's disarming honesty.

As Worthing and Maystone were similarly struck, if the looks on those two gentlemen's faces were any indication.

It was a candour which Christian should no doubt have taken into account when deciding upon his own plan of action in regard to revealing Lisette's identity.

'Bravo, Lisette.' Worthing was the first to recover from his shock, as he gave her a gentle and appreciative clap. 'She has the courage of ten men, Christian,' he added admiringly.

'It takes no courage at all to tell the truth, Your Grace.' Lisette was the one to answer him ruefully.

'It does, in my experience.' Marcus grimaced.

'And mine,' Christian added softly, finding himself once again admiring and not a little in awe of Lisette's determination to be truthful. Even if, in this case, he might have wished her to be a little less so. 'I believe you may safely allow me to deal with any further explanations, Lisette—'

'Helene Rousseau's daughter!' Maystone appeared to have recovered his voice, although he continued to stare at Lisette as if he had seen a ghost, seeming unaware that Lisette still held on to his hands.

'Illegitimate daughter,' Lisette corrected firmly.

'I— But—' Maystone gave a shake of his head as if to clear it. 'Helene Rousseau does not have a daughter.'

'I was as surprised as you obviously are when she claimed me as such only a few months ago,' Lisette asserted regretfully. 'You cannot know how much I have wished since that it was not the case,' she added heavily.

Lisette had resisted that connection from the start. She also felt heartily ashamed of any part Helene might have played in the kidnapping of an innocent eight-year-old boy.

But, having now met Lord Maystone, Lisette felt a renewed anger towards the older woman. It was bad enough that Helene had abandoned her own child to be brought up by strangers, but Helene's crime against Lord Maystone and his family, because of her political machinations—and a crime she had given no indication of caring about these past months— was truly unforgivable.

Lisette gave Lord Maystone's hands an empathetic squeeze. 'I can only apologise again and state how sorry I am for the pain and distress that has been caused to you and your family.'

'Sutherland…?'

Christian had every sympathy with Maystone's slightly dazed expression; Lisette had the same effect on him. Often. 'It is quite true, I assure you,' he confirmed. 'But I also want you to know that I have brought Lisette to England with me for her own protection. Let me assure you she had no knowledge of or involvement in your grandson's kidnapping,' he added just as firmly.

'I do not— This is—' Maystone still seemed at a complete loss for words as he dropped down onto the upholstered window seat as the butler entered with the refreshments, none in the room speaking again until after that elderly gentleman had departed.

Lisette sat down on the seat next to Maystone. 'Unfortunately, as I have found, my birthright does not become any easier to comprehend or accept with time.'

'Would you care to do the honours, Lisette?' Christian indicated the tea tray as a way of changing the subject and easing some of the tension in the room.

She gave him an impatient glance. 'Could you see to it, Christian? Can you not see I am still busy attempting to commiserate with Lord Maystone?'

Christian heard Marcus's guffaw of laughter behind him. Indeed, he had to bite the inside of his own cheeks to stop himself from laughing. Maystone appeared to still be suffering from the shock of Lisette's earlier revelation, this latest social gaffe seeming to pass him by.

'Did I say something amusing?' Lisette frowned her irritation with Marcus's laughter.

Marcus straightened in his seat, still grinning. 'It is only—'

'It is only that I thought you might enjoy pouring the tea,' Christian cut in smoothly.

'Because I am a woman?' Lisette gave a disgusted snort to accompany her dismissive comment. 'Why should I pour your tea for you and your friends when you are more likely to be acquainted with how they take their tea than I am?'

It was a good point, Christian acknowledged. Except he didn't, of course, never having poured tea in his privileged life before, for his friends or himself. Which was no reason for him not to do so now. Although Maystone, for one, looked in need of something stronger than tea.

'I will pour you a cup of tea, Lisette.' Christian proceeded to do so, much to the amusement of his brother-in-law. 'But I think the gentlemen would prefer brandy…?'

'Just a small one,' Marcus accepted drily. 'Then I must hurry home to Julianna.'

Christian was well aware of the fact that it was only Marcus's fascination as to what Lisette would do or say next which had prevented him from departing already.

He finished pouring the tea and carried the cup and saucer across the room to place it on the table beside Lisette; having observed her at breakfast this morning, he knew it was exactly as she liked it—milk and a little sugar. 'Maystone?' he prompted sharply. Really, the news of Lisette being Helene Rousseau's illegitimate daughter was surprising, yes, but not *so* shocking that the older man should still be rendered speechless.

'Hmm? Oh. Yes. Thank you, Sutherland.' Maystone nodded, still staring at Lisette in that bemused fashion. 'A brandy would be most welcome.'

'I do not believe you should be drinking strong liquor when you are injured, Christian.' Lisette frowned her disapproval as she watched him pour the amber liquid into three glasses before handing two of them to his guests and retaining one for himself.

Christian heard Marcus give another muffled laugh. A laugh his friend tried—and failed—to hide behind a look of innocence when Christian narrowed his gaze on him. Lord knew what Marcus would report back to their mutual friends concerning his friendship with Mademoiselle Lisette Duprée. They were not even married and she was leading him about by the nose—

Married?

Where on earth had *that* come from?

Wherever it had come from, it could go back again! He had never met a more opinionated, irritating, bossy, *infuriating* young woman in his life than Lisette Duprée.

Or one quite so desirable.

Well, yes, there was that, and he really should not

have taken things as far as he had in the carriage. Even so, desire did not make up for the fact that Lisette was also—also—

What else was she?

Alone and defenceless.

Apart from that sharp tongue!

Vulnerable and frightened.

Again, apart from that sharp tongue!

She was also about to be used in a game of political chess for which she bore no responsibility or knowledge, but might nevertheless be the one called upon to pay the highest price.

Even that sharpness of Lisette's tongue and intelligence of mind could not save her if that should prove to be the case.

But Christian had just realised a way in which he might do so...

If *he* was prepared to pay the price.

Many families in English society were related to or married into the French aristocracy.

Which Lisette most certainly was not. Instead, she was the illegitimate daughter and niece of two notorious French spies.

Maybe so, but no one chose where and to whom they would be born. Lisette was a victim of her own circumstances, not a perpetrator of them—

Good God, he could not seriously be contemplating doing the unthinkable?

'Christian...?' Marcus prompted sharply. 'I believe you are about to spill your brandy all over the carpet!'

He looked blankly at the man he had known since childhood, his thoughts still too onerous for him to form a sensible or coherent reply.

Was he really prepared to go as far as *that* in order to keep his promise to protect Lisette? For there was no doubting that no one would dare to arrest or harm the Duchess of Sutherland—

'You see.' Lisette stood up to briskly cross the room before plucking the brandy glass from Christian's relaxed fingers. 'I said that you should not attempt to drink brandy in your already weakened state.' She tutted disapprovingly as she placed the glass down on Christian's desktop.

His heavy oak antique desk that had once belonged to a king.

Christian, however, was not the King of England, and if he did decide to tie himself to Lisette Duprée, then he knew it would be for life.

A life spent with an impulsive and totally irrepressible woman who would make a terrible duchess.

'Are you about to take me away and lock me in a cell, m'lord?' Lisette spoke to Maystone with her usual directness.

That gentleman looked startled by such a suggestion. 'I— Why, no, I had not thought of doing such a thing.'

'Why not?'

'I— Well—' Maystone gave a shake of his head. 'I have no evidence— I trust Sutherland's word if he has vouched for you.'

'He has,' Christian asserted sharply, although he

could not help but feel surprised that Maystone had ceded his ground so easily.

Indeed, Maystone still looked befuddled, clearly as disconcerted by Lisette's directness as the next man. And Christian, as the *next man*, was highly disconcerted by her!

Maystone nodded. 'I really need time to consider this…situation before taking any further action.'

'Then perhaps you two gentlemen have visited long enough for today,' Lisette now told Worthing and Maystone politely but firmly. 'Christian is weakened still and needs to rest after his long journey.'

What Christian *needed* was to retake charge in his own household and not have it, and him, dictated to by a mere chit of a girl—

'I believe you are right.' Maystone downed the last of his brandy before rising quickly to his feet and placing his empty glass down on the desk beside Christian's.

Good God, they were all doing it now!

It really was insupportable that Christian's life, his very existence, most certainly the authority he had possessed since birth, was being eroded in just minutes by this bossy and opinionated French miss.

'I shall come back and…and discuss this further in the morning, Christian, once I have had chance to ponder the situation,' Maystone added distractedly.

As far as Christian was concerned, Maystone could 'ponder' all he liked and it would not change the outcome; *he* could not allow Lisette to come to any harm. Indeed, the mere thought of it caused a cold shiver down the length of his spine.

'Mademoiselle Duprée.' Maystone now nodded abruptly. 'Worthing?'

'Definitely time we were leaving.' Marcus nodded after a single glance at the thundercloud he no doubt saw forming on Christian's brow. 'I shall bring Julianna to see you tomorrow morning, Christian.'

After he had no doubt regaled Christian's young sister with all the details of his relationship with Lisette. Including what Marcus suspected might have happened in the carriage on their way from Portsmouth to London; as far as Christian could see, the married couple kept no secrets from each other.

He also knew instinctively that his sister was sure to like Lisette, if only for the fact that she appeared to have taken charge of Christian and his household without so much as a by-your-leave.

'There is no rush for you to leave now,' he assured his brother-in-law hastily. 'Indeed, I was about to suggest that perhaps you might care to take Lisette home to Worthing House with you, so that you and Julianna might act as chaperone—'

'I am not in need of a chaperone—'

'But of course you are, my dear.' Maystone spoke up bravely over Lisette's outraged protest. 'A single unmarried lady does not reside in a single gentleman's house without a chaperone, even that of her guardian.' He gave a slightly bewildered shake of his head. 'Forgive me, Sutherland, I was—I am still—a little shocked to learn of Miss Duprée's…lineage.'

'*Half* my lineage,' Lisette cut in dismissively. 'I fear my father's identity is unknown, and likely to remain so,' she informed him at his questioning look.

'Oh. Well. Yes.' Maystone looked more disconcerted than ever. No doubt at hearing Lisette speaking so frankly of her illegitimacy.

'And I do not intend going anywhere, Christian.' She turned back to him. 'Now that I *am* here—' she gave him a glowering look '—I intend to continue seeing that all my good work of these past three days does not become undone simply because you are too stubborn to call for a doctor.'

'And if I now agree to send for the physician?' Christian challenged.

'Then I still could not leave you here without family or friend to attend you,' she maintained obstinately.

Christian looked at her searchingly, sensing—sensing—ah, yes, there it was—a telltale glitter of tears in those deep blue eyes.

Because he was attempting to save Lisette's reputation by sending her to stay with his sister and brother-in-law?

Admittedly, it would also save his own reputation, but—

There was no *but* to this situation, he conceded heavily; Lisette was the one without family or friends, apart from himself, and to send her away, albeit to stay with his sister and Marcus, would be the height of cruelty after all that she had done for him.

'It was merely a thought, Lisette.' He sighed in

defeat. 'Of course, if you wish to stay here at Sutherland House, then you must do so.'

She blinked, lashes slightly dampened by those tears she was determined not to allow to fall. 'If Lord Maystone does not wish to take me away for questioning as yet, then yes, I do prefer to stay here.'

'Then it is settled.' Christian braced his shoulders before turning to Marcus and Maystone. 'Gentlemen?'

Marcus rose elegantly to his feet. 'I have no doubt you do need to rest following the…the exertions of the journey here, Christian,' he added drily.

Pointedly, Christian acknowledged irritably, knowing full well to what 'exertions' Marcus was referring. As did Lisette, by the becoming blush that had now coloured her cheeks. Maystone still looked befuddled.

And perhaps Christian *did* need to rest; his thoughts of a few minutes ago regarding marriage to Lisette certainly indicated that he was not in his right mind!

It seemed that he was to have Lisette as his guest at Sutherland House after all. And he had not had to fight Aubrey Maystone, verbally or otherwise, in order to achieve it.

His gaze narrowed on the older man as he continued to stare at Lisette as if she were an apparition.

What was wrong with the man?

Perhaps his grandson's kidnapping had affected Maystone more seriously than any of them had suspected?

But, if that was so, then why was he not insisting on taking Lisette into his custody?

He felt a throbbing behind his eyes, as indication that so much thought—and so many unanswered questions—had resulted in him developing a headache. 'Just so,' he now answered Marcus vaguely. 'Do not visit with Julianna too early tomorrow morning, Marcus,' he added wearily as he rang for Evans to show the gentlemen out. 'I have a feeling I will not be at my best until later in the day.'

Marcus's dark brows rose. 'You know your sister almost as well as I; it will be as much as I can do to prevent her from visiting you later today once she knows you are returned from France and injured!'

Yes, Christian did know Julianna very well. He also knew that she had Marcus entwined about her little finger.

'Then I suggest you do not tell her I am injured,' he bit out. 'As to the rest, I am sure you will manage to think of some other manner in which to divert her,' he added ruefully.

Worthing gave a devilish grin. 'I shall do my best.'

Lisette was very aware of Lord Maystone's gaze still fixed upon her as the two gentlemen prepared to leave. No doubt his decision not to arrest her as yet was only because he was still trying to come to terms with the fact that his enemy's illegitimate daughter now stood just feet away from him.

Having now met Lord Maystone, Lisette felt even more ashamed of her connection to Helene Rousseau. The woman was a monster beyond her imagining, to have instigated the kidnapping of this man's young grandson.

She also could not deny the heaviness she felt in her chest at Christian's obvious effort to send her away to stay at his sister's home. Evidence, no doubt, that now he was back in his own household, and despite his earlier promise to protect her, he wanted to be rid of her.

Chapter Eleven

'Do you have everything you need?'

Lisette turned at the open doorway from the hallway into the comfortable bedchamber she had been shown into by the butler just minutes ago, on Christian's instructions.

That same gentleman now leaned against the door frame, looking across the room at her as she sat on the side of the four-poster bed that dominated the luxuriously appointed cream-and-gold room.

A bedchamber fit for a princess.

Or a duchess...

Christian Seaton's duchess.

Except he did not appear to have one of those.

Lisette wondered why that was when he was a handsome man in his early thirties and in possession of a wealth she could only ever dream about.

But perhaps he considered his work for the English Crown too dangerous to risk taking a wife? The fact that Christian had been shot only days ago would seem to confirm it *was* dangerous work.

And the truthful answer to his question was that she did not have *anything* she 'needed'. No home. No money. Her future uncertain. No kind relatives to whom she might ask for help.

She felt wholly disconnected from any and everything that was familiar to her, and her earlier bravado upon arriving at this imposing residence had now totally deserted her.

Added to, she had no doubt, by the memory of Christian's efforts to rid himself of the responsibility of her just a short time ago…

'I believe so, thank you,' she answered Christian in a subdued voice.

'You do not sound as if you do.' Christian favoured his left leg as he stepped further into the room.

Evidence that he was once again in pain?

Lisette stood up. 'Do you wish me to inspect and re-dress your wounds before you retire to your bedchamber?'

'No, thank you,' Christian refused ruefully. He was only too well aware of what that 'inspection' might lead to, despite his disquieting thoughts of earlier and the discomfort of his wound.

A certain part of his anatomy did not seem to give a damn about either of those things and leaped up eagerly in response to Lisette's slightest touch. The very reason he had chosen to leave the bedchamber door open when he entered.

'What am I to do whilst you are resting?' There was a frown between Lisette's eyes.

Stay out of trouble was Christian's first thought, followed by the knowledge that it would be no good to instruct Lisette to do any such thing when trouble, of one sort or another, seemed to follow her around.

Not particularly through any fault of her own, he accepted; Miss Lisette Duprée just seemed to be a magnet for all things troublesome.

'Perhaps you might also rest?' he suggested mildly, determinedly walking over to the window to look down into the square below rather than at Lisette; she looked so woebegone at the moment, it was all he could do not to take her into his arms and offer her comfort.

A comforting that he had no doubt would lead to the deeper intimacy between them that he was trying so hard to avoid now that they were in his London home. For Lisette's sake; all servants gossiped, even if one might wish they did not, and London society was so quick to condemn when it came to the reputation of a lady, no matter how much Christian might continue to publicly claim that Lisette was his ward.

Damn both Marcus and Maystone; one for ignoring his obvious request for assistance, the other for being so befuddled of wits he had not only seemed, but had proved to be, incapable of any action or sensible thought where Lisette was concerned.

Not that Christian would have allowed the older man to take Lisette away with him. He could not have allowed that after his earlier promises, but he could have done with a *little* assistance from one or both of the other gentlemen in regard to this situation.

A situation not of Lisette's choosing, he once again reminded himself heavily.

'I am not tired,' she answered him huskily.

Christian frowned now at the way Lisette kept her face turned away from him. Damn it, if she was crying…!

He was weakened and felt as much at a loss as most men did when confronted by a woman's tears. The more so if they were Lisette's—she had been so stalwart in her behaviour and actions up until now. He could not think of many women who would have acted as bravely as she had done these past few days—escaping out of windows in order to warn him of danger, coming to his rescue after he had been shot, leaving behind her home and country to sail all the way to England to care for him on the journey.

And her reward? She had been bundled into a coach and brought to London against her will. Moreover, she had been made love to in that coach by the very man who was responsible for her present dilemma.

Perhaps, in the circumstances, Lisette was allowed to shed a few tears.

'Come here.' Christian limped across the room to sit down on the bed beside her and take her into his arms. 'No, do not fight me, Lisette,' he soothed gently as she did exactly that. 'Let me hold you,' he encouraged gruffly.

'Why?' Her voice was muffled against his chest as his arms held her too tightly for her to escape.

'Why what?' Christian allowed himself the pleasure of winding one of her silky curls about his finger.

'You so obviously wanted either Le Duc or m'lord to take me away earlier!' she accused brokenly as she finally gave up the fight and her head rested against his chest.

Yes, there were definitely tears, Christian acknowledged as he felt their damp heat soaking the front of his shirt. And not for any of the reasons he had attributed, but because *he* had hurt her feelings earlier. 'I thought only of your reputation,' he soothed, knowing he was not being altogether truthful.

He *had* been concerned with Lisette's reputation, but more so with his inability to resist her.

Good Lord, when he had made love to her in his carriage earlier today, he had not given a care for where they were or that his leg pained and discomforted him. How much less resistance would he have against her once he was completely well again? Even now he was totally aware of the fact that there was only the thin material of her gown between his hands and the bareness of her creamy skin. A fact made possible by his having ripped her chemise to shreds earlier in a fit of passion.

He had never behaved in such a rough and demanding manner with any woman before Lisette.

Had never burned so deeply with lust before Lisette.

She gave a choked laugh now. 'I have no reputation left to lose, Christian.'

'Of course you do. When this is over—'

'I will still be a stranger in a strange land, with no money or family, and the illegitimate daughter of a French tavern owner who is an enemy of your country.'

Christian gave a wince at this unflatteringly accurate description of Lisette's circumstances.

'I know I have previously spoken to the contrary, but…once Lord Maystone realises that I truly do not know anything about my—about Helene Rousseau's plots and plans, perhaps you might consider taking me as your mistress?' Lisette looked up at him with tear-damp eyes.

'What?'

'Until such time as you take a duchess, of course,' she added hastily, no doubt at his horrified expression. 'I should not like to intrude upon a marriage.'

If Christian had been startled by her outspokenness to Maystone earlier, he now found himself completely stunned by Lisette's suggestion of becoming his mistress.

Women simply did not behave in this forward manner—

He already knew that Lisette was not like other women. Indeed, he had never met another like her. Innocent on the one hand, completely practical on the other.

But not so innocent that she did not know that she had only one thing that was truly her own, and practical enough to decide to whom and when she would give it.

'Have you forgotten your claim—"I would rather sell my soul to the devil than be beholden to you for a moment longer"?' He huskily reminded her of the insult she had hurled at him during their heated exchange at the inn yesterday.

If Lisette telling him exactly what she thought of him and his having had no choice but to listen to those thoughts could be called an *exchange*!

'I have said that I do.'

'But you have now changed your mind?'

'Do not mock me, Christian.' Lisette did not appreciate his levity when she had spent the past few minutes considering her future.

She had no real wish to return to France, now that she had been made aware of the full extent of Helene's actions. Indeed, it might be dangerous for her to do so.

But if she was allowed to remain free and in England, then her lack of spoken English would limit her options of employment. Something she intended to rectify as soon as possible, but unfortunately, that would not be soon enough for her to become a companion, governess or even a maid in an English household.

But if she had no choice but to become some rich gentleman's mistress, then she would rather make the choice of that lover for herself. She already knew that she and Christian were physically compatible. Much better, if she had to become some man's mistress, that she at least enjoy the gentleman's attentions.

'Besides, I should not be beholden to you,' she reasoned briskly. 'You would set me up in my own small establishment, and in exchange I would make myself available to you whenever you wish it. That is the way these things are arranged, is it not?' she added with a pragmatism she was not sure she actually felt as yet but hoped to achieve, and certainly now wished to convey to Christian.

The Duprées had been great believers in pragmatism; they had often had need to be on the farm, when the crops had failed or the cows did not provide enough milk to sell.

A pragmatism Lisette was sorely in need of when all she possessed, besides herself, were the few belongings Christian had purchased for her before leaving Paris.

'I have no need of a mistress.'

She looked up at him sharply. 'Is that because you already have one?'

'No, of course I do not—' He broke off in obvious exasperation. 'Lisette, you cannot just offer to become a man's mistress without his first having given indication that is what he wants too!'

Her eyebrows rose. 'Earlier today in your carriage was not an indication of your desire for me?'

'Well. Yes.' He gave an impatient shake of his head. 'Of course it was an *indication* that I desire you, but I— Lisette, I have never set myself up with a mistress—'

'Why not?'

'—and I do not intend to start now. What do you mean—why not?' He scowled darkly.

She gave a shrug. 'I thought all society gentlemen, most especially a duke, took a mistress?'

'Then you thought wrong.' He glowered. 'Neither I nor, to my knowledge, any of my close friends have ever done so.'

'That does not mean you could not do so now.' It was not an ideal situation for Lisette either, nor had it been an easy decision for her to make, but she really did have so very few choices left to her. Once she had told Lord Maystone what she knew—which was very little, and most certainly did not include Helene caring for her enough to respond to blackmail on her behalf—then it was easy to surmise that neither he nor Christian would have any further use for her.

Unless she were to offer her services in some other way.

'I do *not* have need of a mistress,' Christian bit out between gritted teeth.

'Well, certainly not now, when you are incapacitated—'

'Ever!'

'There is no need to shout, Christian—'

'No need to—!' His arms moved from about her before he stood up to glower down at her even more darkly. 'There is every reason to shout when you have just offered to become my mistress.'

'An offer you have clearly refused.' Lisette stood up, chin raised proudly. 'Which means I will have to find some other acceptable gentleman to whom I might—'

'You will do no such thing!'

She gave a wince. 'You are still shouting, Christian.'

'I am about to put you over my knee and administer that spanking we discussed earlier if you do not cease talking of this subject—' He broke off as Evans appeared in the open doorway, accompanied by a wide-eyed maid carrying a pitcher and several towels.

Lisette was unsure who was the most embarrassed: herself for having had Christian's threat to spank her bottom overheard—and possibly some of the conversation leading up to that threat?—or the two shocked servants at being the ones to have overheard that threat.

Christian glared furiously.

'I... I thought Miss Duprée might care for some hot water and towels with which to refresh herself after your journey, Your Grace.' Evans was the first to recover, his expression once again respectfully deadpan.

The situation was so ludicrous, Lisette acknowledged as her initial dismay began to recede, that it was all she could now do to stop herself from laughing. Her efforts not to do so were not helped by the continuing look of outrage on Christian's face.

He breathed in deeply—fighting for control?—

before answering his butler tautly. 'Leave them and go.'

'Thank you, Evans,' Lisette managed to add in heavily accented English, with the addition of a smile, in the hope of making up for Christian's abruptness; it was very kind of the butler to have thought of her comfort in that way.

'Close the door on your way out,' Christian instructed stiffly once the pitcher of water and towels had been placed on the washstand.

Christian considered it shocking enough that Lisette had offered to become *his* mistress, but the idea that she might so much as think of making that same scandalous offer to another gentleman was even more unacceptable.

He would rather accept the offer himself than— *No!*

He was not going to take Lisette as his mistress or anything else. Once the situation with Maystone had been settled then Christian would do everything in his considerable power to help Lisette to find gainful employment. Legitimate gainful employment. In a respectable household. Many women in English society now had French maids, *emigrées* from the years of upheaval in France, and although Lisette might be a little outspoken for such a post, he was sure that Julianna, if she had no need of her services herself, might at least be able to advise the younger woman on how best to behave.

And maybe, from time to time, the two of them might meet, have luncheon or afternoon tea together, so that Christian might see Lisette, talk with her and ascertain that she was happy and being well cared for—

A duke did not have luncheon or afternoon tea with a lady's maid.

Well. No. Perhaps not.

There was no *perhaps* about it; it simply was not done.

Then perhaps Julianna might be persuaded to invite the two of them—

He was taking himself round and round in circles, Christian realised. And Lisette stood at the centre of all of them.

If—when Lisette eventually left his household and became a lady's maid, or perhaps just a maid, then he must accept that he would not be able to see her again.

The thought did not sit well with him.

He could not imagine being unable to look into those beautiful blue eyes or to see the spark of anger that so often lit them. Or to listen to her outrageous conversation; even her scoldings were so much more entertaining than anything any other woman had ever said to him.

As for the effect she had upon him physically…

She had, Christian realised, made a place for herself in his life these past few days. A place that no other woman ever had.

A place that would gape like an open wound once Lisette was no longer there to fill it.

Meaning what?

*That he had to be suffering a fever of some kind—
perhaps his wound had become infected after all?—if
he was once again considering doing the unthinkable!*

He straightened. 'I am sure we will both feel…
calmer, more able to discuss your future, once we
have rested after our journey.'

Lisette could not see that there was anything more
for them to discuss on the subject when she had already considered her future from all angles.

Christian had just refused the obvious choice.

She had no skills, except those of working on
a farm or in a tavern. If the English taverns were
anything like the one owned by Helene Rousseau,
then she was more likely than not, as an unprotected
young woman in a strange country, to end up one
night with her skirts up to her waist and her virtue
lost.

No, better by far to choose that life for herself, to
choose the man for herself, rather than have it chosen for her by some unwashed lout in a dark alley.

She stood up. 'You are right, of course, Christian.
As usual,' she added tightly.

Christian eyed her guardedly; an acquiescent Lisette was decidedly more worrying than the virago
Lisette. 'What are you up to…?'

She opened wide eyes. 'What does this mean—
"up to"?'

Christian wished he felt reassured by those innocent wide blue eyes. Unfortunately, they had the
opposite effect; when Lisette looked innocent then

he could be sure she was about to do something she should not.

He sighed. 'In your case it means—what are you plotting and planning to do this afternoon, while I am resting, that you should not be doing?'

She shrugged. 'I have no idea what you are talking about.'

Yes, definitely plotting and planning… 'You realise you cannot leave here, Lisette?' He watched her closely. 'That to do so would be dangerous?'

Her chin rose. 'For whom?'

Christian frowned his irritation. 'For you, of course. England is rife with French spies— This is not funny, Lisette.' His frown turned to a scowl.

'Of course it is.' She continued to chuckle. 'I am not safe in France; I am not safe in England. Where shall I be safe, Monsieur le Duc?'

With him, Christian instantly answered, and then just as quickly dismissed it again. Lisette was *not* safe with him, or *from* him; he had more than proved that in the coach earlier.

He gave a weary shake of his head. 'I am too tired to argue with you just now, Lisette. Only give me a few hours to sleep and I promise I will be rested enough for you to argue with for as long as you wish to do so.'

'I do not argue with you—'

'You do nothing else!' Christian's voice rose, this time impatiently. 'You are the most contrary woman— I swear that if I said the sky is blue that you would argue it was pink.'

She wrinkled her pretty nose. 'Sometimes it is. Have you never seen the sunset when—?'

'I am going to bed, Lisette,' he announced flatly as he walked determinedly across the room to the door. 'Try to behave yourself in my absence.'

Lisette kept her chin raised high until Christian had left the bedchamber and then, only then, did she allow her shoulders to droop dejectedly.

She had buried all her scruples, her dreams for the future, had done the unthinkable and offered to become Christian's mistress, and he had rejected the idea totally. There had not been the slightest hesitation or doubt. He did not want her.

He could not have told her any more clearly that she had only been an amusement to him in Paris, a diversion on the journey here, one he did not need or want now that he was back in London and was once again every inch the Duke of Sutherland.

'What do you mean she went out, Evans?' Christian demanded. 'Where did she go? And when?'

His butler looked distinctly uncomfortable. 'Miss Duprée went out for a walk, possibly two hours ago, Your Grace.'

'Where?' he repeated forcefully, hands clenched into fists at his sides.

Christian really had been exhausted by the time he had reached his own bedchamber earlier, and he had not even bothered to undress before dropping weakly down on top of the bed and falling into a deep sleep.

His valet had woken him several hours later, armed with a cup of tea to refresh him and hot water in which to bathe. Christian had enjoyed the luxury of the latter long after his valet had completed his shave and the bath water had become cold.

The bandage on his thigh had come off quite easily after his soak in the bath, and he was relieved to see that the wound was healing well once he had removed the soiled bandage upon stepping from the bath. He had also managed to reapply a fresh bandage himself; he certainly did not need any gossip below stairs concerning how he had acquired such a wound.

Once he was dressed he had gone downstairs in search of Lisette, only to be told that she was not there. Which had the effect of completely undoing all the good work of the previous hours of sleep, followed by the relaxation in the bath.

It was also in complete opposition to what Christian had instructed before going to his bedchamber.

He really was going to have to put Lisette over his knee and spank her—

'There was something of a…language barrier, Your Grace, but I believe she did not intend to be out long,' his butler answered uncomfortably.

There would be no 'language barrier' necessary once Christian caught up with Lisette. 'Language' would not be used, but physical retribution.

'To be truthful, Your Grace, I was becoming a trifle worried about her myself,' Evans continued awkwardly. 'I had assumed she was just going to walk about the square, but she has been gone far too long for that to be the case. A young lady out alone…' The elderly butler broke off with a wince as Christian gave him a glowering frown.

Although in truth, he could not hold any of his household responsible for Lisette's actions; she was impulsive and strong-willed to the point where she was a danger to herself and everyone else. Christian could not deny that her impulsiveness and strong will had saved his life a time or two, but he had been perfectly serious earlier when he had warned Lisette of the dangers lurking beyond the walls of this house.

It was not only her identity but also the fact that she was a beautiful young woman, now out and about without escort or chaperone, so leaving herself prey to any of the criminal element that strolled these streets, day as well as night.

'It is not your fault, Evans,' he assured him on a sigh. 'Miss Duprée is…an independent young lady, brought up in the country and used to doing as she wishes. I fear she is not yet used to the ways of the City.'

'I guessed that, Your Grace.' The elderly butler nodded. 'I even offered for her to take young Mary with her for company—the Second Upstairs Maid,' he supplied as Christian looked baffled as to who Mary might be. 'But Miss Duprée indicated there was no reason to bother or disturb anyone and that she would only take a stroll outside in the fresh air.'

A stroll that had already lasted for two hours or more…

'My cloak and hat, if you please, Evans,' Christian requested wearily. 'If I do not return for another two hours then perhaps you had better send out a search party,' he added drily in parting as he swept out of the front doorway of Sutherland House in search of his errant and rebellious house guest.

Chapter Twelve

'It is so *bon* to see you, Davy!' Lisette beamed at the young man walking along beside her, aware that he probably did not understand a word she was saying, but hoping to convey her happiness with the brightness of her smile.

She had badly needed to escape Sutherland House earlier, to breathe in the fresh air, to be free for a while of the worry and intrigue that had surrounded her these past few days.

After leaving the house she had taken a stroll about the square outside Sutherland House, as she had given Evans the impression she intended to do. Which had taken her all of ten minutes to complete, and that included pausing to watch a group of small children playing with a ball, watched over by their gossiping nannies.

Having no child of her own to allow to play, and no English either to join in the conversation, Lisette had then ventured out of the square in search of other entertainment.

It had taken some time to reach the shops, and they had proved to be amusing for a while, but as usual she was only window-shopping, having no money to buy any of the pretty lace or fashionable leather gloves on display inside those windows.

It had been shortly after she had given in to the lure of a much bigger park, and become fascinated with watching the ducks swimming happily about on the pond there, that she had spied young Davy, the assistant to the cook on board *The Blue Dolphin*, strolling by.

Fortuitously, because by this time Lisette had walked so far and for so long that she had absolutely no idea how to find her way back to Christian's ducal home.

Conversation between herself and Davy was, as might be expected, a little difficult, but they had managed, between the two of them, to convey the fact that Lisette was well and truly lost in England's capital and Davy had now generously offered to walk back with her to Sutherland House.

Where Lisette would no doubt have to face a wrathful Christian.

She really had not intended to be out for so long or to walk so far, had thought to be back long before Christian rose from his nap. So that perhaps he would not even need to know that she had been out at all.

Instead she had become lost, and no doubt Christian would have been up for some time now and possibly pacing one of those elegantly appointed rooms in Sutherland House as he contemplated what was to be her punishment for having disobeyed him.

In her defence, she had not actually *agreed* with his instruction earlier not to leave Sutherland House.

A poor defence, to be sure, but it was the only one Lisette had in the face of what she knew was going to be Christian's extreme anger for her having disobeyed him.

'Do you have *la famille*—family in London, Davy?' she prompted curiously as they left the park and began to stroll along the pavement.

'My widowed mother.' He nodded.

Considering that Davy was only aged perhaps sixteen or seventeen, his mother must be a very young widow. 'Any *frères ou soeurs*? Brothers and sisters,' she translated awkwardly.

'Four.' He nodded again. 'Two of each. All younger than me.'

With young Davy no doubt the only breadwinner, Lisette inwardly sympathised, wondering if she dare ask Christian to reward Davy for having returned her safely to Sutherland House.

She already owed Christian so much; what did a little more matter? Besides, she doubted that Christian would wish to make a fuss in front of Davy or Evans.

Once they were alone she had no doubt it would be a different matter…

'How can you have lost her already?' Marcus frowned once Christian had explained the reason for his having called at Worthing House. 'You have only been back in London a few hours!'

A few hours could, when it came to Lisette, as Christian knew only too well, seem as long as a lifetime. Indeed, it seemed like that lifetime since he had left Sutherland House to begin walking the streets in search of her.

His leg ached like the devil, and he had finally given up that search and called upon his sister and brother-in-law at Worthing House, in the tenuous hope that Lisette might have decided to call upon them. An unlikely occurrence, Christian knew, especially as Lisette had no idea where Worthing House even was, but it had now been over three hours since Lisette left to go for a stroll and his anger had been replaced with an uneasy anxiety.

Although he had no doubt that his anger would come boiling back up to the surface the moment he saw her again!

She had the ability, it seemed, to induce strong emotions inside him, be they anger or desire.

'Can you not see how worried he is, my love?' Julianna, glowing with the happiness of her marriage to Worthing and their excitement at their forthcoming baby, now placed a lightly restraining hand upon her husband's arm as the two sat together on the sofa opposite Christian, who sat restlessly on the edge of an armchair. 'Perhaps she has called upon Lord Maystone in the hope of easing that gentleman's mind in regard to her innocence?' she suggested.

It did not surprise Christian in the slightest that

Marcus appeared to have told Julianna all. Indeed, he would have been surprised if he had not; the couple had once lost each other because of a lack of communication. Now that they had found each other again and were happily married, they did not intend such misunderstandings to ever happen again.

Christian wished that he could say he had the same open honesty with Lisette.

Although, to be fair, *he* had been the one mainly responsible for having kept secrets.

'Doubtful,' he answered his sister; he could not imagine Lisette voluntarily calling upon Maystone.

'You do believe she is innocent, Christian?' his sister prompted anxiously.

'Without a doubt,' he confirmed distractedly; he now knew that Lisette was far too headstrong, too outspoken—too forward, he added as he recalled their conversation of earlier—to be in the least proficient at subterfuge. 'She has been gone for *hours*, Marcus.' He gave a shake of his head. 'She is headstrong and impulsive but she is not stupid, and I warned her that it is not safe for her here!'

'Perhaps you should have thought of that before bringing her to England?' Julianna said quietly. 'Although I have to admit to a selfish need to see and speak with her in person, in order that I might thank her for saving my brother's life…'

A sharp reminder from Julianna, perhaps even a rebuke, as to the reason Lisette was in England at all?

Christian sighed heavily. 'I am well aware of what

I owe her, Julianna. I just wish—' His mouth firmed. 'She never listens to a word I say to her!'

'Perhaps that is because you do not ask but tell, Christian?'

His jaw tightened at this second rebuke from his sister. 'Asking or telling; neither seems to make the slightest bit of difference. Lisette will always do exactly as she pleases.'

'Another reason why I shall like her!' Julianna's eyes sparkled merrily. 'But I can see how you might find that...irritating.' She sobered as he continued to scowl.

Christian now gave an impatient snort. 'She is stubborn as a mule!'

'She is also missing,' Marcus reminded softly.

'I am well aware of that fact!' Christian stood up to restlessly pace the room, more worried than he cared to admit.

What if Lisette had been set upon by thieves or pickpockets and was even now lying in a gutter somewhere, injured and alone? Or, worse yet, perhaps she had been accosted by those lower-than-low men and women who dealt in the sale of female flesh?

There were any number of scenarios Christian could imagine befalling the naive innocent that Lisette undoubtedly was, albeit a brave one, and each scenario was more horrifying than the last.

'Perhaps you should return to Sutherland House?' Julianna suggested gently. 'Lisette may have returned in your absence and now be worried about you.'

Christian had already thought of that; he had just needed to vent some of his tension, created by his anger and worry over Lisette's whereabouts, before he saw her again. Otherwise he knew he could not be responsible for his actions the moment he set eyes on her again, no matter where they might be or who might be present when it occurred.

'Perhaps you should go with him, my love.' Julianna smiled at Worthing. 'I am sure that Christian would welcome your...moral support at this difficult time.'

'I believe you mean to say my efforts might be required to restrain him from doing poor little Lisette harm when he sees her again.' Worthing gave a boyish grin, obviously enjoying himself, no doubt at Christian's expense.

'Poor little Lisette, my—!' Christian broke off before he was ungentlemanly enough to swear in front of his sister. 'She is also responsible for causing absolute chaos in my life since saving it!' Christian came back disgustedly.

'Well, yes,' Julianna conceded with a slight smile. 'But is that not better than the boredom and ennui that has occasionally bothered you in the past?'

Christian stared at her dumbstruck for a few moments before turning away. 'If you are coming, Worthing, I suggest we leave now.' He did not have an answer to his sister's probing question.

Mainly because he knew Julianna was in the right of it; who could possibly be bored or suffer from ennui when they had the irrepressible Lisette to prevent from becoming embroiled in her next escapade?

Where the *hell* was she?

If she was not back at Sutherland House when he returned, then he would—

He would what?

If Lisette had not returned, three hours after she had supposedly gone for a simple stroll outside in the fresh air, then something must have happened to her. In which case, neither his anger nor his threats to her would be of the slightest significance.

'I am sure she is safe, Christian—'

'You can no more be sure of that than I am, Marcus!' Christian glowered at his brother-in-law a short time later as the two of them travelled back to Sutherland House in Marcus's ducal carriage, a convenience Christian was more grateful for than he cared to admit, his thigh having now become a continuous and painful throb after so much physical exertion.

He somehow knew, as he stepped down from the carriage outside Sutherland House, that Lisette was not contained within its walls. He would have *sensed* her presence there, would have *felt* that quiver of awareness that always seemed to be in the air whenever she was near.

Lisette had not returned.

He knew he was right when a grave-faced Evans opened the door to him and Worthing.

The elderly butler did not even offer to take their hats and cloaks but instead held out a silver tray towards Christian as he entered the hallway. 'This letter was delivered shortly after you left the house, Your Grace.'

'By whom?' Christian prompted sharply.

'A street urchin, it seemed to me.' The butler gave a shake of his head. 'I sent someone to follow him, but they were soon lost in the warren of backstreets. I also sent someone after you, but you could not be found,' he added apologetically as Christian took the letter without comment before ripping it open and quickly reading the contents. 'Is it bad news, Your Grace?' he prompted anxiously.

Christian's hand curled into a fist, crumpling the letter in his palm as he answered reassuringly. 'Nothing for you to worry about, Evans.' He gave a brief if humourless smile. 'Miss Duprée has merely run into an old acquaintance but will be back with us shortly.'

Evans breathed a sigh of relief. 'I am glad to hear it, Your Grace.'

'An old acquaintance…?' Marcus prompted as soon as the two men had retired to the library with a decanter of brandy. 'I did not think Lisette knew anyone in England but us?'

'She does not.' Christian grimly handed the crumpled letter to the other man for him to read. 'It would seem that Lisette has been kidnapped.'

Marcus looked up after quickly reading the letter. 'It is not a very well written letter and the paper is of a quality—'

'Damn the quality of the writing or the paper, Marcus!' Christian exploded angrily. 'They have Lisette, and that is all that is important.'

'Yes, but who are "they"?' Marcus turned the letter over, studying Christian's name and the address written on the front of it. 'Do you think this can be connected with the kidnapping of Maystone's grandson and the abduction of Bea?'

Griffin Stone had almost run Bea down with his carriage after she had escaped her abductors. The two of them were very recently married.

'It is too much of a coincidence for it not to be,' Christian bit out grimly as he recalled that young lady's harsh treatment during her incarceration. The thought of Lisette being treated harshly was enough to turn the blood cold in Christian's veins.

'But we already have those responsible in custody—'

'Not all of them.' Christian's hand shook as he raised the glass of brandy to his lips and took a much-needed swallow of the fiery liquid before speaking again. 'We—*I* did not apprehend Helene Rousseau.'

'You were not sent to Paris to apprehend her—' Marcus broke off, eyes widening. 'Do you believe that she is capable of arranging something so abhorrent as the abduction of her own daughter...?'

Christian recalled the pistol that had been pressed against his spine that very first evening at the Fleur de Lis, when Helene Rousseau had thought he was paying far too much attention to Lisette. She had seemed like a hen protecting her chick that night— albeit a steely-cold one!—and yet it really was too much of a coincidence to believe there could be two sets of kidnappers in so short a time. Helene Rousseau *had* to be involved in Lisette's disappearance.

The alternative was too disturbing to contemplate.

Christian's jaw tightened. 'It clearly says in the letter that Maystone is to be at Westminster Bridge at midnight tonight if we want to see Lisette again. Why else would they involve Maystone if this was not connected to the kidnapping of his grandson and the abduction of Griffin's Bea?'

Why else indeed...?

How could she have been so stupid, so *naive*, Lisette admonished herself as she looked about the windowless room in which she was being held a prisoner, a dirty handkerchief secured about her mouth, her wrists and ankles bound with thin but strong cord; she knew it was strong because all of her efforts to free herself had proved to be in vain.

As if Davy would really have just been strolling in a London park, when the last time she had seen him had been at the Portsmouth dock as she and Christian departed *The Blue Dolphin*. She should have guessed—*known*—the moment she saw Davy again that it was too much of a coincidence for him to now be in London.

Instead, she had been so pleased to see a familiar face, after realising she was lost, that she had not questioned *why* she was seeing that face.

Lisette had assumed, even as Davy directed her through an unsavoury area of London that she did not remember walking through earlier, that he knew the capital so well that he was taking a shortcut back to Sutherland House. Instead, another man had suddenly emerged from a dark alley, throwing a sack over her head while Davy bound her wrists, and she was then bundled into a smelly cart and taken to the house in which this windowless room was situated.

The sack had not been removed from her head until she had stumbled into the room, Davy remaining in the background as the other man, hat pulled low over his eyes, a kerchief about the lower half of his face, had secured the gag and then bound her hands and feet, before they both departed, Lisette assumed, to another part of this hovel.

She had no idea if Davy was acting alone with his accomplice, in an effort to extract money for her release, or if her abduction had a much deeper significance.

Whichever of those it was, Lisette knew that Christian would be very displeased with her when he learned what had happened; he had tried to warn her of the dangers of leaving the house alone. She, with her usual stubbornness, had thought she knew better and had refused to believe there could possibly be anyone in England who might want to harm her.

Her reward for that naivety was to be held prisoner in this dark room, gagged and bound.

With the added worry that, as she was nothing more than a rebellious nuisance to Christian, he may not feel inclined to pay a ransom for her release even if one should be demanded.

The situation was dire enough to make her sit and

cry. If self-pity had been in her nature. And if she thought it would have done any good.

It was not, and she knew crying would only make her feel more miserable when her mouth was gagged and her hands tied.

No, she had no choice but to remain in this unpleasant place until such time as she was either released or—

Lisette did not wish to contemplate what that *or* might be.

'Well, of course I will go to Westminster Bridge and meet with these people tonight, Christian,' Maystone assured him testily as Christian scowled down at him as he sat in a chair in his own drawing room. 'It is not a question of whether I go or not.'

'Then what is it a question of?' Christian was too restless to be seated himself, preferring to pace the room instead.

The older man sighed heavily, his face pale. 'What might be demanded of me in exchange for Miss Duprée's release.'

Christian was well aware of the demons of hell Maystone had suffered for weeks, when his loyalty to the Crown prevented him from yielding the information demanded of him in exchange for his grandson's safe return.

The same demons of hell Christian had been suffering since he had received word of Lisette's abduction. Which, in actual time, had only been a matter of just over an hour.

It seemed much longer.

As he knew the five hours until midnight would seem interminable.

Christian's mouth thinned. 'Whatever it is they want, you will give it to them.'

The older man looked up at him regretfully. 'You know I cannot do that, Christian.'

Yes, he did know that; if Maystone had been unwilling to give in to blackmail in exchange for his grandson's life, then he was unlikely to do so for a young woman he had only met for the first time earlier today. A young woman, moreover, who was known to be the illegitimate daughter of the same woman who had organised the kidnapping of Maystone's grandson.

'I think we may both safely assume that this unpleasant business does at least confirm Lisette to be innocent of all wrongdoing,' Maystone proffered gently. 'Unless, of course, she was aware of this plan all along and is in cahoots with her supposed abductors…?'

The idea had also occurred—very briefly—to Christian and been just as quickly dismissed. Lisette had been brought to London against her will or intention. And the Lisette who had offered to become his mistress earlier today simply did not have it in her to behave in so underhand a manner.

She was infuriating, rebellious to the point of endangering her own safety, but he believed beyond a shadow of a doubt that Lisette was not, and never could be, a liar.

He glared at Maystone. 'You *will* give these people whatever they demand for her safe return,' he growled.

Maystone surged impatiently to his feet at Christian's accusing tone. 'You know of my limitations in that regard as well as I, Christian.'

'Damn it to hell—!' Christian wanted to put his fist through something in order to vent his frustration and anger.

Every minute that passed was one more minute he could not be sure if Lisette still lived; she would not be the first kidnap victim to have been disposed of shortly after being taken, the kidnappers' only interest in the ransom. His only consolation was that Maystone's grandson had been found unharmed, if badly shaken.

But even that was of little comfort. Worthing had a point earlier; the people who had Lisette could not be the same ones who had taken the boy because they were currently incarcerated in prison, awaiting trial.

'I understand how you are feeling, Christian,' Maystone consoled him.

Christian was not sure how he was 'feeling', so he very much doubted that the other man could possibly know or understand either.

On the one hand, Christian felt almost paralysed with worry as to Lisette's safety.

On the other, he wanted to *do* something—something tangible towards facilitating her return.

He was also furious with Lisette for her recklessness, at the same time as he needed to hold her in his arms and reassure himself that she was safe and unharmed.

So many mixed emotions, all running around inside him, with Lisette at the heart of all of them.

The heart...

Christian was an educated man, and that intellect told him that emotions came from a person's head and not their heart, as the romantics liked to wax lyrical.

But if that was so, then why had his chest *ached* so much since he learned of Lisette's abduction? As if a heavy weight had been placed upon it, restricting his breathing and making him feel nauseous.

'She will not allow her to be harmed, Christian.'

'She?' He looked sharply at Maystone.

The older man sighed. 'Helene Rousseau.'

'We cannot be sure she is behind this.'

'I am.' Aubrey Maystone moved to replenish his brandy glass, holding the decanter up questioningly to Christian and replacing it back on the tray when he gave an impatiently dismissive shake of his head.

'How so?' Christian finally prompted irritably when he could stand the other man's silence no longer.

Maystone looked at him with calm blue eyes. 'Because I believe I now know the reason that I, and *my* grandson in particular, was made the target two months ago.'

'Which is?'

The other man closed his eyes briefly before opening them again to reveal a look of stoic resolve. 'I was not always the elderly man you now see before you,

Christian. I was once a young man very like you and the other Dangerous Dukes.' He gave a self-derisive twist of his lips in the semblance of a smile. 'I too wanted to set right the wrongs in the world, craved adventure, intrigue—'

'I do not see—'

'—was impatient with the caution of others,' Maystone continued pointedly. 'Believed that action was what was needed, not talk and political compromise.'

Christian's hands were clenched into fists at his sides. 'If there is a point to this conversation, Aubrey, then I wish you would get to it!'

The older man sighed. 'There is a point, but it is not one I can share with you just yet. Suffice to say,' he continued when Christian would have interrupted, 'if I am still alive when this is all finally over, I shall be resigning my post.'

'If you are still alive...?'

'Have you not accepted yet that *I* have been the target all along?' He gave a rueful shake of his head. 'A very personal, very definite target.'

'Why should you think that?' He stared at the other man incredulously.

'I have been compromised, Christian, and in a way I could never have expected.' He gave another deep sigh before brightening. 'But we will get your Lisette back to you—'

'She is not my Lisette—'

'No?' Maystone raised iron-grey brows. 'Well, never mind that for now,' he continued briskly. 'For the moment you and I are going to eat dinner together—'

'I cannot eat whilst Lisette is no doubt alone and frightened as to what will happen to her!'

'We will eat dinner together,' Maystone repeated firmly. 'Discuss the weather, and all those other boring subjects that are considered correct conversation in polite society, and then at midnight we will go to Westminster Bridge and retrieve Lisette. Trust me, Christian.' The other man placed a reassuring hand on his arm. 'No harm will come to her.'

Somehow the other man's words of reassurance had the opposite effect on Christian; he was now more worried than ever that before the night was out someone was going to die.

Chapter Thirteen

Lisette knew that in her present circumstances she should not be admiring the beauty of her surroundings as she stood on the bridge between her two abductors. One of which she knew to be Davy, the other remaining silent and hidden beneath that cloak, kerchief and the hat pulled low over his eyes.

She should not be appreciating her surroundings, but it was impossible for her not to be grateful for the fresh air she was breathing into her lungs after the stale air in that closed room. Or to be affected by the atmosphere of the night, with the gentle glow of the street lamps overhead casting shadows on the softly flowing river below.

Of course, she would have been happier if she was not still gagged and had her wrists tied behind her back, but Davy's one attempt to remove the gag had resulted in her screaming so loudly he had proclaimed she had 'fair deafened' him with the noise, before he had hastily replaced it.

A nasty smelly piece of now damp rag, which literally made her want to gag every time the smell assailed her nose.

Still, she was at least out of that dark room, and with only these two men to guard her she had hoped for the possibility of escape.

Except there had been no opportunity to do so as she was pushed back into that uncomfortable cart before being brought here to this bridge, the two men now seeming to be waiting for something. Or someone.

Christian?

Lisette could not think of anyone else who would be in the least interested in whether she lived or died. After her earlier disobedience of his instruction, she was not altogether sure that Christian would be interested either.

But she could hope.

Christian could see the three figures standing beneath a guttering street lamp at the far end of the bridge as he and Maystone alighted from his carriage together. None of them looked to be very big, but he was sure that the slighter one in the middle was Lisette. He hoped and prayed the middle one was Lisette, as much as he hoped and prayed that she was unharmed.

'The note said I must go alone, Christian,' Maystone reminded as he placed his hat determinedly upon his head.

'They may be armed—'

'I too am armed,' he reminded quietly, having hidden a pistol in the waistband at the back of his pantaloons. Not the most convenient of places for him to retrieve it, but it would not do to reveal he was armed from the onset. 'But I doubt it will be necessary,' he added softly, his gaze fixed on the three figures on the bridge.

Christian was also armed with a pistol, but he knew that he would never be able to make his shot anything near accurate from this distance. 'What are you not telling me, Aubrey?' He eyed the other man frustratedly.

Maystone gave him a calm smile. 'Does your Lisette possess a temper, Christian?'

'She is not— Yes,' he confirmed impatiently as Maystone raised mocking brows. 'Lisette has a very fine temper indeed.'

'I believed that might be the case.' Maystone nodded. 'A word of advice, Christian: whatever you do, never be the one to incite that temper.'

'Oh, I believe it is far too late for that!' he murmured drily as he recalled the names Lisette had called him in her tirade both yesterday and again today.

'I have no doubt you are more than up to the challenge.' Maystone chuckled as he held out his hand. 'I am glad to have known you, Christian.'

He slowly reached out to take that hand and return the handshake.

'You are a man any parent would be proud to call his son.' The older man nodded in satisfaction.

'What—?'

'Never fear; I will send Lisette back to you in just a few minutes.' He straightened. 'You will find several letters on my desk at home; if I could ask that you deliver them to the appropriate people if I should not return?'

Christian was liking the sound of this less and less.

'Strangest thing about women,' Maystone mused as he stared across the bridge. 'Softest creatures on earth when they are loved, and the most vicious when they are not.'

'Aubrey—'

'I am not rambling, I assure you, Christian,' he continued briskly. 'Wait here for Lisette.'

'But—'

'You will do as I ask, Christian.' The older man's eyes glowed with determination.

Leaving Christian with no choice but to stand and watch as Aubrey Maystone began to walk across the bridge to where Lisette and her abductors waited.

Of one thing Lisette was certain; the man walking across the bridge towards them was not Christian. This man was not tall or broad enough in the shoulders to be him.

And yet he seemed to be walking purposefully towards them. Just as Lisette could also sense the increased tension in the man beside her, the one whose face was covered by the kerchief. As if he knew and recognised the man, if Lisette did not.

Except she did, of course; once the man passed

beneath one of the flickering lamps, she was able to make out that he was none other than Lord Aubrey Maystone.

A man who had no reason to trust her, and surely had absolutely no interest in saving her.

'Is that really necessary?' He stopped just feet away to indicate the gag about Lisette's mouth and the rope about her wrists.

'She's a screamer,' Davy muttered.

Lord Maystone pinned him with his steely blue gaze. 'You would no doubt scream too, young man, if you had been abducted and held a prisoner these past six hours or more! Remove the gag and ropes immediately,' he instructed authoritatively.

Davy turned to look at his accomplice, as if for direction. A direction he received as the other man gave a dismissive wave of his gloved hand without once looking away from Lord Maystone.

Lisette drew in a grateful breath the moment the gag was removed from her mouth; even the pungent odour of the river was more pleasant than the smelly rag.

She was even more relieved when the cord had been removed from about her wrists. Allowing her to rub the numbed flesh and let the blood flow freely to her fingers as she stepped tentatively away from her abductors, moving more quickly as they made no attempt to stop her.

'You are unharmed, my dear?' Lord Maystone prompted gruffly as she reached his side.

'No thanks to these two men,' she confirmed with

a narrow-eyed and accusing glare at Davy, who at least had the grace to shift uncomfortably.

The elderly man nodded. 'In that case, you may return to Christian while I— You will let her go to him, Helene,' he rasped harshly as the man with the kerchief stepped forward as if to prevent Lisette from leaving.

Helene...?

Lisette turned to look wonderingly at the man— woman?—wearing the kerchief, just in time to see that kerchief pulled down and to find herself looking into the hard uncompromising face of the woman who claimed to be her mother.

She felt the blood leach from her cheeks at the realisation that her own mother had been one of her abductors. 'I do not understand...'

Lord Maystone gave a regretful smile. 'I have only just begun to do so—' He broke off as he quickly reached forward to drag Lisette behind him as Helene Rousseau drew a pistol from the waistband of the rough trousers she was wearing.

'I said you were to come alone,' Helene rasped in accented English, her pistol pointed not at Maystone or Lisette but at someone behind them.

Lisette turned to see that Christian now stood just a few feet away, his own pistol aimed at Helene's heart; his approach had been made so stealthily that none on the bridge, least of all Lisette, seemed to have been aware of him standing there until Helene was finally alerted to his presence.

Lisette gave a wince as she saw the dangerous

coldness of Christian's expression as he continued to aim his pistol at Helene. A cold intensity of purpose that prevented Lisette from gauging his mood towards her.

Although she knew that it could not be in the least favourable, when she had put not only herself in danger with her impetuousness, but now also Lord Maystone and Christian himself.

She had every intention of apologising to him for her reckless stupidity if—*when* they had all escaped from this situation unharmed.

In the meantime, she was still finding it difficult to believe that Helene was in London at all, let alone that she had been instrumental in her abduction. The other woman must have followed on another ship almost immediately after their own sloop had left France.

'Put the pistol down, Helene,' Lord Maystone was the one to instruct firmly. 'Before someone gets hurt. Undoubtedly yourself, considering that Christian is an expert shot and unlikely to miss from such close proximity.'

Helene's nostrils flared. 'It is a pity my men did not succeed in disposing of him five days ago.'

Maystone chuckled ruefully as Lisette gave an indignant gasp. 'It is as well for you that they did not, otherwise I fear we would not be having this conversation at all.'

Helene's eyes glittered malevolently as she now turned her pistol onto him. 'I did not come here to talk.'

'I am well aware of it, my dear,' Lord Maystone

accepted wearily. 'And I am completely at your service, if you could first allow Lisette and Christian to depart, and perhaps this young man?' He indicated Davy, now standing back in the shadows.

'I have no intention of going anywhere,' Christian stated firmly, completely baffled as to Helene Rousseau's presence in London, but totally aware that it boded ill for any who were acquainted with her cold ruthlessness.

'Nor I,' Lisette stated just as determinedly.

That was not his intention, Christian acknowledged with frustration. Although, knowing Lisette's stubbornness, he should have expected it. 'Were it not for your rebelliousness of nature, then none of us would be here at all,' he reminded harshly.

A guilty blush instantly coloured her cheeks, her lashes becoming downcast, but for once she remained silent.

Christian found that he disliked Lisette's silence even more than he had enjoyed her outspokenness in regard to himself these past few days.

As much as he disliked the fact that she remained at Maystone's side once she achieved her release. Perhaps understandably when his own anger must be so apparent. Lisette obviously did not realise it, but it was an anger born of anxiety, rather than anything else.

'As the young people both seem bent on being a part of this conversation—' Aubrey Maystone spoke lightly '—perhaps we might all, with the exception of your young accomplice, retire to the comfort of

Sutherland's carriage for the rest of it? Away from prying eyes and listening ears.'

Helene Rousseau gave him a contemptuous glance. 'I have nothing to say to you.'

'Nothing?' He quirked steely brows.

Her mouth thinned. 'No.'

'Just want the satisfaction of putting a bullet through my heart, hmm?' the older man said drily.

The Frenchwoman gave a hard feral smile. 'I have thought of little else for some time now.'

Christian could see the bewilderment in Lisette's expression and knew that it must reflect his own. Maystone had never mentioned knowing Helene Rousseau personally during all these months they had been investigating her and her brother, and yet it was obvious from the conversation that the two had met before.

An uneasy feeling had begun to settle in the depths of Christian's chest.

'Dear, dear, Helene,' Maystone chided mockingly. 'Has no one ever told you that vengeance invariably destroys the avenger rather than the victim of that vengeance?'

She eyed him contemptuously. 'And yet I am the one standing here with a pistol aimed at your treacherous heart.'

'Oh, I did not for a moment mean that you would not kill me, my dear—' Maystone spoke calmly of his own imminent murder in cold blood '—only that by doing so you stand a chance of losing the one thing that matters to you. Am I right?'

Christian was now standing close enough that he could see Helene Rousseau's eyes narrow in warning. 'Perhaps it *would* be best if we were all to retire to my carriage,' he suggested mildly, his pistol remaining unwavering on the Frenchwoman as he turned to look at the boy lingering in the shadows. 'You and I will talk again, young Davy,' he added.

'She made me do it!' He stepped forward in alarm. 'I only went to the tavern for a drink or two that last night ashore in Paris, and—and— She plied me with free liquor and threatened to 'ave someone 'arm me mam if I didn't do as she asked!'

'Which was?'

'To leave word for her at Portsmouth as to where you and the young lady 'ad gone—er—Your Grace. To follow you and then wait for her arrival. I couldn't let nuffink 'appen to me mam, Your Grace,' he added desperately. 'She's all me brothers and sisters 'ave while I'm away at sea. I mean, I like the young lady well enough, but—'

'You are excused, Davy,' Christian interrupted wearily, having no wish to hear how much Davy 'liked' Lisette. He was also well aware of the methods of persuasion of which Helene Rousseau was capable. 'But a lesson has been well learned, I hope?'

'Your Grace?' Davy wrinkled his grubby brow in concentration.

Christian grimaced his exasperation. 'In future, stay away from French taverns and free liquor.'

'Oh.' The grubby brow cleared. 'I will, Your

Grace. Thank you, Your Grace.' He touched a greasy forelock.

'Just go, Davy.' Christian sighed, waiting until the young lad had scuttled away into the darkness before turning back to the woman who had put the fear of God into the boy. 'I trust he, and his family, need not live in fear of any retribution from you?'

Helene Rousseau gave a dismissive snort. 'He was merely a means to an end and is of as much importance to me as the flea on a dog!'

Christian nodded his satisfaction with her answer. 'Then if we might all adjourn to my carriage…?'

Lisette had to admit to being baffled by all that had happened these past few hours—these past few minutes especially.

Helene in London.

The fact that she and Lord Maystone obviously knew each other.

That Helene stated she now wished to kill him.

It seemed to Lisette that everything that had happened these past few months—the kidnapping of Lord Maystone's grandson, Helene's anger at Lisette's… friendship with Christian—a friendship Lisette had almost certainly put in jeopardy with her reckless behaviour—her own abduction earlier today—had all been leading to this face-to-face meeting between Helene Rousseau and Lord Maystone.

Because of some past wrong Helene believed he had done to her.

The shooting of Helene's brother André, perhaps?

Not personally, of course; Lisette had learned

from one of the other serving girls at the tavern that her uncle André had been gunned down outside the tavern in a street brawl. But perhaps a brawl that had been arranged by Lord Maystone?

That did not make any sense when André Rousseau had met his end only months ago, and Helene's grudge against Lord Maystone appeared to be one of long standing.

And if it was of such long standing, why had Helene not sought vengeance before now?

What had happened in Helene's life in the past few months to bring about this sudden need for vengeance—?

Lisette stilled, eyes widening as she turned to look at the woman who had come to the Duprées' farm and claimed to be her mother less than three months ago.

The advent into Helene's life of Lisette, her illegitimate daughter, was what had changed for Helene Rousseau in these past months.

She was the reason Helene was here seeking vengeance against Lord Maystone.

If that was true, then Lisette could think of only one reason for it being so.

'If you will excuse my sudden movement, Helene?' Lord Maystone remarked conversationally as he stepped forward. 'But I do believe our daughter is about to faint.' He gathered Lisette into his arms as she began to sink gracefully to the ground.

Chapter Fourteen

'You should have told me you were with child.'

'*You* had made it clear to me that you were returning to England to your wife and family!'

'Which I duly did. But that still did not prevent you from informing me that you were expecting my child. I could have made provision for you—and her—'

'I did not want your charity—'

'And what about her? Did she not deserve better?'

'I did the best for her that I could, ensured she was placed with a loving couple—'

'Would the two of you please be silent?' Christian cut icily through the argument that had been going on for some time now. Without any pistols in evidence, thank goodness; he could not be answerable for not placing a bullet in both Maystone and Helene Rousseau himself if he had to listen to too much more of their to-and-fro bickering.

And all the time the object of their argument lay

recumbent upon the chaise in Christian's drawing room, covered with the blanket he had demanded from Evans as he carried Lisette into the house, and still unconscious from her faint at Westminster Bridge.

Christian had wasted no time in putting his pistol away and relieving Maystone of the burden of Lisette, ushering her back across the bridge towards his carriage, uncaring whether Maystone and the woman who was his ex-lover followed him or not. His only concern had been for Lisette.

It still was.

She had remained unconscious for the whole of the carriage ride back to Sutherland House, no doubt from fatigue and the relief of knowing she was free as much as anything else. Even Lisette, with her indomitable will, must have been traumatised by her abduction and imprisonment goodness knew where.

Having subsequently realised, as he was sure she had, that Lord Aubrey Maystone was her father must have been the final straw that had broken that indomitable will.

Christian had to admit to being more than a little surprised at that disclosure himself. How on earth had Lord Aubrey Maystone, a man who worked in the shadows for the government and Crown, even met a woman like Helene Rousseau, let alone—let alone— The idea of the two of them having engaged in an affair twenty years ago was astounding—

'I did try to explain earlier that I was once very like you, Christian.' Maystone gently interrupted his thoughts. 'Twenty-five years ago I was also an agent for the Crown, as you are now. My duties often took me to France, and it was during one of these…forays twenty years ago, for information, that I chanced to meet Helene.'

Christian grimaced. 'It would seem that you did more than "meet" her!'

'Yes. Well.' The older man looked uncomfortable. 'I have never claimed to be a saint.'

'Neither have I—but I do not believe I have ever impregnated a woman and then abandoned her!'

The older man closed his eyes briefly. 'It was not like that.'

'Then pray tell us what it was "like"?' Lisette finally stirred from lying prone on the chaise, her head aching as she sat up. She felt unable to even glance at Christian as he stood beside the window, for fear of the condemnation she might see in his face that her actions earlier had brought them all to this. Instead she chose to look only at the man and woman she now knew to be her parents.

A more unlikely couple she could not imagine— Helene so tall and fierce, Aubrey Maystone several inches shorter, and with an aristocratic face that now softened into lines of concern as he looked across at her.

Her father.

Lord Aubrey Maystone was her father.

The very *English* Lord Aubrey Maystone.

Lisette had been in turmoil as to who her father might be since learning that Helene was her mother;

it did not seem possible, after the fears Lisette had harboured in regard to this English Lord for the past few days, to now learn that he was also the man who had fathered her.

He stood up now, as if he might come to her, but instead he began pacing in front of the fireplace when Lisette glared at him almost as fiercely as Helene was now doing. 'Once I learned earlier today that you were Helene's daughter—' He gave a shake of his head. 'I knew the moment I saw you that you must also be my own daughter.' He looked at Lisette wonderingly. 'You look exactly like my sister—your aunt Anna,' he explained at her wide-eyed look.

Lisette recalled the way he had stared at her when they were introduced earlier. 'I have an aunt…?'

He nodded. 'And several half-brothers and sisters, and nieces and nephews—'

'Let us not become distracted with a list of Lisette's English relatives.' Christian stepped forward into the centre of the room. 'Surely you all must see that this situation is… It is far more complicated than I could ever have imagined.' Although he did have some explanation, at least, as to why Maystone had seemed so befuddled earlier today when he met Lisette for the first time.

And it had also not escaped Christian's notice that Lisette had not so much as glanced in his direction since she regained consciousness.

Because she felt awkward, having now learned of her true parentage?

Perhaps because she now felt uncomfortable recalling their own conversation earlier today, when she had offered to become his mistress?

Or it might just be that she was aware this present situation had come about because she had disobeyed him, and so allowed for her own abduction?

The former she was most certainly not responsible for.

Nor could Christian ever have contemplated taking Lisette as his mistress.

And he was no longer sure Lisette could be held even partly responsible for her own abduction either.

For one thing, Helene Rousseau had obviously been bent on reclaiming her daughter, as well as seeking vengeance on her erstwhile lover. Christian was now convinced that if the older woman had not abducted Lisette when she had, she would only have found another day when she might do so.

As for Lisette disobeying him... Christian had *known* she was upset earlier, after he had rejected her offer to become his mistress.

Just as he had known how headstrong she was.

Consequently he should have had more safeguards put in place to prevent her from straying outside the house. At the very least, he should have alerted Evans to the fact that Lisette might attempt to do exactly that, and to wake him immediately if it should occur. Instead, several hours had elapsed—including his lazing in the bath for almost an hour—before he was even made aware Lisette had left the house.

If anyone or anything was to blame for what she had suffered today, then it was Christian's own arrogance in having believed he could issue a mandate to Lisette and expect her to obey it without question.

She had felt so tiny in his arms earlier, so fragile as he carried her across the bridge. A painful reminder of how close he had come to losing her.

Just the thought of that was indeed painful.

He had, he realised, become accustomed to having Lisette in his life—arguing with her, teasing her, laughing with her, *making love to her.* Even after only a few hours of her presence, his house had seemed empty without her in it.

His *life* would be equally empty without her in it.

But if she really was Maystone's daughter—and the other man appeared to have no doubts on the matter—then Christian knew he had already lost the Lisette he knew. Not to kidnappers, or death, as he had feared earlier, but to the father who would surely now claim her as his own.

There would be a brief scandal, of course—Lisette had been born during Maystone's marriage, after all—but she was not the first illegitimate child to have later been given legitimacy when claimed by her father. Maystone was certainly more than powerful enough to weather such a storm.

And Lisette?

Lisette had already ably demonstrated her own fortitude.

She would possibly object initially, but with time she would no doubt become the polished, the Honourable Miss Lisette Maystone.

And while she might politely acknowledge Christian Seaton, the Duke of Sutherland, at a ball or some other society entertainment, they would meet as polite strangers, would no longer be the Lisette and Christian they had been for these past days.

Arguing. Teasing. Laughing. Making love together.

That realisation was enough to bring back the heavy ache in his chest.

'I do not see any complication; Lisette is my daughter, and I will immediately acknowledge her as such,' Maystone announced predictably. 'Unless, of course, you are still intent on shooting me?' He glanced ruefully at Helene Rousseau.

'Do not mock me, *monsieur*!' Helene glared at him.

'I am not mocking you.' He sighed wearily. 'I am only sorry that my actions twenty years ago have caused such a deep and abiding resentment inside you. You were responsible for the kidnapping of my grandson two months ago, were you not?'

Her face flushed. 'For Napoleon's cause—'

'Not for Napoleon's cause, Helene, but your own,' Maystone corrected softly. 'You no doubt thought to pay me back in some measure for what you considered my cavalier treatment of you all those years ago. You should not have used an innocent child as a weapon, Helene,' he rebuked her. 'I am perfectly willing to pay for my crimes, but Michael and his parents did not deserve to suffer in that way.'

'And what of my innocent child?' Helene challenged.

'If you had told me all those years ago, come to

me after Lisette was born even, then Lisette need not have suffered either!'

'You would not have acknowledged her as your daughter while your wife still lived,' the French-woman said scornfully.

'I would have ensured that she wanted for nothing—'

'You would not have acknowledged her!'

'I will acknowledge her now. And gladly,' May-stone assured her fervently. '*If* you should choose not to shoot me, Lisette will stay here in England with me, as my recognised daughter.'

'And if I do not agree?'

'I will of course listen to your arguments regard-ing the pros and cons of the situation—'

'And then do just as you wish, as you always have!'

'Am I to have no say in this matter?' Lisette now rose impatiently to her feet, having heard enough from both these people who claimed to be her par-ents. 'I am not a sweetmeat for the two of you to fight over. I am a person. With—with feelings of my own.' Tears stung her eyes. 'Three months ago I lived on a farm and believed the Duprées were my parents. I then learned that I was the illegitimate daughter of tavern owner Helene Rousseau. Now I am expected to accept that I am also the daughter of an English lord.' She threw her hands up in disgust. 'What if I should decide I do not wish to live with either of you? If—if I wish to establish my own household? Separate from either of you?'

Lord Maystone—her father—looked disconcerted.

'It really is not the done thing for a single young lady to establish her own household—'

'For an English young lady, perhaps,' Lisette accepted stubbornly. 'But I am not English.'

'You could be, and in just a little time.' Lord Maystone nodded. 'I will hire a tutor to teach you to speak the language, and my daughter-in-law will, I am sure, give her advice on the correct gowns. In no time at all you will be an English young lady, and it will very soon be forgotten that you were ever French—'

'Not by me!' Lisette insisted exasperatedly. 'I *am* French. I am proud to be French. And I will not deny my birthplace to suit English *société*.'

'But my dear—'

'Do not "my dear" me!' Lisette all but stamped her foot in her increasing frustration with this situation. 'A very short time ago I believed you would put me in chains and lock me away, simply because I am Helene Rousseau's daughter—'

'Are you responsible for telling her such a thing, Christian?' Maystone frowned at him.

'He did not need to do so,' Lisette continued impatiently. 'It was to be expected, when I am the daughter of a known conspirator against your English Crown. Except now I am expected to believe that you will not lock me in chains after all, because you are *mon père*.' She gave a shake of her head. 'I cannot so easily adjust to all these sudden changes in my life.'

'Nor should you be expected to do so.' Christian

decided it was time—past time—that he intervened on Lisette's behalf. 'Madame Rousseau, Lord Maystone, I suggest for the moment that Lisette remains here at Sutherland House with me. That she be given time in which to…to come to terms with these sudden changes in her circumstances so that she might then make an educated judgement as to which life suits her best, England or France.'

'Impossible!'

'Impossible!'

At last the older couple seemed to agree on something. Even if it was Christian's suggestion that Lisette should remain here with him.

It was an impossible solution; he had known that before making it. Wanting something did not make it so.

Just as he knew his reasons for making it were totally selfish ones.

He simply could not bear the thought of losing Lisette, of the two of them becoming polite strangers to each other.

'Madame Rousseau.' He turned to look at her between narrowed lids. 'You knew Lisette had come to my home that night in Paris, so why did you not do more to prevent her from travelling to England with me?'

'I followed on the next available ship—'

'Why did you wait at all, when the two of you had argued— I do not appreciate the fact that you struck Lisette, by the way,' he added darkly.

'It was a mistake—an impulse— She is so headstrong, I could not make her see reason,' Helene admitted heavily. 'I deeply regret ever striking you, Lisette. I only wanted to save you from…from making a fool of yourself, as I did over your father.' She shot Maystone a scathing glance.

Christian did not wish to begin *that* particular argument all over again. 'That still does not explain why you allowed Lisette to come to England with me and then followed her.'

Helene's chin rose. 'I came here to take her back with me, of course.'

'Why?'

'Pourquoi?' she repeated. 'I do not understand…'

Christian sighed. 'You do not even acknowledge Lisette as being your daughter, so why would you even bother following her and trying to take her back to Paris with you? Why did you abduct her? In order to bring Maystone to you? So that you might kill him?' Christian continued determinedly. 'Or was it for another reason entirely?'

Helene's eyes narrowed on Maystone. 'He deserves to die. He made love to me then returned to his wife without giving me a second thought, and left me with child!'

Christian's mouth twisted wryly as he glanced at Lisette. 'You really are your mother's daughter.'

Lisette felt the colour heat her cheeks at the memory of the insults she'd thrown at Christian just yesterday.

It seemed so much longer than just a single day

had passed since she verbally vented her anger at Christian at the inn in Portsmouth.

So much had happened in the past thirty-six hours that she really did feel at a loss to comprehend it, to take it all in, let alone make a life-changing decision.

Quite what Christian made of it all she did not like to hazard a guess.

He now gave a shake of his head. 'There must have been any number of opportunities for you to…dispose of Maystone these past twenty years, *madame*. Why should you feel such a need to make him suffer now? To exact your revenge? To think of killing him? Or was it for another reason entirely that you wished to introduce Lord Maystone to his daughter?'

'I do not— He is not— Bah!' Helene threw up her hands in disgust.

Christian gave a rueful grimace. 'Can it be that, in your own way, you do love your daughter? That you wish only the best for her? Even if you have now realised that best is not with you in a tavern in Paris?'

Lisette looked sharply at the woman who had given birth to her; she still could not think of her as her mother. Helene continued to look at Christian, eyes glittering.

'I remember the night we all met at your tavern in Paris, *madame*,' Christian continued softly. 'Your threat to shoot me—a habit you really should think of breaking!—if I should even think of laying so much as a hand upon Lisette.'

Colour darkened Helene's cheeks. 'You— I— You are an English spy!'

'At that moment I was only a man looking at your daughter with lustful eyes.' He shrugged as Lisette gave a shocked gasp. 'I'm first and foremost a man, Lisette,' he excused drily. 'And that night you stood out as pure as a rose amongst lesser, bruised blooms.'

'Helene…?' Maystone prompted softly.

'I do not— I am—' She broke off, her mouth thinning stubbornly.

'I believe, despite everything, Madame Rousseau, that you are a mother who wants what is best for her daughter,' Christian continued softly. 'You were young when she was born, and no doubt it seemed the best thing for all if she was placed with foster parents. But, from the little Lisette has told me, you went immediately to claim her the moment you realised those foster parents had both died. That is not the behaviour of a woman who did not care for her child.'

Lisette had never thought of Helene's actions in quite that way before…

She saw now that Christian was right.

She had no knowledge of Helene until that day she came to the farm for her, no awareness that the Duprées were not her real parents. Helene could so easily have ignored Lisette's existence, and merely thought herself fortunate in no longer having the burden of paying for her child's upkeep.

Instead Helene had taken her to live with her in Paris. Not an ideal situation, for either of them, but she could see now that Helene had perhaps done her best in the circumstances.

'You love me…?' she prompted tentatively.

Helene looked first irritated and then exasperated. 'Of course I love you, you stupid child! Perhaps I do not have the necessary skills to be *votre mère*, but I tried as best I could to protect you. *You* were the one who constantly threw yourself in the path of danger, first with Le Duc and now here again in London.'

'A habit I have also tried—and failed—to curb, *madame*,' Christian drawled.

Lisette gave him a quelling glance before turning back to Helene. 'You believed that following me to England, arranging for me to be kidnapped and then threatening to kill *mon père* in front of my eyes, having just discovered who he was, to be an effective way of protecting me?'

'She would never have shot him, Lisette,' Christian chided gently. 'That was not your intention at all, was it, *madame*?'

'He—'

'I am not interested in what he did or did not do twenty years ago.' Christian spoke firmly. 'It is here and now that is important.'

Helene seemed to fight a battle within herself for some seconds before her shoulders slumped. 'I have tried, these past months, to be a mother to Lisette, but I simply do not— The tavern is not—' She gave a shake of her head. 'She is not happy there, and I am not happy for her to be there either. Not for the reason you suppose, Lisette,' she added softly as she flinched. 'You do not belong in such a place; I knew that from the start. I became convinced of it when the Comte took such an interest in you.'

Lisette frowned. 'If that is true, why did you not simply contact *mon père* and ask him to take me, rather than go through this elaborate charade to achieve your aim?'

'Pride,' Lord Maystone put in gently. 'I believe, my dear Lisette, that when judging your mother you should also consider my own part in all of this. As far as Helene was concerned, I had abandoned her. She is a proud woman. A strong and independent woman. To have asked me for help now would have been—' He looked at Helene. 'It simply could not have been borne.'

'How can you defend her when she arranged for the kidnapping of your grandson?' Lisette frowned.

He smiled sadly. 'I am not defending, only understanding.'

Lisette looked at him with the beginning of a grudging affection; Aubrey Maystone might not have been in love with Helene all those years ago, but he had certainly known her—the woman that she had been and still was.

And Lisette…she *could* understand Helene's need, not only for revenge but also for the assistance of the man who had fathered her child twenty years ago.

She understood it, even if she could never have behaved in such a way herself.

'Helene—' Lord Maystone spoke again '—I promise you I would never have abandoned you, or our daughter, if you had once told me of her existence. I will not abandon you now. Either of you,' he added firmly before turning to Christian. 'There will be questions for Helene to answer to the English Crown, but I believe I have enough favours to draw upon to make those questions less…probing than they might otherwise have been. Your brother André was the main conspirator, was he not?' he prompted Helene.

'I tried as best I could to continue his work after he was killed,' Helene stated flatly.

'Did any of your actions succeed?' he mused.

She sighed. 'You know they did not.'

'You arranged for Christian to be shot!' Lisette reminded exasperatedly.

'It was never meant to be a killing shot, Lisette,' Christian said with certainty. 'Am I right, *madame*? You wished only to disable me enough that I must return to England, in the hope I would take Lisette with me?'

Lisette looked round-eyed at her mother. 'Is this true?'

'He is far too intelligent, that one,' Helene muttered.

'That he is.' Maystone nodded with satisfaction. 'I will take it upon myself to explain all to my son and daughter-in-law in regard to the reason Michael was chosen for abduction. After which, I see no reason why Helene should not be allowed to return to Paris. For you to come back to England to visit Lisette occasionally, if that is what you wish. As long as you first make a promise to cease this war against the English Crown,' he added sternly. 'And your personal vendetta against me, of course,' he said with a grimace.

'And Lisette?' Helene prompted huskily.

Lord Aubrey Maystone, the man Lisette now knew to be her father, turned to look at her. 'I believe that must now be for Lisette to decide…'

Lisette looked at the three other people in the room.

Helene, who loved her but was totally incapable of showing that love.

Lord Maystone, who had learned only hours ago that he was her father but already showed a surprising protectiveness towards her, to the extent he had offered himself up to be shot this evening if Helene would only release her.

And Christian.

Christian, of the wicked lavender-coloured eyes.

Christian, of the wicked hands and lips that reduced her to a limp and satiated puddle every time he took her in his arms.

Christian…

A man—the *only* person here—Lisette knew she could trust completely.

The one she could not bear to be parted from.

A fact she had realised during the hours she had been tied and kept prisoner, when she'd had nothing else to entertain her but her own thoughts. A time when she had realised her heart was breaking at the thought she might never look upon Christian's handsome face and those wicked lavender-coloured eyes again.

Because she had fallen in love with him.

Was so much in love with him that she had even offered to become his mistress, if he would have her.

An offer he had refused.

But perhaps if she were to become Lord Maystone's daughter, this English Miss he wished to make of her, then she might still see Christian occasionally?

She did not wish to leave France, but she no longer had a real home there. Only Helene. But Lord Maystone had said he would arrange it so that Helene and she might see each other sometimes and perhaps, over time, the two of them might come to feel some sort of affection and understanding for each other.

Lisette had no wish to become an English Miss either.

Except…

Except this was where Christian was.

Lisette raised her chin, her decision made.

Chapter Fifteen

One month later

'I hate to say it, old chap, but you have been like a bear with a sore head these past few weeks!' Marcus murmured conversationally as the two men stood at the edge of the dance floor in Maystone's full-to-overflowing ballroom.

Christian's scowl did not lessen in the slightest as he glowered at the young buck twirling past with a glowing Lisette in his arms.

A transformed Lisette, with her fashionably styled red curls and equally fashionable sky-blue silk gown, with matching slippers upon her dainty feet as she danced lightly, and perfectly, by.

She now looked and sounded—he had spoken to her briefly, politely, as she stood at her father's side receiving their guests—every inch the young English society Miss, with not a trace of a French accent to her softly spoken voice, her manner one of perfect politeness.

Tonight was the occasion of Lisette's formal introduction into society, Maystone having decided that, in these unusual circumstances, the 'Little Season' would suit for an introductory ball far better than waiting until next February or March, when the main London Season would begin.

Maystone had organised everything as he had intended, of course. Helene Rousseau had returned to France a few weeks ago, with the blessing of both her daughter and the English Crown. Maystone had resigned his position, and he now spent his time escorting and introducing his young daughter to England and English society.

There had been much talk and speculation these past weeks in regard to the sudden appearance in London of Lord Aubrey Maystone's daughter, and many society families had returned to London for a week or two for the sole purpose of attending this ball, and the opportunity to meet and speak with her.

That the evening was a success could not be doubted, no expense having been spared in Lisette's dress and the beautiful pearls that adorned her ears and her throat, or the champagne and refreshments being served to the guests. Exalted guests, considering there were six Dukes in the room at least; Maystone had invited and made it clear he expected all of the Dangerous Dukes and their wives to attend.

There were also dozens of single young gentlemen literally queuing up to dance with Lisette, or to gather about her when the dancing paused or refreshments were served.

Christian wanted to strangle them all. One by one. Slowly. Thoroughly. Until there was only himself and Lisette left in the room. Perhaps then she might actually say something to him other than, 'Good evening, Your Grace. I am pleased you were able to attend this evening', in that very precise and totally un-Lisette-like English voice.

It had been a little over four weeks—four weeks, three days and two hours, to be precise—since Lisette had made her choice to remain in London and reside at the home of her newly discovered father.

Over four long and tedious weeks—Christian having spent the first frustrating week recovering fully from the wound to his thigh, the following three having been just as frustrating, but in a different way. He had not so much as been able to see or speak a single word alone with Lisette.

Oh, he had called at Maystone House many times once he was fully recovered.

The first time had been in the late morning, and he had been politely shown into the drawing room. Only to then find himself in a room with a genial Maystone and many young and hopeful beaus awaiting the appearance of their young hostess, after having met her the previous evening when she had attended a musical soirée with her father. Lisette had finally arrived, only to ignore his very presence as she sat quietly beside an obviously paternally proud Maystone.

The second time Christian had called it had been in the afternoon, only to learn that Lisette was out at her dressmaker's and not expected back for some time.

The third time had been in the early evening; a time when he had been sure that Lisette must be at home.

He had been wrong.

Miss Maystone, he had been informed by the butler, had gone to the country with her father, to spend the weekend with their family.

That had not been the last of Christian's visits; he had called every two or three days after that, but was always informed that Miss Maystone was either not available or was out.

Leaving Christian to conclude, from the number of times he was fobbed off with one excuse or another, that Miss Maystone had no wish to see him, no matter when he should call.

While Christian was pleased for Lisette that her choice appeared to have been the right one for her, he could not help his own feelings of frustration in not being able to get close enough to so much as speak a private word with her, let alone steal a taste of those delectable pink lips that haunted his dreams every night.

He now turned away from the dance floor and the vision of Lisette laughing gaily up into the handsome face of the young man who was now escorting her back to her father's side.

Lisette was a success.

He should be pleased for her.

He *was* pleased for her.

He was just hellishly miserable for himself. Marcus was right; he had been damned poor company this past month.

But he *missed* Lisette, damn it.

He missed her smile, her impetuosity that had caused her to become involved in so many scrapes—scrapes he had invariably been called upon to rescue her from. He even missed her temper.

Except the Lisette she was now—refined, genteel, every inch the English young lady—no longer appeared to have a temper.

He straightened the cuff of his evening jacket. 'I believe I have had enough for one evening, Marcus. You?'

The other man eyed him impatiently. 'I only came at all because Julianna said that I should, in support of you. We delayed going to the country so that I might attend.' Julianna was now very large with child and would not be out and about in society again until after the babe had been born.

Christian raised haughty brows. 'Support of me?'

Worthing gave an impatient shake of his head. 'You are fooling no one with this act, Christian. If *I* know you are pining for your French *mademoiselle*, then you may be assured that Julianna knew of it long before I did! Besides,' he added slyly, 'Miss Lisette Maystone and my wife are now firm friends.'

'What?' Christian could not think of a worse friendship than one between his interfering sister and the irrepressible Lisette. 'How did the two of them even meet?' he demanded irritably.

'My wife deemed it only polite to call upon Miss Maystone and welcome her to London and into society,' Worthing informed him loftily.

Put that way, it was a generous act on Julianna's part; a welcoming visit from the Duchess of Worthing would ensure that all doors in society would be open to Lisette.

Still, Christian could not rid himself of the feeling that a friendship between Julianna and Lisette was a recipe for disaster.

His mouth thinned. 'Whatever you and Julianna are about, Marcus, I advise you to desist. Any attempt to matchmake between myself and Miss Maystone is a complete waste of your own time and mine—'

'No more so than it would be of my own, I do assure you, Your Grace.' An icily haughty voice spoke behind him.

An icily haughty voice that Christian instantly recognised as belonging to Lisette.

Lisette had looked forward to the night of her father's ball with both excitement and trepidation.

Excitement because it was the first ball she had ever attended, and she was to wear a beautiful gown that had been designed and made especially for her for this occasion.

Trepidation because she so longed to see Christian again at the same time as she felt apprehensive about such a meeting.

She had spent the past month becoming the English Miss expected of her as Lord Aubrey Maystone's daughter. Had learned to speak English as clearly and precisely as any in society. Had attended numerous fittings for all the clothes she was assured she would need as a member of that society. Had diligently followed the instructions of her dance instructor, and the teachings of her father in correct manners and conversation.

All of it working towards this single evening.

The evening she was to be with Christian again, when he would see she could be as refined and lady-like as any of the beauties in the society of which he was such a part.

She had worked and struggled hard to become that lady in these four short weeks.

Only to now overhear him dismissing her as if she were no more than a passing acquaintance he had no more regard for than he did all those other silly young debutantes who reputedly threw themselves at him at the start of every Season in the hope of becoming his duchess.

She had felt hopeful as she sensed his gaze upon her throughout the evening, and had deliberately laughed and flirted with all the eligible young gentlemen her father had invited to amuse her. All in the hope that she might pique Christian into inviting her to stand up with him for one dance, at least.

When he had not she had finally decided it was acceptable for her to ask one of the young gentlemen to escort her across the room to speak with Marcus Wilding so that she might enquire about the health of his wife, whom she now counted as her friend. It was no coincidence that Christian stood at that gentleman's side.

The humiliation she now felt, upon hearing Christian's comment to Marcus Wilding, was overwhelming. And made all the more so because Sir Percy Winterbourne, her current escort, had also overheard the derogatory remark.

Christian turned to look at her now, that haughtily superior expression upon his handsome face as he looked down the length of his aristocratic nose at her, those lavender-coloured eyes as cold as ice. 'I merely meant, Miss Maystone, that to add yet another admirer to those already clustered about you would appear to be entirely superfluous,' he drawled mockingly. 'Winterbourne.' He nodded briefly to the man at Lisette's side.

'How true, Your Grace.' Lisette bared her teeth in a smile.

He had bungled this badly, Christian acknowledged with an inward groan of self-disgust. This was the first occasion upon which he had spoken to Lisette away from the watchful eye of her overprotective father, and he had insulted her. Out of self-defence, admittedly, but it was a poor excuse for his rudeness to the young woman who had, he had no doubt, saved his life on more than one occasion, usually to her own detriment.

He drew himself up to his full height. 'I apologise if my remark sounded...less than polite. It was not intended to be, I assure you.'

Lisette looked up at him sceptically. 'Your apology is accepted, Your Grace.'

'Perhaps as confirmation of that acceptance you might graciously allow me the next dance?' Christian tensed as he waited for her refusal.

'Oh, but—'

'Been meaning to have a chat with you this evening, Winterbourne—' Marcus Wilding interrupted the younger man's protest '—about that fine piece of horse flesh I saw you on in the park this morning.'

'Really?' The young buck visibly preened at this praise from the Duke of Worthing.

'Oh, yes. Be interested to know where you purchased it.' Worthing continued talking as he first drew the younger man aside before stepping away completely.

'It would seem that Marcus has become as much the matchmaker as my sister.'

Lisette turned to give Christian a scathing glance. 'I assure you, I am no more pleased with this arrangement than you are!'

'Ah, there she is…' Christian murmured with satisfaction.

Her look of scorn turned to a puzzled frown. 'Am I keeping you from someone…?'

'Not at all.' Christian grinned widely; the first time he could remember doing so for some time. Four weeks, three days and two hours, to be exact.

'I do not understand…'

Christian could not seem to stop himself from

grinning. 'I am very pleased, very pleased indeed, to remake your acquaintance, Mademoiselle Duprée.'

'I am Miss Maystone now.' Those blue eyes flashed with impatience. 'And I have been in London these past four weeks, if you had cared to call.'

It was Christian's turn to frown now. 'But I have called upon you. Many times.'

'I do not think so,' Lisette dismissed scathingly. 'I recall only the once, a morning visit in the presence of a dozen other people, when you did not speak so much as a single word to me but stood in a corner of my father's drawing room looking down your haughty nose at everyone!'

'But—' Christian broke off to gaze across to where Aubrey Maystone stood in conversation with the other Dangerous Dukes and their wives. As if aware of his gaze, Maystone glanced across to where Christian and Lisette stood talking together, one iron-grey eyebrow slowly rising in mocking enquiry. 'That wily old fox…' Christian muttered, knowing from the challenging look Maystone was giving him that he was responsible for Lisette not knowing of the many visits Christian had made to Maystone House this past month, his only intention to see her again.

'*Quoi?* I mean, I beg your pardon?' Lisette's cheeks blushed a becoming shade of pink at her mistake in having lapsed into her native French.

Christian gave a roar of laughter, relieved to learn that it had not been Lisette avoiding him after all, but the machinations of her interfering father. His laughter caused more than a few heads to turn in their direction; the Duke of Sutherland was not known for his public displays of levity.

'I fail to see what is so funny in my having let down *mon père* by not speaking the King's English?' Lisette eyed him irritably.

Christian sobered a little. '*Mon père* is not "let down" but is the wily old fox to whom I referred.' He smiled wryly. 'Once a spymaster, always a spymaster, it would seem.'

'Are you quite recovered from your injury, Christian—Your Grace?' Lisette corrected hastily. 'Do you have a fever?' She could think of no other reason for his current strange conversation.

'Would you care to take a stroll out on the terrace with me, Miss Duprée?' He did not wait for her answer before tucking her gloved hand into the crook of his arm and striding off in the direction of the doors opened to prevent the room from becoming too stifling.

'Is such behaviour quite correct, Christian?' Lisette cast a furtive glance at the people she sensed were watching the two of them together, the women from behind their fans, the gentlemen openly speculative of the Duke of Sutherland's obvious intention of stealing their young hostess outside onto the moonlit terrace.

'Correct can go hang, Lisette,' Christian dismissed happily. 'If I do not soon taste your delectable lips and touch your creamy flesh, I am afraid I will do something that will never be forgotten, by not only those members of society present tonight but also the heirs that come after them!'

'Christian!' Lisette gasped her shock.

'Lisette.' He stood aside to allow her to precede him out onto the terrace.

She looked up at him uncertainly, unsure of Christian in this reckless mood. 'My reputation will be ruined if I go outside alone with you.'

'So it will,' he acknowledged unconcernedly.

'Can you possibly have drunk too much champagne this evening?'

'First I am fevered. Then I am accused of neglecting you. Now you believe me to be drunk!' He gave a brief laugh. 'I assure you, my dearest Lisette, I am none of those things,' he added huskily.

'But—'

'My wound is perfectly healed, thanks to your initial diligent care, my doctor has informed me. If I am drunk then it is with the pleasure of being in your company again, for I have not drunk so much as one glass of champagne this evening. As for being neglectful...' He gave a shake of his head. 'I was slightly incapacitated that first week, but I have called at Maystone House every two or three days these past three weeks.'

'I have not seen you...'

'No, you have not,' Christian acknowledged drily. 'And I have not seen you, except at a distance once or twice, as you travelled by in Maystone's coach.' Fleeting glimpses that had reminded him of the last time he and Lisette were in a coach together, those memories leaving him hungering for so much more than a fleeting glimpse of her. 'Please step outside with me, Lisette, and allow me to explain.' He looked down at her intently.

Lisette still eyed him uncertainly, so tempted to do as he asked, at the same time aware of the many eyes upon them as they stood in the open doorway, neither in nor outside of the house. 'What is there to explain?' she prompted slowly.

Christian glanced across at her father, the tension leaving his shoulders as he received a slight nod from the older man. Not that it would have made the slightest difference if he did not have Maystone's blessing, but he was glad of it in any case, for Lisette's sake.

He turned back to her. 'How about what a pompous, blind, ungrateful ass I am?' he began, knowing that Lisette would not have seen the look that passed between the two men.

'Blind and ungrateful how…?'

Christian gave a throaty chuckle. 'I notice you do not question the "pompous" or the "ass"?'

'The first is no doubt because you are a duke. The second…?' She gave one of those achingly familiar Gallic shrugs. 'Perhaps for the same reason?'

Christian choked back another shout of laughter. Indeed he was fast reaching a point where he really would shock all in the room, and to hell with them, their heirs *and* his own. 'Please come outside with me, Lisette,' he pressed urgently.

'If you are merely going to upbraid me for my outspokenness to you just now, or some other social misdemeanour I have made, then I would really rather not—'

'*You* may upbraid me, if you wish,' he asserted fervently. 'For what you have perceived as my tardiness, my neglect and what I now believe to have been my *utter stupidity* in not doing this sooner!'

Lisette gave a gasp as 'this' became Christian sweeping her up into his arms before carrying her outside.

From the ballroom at Maystone House.

For all and everyone in London society to see.

Chapter Sixteen

'How can you have been so…so *stupide*?' Lisette glared up at Christian in the moonlight bathing the terrace on which they both now stood, the pummelling of her fists upon his chest finally having secured her release. Her cheeks were flushed, her eyes glittering with temper. *'Imbécile!'*

Christian needed no translation of the names Lisette had just called him.

Nor did he say a word to stop her, but simply wallowed in the pleasure of knowing his Lisette was here, after all.

This was the Lisette he remembered.

And it was because of her return that he could not regret his actions of a few minutes ago. Damn it, he would have done something very like it long before now, if he had not felt as if Lisette had become a stranger to him.

The musicians had drawn to a discordant halt as they lost their place in the music, to openly stare, along with the rest of the people assembled in Maystone's ballroom, as Christian had swept Lisette up in his arms and carried her out onto the moonlit terrace.

Christian knew the chatter he could now hear above the musicians resuming their playing—no doubt having been encouraged to do so by their host—would all be about the two of them.

Scandalous.

Shocking.

Damning.

Very damning for a duke to behave in such a reckless fashion in public.

And Christian did not regret it for a single moment.

How could he, when Lisette was currently berating him, that rapid-fire French he loved to hear spewing forth from those delectable lips.

Instead of being insulted, as she no doubt intended he should be, it was like sweet music to his ears after all these weeks of silence between them.

He leaned back against the balustrade as Lisette paced up and down in front of him, knowing that even she would eventually run out of names to call him.

In the meantime, he could enjoy the sight of her. She really was magnificent when she was in full spate. Her hair seemed a brighter red, eyes sparkling like sapphires, cheeks aflame with colour, her lips a deeper rose, that tiny chin lifted high, her breasts— Ah, those magnificent breasts. *They* were quickly rising and falling above the low neckline of her gown.

Almost indecently so, Christian realised with a

frown. Maystone really should not have let Lisette wear a gown with such a scandalously low neckline as this in public. It was the sort of gown that only a lover should see, or a—

'You are not even listening to me. *Imbécile!*'

Ah, Lisette was starting to repeat herself. Time to attempt to redeem himself perhaps—

'No, of course you are not,' she answered her own question impatiently. 'You are the esteemed Duke of Sutherland; why should it matter to you that you have just completely sullied my reputation—?'

'And my own,' he interjected softly.

'—when men are not held up to the same rules and limitations in English society— *Quoi?*' She frowned as his words finally penetrated her anger.

'I have just sullied my own reputation too, Lisette.' Christian straightened away from the balustrade. 'To such a degree, I believe the only course that might save us both from the derision and pillory of our peers—'

'They are your peers, not mine.' She glared at him. '*I* am not even properly launched into society and already I am ruined. My poor papa must be beside himself!' Her gloved hands twisted together in her agitation.

Christian chuckled softly. 'Unless I am mistaken, your "poor papa" is at this moment filled with self-satisfied jubilation.'

'You really are *ivre*—' She paused, obviously seeking the translation. 'Inebriated. You are inebriated,' she repeated firmly. 'Drunk. Soused—'

'I believe you have made yourself clear, thank you, Lisette,' he drawled. 'And no, I am perfectly sober, I do assure you.'

'Then what on earth possessed you to behave in such a scandalous fashion?'

He shrugged. 'It succeeded in securing your singular attention, did it not?'

Lisette could have cried with pure frustration at the social disaster that had just occurred. All those hours, weeks of excruciating lessons and dress fittings and tedious social visits to her papa's friends, had all been stripped away, demolished by the simple action of Christian sweeping her up in his arms and carrying her from the ballroom.

She would be disgraced, a laughing stock, and her poor papa would never recover from the humiliation caused by his French daughter.

'How could you do such a thing?' Her voice broke emotionally. 'I have tried so hard to be everything that was expected of me. Have suffered through such torments with the dressmakers and milliners and dance instructor, and now it has all been for naught. I am disgraced, will have to retire to the country, become what the English call an Old Maid—' She stopped as Christian gave another roar of laughter.

Indeed, he laughed so loudly and for so long Lisette seriously feared for his sanity.

'Your amusement at my expense is most unwelcome, Christian,' she informed him haughtily when that laughter at last seemed to be abating.

He gave a shake of his head. 'One thing you will never be is an Old Maid, Lisette!'

'You— What are you doing?' she squeaked in surprise as he fell to his knees in front of her. 'You must get up!' She attempted—and failed utterly— to take him by the hands and pull him back up onto his perfectly shod feet. 'I expect only a few words of apology from you, Christian, not this—this— What is it that you are doing?' She frowned her consternation at his unusual behaviour.

'I am trying to ask you to marry me. Not very successfully, I admit,' he acknowledged drily. 'But that could be because the object of my affections is too busy berating me to listen to me— Lisette…?' He voiced his concern as she released his hands to stagger away from him until she could go no further, back resting against the balustrade, hand clasped to her breast. 'Lisette—'

'Remain exactly where you are!' She now held her hands up in warning as Christian rose to his feet with the intention of going to her. 'You— This is— I—' She gave a shake of her head. 'You should not play with me in this cruel manner,' she admonished huskily. 'It is wholly unworthy of you.'

Christian tilted his head to one side as he studied the pallor of Lisette's face. Unless he was mistaken, there were tears in those sapphire-blue eyes, her cheeks were pale, her bottom lip trembling slightly, as if she was barely retaining control of those tears.

He stepped forward. 'Maystone should have

decked you out in sapphires to match your eyes rather than those pearls.'

'He said—'

'Yes?'

She swallowed. 'He said that it was the role of my future husband to give me sapphires.'

Christian would have fought Maystone for Lisette if he'd had to do so, but he knew in that moment that he had not misunderstood the other man's nod of approval just a short time ago; the Sutherland sapphires—earbobs, a necklace and bracelet—were always given to the new Duchess by her Duke to wear on their wedding day.

'He was quite right; it is.' Christian took another step forward, to stand only inches in front of her. 'I do apologise most sincerely if I embarrassed you with my flamboyant method of leaving the ballroom, Lisette. My only excuse is that I was just so pleased to see you, to be with you again, that I wished to express my joy by holding you in my arms again.'

A frown creased her brow. 'You saw and spoke with me two hours ago when you arrived...'

'I saw and spoke to Miss Lisette Maystone,' he corrected huskily. 'It was *my* Lisette whom I came here to see, and now that I have...' He clasped both her hands in his and fell to his knees in front of her again. 'Lisette—darling, wonderful Lisette—will you marry me and make me the happiest man in England? No, not just England—the whole world!'

It was the second time in as many minutes that

Christian had mentioned marriage to Lisette. But he could not seriously be proposing marriage to *her*.

Could he...?

Of all the people present here this evening, Christian knew her true story rather than the one that Lord Maystone had chosen to share with society: a tragic tale of love and loss, resulting in him at last being able to claim his long-lost daughter.

Christian *knew* that story to be completely false. Knew too that her mother had been in the past, but was no longer, thank goodness, an enemy to both England and the Crown.

Dukes did not marry women such as she.

Nor, as she knew to her humiliation, did they take them as their mistress either.

She pulled her hands free of his. 'I have no idea why you have chosen to deliberately humiliate and hurt me in this way—perhaps as recompense for my mother's actions last month, I do not know—but I do not deserve such mockery from you. My father certainly does not deserve for you to have behaved in such a fashion in his own home.'

All humour had gone from his expression. 'Your answer is no, then?'

'There was never any real question, so there can be no answer either!' She moved aside and swept past him towards the doorway, and the humiliation that would now be her lot in life.

'Lisette, I love you!'

Lisette froze in the doorway leading back into the ballroom, her breath caught in her throat, her heart pounding loudly in her chest. Seconds later she felt the heat of Christian's body against her back as he moved to stand behind her.

'Lisette, I love you,' he repeated forcefully. 'I want to marry you, to make you my duchess—'

She spun around in his arms, her gloved hands pressed against his chest as she looked up searchingly into his oh-so-handsome and dearly beloved face, the love he proclaimed shining brightly, steadily in his beautiful lavender-coloured eyes.

She swallowed. 'You love me...?'

'I do,' he stated firmly as he took her hands in his and pressed them to his chest, allowing Lisette to feel the rapid beating of the heart he claimed was hers. 'So much that at this moment I am even prepared to forgive your father for being a wily old fox. Maystone is responsible for us not seeing each other this past month, Lisette,' he explained as she frowned her lack of understanding. 'Every time I called at Maystone House I was either told you were out or unavailable. I believe now that was on your father's instructions.'

She swallowed. 'But why?'

'Because he knew I love you. Marcus knows I love you. Julianna knows I love you. Damn it, I do believe everyone has known I love you except for me!' He gave a self-disgusted shake of his head, his hands tightening about hers. 'Could you not just love me a little bit in return, Lisette?' He looked down at her earnestly. 'I promise if you agree to marry me you will never have cause to regret it. As my duchess you will be the most cherished, the most loved woman in all the world—'

'A duke does not marry a woman like me—'

'What does that even mean?' he dismissed impatiently. 'You are a woman of great courage, honesty and loyalty. A woman who was not afraid to risk her own life to save mine—'

'Helene has said those men were not instructed to kill, only to issue a warning.' Lisette spoke distractedly, huskily, such hope building in her heart she was afraid to let it loose in case her chest was not large enough to contain it.

'*You* did not know that,' Christian insisted. 'Any more than you knew those men would have fled by the time you reached my carriage. You came rushing out into the street anyway, staunched my wound, drove my carriage home, tended my wounds and Pierre's—he is completely recovered, by the way. François sent word just last week.'

'I am glad.' Lisette nodded.

'Lisette…darling Lisette,' Christian groaned. 'I have been such a fool—that arrogant, pompous ass—for not telling you, for not realising how much I love you. I believe I fell in love with you at first sight. I know I could not take my eyes from you, and that I incurred your mother's wrath because of it.' He gave a rueful grimace. 'Each time we met after that I fell a little harder, a little deeper, until my love for you now consumes my every waking moment. I cannot sleep. I cannot eat. Marcus assures me I have been insufferable this past month.'

The hope in Lisette's heart grew to unbearable proportions. 'If you marry me, the illegitimate daughter of Lord Maystone, you will be risking incurring the condemnation of society—'

'I do not give a damn for what society thinks or says.' He waved an impatient hand. 'Besides which, none would dare to gainsay Lord Maystone, his friend the Prince Regent and *all* of the Dangerous Dukes.'

Lisette looked up at him searchingly. 'You believe your friends will publicly support you in this…this endeavour?'

'I know they will,' he asserted without hesitation. 'And it would not matter to me if they did not. I shall marry where and with whom I choose. And I choose you, Lisette. Indeed, if you will not agree to marry me then there will be no Duchess of Sutherland.' His gaze softened. 'Can you not love me just a little in return, Lisette? Will you not marry me and save me from the long and unhappy life of being a Taciturn Bachelor to your Old Maid?'

Hope burgeoned in Lisette's chest, flying free and carrying her with it as she allowed the last of her concerns—for Christian, not for herself—to be satisfied, dismissed as if they had never been.

Christian loved her.

He wished to marry her.

It was more—so very much more—than she had ever dared hope or pray for during this month of not seeing or hearing from him. Her father truly was a 'wily old fox'.

She looked up at him with her own love for him shining brightly in her eyes. 'I believe I have loved you since that first night too, Christian,' she admitted huskily. 'I—'

'You love me?' He pounced eagerly, his hands tightening painfully about hers. 'You *love* me, Lisette?'

'Of course I love you, you silly man.' She reached up to curve her hand lovingly about the hardness of his cheek. 'I love you very much, and of course I will marry you, Christian Algernon Augustus Seaton.'

Christian gave a shout of exultant laughter as he swept her up into his arms and began to kiss her with a thoroughness that took her breath away.

He loved.

And he was loved.

By his outrageous, his darling, his wonderfully unorthodox Lisette.

He asked for no greater happiness than that.

Epilogue

*Six weeks later, St George's Church,
Hanover Square*

'Do stop fidgeting with your necktie, Christian;
you are starting to make me feel nervous too!'

Christian gave Worthing a baleful glance as the
two of them sat at the front of the church awaiting
Lisette's arrival. His beautiful Lisette. Shortly to become his wife, his duchess and his companion for
the rest of their lives together.

'I seem to remember you being in just such a
state on the day you married my sister Julianna,' he
drawled mockingly.

'Yes. Well.' Marcus turned to give his wife an af-
fectionate smile. She sat on the pew just behind them,
next to a heavily veiled Helene Rousseau, here today
to witness her daughter's wedding.

Julianna had given birth three weeks early to
Worthing's son and heir, Peter Matthew Joshua Tim-
othy Wilding. That young man had been left at home

with his wet nurse today, but the three would be united following the wedding breakfast.

Christian was amazed at how quickly his brother-in-law had taken to fatherhood, young Peter with his parents constantly when they did not have other commitments.

All of the Dangerous Dukes were present in the church today, along with their wives.

Zachary Black, the Duke of Hawkesmere, and his lovely duchess Georgianna, their baby son also at home with his nanny.

Darian Hunter, the Duke of Wolfingham, along with his beautiful duchess Mariah, their first child due to arrive on Christmas Day.

Rufus Drake, the Duke of Northamptonshire, and his mischievous duchess Anna. Those two had recently learned that their family was also to increase in the spring.

Griffin Stone, the Duke of Rotherham; often too serious in the past, Griffin had at last found true happiness with his duchess Bea. And, from the look of Bea's glow today, Christian would not be at all surprised if the two of them very shortly shared news of their own increasing family.

All of them were here—all of the women having become fast friends, all of the gentlemen having survived their years as agents for the Crown, before just as happily retiring from that endeavour now they had become married men. Some of them were battle-scarred, admittedly, but they had survived and without exception had found their true, their real happiness in the women they loved and who loved them in return.

As Christian had with Lisette.

Which was why he was becoming more and more agitated as the seconds ticked by after the appointed time of twelve o'clock for their wedding ceremony to begin. *Where was she—?*

Ah.

Christian breathed a sigh of relief as the organ music began to play in announcement of his bride's arrival, he and Worthing both standing as the Vicar moved into his place at the altar.

It was too much to expect Christian not to turn and look at the woman he loved and who had consented to become his wife, his duchess.

Lisette walked slowly, gracefully on her proudly beaming father's arm, a vision in white, the smile upon her lips only for Christian. The love glowing in her eyes only for him.

His Lisette.

The woman he loved and was about to happily pledge to love and cherish for the rest of their lives together.

* * * * *